THE BELIAL BLOOD

Book 4 of the Belial Rebirth Series

R.D. Brady

"If we believe that god is the creator of evil, maybe there is evil also in heaven, if that is the case, we are not out of the woods yet."

— BANGAMBIKI HABYARIMANA, PEARLS OF
ETERNITY

PROLOGUE

JERUSALEM, ISRAEL

1186 AD

LIGHT FROM THE TORCHES FLICKERED OFF THE TEN-FOOT-TALL brass pillars that led to the subterranean levels beneath the Temple of Solomon. Templar Rowan of Macedonia stepped through from the hallway to the space that had been cleared six months earlier.

These halls dated back to Solomon's time, safely entombed for centuries. The temple on the surface hadn't fared as well. The crown jewel of Solomon's reign and the resting place for both the Ten Commandments and the Ark of Covenant, it had only stood for four hundred years before the Babylonians destroyed it under the command of Nebuchadnezzar.

Over the years, the temple had been rebuilt, with King Herod finalizing the last of the work on the temple and expanding the Temple Mount. But the Romans had put the final nail in the coffin of Solomon's architectural legacy, destroying the last pieces of the surface temple. The area had then languished as a garbage dump for decades until it had finally been cleared and the Dome of the Rock and Al-Aqsa Mosque had been created by the Muslims.

In all that time, nearly two thousand years, the subterranean levels of the original temple had remained untouched. It was only when the Templars arrived that the ancient temple's hidden chambers were uncovered in 1099. And it was fitting they did so. After all, while they were known simply as Templars, their full name was Poor Fellow-Soldiers of Christ and of the Temple of Solomon.

The Templars had fought a hard-won battle to reclaim the holy site, but now, in the waning days of this decades-long battle, the Templars knew that their end was near. The Muslims' highly skilled military leader Saladin's strategies and machinations made it clear that Jerusalem would once again fall from Christian hands. It would be a matter of days, a fortnight at best, before their forces were overtaken. Then the site would return to Muslim control.

But at least the excavations had proven fruitful. Ancient treasures long buried had been excavated and many already taken safely from the Holy Land and back to Europe. Excavation continued, the work too important to stop. Preparations to take the remaining finds continued unabated, and they would right until they were forced to flee.

But Rowan wasn't interested in anything that had been already found. She was focused on one incredible relic still to be unearthed.

A cool breeze cut across Rowan's skin, causing a few strands of her long dark hair that had come undone from her braid to tickle the back of her neck. The sensation was like ice-cold fingers running against her skin. She shivered.

A great beast of a man, Philip of Cornwall, ducked under the archway to join her, his large biceps bulging even without effort. Behind him, eight diggers stood, all novice Templars, shovels and picks held in their thin arms. They looked through the archway with trepidation.

With an impatient wave of his arm and a growl, Philip ordered them through. "Come." Rowan left the command of the novice Templars to him, stepping forward to embrace the moment.

Philip shot a glance in her direction but made no comment. He knew better than to ask after her welfare.

Rowan had joined the Templars ten years ago. The first year, it had not been easy. The fighting and grueling lifestyle she had no problem with. Keeping her fellow Templars from uncovering her gender, that had been much more difficult.

But she'd been careful to keep all of her padding in place and wear a mask as much as possible. She spoke only when absolutely necessary to keep up the subterfuge. But two years in, her gender had been revealed when she'd taken a wound on the battlefield. The blood loss had rendered her unconscious. By the time she'd regained consciousness, she was already being tended to by Philip.

In that tent, she'd met his eyes across the darkness. The flames of the candle by which he worked flickered across the shadows of his face. "So now you know."

He'd finished wrapping the bandage around the wound at her ribs and tied it tight. Rowan winced but said nothing more.

Philip leaned back, his gaze still on her. "I have known almost from the moment you joined the Templars. Your reasons are your own. But you have saved my life and countless others many times over. You are a brother regardless of what sex your body claims."

Relieved at his response, Rowan sucked in a breath, knowing that she should not be surprised. Philip had proven to be an admirable and respectful brother in arms. The two of them had often found themselves side by side, fighting through some of the thickest of their battles. Yet he never claimed a life he didn't have to.

Since that moment, he'd kept her confidence and never asked

why a woman would join the Templars. But that reason was hopefully down this long hall.

The flames of their torches flickered, the cool breeze coming yet again from the stairs.

Philip gave her a sidelong glance. "Are you sure you are ready for this? What they have found so far, it chills a man's soul."

Rowan straightened her spine in response. She'd not been cowed by the discoveries thus far, terrifying though they may have been. Books of spells and demon writing. They had already been scurried away to Europe by the Templars.

But she could not allow this next treasure—if it was what she'd sought—to be taken away as well. That much power could not be given to the Church of England. It could not be delivered into the hands of men.

Rowan met Philip's gaze and gave him a small smile. "Is that your own fears that you're speaking of, Sir Philip?"

He grunted, a smile now upon his lips. "Who raised a woman such as you?"

It was an interesting question and not one she could easily answer, not even to someone as trusted as Philip. The Great Mother stayed in the shadows, as did her followers. But they had been a part of history in so many ways, sitting on the sidelines and intervening when necessary to make sure that the great evils of the world did not overtake it.

And to protect the knowledge that ambitious men would use for their own ends. The knowledge held within this subterranean dungeon was perhaps the greatest they had yet uncovered.

If, of course, the rumors proved true.

The latest discovery acted as a buffer against her fears that all her time with the Templars had been wasted.

She shook her head, bringing her attention back to the task at hand. The diggers had uncovered a door. They had cleared the area around it and wiped it down to reveal its inscriptions. But one look at what was written there, and they had refused to go any further, running from the site and presumably refusing to return.

Rowan thought she might hold the same amount of fear as those diggers. But for her, turning and running was not an option. She needed to see what was here. She needed to take it into her possession and keep it safe from the powers of the world. They were not ready for this power, and in all likelihood, never would be.

The door lay down a stone-paved hallway. Large arches framed the space up ahead and kept the ground from caving in on them.

Even just this subterranean area was a marvel of construction. It had stood for nearly 2,000 years. What skill it took to create.

If the legends were true, it was only with the aid of demons that King Solomon was able to create such a place. It was during his reign that the ring was given to him. He became the ring bearer, able to control the fallen angels. But he later abused that power, turning his back on what was right—and his power was stripped from him.

The ring never again fell into the hands of someone such as Solomon. It never again fell into the hands of a man.

Another chill rolled through Rowan, but this time it wasn't from the air. This chill was inspired by the thoughts running through her mind as she caught sight of the door that had sent the diggers running in terror. It was made of metal and lay closed with thick metal bands across it.

She stepped closer, placing her torch only inches from its surface to read the inscription there.

"What does it say?" Philip asked.

"*The poison that would destroy men's souls resides within. This door must never be opened for the sake of all the world,*" Rowen said softly.

Philip's jaw hardened, and he glanced at her. She met his gaze and gave him a nod. The warning could only allude to one thing: the grimoire of Asmodeus, the head demon who had aided

Solomon. Philip turned to the six young Templars who had followed them down the hall.

From the widening of their eyes and the tremors in their hands, they had heard Rowan's translation. But they were desperate to join the ranks of the Templars and escape the lives they'd had up to this point. Poverty, abuse, and hopelessness drove them to what they thought would be a life of adventure and riches.

How foolish the young were.

Clasped between the Templars was a heavy log, ropes attached to it to allow them to use it as a battering ram. She nodded at the men and stepped back. "Take it down."

She and Philip stepped out of the way, allowing the men access to the door. She would have preferred to have opened it on her own. But it would take more than just the strength of her and Philip to take this door down. She'd already slipped down and tried it.

She watched the men as they swung the log back and then rushed it forward. It crashed into the door with a thud. Dirt and rocks rained down from the ceiling at the hit.

"Again," Philip ordered.

The men hit the door four times, five times, twelve before the first movement occurred. Rowan sucked in her breath as the next three hits created an opening two inches wide. She leaned forward, careful to stay out of the other Templars' way but wanting to see inside.

She held her breath as three more hits created enough of an opening. Her torch led the way she thrust it inside and glanced into the space.

The room beyond was set up as a living chamber. A small table with one chair sat to the right, a candle burned down in its center. And sitting at its edge was a single book. Slipping inside, she quickly picked it up, but it crumbled in her hands. *No.*

Her mouth fell open in dismay, and then her eyes spied the

room's last occupant. They lay on a cot at the back of the small space.

Crossing the room on silent feet, she walked toward the body. It had been here for nearly two thousand years, yet it was remarkably preserved. She could still make out the woman's alabaster skin and her long dark hair. Her eyes were closed as if she were simply sleeping.

Behind her, the scrapes and grunts of the men told her that the door was now open, allowing them passage.

Rowan's shoulders dropped as she looked at the figure on the bed. This was not what she'd hoped for. But perhaps it was for the best.

The Templars crowded into the room, walking toward her. Philip was the last in, looking over the group.

Which was why he did not see the eyes on the bed open.

Rowan's eyes grew large as she met the gaze of the creature before her.

The Templar next to her, a boy who'd been with the Templars for only six months, let out a gasp. "My God, it's—"

The rest of his statement was cut off by a gurgle of blood as Rowan's sword cut through his neck.

She whirled, slashed, and plunged her sword into the remaining five Templars before they even had time to breathe. She turned to Philip, the blood still dripping from her sword, and placed it at his neck before he even had a chance to reach for his. She looked into the dark eyes of the man she thought of as family. "I need to know where your allegiance lies."

He met her gaze, unflinching. "It lies with the Templars and our mission for the Holy Father."

She slid the sword through his throat. His eyes bulged wide. The blood loss was massive, but she sliced again to the other side to hasten his death, not wanting him to suffer. He grabbed at his throat, his eyes full of betrayal.

With a cry, she dropped her sword and caught him, lowering

him to the ground. She cradled his head in her lap. "I am sorry, Philip. But this can be trusted with no one, not even someone I love."

He grabbed her arm, leaving a bloody print there as the life drained from his face.

Rowan held him, leaning down and kissing him gently on the forehead, tears pressing against the back of her eyes. She'd known that this mission would be difficult. It had taken her from her family and her friends for years.

But then Philip had filled that void in her life. A void that now lay gaping open. Her heart felt heavy at what she'd done, even though she knew there was no other way. Gently, she untangled herself from him and lay him gently on the floor, crossing his arms over his chest.

Glancing over her shoulder, she stared at the figure on the bed that now sat up.

The woman gestured to the water satchel at Rowan's waist. Standing, she handed it over. The woman took a long drink. Closing her eyes, she held the back of her hand to mouth. Blowing out a breath, she opened her eyes with a nod. "What will you do with me?"

Rowan knelt down. "Keep you safe from those that would use you."

"Can you do that?" the woman asked.

Rowan stood and extended her hand. "We shall see."

CHAPTER 1

PRESENT DAY

KYMI, GREECE

D̲RAKE'S ALIVE. D̲RAKE'S ALIVE. D̲RAKE'S ALIVE.

The words rolled through Delaney McPhearson's brain in an unending loop. She sat against an old truck on the dock of the warehouse. The Mediterranean Sea rolled by slowly on her right, but it barely registered. She'd been sitting in the exact same spot for fifteen minutes.

By some miracle, the police had not shown up yet. The grenades used by David Okafor should have caused more than a few calls to law enforcement. But someone seemed to be looking out for them. Even in her shocked state, she could see the people of the neighborhood slowly walking up to see what all the commotion was about. The authorities would be here soon, which meant they needed to leave.

Yet she still sat. *Drake's alive.*

Laney was the only one not moving. Around her, Jake Rogan

was organizing the collection of all weapons and casings. Jen Witt was seeing to the wounded, all of whom, due to their Fallen natures, were already healing. None of the non-Fallen in their group had been harmed.

Vaguely, she noted David arriving in the van with Danny Wartowski, and they both immediately start loading their supplies into it. Danny had been sent blocks away to keep him out of harm's way. Molly McAdams had been with him, but she had returned, no doubt seeing something on the feeds that made staying away from the fight impossible. Now she helped Jake organize supplies and people.

Max was working with the newest member of their group, Danny's brother, JW Carter. It looked like the two of them were wrapping up a body, one of Gedeon's people. With surprise, she looked around and realized it was the only body of Gedeon's people left behind. They had taken the others with them when they escaped.

Laney watched all of it through a fog, as if her mind could only work at half speed. They had fought against Gedeon, and although they hadn't succeeded in destroying him, they had definitely put a wrinkle in his plans. That had been the intent: to take Gedeon by surprise, and if possible, defeat him.

But that intention had flown out of Laney's mind once she caught her first sight of Drake. He'd appeared as if from nowhere, standing between her and the blow from Gedeon that could have very well ended her. And then almost as quickly, he was gone.

Even now, it seemed like a dream. Part of her believed he was just a figment of her imagination, it had all happened so quickly.

But in her gut she knew that it had been real. She ran through it again in her mind. She'd been fighting with Gedeon in an alley just two warehouses over, on her own and tracking him. But Gedeon had gotten the jump on her. And she knew that she wasn't going to be able to stop the hit that was coming her way.

But then, somehow Drake was there, standing between her and Gedeon, protecting her.

Her mind had short-circuited in that moment, and it had yet to return to normal. She wasn't sure it *would* return to normal.

She blew out a shaky breath as she recalled Max arriving to help her. His appearance forcing her to choose between protecting Drake and protecting Max. And she'd had to go for Max. But in that moment, Gedeon had managed to get away with Drake.

Even with the molasses level of speed her thoughts were currently operating at, she knew that was wrong. Drake was incredibly powerful. He was the archangel Michael. But Gedeon had somehow overpowered him. Pushing through the sludge of her mind, she pictured the scene again. Gedeon had had something in his hand, something he'd plunged into Drake's arm. But it hadn't been a weapon, or at least not a knife. It had been a needle. He'd somehow weakened Drake with that needle. But what could possibly do that?

Was it the Omni? She thought Drake was immune to that, but perhaps she was wrong.

She needed to speak with Danny and Dom about that. But she didn't think that the Omni was capable of robbing an archangel of its powers. And besides, Dom said the Omni didn't work anymore.

She supposed it was entirely possible that Drake had been weakened already. Maybe returning had somehow drained him of his strength. But that thought led to more questions: How was he back? And how had Gedeon found him?

A weight settled over her shoulders. She looked up into David's dark-brown eyes. He smiled at her, his voice soft. "Laney, everybody's ready to go. I'm going to help you to the van now, okay?"

Laney looked around and realized that everyone was indeed

gone. David was crouched next to her, ready to help her up. Jen stood just a few feet away a worried expression on her face.

Laney let David help her up, surprised at how weak her limbs felt. "The plane?" she asked.

David slipped a hand around her waist. "Yes. We're going to head back to the States. The rest of the group has already headed out to the airfield. There's another car waiting for you, me, and Jen."

They needed to get back to the States. She knew that. But she couldn't go. Not yet. She stopped and shook her head. "I'm not going back."

David paused, flicking a glance at Jen, who took a step forward. "What do you mean you're not going back?" Jen asked.

Laney shook her head again. "I'm not going back, not yet. I need to find out about Drake. I need to know how he came to be here."

"And how do you intend to do that?" Jen asked.

"By visiting Ephraim Pappas's place."

CHAPTER 2

BALTIMORE, MARYLAND

THE SMELL OF SMOKE WAFTED THROUGH THE AIR. NYSSA RAN, HER legs churning beneath her as she sprinted down the hallway.

She could hear the sound of feet behind her, heading toward her. The heavy thuds grew closer no matter how fast she ran. The hallway ended, and she ducked into a stairwell, racing down the ancient stone steps. At the bottom of the stairs, she burst into a hallway and came face-to-face with a mirror. She stared at her reflection, her eyes growing wide, her mouth falling open, and her reflection did the same.

She did not recognize the woman staring back at her. The woman was in her early forties with long red hair and bright blue eyes. Wrinkles were at the edges of her eyes, and freckles dotted her skin.

Nyssa took a step forward, and the reflection did the same.

"Who are you?" Nyssa asked.

"You know who I am," the reflection answered her.

Behind her, movement stirred.

An impossibly tall man ducked under a doorway wearing a

leather vest, two swords strapped across his back, a hammer of some sort in his hand, and a strange helmet that Nyssa could only recognize as old upon his head. He smiled, showing off a mouth full of yellow-and-brown-teeth dotted with black before he raised the hammer and swung.

Nyssa burst up from her bed, her heart pounding as her eyes flew open. Pale pink walls greeted her, along with the familiar star stickers glowing along the wall in her bedroom.

A dream, it was just a dream.

She lay back against the mattress, but the bed was too warm, and she didn't like the feeling of vulnerability that came with lying flat on her back. She slipped off the edge of the bed and sat on the ground, her knees pulled up to her chest.

Another nightmare. Why did she keep seeing these things? She didn't know these people in her dreams. And she didn't understand why she kept dreaming of different times.

At first she thought maybe it had been from a movie or a TV show she'd seen. But the dreams kept coming, these visions of the past that she didn't recognize. And yet in each of the dreams, she was there, always an older version of herself.

What is going on?

She didn't ask the question out loud. She didn't *want* to ask the question out loud. As much as the dreams terrified her, on some instinctual level, she knew that the answer to that question would terrify her even more. She'd seen the watchful looks of her dad and Uncle Patrick. They knew something. Or they suspected something. Yet neither of them had said a word about it.

And that perhaps terrified her more than anything.

She and her dads, which was how she thought of them even if she called one Uncle, they talked about absolutely everything. She knew all about the Fallen. She knew about Laney being the ring bearer, the one with the ability to control the Fallen and all of the abilities that she had. She knew all about reincarnation and the fact that people lived lives over and over again.

THE BELIAL BLOOD

The reincarnation conversation actually made her feel better. She liked the idea that she went through these lives with these people over and over again. There was a comfort in that.

But for some reason, she couldn't bring herself to ask about the nightmares. Because she had a feeling deep down that the answers to that were going to change everything.

The clock on her side table proclaimed it was 4:30 a.m.

She groaned, staring at it, knowing she wasn't going to be able to go back to sleep. She knew from experience that it would be hours before her mind would shake free of the dream and let her return to the world of sleep.

The rumble of her stomach reminded her that she hadn't eaten much last night. There'd been plenty of food, but she'd been too worried about all of the others going to Greece. Laney was capable, but she'd already lost Laney for years once. She didn't want to lose her again.

She'd stayed up late last night waiting for word but hadn't heard anything. But if everything went according to plan, they'd be returning home later today, tomorrow at the latest.

Unless something happened.

A twinge of unease rolled through her at the idea. But there was nothing she could do about it.

Nyssa wasn't sure where the unease came from, but it wasn't new. It had been building over the last few months. She wanted all of the people that she loved to be near her and to *stay* near her. She didn't want to take the chance of them being out of her sight. She didn't understand why she'd suddenly started to feel this way. She'd mentioned it to her dad, and to her horror, he'd gone off on a lecture about hormones and the changing needs of a near-teenage girl.

She'd blocked that conversation from her mind even as he was still talking. She loved her dad, but he really needed to stop reading all those self-help books.

Her stomach rumbled again, and her butt was getting a little sore from sitting on the ground. She pushed herself up and grabbed her pale-blue robe, throwing it on. After a moment's hesitation, she grabbed her old bunny and shoved him into the pocket of her robe. She knew she was getting too old to care about things like stuffed animals. But some days, when it was dark and you just had a horrible dream, a girl needed her stuffed rabbit.

Opening the door quietly, she padded softly down the hall and stepped over the one creaking floorboard just outside her dad's room. Making her way down the stairs, she paused for a second to listen at her uncle's room, but everything was quiet inside.

Passing by, she headed into the kitchen. She flicked on the light over by the counter, not wanting to put on the big overhead light.

She opened up the cabinet and grabbed a glass, placing it on the counter before heading to the fridge and opening the door. She'd just pulled out the milk when a voice with a strong Scottish brogue spoke from behind her. "Trouble sleeping?"

Nyssa turned to see her uncle Patrick in his wheelchair, rolling toward her. He smiled, but she couldn't help but think that his face looked thinner than it should, his skin paler. He'd lost the use of his legs years ago to a bullet. Despite Henry sending Patrick to every doctor and specialist out there, there'd been no hope for him. His legs would never heal.

Nyssa hadn't really thought much about Patrick aging as she was growing up. To her, he was always kind of old, as if that was one consistent age. Besides, he was Uncle Patrick, a constant fatherly presence in her life.

But now that she was getting older, she worried about what it all meant. She worried that one day he would no longer be in her life, and she couldn't accept that possibility—he was too important to her world. Almost all of her early memories had him in it. The idea of him being sick and her being unable to help him ... it shook her to her core. And after the dream she just had, those thoughts were not welcome. Normally she could shove them away, but after that dream, they bled into her consciousness.

Patrick's smile shifted, his blue eyes filled with concern. "Nyssa? Are you all right?"

Swallowing hard, she nodded. "I just ..."

The tears came from nowhere. One moment she was fine, and the next, little rivers of water were cascading down her cheeks and splashing onto her robe.

Patrick rolled up to her and pulled her into his lap. Without hesitation, she wrapped her arms around him and cried, not sure exactly what she was crying about but unable to stop the tears from flowing.

Patrick didn't say anything. He didn't press her for answers or an explanation. He simply held her, rubbing her back and telling her it would be all right.

Nyssa listened to the rumble of his chest as he spoke and felt comfort in the warmth of him. He'd always been a spot of warmth in her life.

Finally, her tears subsided, but she didn't rush to step away from him, and he seemed in no rush to make her go.

"Do you want to tell me what that was about?" he asked softly.

Nyssa shook her head and finally stood back up, wiping her tears. "I just had a bad dream."

"You seem to be having a lot of those lately."

Nyssa shrugged and turned back to the counter, pouring herself a glass of milk with a shaky hand. She glanced over her shoulder. "Do you want me to put on the kettle?"

Patrick smiled. "Of course I want you to put on the kettle."

Nyssa grinned back at him. "One of these days, maybe you'll drink something other than tea."

"That's sacrilege, child. May the tea gods forgive you."

Nyssa laughed, the weight on her shoulders lightening just a little. Then she thought of Laney and the others. "Has there been any word from them?"

"Oh, yes. They called about an hour after you went to sleep last night. Everyone's fine. Most of them are heading back."

"Most?"

"Laney, Jen, and David need to check out one more thing. Then they'll be on a plane home as well."

"Is it dangerous?"

Patrick paused for a moment before answering. "I'm afraid everything associated with this group is a little dangerous. But those three are highly capable. And the others wouldn't have headed back if there was still serious danger."

Grabbing the kettle and filling it, Nyssa nodded. Patrick was right. They were capable, and she knew for a fact the others wouldn't leave if they thought something might happen.

As she placed the kettle on the stove top, Patrick rolled over to the fridge and started pulling out ingredients. "You look like you need a good breakfast," he said.

Nyssa raised her eyebrows. "It's only four thirty."

"Yep, but you and I are up, so it's breakfast time," Patrick said as he placed some ham on the counter. "Get the pancake bowl down."

Nyssa pulled open the cabinet and reached for the large red bowl they used every weekend to make pancakes and then grabbed the whisk from the utensils drawer.

For the next ten minutes, she and Patrick worked together making breakfast: eggs, pancakes, a side of ham. Patrick even grabbed a bunch of fruit and created individual fruit bowls for each of them.

Nyssa stared at all the food, shaking her head. She'd never had one of those Italian grandmothers who shoved food at her every time she came over, but her uncle Patrick and her dad definitely made up for it with the amount of food they thought she could ingest.

Although her stomach gurgling seemed to suggest that this

morning, she might actually be able to make a good-sized dent in it.

"I thought I heard you two down here," Cain said as he strolled into the room with his dark-blue bathrobe over his pajamas. He walked over and wrapped an arm around Nyssa, kissing her on the forehead. "Morning, sweetheart."

She leaned into him for a moment, wrapping an arm around him as well. "Morning, Dad."

Cain headed straight for the coffee machine and made himself a single cup. Neither Patrick nor Nyssa said another word to him until he'd had at least a few sips. It was an unspoken rule in their house that her dad needed those few sips to truly join the world of wakefulness.

When Cain put the mug down on the counter, his blue eyes focused on Nyssa. "Another bad dream?"

Nyssa nodded, her jaw tight. "Yes."

"Do you want to talk about it?" he asked.

Nyssa shook her head. That was the last thing she wanted to do. The memory of it was already fading, and that was exactly what she intended to let happen. "No, not really."

Nyssa turned back to the counter. But she flicked a glance over her shoulder and caught the look between her uncle and her dad. The words flew from her mouth before she could stop them, much like the tears had rolled from her eyes earlier. "Why do you guys always give each other a look whenever I mention my dreams?"

Her dad's face flashed alarm before he covered it with a shrug, not meeting her gaze as he grabbed his mug and headed back to the coffee machine. "It's just because we're worried about you. You seem to be having these dreams a lot."

"And that's all it is? You're just worried about me because of the dreams?" she pressed.

Patrick opened his mouth to say something, but her dad cut

R.D. BRADY

him off. "Of course that's all it is. We just want to make sure that you're all right. You are all right, aren't you?"

Nyssa looked between her dad and uncle and knew that they were lying, or at least that they were keeping something from her. So, she did the same. "I'm fine."

CHAPTER 3

SPORADES ISLAND, GREECE

The home of Ephraim Pappas was located on the Sporades Island of Skyros. The Sporades island chain consisted of twenty-four islands. According to legend, the gods created the islands by tossing colored pebbles into the Aegean Sea. Laney could see why people would believe that. It was really beautiful.

Jen directed the speed boat toward the dock of Ephraim's villa. His home was set right on the edge of the Mediterranean, with long glass windows along the front of the house framed by white stucco walls and timber beams. Somehow the house managed to look both old and modern at the same time. It was as if it had always existed in this particular spot, yet with all the modern conveniences.

All three of them kept a close eye on the villa and the surrounding rocks, but there was no movement, no sound.

"I don't think anyone's home," Jen said.

"Doesn't look like it," Laney agreed.

David let out a low whistle. "Ephraim might be an evil mastermind, but he's definitely got a beautiful lair."

Laney grunted. She wasn't sure how much of a mastermind Ephraim was. She had a feeling he was more of a stooge.

Jen deftly worked the boat next to the dock. David jumped out and tied it off. And then Jen cut the motor once they were secure. She walked up to Laney, linking her arm through hers as Laney stood. "You sure you're all right?"

Laney knew her friend was worried about her. Jen had argued that they should hold off on visiting Ephraim's home until Laney had a little time to recover from her shock.

In truth, Laney couldn't blame her. She was a little worried about herself. She knew she wasn't firing on all cylinders right now. But the boat ride over had cleared away a lot of the fog. Even if she wasn't one hundred percent, they needed to get there and see what exactly was going on.

Besides, she had a feeling this shock wasn't going to wear off anytime soon. She patted Jen's hand. "I'm okay. I promise. I just ... I need to see what's going on here. Wouldn't you if it were Henry?"

"You know I would. So let's go see what we can find out." Jen hopped onto the dock, and Laney followed, casting a glance around. A helicopter flew by overhead with Jake at the stick. Once he'd heard about their change of plans, he'd decided to stay with them as well and managed to commandeer a helicopter. He and Danny were in it right now.

Danny had already relayed that there were no heat signatures inside the home. Although he wasn't sure how deep the home went, so he couldn't swear that was the case for the lower levels.

A wind blew in from the sea, pushing Laney's hair back as she pulled her Glock from its holster. And although the air was warm, a chill crawled up her spine. She followed Jen along the dock and headed toward the house, scanning the beach for any signs of life.

It was obvious people had been here recently. The footsteps in the sand were clear. And with the way the wind was whipping around, they would have blown away if they had been here for a while.

"Looks like people left in a hurry," Jen said, kicking at an empty gasoline container.

David grunted. "Yeah, to try and kill all of us."

Jen grinned. "Ah, but they failed."

David smiled back at her. "Yes, they did."

Laney didn't take part in the banter. She was too focused on the building ahead of them. Drake had been here. She could feel it.

She'd been missing him all this time, and he'd already been in this world. If she'd known he was here, she would have stopped at nothing to get to him. How had he come back without her knowing? Why didn't anyone tell her? Why didn't she just know?

Anger crept along the edges of Laney's thoughts. She never placed herself in a special category because of what she'd done, of the sacrifices she'd made. But was it really too much to ask for someone to give her a heads-up that the love of her lifetimes was alive?

Taking a deep breath, Laney tried to shove the anger away. It was a useless emotion. It would change nothing. But a small kernel took up residence in the corner of her mind, refusing to budge.

The three of them headed to the front door. Jen and David stayed in front of Laney, and she didn't argue with the arrangement, knowing her friends were trying to protect her, and not just from her reduced thought processes. They were worried about what they would find inside and what it would tell her about Drake's captivity.

Even as she worried about that, she couldn't help but be annoyed that this was where Gedeon had been hiding out. Why had Ephraim helped him? And how did the two of them even meet? And how did Gedeon get to Drake before she did?

Once again, she pictured him from the alley, those eyes she

knew so well looking into hers. *How did you get here? And how did you break out?*

Laney hurried into the front door behind Jen and David as they yelled that it was clear. She stepped into a beautiful home with rounded arches and pale-yellow walls. The walls were rough and looked to be very old. From the exterior, she hadn't realized just how old, but it was obvious she'd underestimated its age significantly. The tiled floors were pretty clean, indicating someone was cleaning them regularly, although there were some traces of dirt that seemed to indicate yet again that people had left in a hurry.

The first floor contained the usual assortment of rooms: a large living room with windows that overlooked the sea, three bedrooms, and a kitchen that overlooked an infinity pool in the back.

But Laney's eyes were drawn to the staircase that led to the basement area.

Her gun held carefully in her hand, she shook her head of thoughts and focused on what she was doing right now. She needed to be on point. There could still be surprises below, and she couldn't save Drake if she was dead. "Let's check the basement."

Jen nodded, taking a step toward her as David spoke. "I'll loop through the first floor again, make sure there's no surprises, and then join you."

With a nod, Laney started to descend the stairs with Jen right behind her. The first floor they came to had a long hallway situated similarly to the hallway above. They stopped at the first room on the left, which looked like an intelligence operation. There were four tables set up with computers and large monitors. The computers were all off but intact.

"Definitely left in a hurry," Jen said, glancing at the computers.

"They probably thought they'd run over to the mainland, take care of us, and then head right back."

THE BELIAL BLOOD

Jen smiled. "Too bad for them. Once we clear this place, we need to get Danny down here to see what he can find on these."

"And hopefully, they were careless enough to leave some info on them we can use to track them down."

The two stepped out of the room and checked out two of the other rooms: one was a bedroom with two cots and the other a large storage room. The third door was more interesting—and more nauseating. Inside was a large metal table with straps for someone's legs, arms, and head. Medical equipment was along the side of the room along with a cabinet.

Jen flicked a glance at Laney. "That's not good."

"No, it's not."

Jen walked over to the cabinet, opened it, and shook her head. "Empty."

Laney looked at all of the equipment and knew that they needed to document everything to figure out exactly what had been going on here.

"There's one more level," Jen said, nodding back to the hallway.

Laney had noticed the other stairwell as well. With one last look at the equipment, she nodded and followed Jen out of the room.

As they were hurrying down the hall, David joined them. He flicked a glance in the room as Laney stepped out. He winced. "That's disturbing."

Laney just nodded as she followed Jen down the stairs.

The third subterranean level was rougher than the second one. The floors were made of dirt and uneven, the walls made of rough plaster or even just stone in parts. This level was obviously the oldest and hadn't been touched much by renovations.

The first two rooms were store rooms that held food supplies and little else.

But the next room had obviously been used as a cell of some sort. There was a chain along a wall that had a restraint at the end that could be used around someone's ankle. A bed was pushed against one wall in the corner, and a bucket for relieving themselves was in another. The only other furniture was an old wooden chair next to a table with books that had been set up against the wall closest to the door.

Laney frowned as she looked at the papers and books on the table. Jen peered down at them as well. "Those are genealogy tables."

"I wonder if this is where Professor Moeshe Peretz was," Laney said, thinking about her uncle's colleague who'd gone missing.

"I wonder where he is now," Jen said.

They met each other's gaze, but neither said what they feared: that the professor was long dead.

David had wandered to the end of the hall to check out the remaining rooms. He called down to them. "You two are going to want to check this out."

Leaving the books and papers behind, Laney hurried to the end of the hall. There was only one more room, and David stood at its entrance, the door thrown open.

"I don't know what to make of this." He stepped aside, staying in the hall so that Laney could look. Laney frowned at the move, wondering why he didn't just step into the room.

But when she reached the doorway, she understood. The room was small, only about ten feet by ten feet. But the majority of the floor was taken up by a large design arranged in a circle. Symbols had been painted along the edge of it, and one large one sat in the middle. They looked almost like runes, but a little different.

And they looked like they'd been painted in blood.

There was nothing else in the room. A small window with bars on it in the back corner but absolutely no furniture.

In her gut, she knew this was where Drake had been held.

Jen stepped into the doorway next to her, frowning at the symbols. "I don't recognize these. Do you?"

"No. We need to document everything. Every book, every

symbol, everything. And we need a sample of that blood. Maybe my uncle will have an idea about these."

Jen shook her head as she knelt down, peering at some of the symbols. "I don't think your uncle is going to be able to help us with these. I think we need someone who's been around a lot longer."

Laney nodded, knowing in her gut that Jen was right. Cain would probably be the best bet on deciphering them.

"I know I'm not really as knowledgeable about these things as you guys," said David, "but, uh, that kind of looks like a witch's circle. You know, used to like, summon a demon or something."

Jen met her gaze. And Laney knew she was thinking the exact same thing.

"Or hold one in place," Laney said softly.

CHAPTER 4

Grudgingly, Laney had to admit as she finished the second sweep of Ephraim Pappas's home that it was a truly beautiful building. Danny had shared that it had been here in one form or another for over three hundred years. Laney was a sucker for homes with history. She wondered what its walls had seen over the centuries. Would the original inhabitants be disgusted by what Ephraim had done here or honored?

It had been two hours since they'd first arrived. Jake and Danny had landed the chopper on the helipad out back and had joined them inside to document it.

There was no sign so far of Pappas or any of his people. In their haste to leave, they had left behind all of the notes in the cell downstairs. It was clear they were written by Moeshe Peretz. Now she sat back in the professor's cell, flipping through them. He'd obviously been tracing the descendants of Jesus.

The idea that Jesus had a family was incredibly controversial. Contrary to religious teaching—which in fairness, did not rule out the possibility—there was a great deal of research that supported the idea. And not just that Jesus had a wife, but brothers. In fact, he was said to have had multiple brothers: Joseph,

Judas, James, and Simon. In fact, the tomb of one of his brothers had been found, and they were even able to extract DNA evidence from it.

On its face, the idea really shouldn't be controversial. Given the time period and the fact that he was called Rabbi, it would have been more unusual if he hadn't had a family.

The professor had focused his research to the descendants of the Merovingians, the priest kings who'd lived in a land that straddled the boundary between present-day France and Germany. They had been a rather mysterious group of rulers, if they could even be called that. From Laney's understanding, they were really more figureheads than the actual power in that part of the world.

Legend had it that when Mary Magdalene escaped from Israel, she was pregnant. Giving birth to a daughter in Egypt, she, along with her brother and Joseph of Arimathea, had then gone to the French coast. Later, a dynasty of priest kings had come from that same region, people with special abilities.

She sat back as she stared at the genealogy tables. This really wasn't her area. She couldn't make heads or tails of it to see whether or not the professor had been on the right track.

But she would need to bring all of it with her. She stood up and grabbed the box that she'd found in one of the storage rooms and started placing all of the professor's research into it. She'd take it back to the States and find someone to go through it for her.

Jen stepped into the doorway as Laney was packing the last few pieces of paper. "I'm almost done here."

"Good, because I think you're needed elsewhere."

Laney frowned, securing the lid. "What do you mean?"

"Just got a call from Chandler headquarters back in the States."

Laney's heart began to race. "Is everything all right?"

"Yes, yes, everybody's fine. In fact, it seems we're adding one to our rescue efforts."

Laney frowned again. "I don't understand."

Jen nodded to the box. "It seems the professor has been found."

"What?"

"Peretz. Drake helped him escape. He's waiting for us back at the mainland. He called Chandler HQ and asked to speak with your uncle. The call was put through. And it turns out that Moeshe was here but escaped with the help of a very charismatic blue-eyed individual."

Drake. "Drake helped Moeshe escape?"

"According to your uncle, he literally carried the man out of here. When they got to the coast, he told Moeshe that he needed to hide and to speak only to your uncle. He took refuge at a church and called from there. The priests are keeping his existence from the authorities, but it's possible that someone overheard the call. We should get there now."

"I'll go." Laney started for the door but then paused, looking around the professor's former room.

Jen nodded to the room. "Jake, Danny, and I will finish up documenting this place. You and David take the chopper and go get the professor before anybody else figures out that he's at that church. We'll be only a few minutes behind you on the boat."

Laney nodded, already heading for the door.

"And Laney?" Jen called.

Laney flicked a glance over her shoulder. "Yeah?"

"Be careful."

Laney wanted to say that she would, but careful was not an option with Gedeon still on the loose.

CHAPTER 5

KALUSH, UKRAINE

Delaney McPhearson had bested him. Gedeon rolled his hands into fists as he stared out at the open, barren field that surrounded their new safe house. As soon as McPhearson had gained the upper hand, Gedeon knew the safe house in Greece was burned. He had barely escaped, a few of his people had been killed. A few he'd had to kill himself. It would have taken too long for them to heal, and he did not have that kind of time.

But he knew McPhearson's people had one of the bodies. He wasn't sure what they could do with it. He was not familiar with the nuances of the science of this time, but he knew it could pose a problem.

Or more accurately, another one.

Delaney McPhearson was living up to her reputation. He could see now why she caused Samyaza so much trouble. A wind blew, stirring the air and sending the stench of cow manure toward him. He curled his lip in distaste. Now he was stuck here for the time being, although arrangements were already being made for them to head to another safe house. They should be there within twenty-four hours. Which meant he only had to put up with this stench for that long.

He stared out over the dead-looking land and found himself missing the Mediterranean Sea. He'd never understood why humans found themselves enamored with the water. But now that he'd spent time next to it, he had an idea why.

He supposed it was one of those intangibles about existence on this planet.

Pappas's home had been an excellent hideout, although now it was no doubt crawling with McPhearson's people. Gedeon had no idea where Pappas was. He'd left him at his home, but seeing as how Michael had made a break for it, he'd no doubt killed the man on his way out.

It was a loss, but only a small one. And there was a chance the man had survived. He was a cockroach after all. He'd had two of his people slip back to the island to take care of him. Gedeon didn't like loose ends.

But Pappas had been nowhere to be found.

McPhearson's people had been moving in, and they'd had to abort.

But Gedeon wasn't truly worried about Pappas. He wasn't a danger. He was too scared of them to do anything but keep his mouth shut and stay hidden.

Gedeon stepped outside of the small home and walked to the old garage set about two hundred yards from the house. It was an ugly concrete structure built in the mid-twentieth century. There was nothing aesthetically pleasing about it. It was gray and square.

Gedeon curled his lip at the sight of it. All of the beauty in this world, and humans created things like this. That alone made it clear that they were not truly the chosen ones.

But he supposed it was a perfect location for his current guest.

He nodded at the guard on duty by the door. There was another one at the back of the building. His guest would have round-the-clock security. No mistakes would be made. It still

THE BELIAL BLOOD

boiled his blood that he'd been able to escape before. He'd underestimated him. Distracted by Delaney McPhearson's arrival, he'd let down his guard for just a moment, and Michael had seen the weakness and exploited it.

It gave him pause, realizing that it was the combination of the two that had created the weakness. That was what had almost allowed his prisoner to escape and McPhearson to succeed.

But it was also that very coupling that had turned the victory back toward him. Gedeon had been able to escape because he'd had Drake there as a shield. Although he'd thought he had the drop on McPhearson, he was beginning to realize now that he'd vastly underestimated the woman. And that underestimation had cost him almost all of his soldiers.

He'd not expected McPhearson and her people to wait for him to come to them. He'd thought that they would undeniably head straight for him.

But he'd been wrong in that, brutally wrong.

And now he would have to replenish his ranks. Yes. He'd underestimated her even while telling himself all along that he hadn't. It was galling.

And then, of course, there was the question of Lilith. Seeing her, even on a screen, it had thrown him.

But it wasn't purely for him that he needed to find her. She had a critical role in the upcoming battle. And he needed to keep her safe until she played her part. He should have focused on that. But seeing her so unexpectedly . . .

It probably also affected his strategy in Greece. But losing had a way of bringing issues into stark relief.

Besides, all was not lost. He had gained perspective, and he still had his prisoner to keep him company. He nodded at the guard, who swung the door open. Gedeon stepped inside.

His prisoner sat in the middle of the room, knees pulled up to his chest, his arms around them. He'd made the cell much smaller this time so that Gedeon had more room to walk around the edge of his restricted area. He smiled as he did so now. "Like your new accommodations?"

"I've had worse. And besides, I won't be here for long."

"You won't be able to escape again. I've made sure of it."

Drake grinned. "Yes, but Laney knows that I'm here, or at least she knows that I'm with you. It's only a matter of time before she finds me, which means she'll find you."

Gedeon chuckled. "You think she will come for you? She chose to save that boy rather than save you."

Now Drake laughed. "All these years you've been on this world, and you still don't understand how humans work. She'll come for me. I have no doubt about it."

Gedeon smiled. "It won't matter. By then, I'll have everything I need."

For a split second, he saw the confusion on Drake's face before he covered it. "What are you talking about?"

Gedeon laughed out loud this time. "Oh, the great Michael doesn't know? You are supposed to know all. You are supposed to be the greatest soldier amongst us all. And yet look at you, sitting here helpless, powerless."

Drake simply smiled at him. "Well, if you are so great, why don't you explain to me your little plan?"

"I don't think I will." He smiled back. "But I will share that I have plans for your love. I expect she will come for you. In fact, I'm counting on it."

CHAPTER 6

KYMI, GREECE

THE CHURCH THAT MOESHE HAD TAKEN REFUGE IN WAS GREEK Orthodox and located less than a mile from the warehouse.

David flew them over the Mediterranean. The sea was calm below them, and people were out boating and enjoying the afternoon. Appreciating their experience, Laney felt no longing to be one of them. She'd learned long ago there was no point in longing for impossible things.

When they approached the shore, they made a pass of the warehouse and saw the police scouring the area. Apparently someone had finally called in the gunfight, not that Laney was surprised. But being that none of her people had contacted her, she had to believe that they had all gotten out safely.

She felt a twinge of guilt at that subterfuge, but experience had taught her that authorities weren't always on her side, even when she was on the side of the right. And she simply didn't have hours and hours to cut through the red tape of the locals.

David nodded toward the activity below. "We're going to have to deal with that at some point."

"Yeah, I know. But exactly how are we going to deal with it? Who are we going to let into our little circle of trust? Can you think of any government we can fully trust?"

David laughed. "Individuals within the governments, yes. Unfortunately, there is not a single government entity that I even partly trust."

Laney sighed, knowing he was right. There were too many individual forces at play and competing ambitions within governments. It seemed as if the people who had the most ambition went into government leadership, which also meant that many of them had the most self-interest. And that self-interest, when pitted against national interest, or even world interest, oftentimes won.

And Laney couldn't take the chance of that, not right now, not until she had a better handle on what was going on. So for right now, she had to keep the authorities at arm's length.

It wasn't going to be easy. And it didn't make her feel good. But she simply couldn't take the chance.

For a moment, she thought of Nancy Harrigan. Of all the government officials she'd come across, Nancy was the one that she trusted the most. She'd been the secretary of state, and in fact had been the first person that Laney had seen when she'd opened her eyes after the events in Egypt.

If there was anyone in government that Laney trusted, it would be Nancy.

But Nancy was no longer in the US government. She was now the secretary general of the United Nations. But the United Nations wasn't a world government.

Founded in 1945 after World War II, the UN at their heart were designed to keep peace across the globe. Their charter included developing friendly relations among nations and promoting social progress, better living standards, and human rights. They had 193 sovereign states as members, each with their own interests, making getting anything done difficult. They had two main mechanisms for enforcing their resolutions: economic sanctions and the deployment of security forces.

But the larger nations curtailed the UN's power. They gave them enough power to keep the smaller countries in order, not the big ones. However, Nancy might be someone she could call in the future to help them figure out who exactly they could trust.

"There's the church," David said, cutting into her thoughts.

Laney glanced down at the building. White with a pavilion that had a row of arched entryways and a bright blue roof, it was beautiful. Very different from the Catholic churches she was used to, and there was a hint of Spanish or maybe Middle Eastern influence in its appearance.

She was a little worried about the fact that they were in a chopper and that the police had no doubt seen them. But hopefully they would be able to get in, get the professor, and get out before the police tracked them down.

It would have been better if they had taken a boat, but they couldn't take the chance of Gedeon and his people rediscovering the professor before they reached him. And the boat would simply take too long. So they had to risk the chopper.

David set them down in a small field just behind the church. A group of people from the church rushed out back to watch them slowly land.

Laney was already out the door as David started shutting down the engine.

"Can you and Jen, just once, wait until I've actually shut the chopper down before you dive out the door?" David called out as Laney shut her door.

She grinned at the disgruntled statement. Quickly, she crossed the open lawn and took a deep breath. Ever since her return, she wasn't sure how people would react to her. She wasn't really sure what the world thought of her.

She headed toward the group standing at the back of the church. They stayed under the pavilion, standing framed in rounded archways. There were five of them, all men, two of them in black priestly garb.

Laney focused on the oldest of the group. His skin was lined, and he had a long gray-white beard. The man waited for her to approach with a steady gaze.

She stopped when she was only two feet away. She got no sense of threat from the group in front of her, but she was still wary. The older priest spoke before she did. "Dr. McPhearson, I'm Father Ezekiel. We've been expecting you."

CHAPTER 7

FATHER EZEKIEL USHERED THE OTHER PRIESTS AWAY. AFTER A FEW long looks at Laney, they did, most of them glancing over their shoulders for one last look before disappearing inside.

"I apologize for their interest," Ezekiel said as he walked with Laney along the long patio toward a set of thick heavy double doors. "We were quite surprised to see you step out of the chopper."

"But you said you were expecting me."

The man smiled. "We were expecting someone, not necessarily you specifically. I have to admit, I have read about your adventures. You have lived a very colorful life."

That's an understatement, she thought, but out loud spoke politely, "Yes, I have."

"I wonder if you have given thought to the greater meaning of your life. Of where you fit in God's plan."

Apparently the priest wanted to skip the small talk and head right to the deep stuff. Laney wasn't actually bothered by the question. And it was one she had pondered more than once. "I have thought on that quite a lot, actually. And I'm not really sure. I find that situations crop up and I don't have time to think about their greater meaning. So I tend to have to go with what I think is right. What I think will be the best for the most people."

The priest stopped and stared at her, his gaze intent. "Even at the cost of your life?"

Laney nodded. "Even at that cost, yes."

He stared into her eyes for a longer moment as if searching for something before he smiled and continued forward. "You are a remarkable young woman. You have been through so much, seen so much, suffered so much. And yet, still you are here."

That statement Laney had an answer for. "That's because of the people I have around me. Without them, none of what I have accomplished would have happened."

"Yes, you are lucky to have found such a group. Not everyone is."

"I'm aware of that, and I am grateful."

The priest stopped and studied her again, tilting his head to the side. "You are, aren't you?"

He continued to walk and Laney fell in step next to him once again. "The man who you are coming to see, he would not tell us his name and was obviously in great distress. I hope that you will not cause him any more distress."

"That is not my intention. And yes, he has been through a great deal."

The priest nodded as he opened the door, and they stepped inside, the air growing noticeably cooler thanks to the pale stones on the floor and walls.

The priest led Laney down a hall, bypassing several closed heavy wooden doors and a few that opened into offices. He stopped at the last one on the right. The door was open, and a younger priest stood inside along a bookcase. On the opposite side of the room was an old pale couch. A man lay on it, a light blanket over him, his eyes closed.

Catching sight of Laney and the older priest, the young priest

THE BELIAL BLOOD

hurried across the room. casting a quick glance over his shoulder. "He is asleep."

Father Ezekiel nodded, keeping his voice low. "Very well. Why don't you stay out here while we speak with him?"

The priest nodded, his eyes finally focusing on Laney's face and widening. His mouth popped open just a little as he stepped aside to allow them to enter. He moved to stand outside the door.

Father Ezekiel walked across the room and crouched down, gently touching Moeshe's shoulder.

It took a few shakes before Moeshe's eyes flickered open. The poor man must be absolutely exhausted. In his late seventies, his skin had a thin quality to it, and he only had a few hairs remaining on each side of his head.

As he sat up, Laney tried not to gasp at how thin he was. He'd only been gone for a few days, but it was obvious that he'd lost weight. His cheeks were gaunt, and the suspenders that held up his pants looked more like a necessity than a fashion choice.

But that frail body held the mind of a well-respected academic. He specialized in genealogy, but he had a varied academic background. He'd first started his career researching French and German royalty. They had thought that was what had attracted Gedeon to him.

The priest reached to the side table and handed Moeshe a pair of glasses. Moeshe placed them on his face, blinking a few times as he looked at the priest who spoke with him quietly, then his eyes drifted past him and locked in on Laney. His mouth dropped. "You're Patrick's niece."

Laney stepped forward. "Yes, I'm Delaney McPhearson. My uncle said you were looking for me."

He nodded, flicking a glance at Father Ezekiel, and then closed his mouth.

"Father, if you could give us a few minutes? Also, a colleague of mine will be looking for me," Laney said.

Ezekiel looked between the two of them and nodded. "Yes, of

course. We will show him to you when he arrives." Ezekiel stepped out of the room and took the young priest with him as he headed down the hall.

Laney moved over to the professor, concerned about how frail the man looked. "Are you all right, Professor? Were you hurt?"

The man shook his head, but there was a tremor in his hands. "No, not physically. But it was difficult."

Laney sat down gently on the couch next to him. "We'll get you somewhere safe. Somewhere where they will not be able to find you."

Moeshe looked into her eyes. "Can you guarantee that?"

"No. Neither can anyone else. But we will take every precaution."

"These men." He paused, shaking his head. "I'm not even sure if they can be called that. They're so powerful. And the way they move ... are they ... They look like Fallen."

"They're not Fallen. But they do have the same powers."

"Oh." He studied her for a long moment, his eyes full of intelligence and understanding. "I see."

And Laney had the feeling that he did indeed.

David appeared in the doorway. "Laney, we need to get moving. That chopper is not going to stay unnoticed for long."

Laney stood up and then reached down to gently help the professor stand as well. "Professor, we have to take a short walk. And then we will have a short ride in a chopper before we head back to the States. Once there, we'll arrange for you to be put into protective custody."

"Custody of the US government?" the professor asked.

Laney met David's gaze. He shook his head. "Not exactly. We'll find a place for you that the government knows nothing about, that no one knows anything about. I believe it will be safer that way."

They had made it to the hallway and were now headed down it

THE BELIAL BLOOD

toward the same door that Laney had entered from. Father Ezekiel stood there with the younger priest, waiting for them.

Flicking a glance at the two priests, Moeshe lowered his voice. "My research. It was back at that ... that house. I'm going to need my research. Did you see it?"

"Yes. It looked like you were studying the genealogy of the Merovingian line."

Moeshe nodded, and David stepped on the man's his other side, taking his elbow, as he seemed to slow.

Laney herself was trying not to hurry the man along, but she felt time slipping away. "We found the research. We've boxed it up, and it will be coming back to the States with us."

Moeshe exhaled noticeably. "Thank goodness."

They had reached Father Ezekiel at this point, so Laney shifted her focus to the two priests. "Thank you, Fathers, for taking care of him. We'll see that he's safe from this point on."

"God be with you, child," Father Ezekiel responded. "Although I believe he already is."

Laney nodded her thanks and hoped that the priest was correct.

Laney and David walked with Moeshe across the courtyard of the church. Laney leaned her head closer to Moeshe. "Why are they searching out the Merovingians? Is Gedeon looking for a descendant of Jesus?"

Moeshe's eyes lit up with excitement. "So you understand. Yes, that's exactly what they were looking for. Although I don't know why."

"I'm going to go get the chopper started," David said, giving Laney a look that indicated she needed to keep Moeshe moving as fast as the man could manage. Even now, Laney could hear the sirens in the distance.

But the local police were not her greatest concern or thought at the moment. "How did you escape, Professor?"

"A man. He came into my cell and told me we had to leave. He

43

carried me part of the way. He was very strong. We took a boat, and when we reached the shore, he told me to hide."

"Where did he say he was going?" Laney asked.

"To see a girl. Did he find her? Is he all right?"

"Yes, he found her," she said softly. "But I don't know if he's all right."

CHAPTER 8

KALUSH, UKRAINE

Drake smiled until the door closed behind Gedeon, and then the smile dropped from his face. Laney was all right. Drake hadn't known until this moment. When Gedeon had dragged him away, he had tried to fight, but Gedeon's power far outstripped his own.

He let out a shaky breath, gripping his hands together. She was okay. Even as he knew that, he felt the terror of those moments, seeing Gedeon swing at Laney. Darting forward, he had worried he wouldn't make it in time. That he would lose her.

And Drake knew he would be lost if she was gone.

But for those few glorious seconds, he'd been able to see her, to hear her voice. He pictured the look of shock on her face followed by the look of love. He'd read the indecision in her face before she rushed to save the boy.

In lifetimes past, he would have been angered by her choice. Now, he knew that was who she was. She would always protect the weak. And she did not know in that situation he was the one who needed protecting.

She knew now, though, and what he told Gedeon was true: She would look for him. And she would find him. He knew that just as strongly as he knew if their positions were reversed, he would do the same.

He just needed to survive long enough for her to find him.

CHAPTER 9

KYMI, GREECE

The police arrived just as Laney, David, and Moeshe were taking off in the chopper. Laney radioed ahead to the others to tell that they needed to be ready to go as soon as they touched down. The police were following them to the airfield, and Laney had no doubt they were calling ahead as well.

When they reached the airfield, Jen was waiting in a van for them. They hustled into it, with Jen practically carrying Moeshe and dumping him inside. She drove them straight onto the runway, where a small private jet was already warming up.

Laney stepped out of the van, helping Moeshe up the stairs. He'd fallen asleep almost as soon as he'd been buckled in. Laney crawled into a seat next to Jen as David taxied down the runway. Danny was in the back of the plane working on his computer, and Jake was in a row across from him doing the same.

"Did you guys get everything?" Laney asked.

Jen nodded. "And Jake and Danny have already started scanning the documents into Danny's computer. They want to make sure they have backups of everything. Just in case."

A wise precaution, especially given their track record.

"Where do you think Ephraim Pappas is?" Jen asked.

Laney shrugged. "Probably at the bottom of the ocean. I don't see why Gedeon would keep him around. He served his purpose, and now that we know that Ephraim is part of this and have all of his properties under watch, I don't see that there's any utility in the man."

Jen stretched out her long legs. "Can't say I feel bad about that."

"Me either."

Jen was quiet for a long moment. "So how are you feeling about seeing Drake?"

Laney's chest clutched at the mention of him, and immediately the image of him from the alley returned. "I don't know how to answer that. It all seemed surreal, like a dream. It happened so fast that I'm even beginning to wonder if it was Drake or someone who just looked a lot like him."

"But in your gut, you know the truth of who it was."

Laney nodded. "Yeah, it was him. I just don't understand how. How is he back, and how did Gedeon, of all people, find him?"

"I'm more interested in how Gedeon was able to weaken him. You said he injected him with something?"

Laney nodded. "Yes. I'm not sure what it was. I'm going to speak with Dom when we get back and see if the Omni could impact archangels, although it seems unlikely."

"So what could it be?"

"I don't know. In fact, a lack of information is all we seem to have right now: we don't know how Drake came back, we don't know how Gedeon found him, and we don't know how Gedeon managed to weaken him."

Jen settled back in her seat a little more. "If whatever it was is something that can weaken an archangel, I have a feeling that might be something that we might need."

The tone of Jen's voice made Laney glance sharply at her. She wasn't just talking about Gedeon. "You think more archangels are going to enter this fight—and on the other side?"

Jen had already closed her eyes. She slid them open a little bit. "Don't you?"

Laney wanted to argue that no, of course the archangels wouldn't become involved in this. She couldn't say that for sure, though.

But there was precedent for the angels going to war, and not just the war that resulted in the angels being cast out. And if that was the case, they needed a weapon that could be used against them. "We need to get the parts of the Arma Christi back. We need to get that weapon away from him."

"Well, then we'll kill two birds with one stone," Jen said.

"What do you mean?"

"Gedeon went to a lot of trouble to take Drake, not to kill him but to *take* him. Which means that Drake is important to him. And so is the Arma Christi. Gedeon's going to keep them close to him and close to each other. Which means if we find one, we find the other."

"And then we get them both back."

Jen smiled closing her eyes one more time. "Yes, we do."

CHAPTER 10

THE TRIP HOME HAD BEEN QUIET. LANEY HAD EVEN MANAGED TO get in a little sleep, although her dreams had been filled with Drake. Each time she woke up, she agonized over and over again about what she could have done differently.

But the truth was there was nothing she could have done differently. Max had been in trouble. And the only other option would have been to let Max be killed. And that would never, ever be an option.

Laney didn't regret her choice. But like so many choices she'd made before, she just wished she didn't have to make it.

Once back in the United States, David packed Moeshe into a car to take him to a secure location. After bundling the professor in the passenger side, he closed the door and turned to Laney. "I'll be by tomorrow to help with the plans."

Laney hugged him and shook her head. "No. Take the day at the very least and spend it with your family. Finding Gedeon is going to be a marathon, not a sprint. We'll get the analysts working and see what happens. And if anything critical pops up, we'll let you know. But spend some time with your family, David."

"Are you sure?"

THE BELIAL BLOOD

"Positive. And thank them for sharing you with us. I don't know how we would have done any of this without you."

David grinned. "I have been pretty amazing, haven't I?"

Laney laughed. "Yes, you have. Now go give those beautiful kids a hug for me."

"Will do. And Laney, we'll find him."

Emotion closed Laney's throat, so all she could do was nod.

Waiting until David drove off, Laney turned back to the plane. Jake stood waiting for her. Jen and Danny had already headed back to the estate with a truck full of papers and computer equipment.

Jake leaned against the Explorer that one of the security personnel had left for them. "You good?"

"Yeah, I'm good," she said, then climbed into the passenger seat.

Jake settled in behind the wheel and started the car. They headed toward the airport exit. Neither of them spoke for the first few minutes. "We'll get back him, Laney."

She gave a small laugh. "Everybody keeps saying that. But we don't know that that's true."

"I know it's true."

Laney glanced over at him. "How?"

He flicked a glance at her before returning his attention to the road. "You've been through too much not to get Drake back, Laney. You *deserve* to get Drake back."

"Not everybody gets what they deserve in this world."

"That's true. Horrible things happen to people all the time. But I feel like you've had more than your fair share. And it's time that you got something back rather than just giving. We *will* get Drake back. All of us are going to make sure of that."

Laney knew that he couldn't promise that. It was a long shot that Drake would come back to her. But it had also been a long shot that she would see him again in this life. And yet she had. So maybe, just maybe, Jake was right.

The estate was dark by the time Jake and Laney rolled through its front gates. Jake drove slowly down the main drive toward Share-croppers Lane, which was a block of cottages that had once been the homes of the sharecroppers on the original estate.

Years ago, when Laney had first arrived at the estate, it had had a dozen or so little homes that had been used as guest quarters for incoming guests as well as a place for employees to stay overnight if they ever had an ongoing project that required it.

Since that time, it had blossomed into its own little neighborhood. The McAdamses lived across the street from Cain and her uncle Patrick, whose cottage was right next to Laney's. Danny had his own place close to Dom's at the end of the block. Lou and Rolly had a home, as did the McAdamses' three eldest. A few of the guys on the security force had homes there as well as did a half dozen others. In the time she'd been gone, Mustafa and Yoni had even taken up residence there with their families. David and Rahim also had a place that they stayed in at least one weekend a month.

There was a sense of community here that Laney really loved. As a child, it had been just her and her uncle. They'd had all of the priests from the diocese, of course, but she'd longed to have a big family.

And now she did. She had a large extended family that she loved with all her heart. But with that love came a deep worry about how the current events, and the events yet to unfold, would affect all of them.

But while she felt part of this place, she felt separated from it. Everyone here had moved on with their lives. Laney had, at least on the professional front. She was constantly starting new projects and new endeavors, or she was before she was ripped out of the timeline.

But besides Cleo, she didn't have that close personal relation-

THE BELIAL BLOOD

ship that all the others had managed to develop. Even her uncle had found Cain. It wasn't a romantic relationship by any stretch of the imagination, but it was clear that those two were partners. But Laney didn't have that with anyone, not since Drake.

And she wanted that again. She wanted Drake again.

Now she just had to find him.

CHAPTER 11

MASSA, ITALY

THINGS WERE FALLING INTO PLACE. IT HAD TAKEN A FEW HOURS, but they finally had a location more fitting. They were in a villa in the Tuscany region of Italy in the town of Massa. Grape fields extended across the southern slope of the land as far as the eye could see. Colorful tiles and tapestries adored the floors and walls. The estate sat on over a thousand acres, providing more than enough privacy for what they needed.

Plus, he now had basement room set up for his prisoner.

Gedeon smiled as he walked down the stairs to his prisoner's new accommodations. He made his way down a small hallway and opened the door.

This room was a little bigger than the last one, but Gedeon had had the containment circle made smaller.

Drake sat in the center, his knees practically at his chin. When Gedeon walked in, he nodded toward the smaller circle. "Afraid I might escape again and reveal everything?"

"Nope. But I've decided to take a lesson from your beloved." He turned to the door. "Bring him in."

The door opened. One of his guards stepped in, pushing a young boy no more than twelve years old. The boy looked around furtively, his eyes wide, his skin marred with dirt.

Drake narrowed his eyes. "What is the meaning of this?"

"Ah, something else you don't know. Well, let me explain this to you. Delaney McPhearson saved that other boy instead of saving you. So this is my little insurance package. If you attempt to escape, I will kill him. If you allow someone to rescue you, I will kill him. How much do you think your beloved Delaney will think of you if you sacrifice a child for your own freedom?"

"I'll simply take the boy with me."

Gedeon walked over and hauled the boy up into his side. The boy winced.

"Are you sure you'll be able to? As soon as I hear that you've caused trouble, I will take a knife to his throat." Gedeon grinned. "Your move, Michael."

Drake narrowed his eyes, saying nothing.

Gedeon smiled. "Good, we understand one another. Now I have some plans to make." He pushed the boy toward the corner of the room and tied him to a metal pole. "I think I'll leave you two to get to know one another a little better. Take all the time you want."

Gedeon nodded at the guard, who stepped into the room as Gedeon stepped out. Gedeon closed the door behind him and headed toward the house. He'd no doubt that Michael would attempt to defend himself against caring for the boy. Gedeon shook his head. Michael, the true Michael, wouldn't have even given the boy a thought. Sacrificing the boy for the greater mission would have been a given.

But this new Michael, this weaker Michael, would worry about the child. He would worry about the child's immortal soul and, Gedeon supposed, his own.

He would never allow the child to be killed in his place. And Delaney McPhearson would never allow it either.

Gedeon shook his head. Such weakness. He walked back into the kitchen and then headed to the dining room. "Report."

The dining room was set up as Lucius's command center. A row of tables were aligned against the back wall with four different individuals sitting at computers running God knew what.

Lucius stepped away from the report he was reading over the shoulder of one of the analysts and turn to Gedeon. "We have eyes on most of McPhearson's people."

Gedeon frowned. "Most?" he asked.

"Yes, the spy, David Okafor has proven difficult to pin down."

"And the professor?"

"There's been no report of him since he was taken from the island."

Gedeon drummed his fingers along the table as he took a seat. They had no doubt brought the professor's research with them. And while he didn't have confirmation, he was pretty sure that they would have the professor as well. So now, what was he to do?

"Were you able to get the schematics on the Chandler Estate?"

Lucius nodded, grabbing a tablet and walking over to Gedeon as his hands flew over the screen. "Yes. It's impressive. Henry Chandler has really made a fortress."

"It cannot be hacked?"

"Everything can be hacked. But the ability to do so is beyond our abilities here."

Gedeon stared off through the window, his only view that of the ugly garage.

But he wasn't focused on the here and now. He was focused on his plans for the future. He needed to take down those defenses. And he knew someone who could do it, although he hadn't been planning on moving this person into place quite so soon.

But there was no helping it. And besides, he'd waited long enough. "I'm going to need you to send those schematics to someone. He'll take care of the defenses for us."

CHAPTER 12

BALTIMORE, MARYLAND

JAKE PULLED UP IN FRONT OF THE COTTAGE HE SHARED WITH MARY Jane and Susie. Molly and the boys lived in the house next door.

Jake turned off the engine but made no move to step out. "You going to be all right?"

She nodded, placing her hand on the handle. "Yes. I'm going to start looking for Drake. I'll call the analyst and see what—"

Jake reached out a hand and patted her forearm. "Not tonight, Laney. The analysts are already doing everything they can. And you've been through a lot. You need to get some sleep. In fact, I'd really like it if you took a sleeping pill and got a serious night's sleep. Nothing's going to change tonight. If anything pops up, you will be the first that they call. Give yourself tonight to just accept everything that's happened."

Laney's hand fell away from the door handle. Jake's words seemed to seep into her bones. He was right. She needed to wrap her head around seeing Drake again. She needed to let herself feel everything that she'd been pushing away for the last few hours.

And then tomorrow she could take charge of the search. She squeezed his hand. "Thanks, Jake. Have a good night."

"You too, Lanes," he said as he stepped out of the car.

She walked across the street to her uncle and Cain's home. A dark shape sat waiting for her. Cleo walked across the street, and Laney sat on the curb and hugged her tight.

"I missed you," Laney murmured into her fur.

Sad? Cleo asked.

Laney pictured Drake, and Cleo buried her head into Laney's chest. *He's back?*

"Not yet. I lost him again."

You'll find him.

Laney didn't have the strength to argue, so she just sat with her arms wrapped around her. Finally the cold pavement forced her to move. She crossed the street, Cleo a warm presence at her side. Laney started up the front path, but Cleo started to nudge her toward the backyard.

Laney looked down at her with a frown. "What's going on?"

Nyssa. Cleo headed around the side of the cottage and toward the back. Laney followed her.

It took her a moment to pick out the young girl sitting on the bench at the back along the rock wall. The lights on the porch were on, but everything else was bathed in shadows. And Nyssa sat quietly, absent any electronic gadgets that normally would light up any darkened space around her.

"Nyssa?"

The young girl's head jerked up, and her mouth fell open. "Laney." She burst to her feet and sprinted across the space, barreling into Laney and wrapping her arms around her.

Laney hugged her back just as tightly, content for just a moment to exist in this present. No future, no past, just now. Standing with her arms wrapped around Nyssa, she felt that connection that she thought she was missing. Nyssa released her a little bit to look up at her. "You're all right? You're not hurt?"

Laney pushed back the strands of Nyssa's red hair that had fallen into her face. "I'm fine. No harm done. What are you doing out here by yourself?"

Nyssa tried to step away, but Laney kept her arm around her shoulders and led her back to the bench.

"Nothing. I just … I was just sitting," Nyssa said.

Laney sat down next to her and took her hand, turning toward her. "Is everything all right?"

Nyssa blew out of breath. Laney worried for a minute that she would hide whatever was rolling around inside that brain of hers, but then Nyssa spoke. "I don't know, Laney. I mean, I keep having these nightmares."

Laney's chest tightened. "Nightmares?"

Nyssa nodded. "Yeah. They started, I don't know, maybe six months ago?"

"Are they the same nightmare or different ones?"

"Different, always different. But I don't recognize any of the people in them, and at the same time I just, I kind of know that they're about me." She shook her head. "It doesn't make any sense. I mean, in them I'm old, like *really* old, like thirty."

Laney struggled not to roll her eyes or feel insulted at the slight. She failed. "Oh my God, you're ancient."

A smile cracked along Nyssa's lips. "Yeah, practically a senior."

Laney laughed out loud. "Brat."

Nyssa smiled at her again before the grin faded.

"Why do these nightmares have you so worried?" Laney asked.

Pulling her knees into her chest, Nyssa wrapped her arms around them. "I don't know. They feel, I guess, different from other dreams. And I just …" She shook her head, resting her chin on her knees.

"And you just what?" Laney asked softly.

"I just have this feeling that something's coming. I know it's crazy. I know I'm not like Max. I don't sense things, but I just can't shake this feeling that something's coming and that it's going to change everything."

In three months' time, she would turn thirteen. Which, for a normal girl or boy, meant that they were entering their teenage years and all of the changes, physical, emotional, and otherwise, that came along with it.

But for Nyssa it meant something so much more. When she turned thirteen, she would be gifted with all of the memories of her past lives as Lilith. Laney desperately wanted to keep that from her. She didn't want her to be burdened with those memories. She wanted the young girl in front of her to just have a life that was carefree, that was easy.

Eons ago in her first life as Lilith, she'd decided that humanity needed to be mortal. They needed the specter of death hovering over them to truly appreciate the lives that they were living.

That difficult choice came with a consequence that was to humanity's benefit: Everyone would be reborn time and time again with the opportunity to finally understand and appreciate what this existence was all about. Each of those reincarnations would happen without the burden of the memories of their past lives. And with each life, they had the opportunity to get it right and end the cycle of reincarnation.

But for Lilith, each time she was reborn, when she became a teenager, all of the memories of her past lives returned with her as well. More than that, she often had to sacrifice herself to replenish the promise. It was a grueling existence.

Twelve-year-old Nyssa knew none of that. As far as she was aware, she was just a normal adolescent girl. They had agreed that they wouldn't tell Nyssa until it was absolutely necessary, although all of them had hoped that it wouldn't be until she actually turned thirteen. They had all hoped that her life would be quiet and peaceful up until that point.

In fact, they had often discussed how they would help her after it happened so she could continue a normal life once her memo-

THE BELIAL BLOOD

ries returned. Normally, she would have to leave once her memories returned because there were people and groups, usually Fallen, who would want the benefit of those memories. And they would stop at nothing to get to her. To keep those she loved safe, Lilith had to leave.

But everyone in her life right now was used to danger, the Fallen no longer existed—at least with powers—and there was nowhere safer for her than with them. They had planned for how to convince her to stay and let her just be a young girl, burdened with past memories but surrounded by those who loved her.

But those hopes of a better life for Lilith in this existence were looking more and more naive. And it looked like they were going to need to have another conversation about whether or not Nyssa should be told about what was coming. Her other lives were already bleeding into this life, at least during sleep. And Laney wasn't sure if it was kinder to let her know what was coming or let her simply stay worried about unusual dreams.

Nyssa's phone buzzed, breaking into the moment. She pulled it out of her pocket and glanced at it.

"Who's that?" Laney asked.

"It's Susie. She just downloaded the latest Haley Mills album. She wants me to come over and listen to it." Nyssa didn't move, just stayed where she was on the bench.

"So why aren't you heading over there?"

Nyssa shrugged. "I don't know."

"Did you and Susie have a fight?"

"No, nothing like that. I just … I don't know if I'm in the mood to do that."

Laney studied the young girl in front of her. She looked like she had the weight of the world on her shoulders. And one day in the not-too-distant future, she quite literally would. But that day wasn't today.

"All right, I need you to listen to me. You are a young girl. And yes, right now your dreams are disturbing, but other than that, your life's going along pretty well."

Nyssa rolled her eyes. "Laney, half the people I know were nearly killed within the last week."

Laney winced. She'd forgotten about that. "Yes, but they're all still alive. And the same is true for Susie."

Nyssa tilted her head with a frown. "What?"

"Jake's been in the thick of things. Molly's been in the thick of things. All the other people that Susie has come to care about have been in the thick of things too. She's just as worried about them as you are. And maybe she's looking for someone to help distract her from her worries."

"I never thought about it like that."

"And take it from me, when things are dark and difficult, it's always better to be around people that you care about, especially people that can make you laugh."

"Like Drake used to make you laugh?"

A warm glow settled in Laney's chest. That was one of the things that she loved the most about him. When everything was falling down around their ears, he could, in the middle of all of that darkness, make her laugh. "Yes, like Drake made me laugh."

"I overheard Uncle Patrick and my dad talking. Drake's alive?"

Laney nodded.

"But he didn't come back with you. He was taken again?"

"Yes."

Nyssa reached out and took Laney's hand. "You're going to find him."

"I hope so."

Nyssa shook her head. "No, you're going to find him. Laney, you were gone for years, and we all thought the worst. You faced down the head of the fallen angels and managed to bring the world back from World War Three. Do you honestly think you can't find Drake? If he's back in this world, then you're going to find him."

THE BELIAL BLOOD

Laney tried to tell herself that it was just a juvenile optimism shining through Nyssa's voice, but she could hear the creep of something older, of some*one* older in Nyssa's words. She looked into Nyssa's eyes, and for a moment the eyes that looked back at her held the knowledge beyond that of a twelve-year-old girl.

"I think you're right," Laney said softly.

Nyssa's cell phone buzzed again, breaking the moment.

All evidence of the old soul inside her gone, Nyssa rolled her eyes as she pulled out her phone. "Susie again." She quickly typed back a message and then stood up.

Laney stood up as well. "Heading over?"

"Yeah. Can you tell my dad and Uncle Patrick?"

"I'll let them know. Go on. Have fun."

Nyssa took a step away from her and then turned and wrapped her arms around her one more time. "Thanks, Laney. I'm glad you're back."

Laney hugged her back and watched as Nyssa disappeared around the side of the house. "I'm glad I'm back too."

CHAPTER 13

The lights were on in the kitchen, shining brightly as Laney opened the back door and let herself in. Her uncle Patrick and Cain, who'd been chatting good-naturedly while drying dishes, both turned around with a smile.

"Laney!" her uncle said as he dropped the dish towel back on the counter and rolled over to her.

She quickly made her way over to him and hugged him tight. "Hey, Uncle Patrick."

He released her, grinning up at her. "You don't look too worse for wear."

"Well, not all injuries are quite so obvious."

He frowned, looking up at her. "We heard about Drake. Are you all right?"

"As all right as I can be," she said as she shifted to give Cain a hug as well.

Cain looked beyond her toward the backyard. "Is Nyssa with you?"

"No. She headed over to Susie's. Something about listening to some music."

Cain nodded. "Yes. Haley Mills's new album came out today."

THE BELIAL BLOOD

Laney stared at him. "How do you know that?"

Cain shrugged. "I'm the father of an almost teenager. I need to know things like that."

Patrick rolled himself over to the island. "We saved you some dinner. We thought you might be hungry."

Food had been available on the flight from Greece, but Laney hadn't had an appetite then. But right now as she took in the covered plate, she felt her hunger rising. "Depends. What have you got there?"

Patrick pulled the cover off, revealing a gorgeous-looking Mediterranean salad and some challah bread.

Cain opened up the fridge. "And I've got a steak in here for you. If you give me just a few minutes, I'll throw it on the barbecue out back."

Laney nodded. "Actually, that sounds great."

While Cain prepared her meal, Laney slipped next door to grab a shower and a change of clothes. By the time she returned, her food was sitting waiting for her on the table, along with a side of baked red potatoes.

Laney slid into the booth and Cain, and her uncle sat across from her, eating some challah bread along with a spicy tomato dipping sauce.

Laney focused on her food while Cain and Patrick spoke quietly about whether or not they should invest in a new dishwasher. Apparently, their current one was giving them fits.

Laney appreciated the fact that they weren't delving right into their usual array of questions for her. She wasn't up to answering them quite yet. She really needed to fill her stomach first.

Finally, she cleaned her plate, placing her knife and fork in the center of it and wiping her mouth. "I desperately needed that. Thank you."

"Would you like a little dessert?" her uncle asked. "We have lemon meringue pie."

Laney groaned. "I don't think I could fit another bite."

65

R.D. BRADY

"Well, maybe in a little while you'll have some room," he said, his eyes twinkling. He knew lemon meringue was one of her all-time favorites. And she had no doubt that was exactly why he'd bought it.

"So, we spoke with Max. He was the one who told us Drake was there," Cain said.

Laney nodded. "He showed up when I was tracking down Gedeon. In fact, he placed himself between me and Gedeon. He saved me again."

Patrick leaned across the table and squeezed her hand. "Max also explained that Gedeon took Drake."

Laney nodded, the hurt rolling through her again and the helplessness. "Yes. I went to help Max, and by the time I turned back, Drake and Gedeon were gone."

"Do you have any idea where he might be?" Cain asked.

"Not yet. But Henry has all of his people on it, and Danny is going through all of the information we gathered from Ephraim Pappas's home. Oh, which reminds me: your colleague Moeshe, David has him set up in a safe house somewhere. I'm not even sure where."

"Oh, that's good," her uncle said. "When I received his call, I was worried. Moeshe, he's an unusual character, but he's very dedicated to his work."

Picturing the eccentric academic, Laney smiled. "Yes, he is. He wanted to make sure that the research he'd been working on for Gedeon was brought to the safe house. He wants to continue the research."

"That doesn't surprise me. Moeshe is one of those types that when he gets intrigued by an idea, he doesn't let it go until he's figured it out," her uncle said.

"Reminds me of some other people I know," Cain said dryly.

Laney wasn't sure if he was referring to her uncle or herself but it applied to both of them equally. "He's trying to find the descendants of Jesus through the Merovingian line."

THE BELIAL BLOOD

Patrick exchanged a glance with Cain. "We thought as much. Gedeon is going to need that descendant in order to complete the Arma Christi."

"We still think he's going to be trying to create a weapon out of it?" she asked.

"It's the only thing that makes sense. And you need to keep that from happening," Cain said, his eyes intense.

Laney looked between her uncle and Cain. Something was off here. "What's going on? What aren't you telling me? Is it about Nyssa?"

Cain spoke quickly, much too quickly, as if he was grasping onto the change of conversation. "She's been having the nightmares. She's starting to remember her past lives."

"I know. Do you think we should warn her about what's to come?" Laney asked.

Cain shook his head. "Your uncle and I have gone back and forth on this I don't know how many times. But telling her won't change anything. And it might rob her of some of the happiness she could have these last few months. So, no, we don't think we should tell her."

"But it's possible that Gedeon is looking for her. Don't you think we need to warn her?" Laney asked.

Shaking his head, Cain leaned forward. "To what end? You and Henry have locked her down. This place is probably the safest place on the planet for her. We're not going to let her out of our sight. And no one is going to be able to get to her here. Telling her won't change anything. There's nothing she can do to keep herself safer than what we can do for her."

Laney knew that Cain was right, but it still felt wrong. Shouldn't she tell Nyssa? Warn her? But at the same time Nyssa was still just a girl. What more could she really do to protect herself?

"She's still a child," Patrick said, as if knowing what Laney was thinking. "She doesn't need the burden of this. That's ours to take on for her."

And that Laney completely agreed with. One day, Nyssa would no longer be a child, and that day was rapidly approaching. But right now they did need to do everything they could to keep her safe, and that included keeping her ignorant of what was to come.

Cain flicked a glance at Patrick and then returned his gaze to Laney.

Laney studied the two of them. There was a seriousness to them, and she didn't think it was all about Nyssa. "Something else is going on, isn't it? What is it? What aren't you telling me?"

Patrick opened his mouth and then shut it. He let out a breath. "Trust that we will tell you what's happening when you need to know."

Cain continued. "And right now, there's no need to share this with you. There's no need for you to worry about something else. Once you find Drake and we have a better idea of what's going on with Gedeon, then we can talk."

Laney looked between the two of them. "But you'll tell me if it's something that I need to be worried about, right? You won't keep it from me?"

"Of course not. We'll tell you if there's anything you can do."

The phrasing brought Laney up short. They'd tell her if there was anything she could do? That meant something was coming. They just weren't sure if she could help or not.

Worry gnawed at her gut. There were so many possibilities: her uncle's health, Nyssa, the Arma Christi, Gedeon. With these two, their worries could be just about anything.

She gripped her glass and took a long drink of water, shoving the worry aside. She'd find Drake, and then she'd make them tell her what was going on. And she would find a way to make sure she could do something about it.

CHAPTER 14

MASSA, ITALY

THE BOY SAT CURLED UP IN THE CORNER OF THE ROOM AS GEDEON shut the door with a bang. His long dark hair fell onto his dirt-scuffed cheeks. With his head bent forward, it also covered his eyes.

His legs stuck out from underneath his shorts, showing that the boy was slim bordering on malnourished. His clothes were old and stained, the shorts threadbare. The top was too large with the neck stretched out. It was obvious the boy didn't come from money.

Drake kept his voice soft. "What's your name?"

The boy sniffed, looking up. He wiped at his nose with the back of his hand. "Arturo."

"Arturo. It's nice to meet you. My name's Drake."

"Drake?"

He nodded.

Arturo frowned, flicking a glance at the door. "They called you something else."

Drake grinned. "I'm sure they've called me a lot of something elses."

A small smile slipped onto Arturo's face before it disappeared. "No, I mean a different name. They called you Michael."

"In a different life, that was my name. How did you come to be here?"

Arturo's chin trembled, and he took a shuddering breath as he looked around the room.

Drake had no doubt he was looking for a way to escape. But he was too small to reach the window, and with the sigil on the floor, Drake would be unable to help him. Besides, Drake was as weak as a human right now, and against Gedeon and his people, well, it just would not end well for either of them. "I'm afraid there's no way out of here if that's what you're hoping to find."

Shooting a glance at the guard by the door, who looked extremely bored, Arturo shook his head quickly. "No, no, I wasn't."

The boy was scared of the guards and scared of Drake. Drake couldn't blame him. He didn't exactly look like someone you should trust. Drake could only imagine the treatment the boy had received at the hands of Gedeon and the others.

As worry for Arturo's mental state wormed through Drake, he couldn't help but wonder at it. Back when he'd first met the humans, he would have thought nothing of a boy like this. He barely would have registered on his consciousness, an obstacle that needed to be removed.

But now, as he stared at Arturo, he couldn't help the empathy that bubbled up in him at the boy's plight. And at the same time, he found himself curious about the life the boy had led before he'd arrived here. Was someone looking for him? Had someone been killed when they grabbed him?

He was also worried about what this experience might do to the boy. But more than anything, he was worried what would become of him when Gedeon no longer had a use for him.

THE BELIAL BLOOD

That reaction was a far cry from him eons ago, or even just a few decades ago. Laney was responsible for all of those changes. She'd opened his eyes and opened his heart, even though as Helen she'd started the process.

But it was in this lifetime that he truly understood what it meant to care and to sacrifice for someone else. Laney, she embodied that. And Drake couldn't help but be influenced by it. Seeing the people that she cared for and seeing how she cared for people she didn't even know, it was hard not to try and figure out why.

And once he did, he started seeing all the connections that humans had to one another. The love, the laughter, the joy. And the heartache. All of it made up the human experience and human connections.

And once Drake's eyes were open to that, he'd started to feel those connections as well.

As he stared at this young boy, he couldn't help but worry about the family he may have left behind or perhaps the abuse that he'd escaped. There was a haunted look in the boy's eyes that worried Drake, and he found his heart leaning toward him.

"How did you come to be here?" Drake asked again.

Arturo sniffed. "I was walking home from school. It was late. I don't know what happened. Someone just grabbed me. They moved so fast." He lowered his voice. "I think it was a Fallen."

"Not quite, but they are something like that," Drake said.

Arturo looked around. "My mom is going to be so worried. It's just her and me. I need to get back to her."

"I'm afraid you're going to be here for a little while," Drake said gently. "But not forever. And when I leave, I'll make sure you come with me."

The boy looked at Drake curiously. "Why can't you leave? Why don't you move from that spot?"

Drake nodded to the sigils painted on the floor. "Do you see those?"

The boy nodded.

"Together they create an ancient jail cell. The knowledge of it is lost to the world now, but Gedeon, he remembers."

The words stirred a memory from the far reaches of his mind. Drake scoffed. "In fact, I think Gedeon might've invented them. He is keeping me here with them. But have no fear. I will escape."

The boy looked dubious, and for good reason. Drake surely didn't look like he could accomplish much. Plus, right now he was desperately in need of a shave and a haircut, not to mention a shower, although Drake himself had gotten used to his own stench.

Mostly.

He did, however, feel bad that the poor boy was being subjected to it. But right now, he needed to give the boy something that he desperately needed. He leaned forward, staring into the boy's eyes. "Don't let these trappings fool you. They only put them here because I am too powerful otherwise. And soon I will find a way to escape."

"And you'll take me with you?"

"Yes," Drake said, sealing the promise.

CHAPTER 15

BALTIMORE, MARYLAND

Up ahead, Cain closed the door after Laney slipped through it to head back to her home. Patrick rolled down the front hall toward him.

Laney seemed good, all things considered. He knew seeing Drake had both broken her heart and healed it simultaneously. He also knew she would find him. There was no one more determined than his niece. But he worried about the toll it would take on her.

She'd stayed chatting with them for an hour before Nyssa reappeared, then the four of them had curled up in the living room and watched a movie.

It all seemed so normal. And he wished more than anything that their lives could be more of these moments of normality, when there was nothing more to worry about than whether or not the popcorn would run out before the end of the movie.

Nyssa was now asleep upstairs. Cain had gone and checked on her before Laney left. She was going to bed earlier and earlier, mainly because she wasn't sleeping at night, and her body was desperately in need of rest.

Cain shut the door and leaned against it for a moment, not moving, his gaze on Patrick.

"Did we make the right choice? Not telling her?" Patrick asked.

Shaking his head, Cain pushed off the door. "I don't know, Patrick. I don't know."

Laney had asked if there was anything more that they were keeping from her. And there was, but Patrick agreed with Cain that it wasn't yet the time to tell her. Not when she'd just found out about Drake returning. Once she found Drake, they'd sit down and tell her everything.

Once again, he went back and forth over whether it was the right thing to do. He didn't like keeping things from Laney. But he also didn't like adding to her burden. He'd seen how lost she'd been since Egypt, no matter how hard she tried to hide it. He could not add to that, not when there was a chance they were wrong.

If they had defeated Gedeon in Greece, they could have been wrong. But the more he researched the topic, the more convinced he was that they had interpreted everything correctly.

But he did want to put it off. Nothing would change, either for better or worse, by telling her now.

Once she found Drake, they would give her some time to enjoy him being back, and then they would sit her down. They would tell her about their worries for the future, the worries that Gedeon's arrival heralded a much more dire future than any of them realized.

Maybe one that they couldn't prevent.

CHAPTER 16

It had been three days since she'd returned from Greece. Three days of searching for Drake and finding absolutely nothing. They had no sign of any of Gedeon's people either. He disappeared from Greece just as seamlessly as he'd slipped into it.

Laney sat back in her desk chair on the third floor of the main headquarters of the Chandler Estate. Her office made up one-third of the floor. Henry and Jake each had offices that took up the remaining thirds. The three of them, the triad that had started all of this. And now the three of them were all running around like chickens without their heads, trying to figure out where Gedeon had gone and what his plan was.

She pushed back from the desk and walked to the long picture window along the back of her office. Outside the window were the rolling hills of the estate. It was such a picturesque scene. Usually, it brought her a sense of calm.

But not today.

Unable to find any thread to pull on to help her track down Drake and Gedeon, Laney turned her mind to other frustrations in her life. The emergence of Gedeon and the return of Drake meant something. There was something going on, some greater plan that she was completely in the dark about. And she had a feeling her uncle and Cain weren't.

As much as she wanted to sit them down and get them to tell her exactly what Gedeon intended, she simply couldn't seem to work up the energy to shift her focus. Because right now Drake was all that mattered, even if she was just spinning her wheels looking for him.

Part of her felt selfish for even indulging herself this way, but she couldn't help it. Once she'd seen Drake, her whole world had shifted. And all she could focus on right now was finding him again. She would not leave him in Gedeon's hands.

The body they'd brought back with them had held no answers. In fact, according to Dom, it was indistinguishable from a human body. He wanted to consult with a colleague, but they were holding off for now until they ran more tests. Laney didn't want to let anyone else know what they had in their possession.

Which left the Omni as a possible link to the solution Gedeon used on Drake. Dom was running tests on the Omni down in his shelter as he'd been for the last three days. Her phone beeped, and she quickly walked over to the desk and pulled up the text from Dom. It was short, sweet, and devastating.

No luck.

Laney tossed the phone back onto the desk. *Damn it.* Dom had had one last test that he'd wanted to try this morning. It had been a long shot, but it had been the last option available to them.

And that was information they desperately needed. Because if that substance could weaken an archangel, whatever he had could probably kill a Fallen or a full-fledged archangel.

While to the general public the Fallen and archangels might appear similar in strength, the reality was that archangels were much stronger. Laney could tell the difference because she could feel that strength. The tingle that let her know that a Fallen was near increased nearly tenfold when it was an archangel.

The first time she'd come across one, she'd been sent to her

THE BELIAL BLOOD

knees by the power of the signal. So what could possibly weaken one, especially one like Drake? Drake, the strongest and most powerful of the angels?

Laney and the others had had some long conversations trying to parse out possibilities. Jake had suggested that maybe when Drake returned, he hadn't returned at full power. She supposed that could be true, but until they found him, they wouldn't know for sure.

As she ran a hand through her hair, Cleo looked up from her spot in the corner of the room. *Fresh air?*

Laney wanted to say no. She wanted to say that she needed to stay here, that she needed to work. But the truth was she was at a dead end. She didn't know where to turn or what to do.

She also knew that sometimes taking your mind off of a topic led to ideas that would come no other way, although she doubted that would be the case now. Nevertheless, she nodded. "Yeah. Let's get out of here."

The two of them made their way down the long circular stair-well that wrapped around the main foyer of Chandler HQ and then walked across the black-and-white-tiled floor, stepping out into the bright sunshine. Squinting against the light, she pulled her sunglasses from her pocket and slipped them on as she and Cleo started to walk without any real direction in mind.

Two other cats appeared on the horizon. Cleo's head perked up at the sight of them. Laney nodded, knowing she needed to be with them. "Go ahead. I'll be fine."

Back soon. Cleo took off at a run to join her pack mates.

Laney watched them go. It was good to see Cleo spending time with the other cats.

There weren't many left now. None had reproduced in the last few years. The government had declared that they weren't allowed to reproduce. They weren't supposed to exist. They were the crazed creation of a brutal Fallen. But Laney couldn't help but think that the world would be a much sadder place when such beautiful creatures were no longer around.

With a sigh, Laney turned and headed across the open field. Sending her thoughts off in that direction was definitely not going to be a pick-me-up. Without any destination in mind, she wandered across the estate, shoving any thoughts of Drake, Gedeon, or any of the current issues from her mind.

Instead she focused on the trees and the flowers as she passed them. She looked up at the sky and focused on the clouds, trying to see shapes in them. She kept her attention on anything that would keep her ingrained in the present and keep the future and the past far away from her.

For an hour, she walked and managed to shove all of her thoughts and worries from her mind for at least half that time. As a result, by the time she reached Sharecroppers Lane, she was feeling much more relaxed and a little drowsy. Perhaps she'd take a nap and that would help spur something. Lord knew, she wasn't sleeping all that well at night.

As she walked along the back of the homes, she spied her uncle and Cain in the garden behind their cottage.

"Laney, hey," her uncle called out.

Laney turned toward them, forcing a smile on her face. "Hey, yourself."

Cain, who was digging up a potato plant, raised his eyebrows. "So you finally decided to leave the office during daylight hours."

Laney shrugged as she hopped over the rock wall. "I wasn't getting much done. I seem to be spinning my wheels."

"Well, pull up a seat and tell us about it. Maybe we can help," her uncle said.

Laney walked over to where he sat in the shade and took a seat on one of the Adirondack chairs next to him. "I don't know how. I keep trying to figure out what it is that could steal the strength of an archangel."

"I take it Dominic's latest test wasn't successful?" her uncle asked.

"No, sadly, it wasn't. I just don't have any other ideas."

Her uncle gave her a sympathetic smile as he poured her a glass of iced tea and pushed it toward her.

A basket filled with his garden haul in his arms, Cain walked over to join them. Placing the basket on the ground, he pulled up a chair. "I've been wracking my brain trying to think of something. But I'm afraid nothing comes to mind."

"Ugh, if the person who's been alive longer than anyone else in human history doesn't have any ideas, I have no idea where else to look or even what to search for."

Cain who'd been in the process of drinking his own iced tea, paused the glass halfway to his mouth.

A tingle of possibility rolled over Laney. "You've thought of something."

"Not something, but someone," Cain said slowly.

"Who?" Her uncle asked.

Opening his mouth, Cain quickly closed it, looking indecisive.

"What's wrong?" Laney asked.

"Nothing, exactly. It's just, I'm not sure whether I should get them involved."

"Well, who are they? Could they know about the liquid?" Laney asked.

"If anyone is alive that knows, it would be them," Cain said before falling silent again.

Laney leaned forward. "Cain, we need to know. If not for Drake, for what Gedeon has planned. If Gedeon can use it against Drake, then we can use it against him. Right now, we have no weapons. We need something."

Her uncle stared at Cain. "And we need to protect Nyssa. Finding this serum may be the only way."

Cain stared right back, the two of them having a long silent conversation before Cain finally took a drink. He let out a breath and nodded. "You have to understand, I've kept them away from all of this. I've kept their identity secret for so long, it's hard to break that habit."

He stared off into the backyard, but Laney knew he was seeing something else. "You'll find them in Rome. I'll give you the address. But take care. They've been through a great deal in their long life."

There was no inflection on the word *long*, and yet Laney heard something in Cain's tone that had her narrowing her eyes. "How long have you known them?" Laney asked.

"Only about three thousand years."

Laney's jaw hit the ground. "There's another immortal?"

"Not exactly," Cain said.

"But this person, they're almost as old as you?" her uncle asked.

Cain shook his head. "No, they're older."

CHAPTER 17

MASSA, ITALY

"Did they take you from someone that cares about you too?" Arturo asked. The boy sat in his corner of the room, his thin legs crossed, his knobby knees sticking out.

It had been three days since Gedeon had shoved the boy into his prison. Each night, he would pull him away. At first, it had been difficult to get the boy to say much. But yesterday, he and the boy had talked a great deal about his life and just life in general. He'd been returned to Drake a few hours ago. Now the boy had lost his fear of Drake and wanted to know more about his life.

Drake paused, once again trying to recall how exactly he'd ended up in Gedeon's clutches. He really had no clear recollection of what had happened. There were vague flashes of memories, but that was all. The last true concrete memory he had was of fighting with Laney in Egypt, of wresting control from the command that controlled him and giving her the chance to end him.

And she had.

He didn't hold any ill will toward her because of it. In fact, he was proud of her. Yet again, she'd overcome impossible odds in order to succeed.

His heart also broke at the idea of her having to take that step. He wished he could have kept it from her. He knew how devastating that must have been for her. And he marveled that she had been able to do it. He wasn't sure he would have had the strength to do the same, if their places had been reversed.

But when he was under command, there was nothing he could do. He was still shocked that he had been able to wrench himself away long enough for Laney to kill him. During all of his time as Michael, he was awake and aware but powerless. He'd seen the look of horror and devastation on her face when he killed Henry.

Henry was a good man. A good brother. He didn't deserve that. But then, none of them deserved what they had been put through. And in Drake's long time on this planet, he was more than clear on one fact: those who deserved to be treated horribly rarely were.

"Is there someone that's missing you?" Arturo asked again.

Once again, Drake pictured Laney's face, the sun shining against her red hair. "Yes, there is."

"Were they there when you were taken?"

Drake shook his head. "No. In fact, she didn't even know I was taken until not that long ago."

"How come she didn't know?"

"Because she thought I was dead."

"Why would she think that?"

Because she killed me, he thought but didn't say out loud. He seriously doubted that would ease the boy's fears. "Because she'd been told I was."

The boy nodded. Drake's mind shifted back to waking up in that cell in Greece. Before that, a wall of fog, a feeling of loss, then rough hands grabbing him, and that was about it.

He wasn't sure if he'd ever get those memories back. He didn't even know how much time had passed between Egypt and now.

But Laney had called that young man on the dock Max. Max had been a child no older than the boy who sat in this room with him now when Drake had last seen him. Which meant that years had to have passed.

He had no memory of any of that time.

Laney looked a little older but not by much. The truth was she looked incredible. The maturity on her face, it suited her. She was an old soul, and now she seemed to fit in that soul perfectly.

He never understood the human world and its obsession with young females. As females aged, they grew more into who they were meant to be. Their faces took on the experiences they had been through. And Laney, she'd only grown more beautiful, which was not something he thought was possible.

Drake realized he'd drifted off into his thoughts. In his time in captivity, it had been something that he did often. It helped to pass the time.

But the boy was staring at him, and he had a feeling that perhaps he'd missed a question. "Did you say something?"

The boy nodded, flicking a glance at the door. "I asked if you were like them."

"What makes you think I am?"

The boy scooted forward just a little bit and tapped the sigils.

Drake grinned. "Ah yes, my little prison. Well, I suppose I am like them, although not exactly like them."

"Are you as strong as them?"

"Usually, I am stronger. But unfortunately, I'm not at my normal strength right now."

"Is that because of the shots?"

"What do you know of the shots?" he asked.

The boy ducked his head. "I heard them speaking."

"Well, yes, the shots keep me weak."

"But if you didn't have the shots?"

"Then I would be stronger than all of them."

"So, you're all connected somehow, like family?"

Drake paused for a moment, trying to figure out how to explain how they were related. It was a complicated topic and perhaps not one that this boy was up for hearing. "Yes. We are family of a sorts." He pictured Gedeon. "A very distant, dysfunctional family at the moment, it appears."

"Do you have a lot of family? Brothers and sisters?"

"Dozens upon dozens."

Arturo leaned forward, his body having relaxed the more Drake talked. "Will your brothers and sisters be looking for you? Will they help you?"

The question brought Drake up short. He hadn't considered his brothers' and sisters' roles in all of this in a long time. The angels that were here were lower angels, less powerful than he and the other archangels.

But Gedeon seemed to have stepped out of bounds. He'd gone beyond what should have been allowed. Would his brothers and sisters step in? *Could* they even step in?

The answer came to him quickly. It was impossible. They would not do that without a command. And he didn't think a command would be coming.

Although he supposed the idea that they no longer had free will was not entirely accurate. Gedeon certainly seemed to be working from his own playbook.

The boy watched him expectantly.

Drake shook his head. "No. They will not be looking for me."

"Are you sure? I mean, I don't have any brothers or sisters, but I think if I did, they would want to help me."

Drake studied the boy for a moment, picturing his own siblings. It had been so long since he'd seen some of them.

But Arturo wasn't wrong in his insight. If they knew what he was being put through, would they intercede? In his gut, he hoped the answer was no. Because if they did in fact intercede, it would mean the beginning of only one thing: a war in Heaven.

THE BELIAL BLOOD

A shudder ran through him at the thought. "I hope not, Arturo. I hope not."

CHAPTER 18

BALTIMORE, MARYLAND

As soon as Cain shared where they needed to go, Laney was a flurry of movement. She arranged for the plane, packed a bag, and called the only person who she could, in good conscience, take.

She and David landed in a small airport outside Rome only five hours later. Before touching down, Laney had donned a wig and glasses to try and throw off anyone who might glance her way. David had had to settle for a simple baseball cap. Neither disguise was all that impressive, but it was all they could do on such short notice. And they didn't plan on staying in Rome for longer than a few hours anyway. If all went well, they would be in and out before anyone realized they were there.

Laney just hoped that their luck was a little better than what it had been lately.

They quickly jumped into the car that David had arranged to be waiting for them at the airport. Pulling out of the airport, Laney couldn't help but glance around. It was quiet. Laney said as much to David.

THE BELIAL BLOOD

"It's Sunday morning. Not much happening today."

Laney shook herself, realizing he was right. With all the hubbub, she hadn't realized that it was the weekend, the time when normal people took a break from their daily lives.

Hopefully soon they would figure out a way to take down Gedeon, and then she, too, would be one of the normal people sitting around lazily reading the news on a Sunday morning while having a late breakfast.

And having the news have absolutely nothing to do with her.

David expertly drove them through the outskirts of Rome and into the city itself. He'd lived here from the age of ten until the age of eighteen, when he'd gone away to college. After that, he'd lived in so many cities across the globe that Laney doubted he could even remember them all. In fact, as far as she could tell, Rome and DC had been the longest he'd stayed anywhere. Actually, on Luiz's ranch in Peru after the war with Rahim had been the longest he'd stayed anywhere for a consecutive time since his childhood.

"Do you ever get sick of it?"

David frowned, flicking a glance at her before returning his eyes to the road. "Sick of what?"

"All the moving around. All the travel."

He whipped around a small moped that made Laney suck in a breath as he tore down a small alley that looked barely wide enough for the car. "Yes and no. I love Rahim and the kids. They're my life. But I do like being able to occasionally go off to some foreign land for a few days before returning home. But as to whether I would trade my home with Rahim for the life I lived prior to the kids coming along? No, never."

Laney smiled, liking that David was embracing his home life.

"What about you? Do you miss all of this craziness?" he asked.

Laney opened her mouth to deny that she did, but then she shut it and thought for a moment. "I don't miss the people I love being in danger. But my life has become quiet, and not always in a good way. This reminds me of back when …" She paused, Drake's face flashing across her mind. "In a strange way, it makes me feel closer to him to be doing stuff like this, rescuing people."

"Being on the edge of death?"

She shrugged. "Perhaps that as well. But it doesn't mean I won't do everything in my power to make sure we get back to the quiet days."

"That I have no doubt of."

David slowed as he made a left, and Laney recognized the neighborhood near the orphanage. Two more turns, and David was pulling up to a parking spot just down the street.

"How do you want to play this?" Laney asked.

"I haven't contacted anyone from here, not even Bas. It's too great a risk. I have no doubt that their phones are being monitored. But it's unlikely that the orphanage itself is being watched. There are too many places that you or any of the people associated with you could be. The orphanage is a long shot for us to visit, especially now."

That was true. But she still couldn't help the small shiver of worry that crawled over her as she scanned the neighborhood.

"Well, let's get this over with," David said.

Laney reached out and grabbed his hand. "Are you sure you're all right with this?"

David shrugged, not quite meeting her gaze. "It is what it is. I would like to hear the story, though."

Laney and David quickly exited the car and made their way down to the orphanage gate. There was a large bell situated next to it, which David rang.

An older man came hurrying from the side of the building where he'd been raking leaves. His face broke into a smile as he caught sight of them. "David."

He opened the door and then took a look at Laney. His mouth dropped open. "Delaney?"

Laney smiled. "Hi, Rosario."

A smile burst across the caretaker's face as he hugged her tight.

"We'd been praying for your safe return. I read the newspaper articles about you reappearing, but I never thought that you would be here of all places."

He stepped back, looking between the two of them. "You must be here to see Angelica. Or is Sebastian joining you?"

David shook his head. "Actually, we're here to see Sister Cristela."

CHAPTER 19

ROME, ITALY

UP AHEAD WAS THE MAIN BUILDING OF THE SCHOOL OF THE HOLY Mother, covered in white stucco. A large wooden cross dominated the wall on the left of the front door. Rosario had returned to his leaves, although he made Laney and David promise to stop in and say hello to his wife Sylvia in the kitchen before they left.

David opened the door, and he and Laney stepped into the front foyer.

Laney's gaze immediately shot to the pope statue sitting in an alcove across from the door. At first glance, it could be any number of popes that had been appointed by the cardinals. But a closer inspection showed the more feminine attributes to this pope's face. It was a statue of Pope Joan, the only alleged female pope and a Follower of the Great Mother.

Rosario had explained that Cristela was in the library working on a book drive for the orphanage. David led the way down the hall as Laney pulled off her wig. They passed classrooms and a few supply closets before David stopped in an open doorway.

Her shoulders hunched, Sister Cristela sat at the desk, flicking a glance between the laptop screen and the legal pad on the desk in front of her. Her hands were still gnarled from arthritis, and the hair underneath her white wimple was pure white and curly. Laney hadn't seen her for at least seven years, but she didn't look like she had aged a day in that time.

Which would be fitting.

David knocked, and Cristela's head jerked up. Her mouth fell open, and she clapped her hands as she smiled. "David!"

She pushed back her chair and shuffled around the desk. David hurried over to meet her and hugged her tight. "I didn't know you were coming. Angelica didn't say anything," Cristela said.

"That's because she didn't know. We made this trip a bit spontaneously." David gestured toward Laney.

Cristela looked over at Laney and frowned. Pulling the glasses that hung on a chain around her neck up and onto her nose, she let out a burst of surprise. "Delaney. Oh, my goodness, girl, it is good to see you."

She reached out a hand, and Laney grasped it tightly. The nun's skin felt so thin. "It's good to see you too, Cristela."

Cristela beamed at the two of them. "So, what brings you to us today? Are you waiting for Angelica and Sebastian?"

Laney closed the door behind her, and David stepped toward one of the chairs in front of the desk. "Actually, we came to speak with you."

As she gestured to the chairs, Cristela looked between the two of them. "Me? Why, I'm honored. What can I do to help you?"

Laney took a seat in the chair, not sure how to start the conversation. "There was a situation in Greece. We learned that there is a serum that can be used to weaken an archangel."

Nodding slowly, Cristela sat down. "I read about that. Horrible, horrible what is happening."

"Yes," David said slowly. "But we have figured out who is

behind the attacks, and it's not a Fallen after all. It's an angel. He goes by the name Gedeon Malik, but his real name is Samael."

Laney studied Cristela closely, but she showed no reaction to the name. "Have you heard of him?"

"The angel of death." Cristela's voice was somber. "He's not a good person. But why have you come to me?"

Laney leaned forward. "Because we need to find more of the serum that he used against ..." She paused. "Another angel. We need to find its source."

Cristela's gaze shifted for a moment between the two of them. "I'm afraid I don't understand."

David leaned forward as well, his eyes intent. "We need to know where to get more of this serum. It may be the only way to stop Gedeon."

"But why are you coming to me?" Cristela asked.

Something in her tone had shifted. Laney waited until Cristela met her gaze. "Because we know that King Solomon told you how to make the serum."

CHAPTER 20

Cristela let out a laugh. "King Solomon? Exactly how old do you think I am?"

"Pretty old," Laney said. "And we know that you've spoken with King Solomon. In fact, we know that you knew him very well."

Cristela looked between the two of them, her brow furrowed before she turned to David. "David, what's going on? What is this craziness?"

David crossed his arms over his chest. "Could you answer her question, please, Sister?"

Cristela's gaze shifted back to Laney, and there was something in her gaze now, a shrewdness that hadn't been there a moment before. Laney kept her face blank, not wanting to show anger or annoyance but just simply waited for Cristela to answer.

Finally, Cristela sat back in her chair, blowing out a breath. "It was Cain, wasn't it?"

David let out a little gasp of surprise, but Laney nodded. "He pointed us in your direction."

Cristela shook her head. "I knew that was him in DC all those years ago. But it seemed so unlike him. He helped you on coronation day."

"He's been helping me ever since. In fact, I consider him part of my family now."

Cristela raised her eyebrows at the remark. "Well, now it seems he's finally figured out how to join the human race again. That's good. How is he doing?"

Laney paused before answering, picturing Cain as she had first met him and how she'd last seen him. "He's good. He is no longer cursed. His eyes, they're blue."

A smile worked its way across Cristela's face. "That is very good to hear. I always thought that punishment was too extreme. After all, he's hardly the only one who's murdered someone. If they went around cursing all the murderers with immortality, well, this planet would be awfully crowded."

Tension lined across his face, David cut in. "So, it's true? You've been around since Solomon's time?"

Cristela nodded slowly. "Oh, I've been around much longer than that. But I've been on Earth since Solomon's time."

"And what is your name?" Laney asked.

"It has been so long since I've heard it. But even if I said it, it would have no meaning for you."

"But Solomon, he gave you a name," Laney said.

Cristela nodded.

"You're the demon that Solomon locked up underneath the temple," Laney said.

Cristela opened her mouth, looking like she was going to argue the point and then simply nodded. "Yes. He called me Asmodeus."

CHAPTER 21

Laney's mind whirled. Asmodeus had been the king of all demons. He'd been, or she supposed, *she'd* been in charge of ordering the other demons to help build King Solomon's temple. King Solomon was said to have captured Asmodeus and then in exchange for Asmodeus's help to build the temple, Solomon said he would release Asmodeus once the construction was complete.

But Solomon lied. Once the temple was complete, he kept Asmodeus locked up, and then as a final insult was said to have sealed Asmodeus underneath the temple so as to always have the demon in his power.

"I don't understand," David said. "How are you here? How did King Solomon capture you? And *what* exactly are you? I don't believe for a minute that you're a demon."

Cristela gave him a small smile. "That's because I am *not* a demon. I am, however, an angel. It was my job to guard a special well here on Earth. I would travel down once a day to check on the well and make sure that it was safe before returning to Heaven. It was an enjoyable duty.

"Each trip offered me a glimpse of humanity up close and personal. And unlike my brothers and sisters, I enjoyed those glimpses immensely. For the longest time, I never interacted with anyone and always kept my distance. Eventually, though, I spoke with humans on occasion and even began to mingle with them regularly, although I never revealed who I was to them, of course. I manned that well and guarded it for centuries before Solomon came along."

Laney frowned. She remembered in the Bible telling of Asmodeus that he had, or she had, in fact, guarded a well. "What's so special about that well?"

"It was created to give humanity a chance to protect themselves against the angels should they turn against God. The Fallen were on Earth, and should they ever band together, God wanted a way for humans to protect themselves."

"So, it wasn't just water in the well?" David asked.

"No. It's called ..." Cristela gave them a small smile. "Well, you could not pronounce its name. The closest in the human tongue would be Inceptus."

"To begin," Laney said, translating the word from Latin.

Cristela nodded. "Yes,. The Inceptus was a way to strip a Fallen or a full-blooded angel of their powers, at least temporarily."

Laney sat back stunned, picturing Drake. That was what had been used on him, it had to be. "It could be used on an archangel as well?"

Cristela nodded. "A great deal was learned after the Fallen rebelled. As they say, fool me once ..."

"How did you come into Solomon's possession?" David asked.

Cristela sighed. "Over time, I had gotten less vigilant in my journeys to Earth. Like I said, I'd started interacting with humans on each trip. I liked them. They were so different from my brothers and sisters. So full of life. At first, I would go for long walks and spy on families or even sometimes walk through the villages just to see them interact. Such a strange combination of love, anger, laughter, and confusion.

"Humans were complicated creatures but what they definitely

were not was boring. So as time went on, I began to look forward to my interactions with them. But what I underestimated was their ambition and their guile."

Cristela broke off, her eyes looking troubled. And Laney couldn't help but feel for her. She sounded almost like a child who'd been taken advantage of.

Cristela continued. "Solomon and his men captured me one day."

"How? You were an angel," David said.

"They forced my mouth open and poured the liquid from the well down my throat. I had no choice but to swallow it, and as I did, my powers fled me. I had enough to throw them off me, but by the time I stood, I was no more powerful than a human."

"What did he want?"

Cristela let out a bitter laugh. "What did he want? What *didn't* he want? By the time I met Solomon, his kindness and goodness were gone. They were replaced with ambition and greed. He wanted everything. He told me he wanted me to build him a temple to honor God, but I could see that it wasn't God he wanted to honor; it was himself. I refused, of course, and they beat me. But I would not help them. I could not."

She took a shuddering breath, and it was clear even all those years later, the memories haunted her. "They dragged two young children in front of me. Without a word, Solomon flicked his fingers, and the guard slit his throat." Cristela closed her eyes. "I can still hear his sister's screams."

"Solomon told me if I did not do what he wanted, he would kill her as well. And then he would drag in child after child and destroy all of their lives until I gave in. I didn't want to help him. I didn't want to do anything for him. But a building, a simple building, is not worth the lives of innocent children. So, I gave in. I told him how to build the temple." She took a deep breath. "I told him how to control the demons."

Laney reached for the ring around her neck, pulling it out. "And this?"

"I crafted that."

The words fell with a thud. All these years, Laney had never wondered who had crafted the ring of Solomon. The symbol, the ring, it had been such a part of folklore that she had never considered it. It was like wondering who had made the material for Superman's suit.

But more than that revelation was the feeling of loss that radiated from the nun. Even now, thousands of years later, Laney could feel Cristela's pain at the loss. And anger at Solomon rolled through Laney. Men and their ambitions.

"How long were you held by Solomon?" David asked.

"Too long. I was still sealed up beneath the temple just before he died. And I remained there for over two hundred years, barely alive."

"No one found you? How is that possible?" David asked.

"Solomon had all those who knew of the room where I was held put to death, and those who entombed me there were killed as well. Once Solomon died, there was no one left to remember me."

"How did you get out?" Laney asked.

Cristela met Delaney's gaze. "It was a Follower who freed me. She had joined the ranks of the Templars. The Templars had excavated underneath the Temple Mount and found the foundations of Solomon's temple. It was all that remained of the temple after the destruction over the years."

"I'd hoped with each attack on the temple and the rebuilding that someone would find me, but they never did. I lay there wasting away until that Follower found me. She knew immediately who I was. And she killed all the Templars with her to keep my secret."

"Why did she do that?" David asked.

"Because while many of the Templars were good and honest

THE BELIAL BLOOD

individuals, those they reported to were not. The Follower knew that if I was taken back to Rome, or if news of me was taken back to Rome, I would once again be put in chains. I would once again be used for the ambitions of men. And she knew that that could not be allowed to happen.

"So she hid me, and I stayed hidden for a long time. And then one day the Followers I had taken refuge with grew sick. There had been an illness in a village. Within a week, they were all dead, and I was on my own. I wandered the land."

Laney cut in. "Why didn't you just go back home? Solomon was no longer feeding you the wine, so you had your powers back."

Cristela shook her head. "I don't know how long it takes, but eventually when you have been given the liquid enough, your powers are gone entirely. I age but incredibly slowly. Yet all the abilities I had before, I haven't felt them in thousands of years. Beyond my long life, I am in every way human."

Laney sat back, staring at Cristela. Human. She was an angel made human. "This well, the source of the wine, do you know where it is?"

"At the time I was taken, it was located near the city of Ophir. That name no longer has relevance in this time. But I do know where it would be in the current time."

Cristela looked between the two of them, and the joy that had building inside of Laney began to dwindle. She shook her head slowly. "It won't do you any good. The well needs constant tending to maintain it. And it hasn't been tended to in thousands of years. It will be completely dry by now."

Laney sat back, her hopes crushed.

"How, then, was Gedeon able to get some?" David asked.

Laney looked over at David in surprise and then sat up. That was a really good question.

Cristela shrugged. "That I do not know. I just know that the well that I once used will have long gone dry."

"Are you sure? Is it possible that it was reconstituted? After Egypt, a great many things changed."

Cristela paused. "That is true. I haven't been there since the events in Egypt. Truth be told, I haven't been there in 500 years."

The words fell easily from Cristela's lips, yet they were shocking nonetheless.

"We need to go check. We need to make sure," Laney said.

"You are committed to this course of action?" Cristela asked.

Laney and David nodded.

"There is a small chance—very small, mind you—that a small amount of the serum you seek may still exist."

"Can you give us directions there?" David asked.

Cristela nodded. "Very well. Give me thirty minutes. I have to decorate the cookies with the children. And then I will be ready to go with you." She stood up slowly, incredibly slowly.

David leaned forward, no doubt thinking the same thing Laney was: If they waited for Cristela, this trip was going to take a lot longer, and not just because of the thirty minutes. She was not a fast-moving woman.

"You could just give us the directions, and we could go and check," David said.

Cristela gave him a smile indicating she knew exactly what he was really thinking. "I know I am slow. You try being alive for thousands of years and we'll see how fast you move. But that is not the only reason. You will not be able to find it without me. I have to go. There is no other choice."

"Where are we going?" Laney asked.

This time, when Cristela smiled, her face took on a much younger appearance, her eyes lighting up. "To the place where I first entered this world: the Corycian Cave."

The name jolted Laney. "The Corycian Cave? But that's where ..." Laney stared at Cristela as the ramifications of the location hit her.

"Yes. That is where I first made myself known to this world."

THE BELIAL BLOOD

David looked between the two of them. "What am I missing?"

"The Corycian Cave is perhaps the most famous cave in all of Greece. It was home to the Oracle of Delphi." Laney met Cristela's gaze. "*You* were the Oracle."

Cristela nodded. "Yes."

CHAPTER 22

After they finished frosting the cookies with the children, Cristela packed a small bag, and they were on their way to the airfield. Laney looked at the bag, and Cristela smiled at her. "Just in case it takes longer than we think."

Once they were up in the air, Cristela's eyes closed almost immediately. Now she dozed, her breaths soft. Laney watched her, trying to wrap her head around the idea that she had come across yet another immortal. Cristela was not what one would picture as an immortal. She was so … normal. Yet she had been alive for perhaps longer than even Cain.

Now as she stared at her, Laney's mind reeled at what she had told them: She had been the Oracle at Delphi. Laney liked to think that nothing could shock her anymore. But that definitely did.

There was almost something sexy about the idea of an oracle, and yet looking at the small birdlike nun across from her, it was hard to reconcile that the two were one and the same.

She supposed the idea that the oracle started as someone trying to help people made sense. But she couldn't help but wonder how the mission had changed with the oracle only accessible to people of a certain rank.

Cristela shifted, her eyes slowly opening. She looked around in surprise before her gaze met Laney's and her shoulders relaxed. "Oh, right. I was confused for a moment as to where we were."

"We should be landing in another thirty or forty minutes."

Cristela nodded, sitting up with a wince. She straightened out her habit and then looked over at Laney. "You look like you have some questions for me."

"If you don't mind."

"Not at all. It's actually quite nice to talk about these things. I've never really had the opportunity to do so. Except, of course, with Cain every few hundred years or so. So ask your questions."

"We believe Gedeon is trying to assemble the pieces of the Arma Christi."

A gasp escaped Cristela. "He wouldn't."

"He's gathering the pieces, but we're not sure what it will do. It's a weapon, isn't it?"

"Yes," she said, her eyes troubled. "It can kill an angel."

Laney frowned. "See, that's what I don't understand. Angels can be killed. I've killed them."

"Yes, that's true, at least their physical bodies can be killed. But their souls remain intact. They can be reborn. In that sense, we are immortal. But the Arma Christi, it destroys the soul as well. An angel would simply cease to be."

"Why would Gedeon want such a weapon? Who would he be targeting?"

"That I do not know, but he cannot be allowed to use it. He cannot be allowed to create it."

"We're trying to stop him, but it's not that easy. We're not even sure what the process would be to create the weapon, so it feels like we're always a few steps behind."

Cristela's dark eyes studied Laney for a long time before she sighed. Reaching down into her bag, she pulled out a small notepad and a pen. She scribbled for a few minutes, then ripped the page off and handed it to Laney. "This is how the Arma

Christi is formed. Be careful who you share this knowledge with."

Laney took the paper and met Cristela's gaze. "Why are you trusting me with this?"

Because the world is going to need you. And there may come a time when you need it."

The paper and the responsibility behind it felt heavy in Laney's hand. She glanced at the list but only to see if she could read Cristela's handwriting. But it was clearly written, so she shoved it into her pocket. She would deal with that later.

Wanting to switch to a lighter topic, she asked, "How did the Delphi Oracle continue after you'd been taken?"

"Oh, one of the attendants to the oracle took over. As an oracle, I always had attendants who helped with matters. I wasn't there all the time. I would come in and provide a reading or two. Return to tend the well and then return to Heaven. It was how it all worked, and then once I was taken, the attendants continued to provide the readings. No one knew that I was gone."

"But those readings, they weren't actually prophecies, then, were they?"

"That cave, it has a particular gas that is emitted from it. It causes trances and abilities to see beyond what human eyes can see. So yes, they were actual readings. The attendants were chosen because they were sensitive to such things. They just need a little more help to bring those abilities out. So the readings continued for centuries after I was gone. Until I returned."

Laney knew the region's underlying rocks were composed of oily limestone fractured by two hidden faults that crossed exactly under the ruined temple. The faults allowed ethylene to rise to the surface to help induce visions. Ethylene was a sweet-smelling gas used as an anesthetic but also produced feelings of euphoria.

"You went back? Why return? Why not go somewhere else?" Laney asked.

Cristela sighed. "I had nowhere to go. My abilities were gone. I could not return to Heaven. The well had long since dried up, and I needed something familiar. I stayed as the oracle for a short while until I learned the Templars were looking for me."

"The Templars? But weren't they long gone by the time you were released? And how did they find you? And why would they be looking for you?"

"I'm not sure. I believe someone might have seen Rowan and I as we left the temple. We had rushed out into the night, and she told me not to look back. I didn't. But I had the sense that someone was following us. So I went and stayed with Followers. When the Templars found me, I managed to slip away, but I knew I needed to reinvent myself, and that's what I did. I slipped between towns and villages until I heard that the Templars had been disbanded and killed. Even then, I knew that there had to be some holdouts hiding away. So, I stayed in the shadows for another 200 years before finally allowing myself to set down some roots."

"It must have been a lonely existence."

"It was at times. I would put down some roots, sometimes for a year or two. Those years were a balm to my soul."

Laney couldn't help but think of Cain and all the wandering he'd done during his life. The lack of connection had hurt him. But Cristela sitting across from her, she seemed to be so at peace.

Cristela tilted her head now as she watched Laney. "Those are not the questions I thought you would have asked."

Laney frowned. "What did you think I would ask about?"

"Well, Michael, of course."

CHAPTER 23

Laney sat back, stunned. "You knew him?"

Cristela smiled. "Of course. I was one of the most trusted."

"You were an archangel."

Cristela gave her yet another smile. "Yes. It was how I was given such freedom. I suppose I was an experiment of sorts. To see how interacting with the humans on a regular basis would affect us. I'm not sure if I confirmed or refuted the hypotheses, but it definitely affected me."

The questions were all on the tip of Laney's tongue, and yet something held her back. She wasn't sure if she wanted to know what Michael had been like.

"I see fear, and I understand it. As angels, duty is the most important priority. In fact, it's the only focus. Nothing else is considered. That was more true for Michael than any of them. At least until the fall."

Laney knew that Michael had been devastated when his brothers had chosen to fall, that he couldn't understand it. It was that act that led him to eventually be born as a human, as Achilles. He'd wanted to see what life was like as a human. He'd wanted to understand what it was that his brothers and sisters had been so drawn to.

"You know, I saw you. I was in Sparta for some of Helen's reign, at least early on. I went to see Michael."

Laney's breath hitched. "You were there?"

Cristela nodded. "Yes, and he was so different than the Michael that I knew. He was full of life. He was full of laughter, and he was so in love."

Warmth spread through Laney.

"I think that was what truly changed him. He fell in love with a magnificent woman, one who was strong and capable and who also understood duty. She had compassion and empathy, and those unfortunately, are qualities that many of my brothers and sisters lack. They are decidedly human qualities."

"Have you seen him since?"

Cristela nodded again. "I caught his show in Vegas once."

Laney didn't think she could be more shocked if Cristela had said that she had become a stripper. *"You* were in Vegas?"

Cristela's laugh burst through the plane. "You appear more shocked by that than the fact that I've been alive for so long."

Laney's mouth fell open, and she had to grin in response. "Yeah, I guess I sort of am."

"It was a very good show. But I could tell he wasn't entirely happy. It is good that you have found each other again."

"We haven't. He's gone, or sort of."

Cristela nodded. "I know he's returned. I felt it."

"You can feel the angels?"

"Not in the way you do. But for some, I can feel when they are on this planet. Michael is one of them."

Laney leaned forward. "How is it possible that he did? I thought he was gone."

Cristela frowned. "I do not know, and the fact that Gedeon has him troubles me."

"You know Gedeon as well?"

"A necessary evil. But I have to say I have questioned exactly how necessary he has truly been."

It was strange. She could tell Cristela had doubts about the role that the angels played in humanity's existence, much the way her uncle had struggled through the same process. All these people of great faith who were now struggling to reconcile what they knew with what they had been taught or with what they believed. "Does it change what you believe?"

There was no doubt in Cristela's response. "No. But questioning whether things could have been handled differently— there is nothing wrong with that. Perhaps I question the choices, but not the reasons underneath them. Humanity should be tested. It should see what its limits are. But I feel that Gedeon has strayed too far from his mission. He has taken it upon himself more and more to craft these tests, and the cruelty and callousness in them —I do not approve of that."

"He was the one who determined the nature of the tests?"

Cristela nodded. "All angels are given their missions. But how they carry them out, that is up to the individual angel. Gedeon chose what he did. His actions are his own."

"How then is all of this okay? How could anyone think that this is part of a plan?"

A troubled look slid across Cristela's face. Her hands shook as she placed them on the armrests. "I don't believe this is part of anyone's plan but Gedeon's."

David's voice over the PA system broke into their conversation. "Okay, ladies. Buckle up. We're coming in for a landing, and we're coming in hot."

Cristela looked up an alarm.

Laney rolled her eyes. David's chuckle came across the speakers a second or two later. "Just kidding. But we will be landing in about ten minutes. So make sure your seatbelts are on and your trays are stowed in the upright position."

Cristela narrowed her eyes, glaring up at the speaker.

THE BELIAL BLOOD

"That boy takes nothing seriously," Cristela said as she tightened her seatbelt, but there was amusement in her tone.

Laney was more focused on what Cristela had said before David's interruption. If Gedeon wasn't under orders? Then what exactly was his plan? And how come the other angels were helping him?

CHAPTER 24

MOUNT PARNASSUS, GREECE

THE AREA AROUND THE CORYCIAN CAVE WAS BEAUTIFUL. Long rambling hills covered with rocks, trees, and even the occasional goat. A dozen or so tourists were heading up or coming down from the dark cave.

"I'll take care of that." The clouds darkened. Lightning flashed and a torrent of rain opened up. Sheets of rain pounded the earth. The tourists made a mad dash for their cars. They waited for twenty minutes, no doubt in the hope that the storm would pass. Laney added some wind, rocking their cars. They quickly headed down the mountain.

David grinned. "Very theatrical."

"I aim to please," she said, stepping outside. Now the ground was wet as she led the way, with David helping Cristela up the path toward the cave.

Cristela stopped, looking around, her eyes wide.

"Does it look at all familiar?" David asked.

"Yes and no," Cristela said. "So much has changed. But it feels the same."

THE BELIAL BLOOD

Laney was glad for that at least. She started toward the main entrance of the cave, but Cristela called out, "We're not going to go that way. We're going this way."

She pointed to the left. There didn't seem to be any path there, so whatever way Cristela knew of, it wasn't well tread.

Laney let David and Cristela go first and followed them around the side of the mountain. Laney worried about the older nun's stamina, but she seemed to be handling it pretty well. If anything, she seemed energized by the adventure. Although Laney had a feeling she would be sleeping the entire way home.

"Where are we going?" David asked.

"There is a secret entrance. It is how I slipped in and out. It is where Solomon caught me," Cristela said.

"How did that happen?" David asked.

Cristela sighed. "I was foolish."

The delegation from Scythia left the cave, and the oracle stretched. "Is that the last one?" she asked, her brain finally beginning to clear from the gas.

Her two attendants had covered the hole where the gases were emitted ten minutes ago. The effects lingered for at least that long. It helped with the readings, but for her it wasn't necessary. But as she didn't want anyone to know that, she used the gas. Besides, it did help her focus more quickly.

The latest readings had not made the Scythian dignitaries happy. But she didn't change her readings based upon her audience. She provided what she saw, no more no less.

Eupraxia nodded, hurrying over to her side and helping her stand. "Yes, Oracle. That is the last one."

The oracle leaned down and ran a hand over Eupraxia's face. She was such a beautiful child. Only ten years on this planet, but love, understanding, and wisdom filled those big brown eyes of

R.D. BRADY

hers. "Thank you, my dear. I think I will take my leave of you. Have the other priestesses taken their places?"

"Of course, Oracle." She hesitated. "Where do you go when you leave us?"

The oracle was happy to hear the question. She had been working on building Eupraxia's trust and confidence. The fact that she would ask such a question was a sign that it was working. She had found the girl two years ago, beaten and half starved by her family.

The oracle had saved her from that wretched home and brought her to be one of her attendants. She had seen her blossom both in spirit and body since that time. She was truly a kind soul without a thought of violence in her mind, despite her difficult upbringing.

She was a gift to the world.

The oracle leaned down and kissed her cheek. "I go to see to my duties and to visit my family."

"Could I go with you?"

"Perhaps one day. But not quite yet."

Accepting the statement, Eupraxia nodded, her eyes shining. "I look forward to the day when I can go with you."

And the oracle found that she looked forward to it as well. She removed the veil from her face and handed it over to Eupraxia as they walked toward her room.

Her other attendant, Tasenka, was waiting for them. She had laid out the oracle's clothes, a simple linen shift and well-worn leather sandals along with the satchel that the oracle always carried.

She quickly got changed into the clothes, laying the silk garments on the bed. As soon as she placed a piece of her wardrobe down, one of the girls would whisk it away.

Fastening the belt around her waist, the oracle sat down on the edge of her cot as she put on her sandals. She flicked a glance to her bag, then reached her hand in and pulled out a small jar.

THE BELIAL BLOOD

Tilting her head, Tasenka glanced over. "What is that, Oracle?"

The oracle grasped the jar in her hand. "This is a gift from the gods to humanity. It is a way to protect themselves when there is a great danger that must be faced."

"Will it be needed soon?" Eupraxia asked, her eyes troubled.

"It will be—"

A vision flashed across the oracle's mind. She fell back on the bed, her eyes slamming shut as she stared at visions long in the future. Violence and death soaked a modern world made of steel and glass. It felt like forever as she watched the violence unfold.

"Oracle! Oracle!"

As the oracle finally opened her eyes, Tasenka and Eupraxia were at her side, pleading with her, tears rolling down their cheeks The oracle reached up, feeling weak as her heart pounded. She gripped Eupraxia's hand. "It's all right. I'm fine. Just a vision."

The two girls hurried to help her sit up. "You've never had one like that before," Tasenka said.

No, she hadn't. "It was disturbing."

"Is there anything we should do?" Tasenka asked.

The oracle looked down at the bottle still in her hand. "Someone will have need of this one day."

"What should we do?"

The oracle smiled. She leaned forward and kissed each attendant on the forehead. "There is nothing for you to do. It is merely something for me to take care of. There is nothing to worry about. It will not affect either of you. It will be long in the future."

The two girls looked up at her, their faces so young. Humans lifespans were so short compared to angel's that the oracle couldn't help but be grateful for whatever short time she was able to spend with these two wonderful creatures.

Unfortunately, it was time for her to go. The well would not wait. "I must go now."

Eupraxia's face fell, and the oracle's heart clutched. She did hate leaving her. It was different for Tasenka, whose mother was one of the priestesses. But the oracle felt a close connection to young Eupraxia. "I will be back soon. Before two nights' time has passed."

Eupraxia nodded.

There was nothing for the oracle to do, so she simply wrapped an arm around the young girl and hugged her tight before walking across the room. She shifted a tapestry aside and slipped into the path cut into the stone behind it. No one but her attendants knew of the secret passages underneath the cave. There was a series of them that allowed her to leave and return without anyone noticing.

She stepped into the hallway, the floor consisting of hard-packed dirt, and walked quickly down. Torches had been lit and would continue until just before the exit. She would extinguish the last few so that when she stepped outside it was completely dark.

The picture of Eupraxia's face swam through her mind, but she pushed it aside as she thought about the visions that she'd had the last few days. There had been many.

But the one she focused on was the visit from King Solomon just two days earlier. For some reason, the look in the man's eyes left her unsettled. She wasn't sure why that was. She had met many a leader over time. But Solomon, there was something in his eyes, ambition, or perhaps ownership. He wanted something from her, and although he had said his goodbyes without any sort of difficulty, the oracle knew in her gut that it was the not the last time she would see him.

She gripped the handle of her satchel tighter. She needed to take care of the bottle. The Inceptus needed to be safe. The vision she had just had, it was years and years in the future, and yet somehow, she felt this urgency, as if it were just around the corner. Which made no sense. The advances she had seen, they could not be coming anytime soon.

Her mind caught up in trying to parse out the meaning of the last few days, she didn't hear the scuff of the sandal until it was too late. A large hand darted out from an alcove and slipped around her mouth before pulling her taut against a warm body. "There you are, Oracle. I've been looking for you."

The oracle didn't hesitate. She slammed the heel of her sandal into the man's instep. He let out a cry, and she heard the crunch of bone. She turned around and grabbed the man by the throat, pushing him up against the side of the cave.

And she recognized him. He had been with Solomon.

Without a word, the oracle snapped the man's neck and let him drop. She hurried down the hall and pulled the bottle from her satchel. She placed it in a small alcove and then covered it with a rock that blended seamlessly into the walls around it. Then she pushed a little harder, sealing the rock in place. She had created this hiding place eons ago, and unless one knew where to look, it would be impossible to find.

Letting out a shaky breath, she paused, looking back toward the cave. Should she return? She flicked a glance toward the exit, which was only a short distance away. She blew out the torch nearest her. No, she needed to get to the well. Maintaining the well was more important, and she could double back around to make sure that the caves and her attendants were all right.

She hurried forward, and in the dark the large rock that guarded its way slid open. It was pitch black out, and nothing but the night sounds greeted her. She stepped outside. Liquid splashed in her face.

Her mouth was open, and some trickled down her throat. Her eyes widened as the familiar scent caught her attention. "No."

But her protestations did nothing to keep the liquid from seeping into her. The Inceptus.

Torches flared to life. A group of men stood in a semicircle around the entrance. The oracle darted forward, but her speed was a quarter of what it normally was. Weakness rolled through her.

Nevertheless, she slammed her foot into one of the men nearest her, and he went flying back, landing twenty feet away with a sickening thump.

Two other men gripped her by the arms. A third splashed more liquid in her face, and then one held her by the throat, pulling down her jaw as the other forced the liquid down.

Choking, she gagged, but there was no stopping the liquid from doing its damage. Her struggles weakened. She closed her eyes, slumping in the arms of the men who held her. So stupid. She should have returned to the cave.

"Good evening, Oracle." The man stepped out from the group, his piercing blue eyes staring at her. His long hair was pulled back in a ponytail, and the look of ownership that she had seen on his face two days earlier now stood out with even more resolve.

King Solomon leaned forward. "You and I are going to do great things together."

"Solomon had found the well. His people followed me one day, and I had not realized it. I do not know how that was possible, but I suppose I had become less guarded over time."

"There was never an opportunity for you to escape?" Laney asked.

"There were a few. But Solomon, he guarded against that."

Laney didn't want to ask, but she knew she had to. "How?"

"He slaughtered one of my attendants, Tasenka. But one he brought with him."

"Eupraxia."

Cristela nodded. "That beautiful child was given as a gift to one of King Solomon's generals. She was his insurance that I would do what he said. Within a year, I'd made the ring, and he could control the Fallen. By then, he could also control me. I had been so weakened by the Inceptus that I had none of my powers.

He kept me there as I helped him build his temple, and then once he realized his own mortality, he had me hidden away, and those who had buried me had been killed. I lay in that tomb for hundreds of years until Rowan came and let me out."

The horror of what she'd been through crawled over Laney's skin, and yet Cristela seemed so at peace.

"How are you not crazy?" David asked.

"Oh, I went crazy for a short while, but then I just gave in to what was happening. With my visions, I knew that eventually I would be freed. So, I lived inside my own mind. Centuries passed, and then I was outside once again. And now, I have slowly aged as time has gone on. I do not know how much longer I have left on this planet. But I do plan to enjoy myself."

She stopped at the back of the mountain at a space overgrown with bushes. She frowned, staring at it. "I believe this is where the entrance was. But I'm not sure how we're going to get to it."

Laney slipped in between the bushes. She reached the edge of the rock face, and David stepped next to her. The two of them inspected the space, looking for any sort of opening. Laney wasn't seeing anything. Perhaps Cristela had the wrong spot? It had been so many years after all.

Then David called out, "I think I have something."

Laney slid along the edge of the rock toward him. It did look like there was a slight ridge along the edge of where David was pointing. She followed with her eyes and eventually made out the outline of a rock.

But after glancing down at the ground, it was clear to Laney that the ground had built up around it over the years. They wouldn't be able to move it without a backhoe.

"Come on," she said to David.

The two of them slipped back out through the overgrowth.

"Did you find the opening?" Cristela asked.

Laney nodded. "It's overgrown. We'll need to get some equipment in here."

Cristela shook her head. "I don't believe you have time for that. You need to get it out now, and then you need to get back to the United States."

Laney frowned, staring at the small nun. "Why? Did you see something?"

Cristela gave a small laugh. "No. My visions, I haven't had them for years. But there is something gnawing at me, telling me that you need to return home. I believe you should be able to open it, yes?" Cristela's eyes bored into Laney's.

Laney looked back at the rock face and then at the nun. "How far away is the hiding spot of the Inceptus?"

"At least a good sixty yards."

Laney nodded. "Okay, then. Let's back up."

The three of them backed away from the rock face, and then Laney looked up at the sky, the clouds rolling in and the sky darkening.

"I'm not sure if I hate when you do this or love it," David mumbled.

Laney smiled. Personally, she loved it.

Taking a deep breath, she called on the power within her and stared at the rock face. Two lightning bolts slammed into the side of the mountain.

Rocks and debris blew through the air. Laney turned her head as she was pelted by dust and small pieces of rock.

David coughed, waving the air in front of his face. "Did you get it?"

Laney peered through the dust and saw a gaping hole in the side of the hill. She grinned. "I got it."

David pulled flashlights out of his pack and handed one to each of them.

Helping Cristela over the debris at the entrance, the three of them stepped inside.

"It will be on the right-hand side," Cristela said.

Laney nodded as she scanned her flashlight over the walls.

THE BELIAL BLOOD

There was no blemishes or graffiti or anything that indicated anyone had ever been in here.

"I sealed these tunnels when I returned as the oracle. I knew that I needed to keep the Inceptus safe." Cristela seemed energized by the uncovering of the tunnel, and she walked down the space quickly. She stopped about sixty yards down and started scanning the rock face intently.

Laney and David added their own the light from their own flashlights to aid her. Finally, Cristela let out a little cry. "It's here."

She nodded toward a spot that was just above Laney's eye level. Laney reached up and wiped away the dust. Two intertwined triangles had been carved into the stone.

"The seal of Solomon," David said.

Cristela snorted, a rather unusual sound coming from the little nun. "Solomon's. Please. That symbol existed for eons before him. His name just became associated with it. In fact, if the ownership of that symbol goes to anyone, it is certainly not Solomon."

"It's Lilith's symbol," Laney said softly as she traced the design in the rock.

"Yes, she deserves the credit much more than Solomon does." Cristela reached up and carefully turned the rock and then pulled it free. She reached up toward the empty space and then grunted. "It appears I have shrunk. Stupid body. Will one of you reach in there, please?"

David reached in and pulled out a burlap fabric carefully. He unwrapped it, and within it was a small stone jug with a stopper still intact.

Laney peered closer at it and realized that wax sealed the stopper in place.

"Is it still in there?" David asked.

Cristela smiled as she shook the stone jar before handing it to Laney. "It is, and now you two need to get back to the States."

119

CHAPTER 25

BALTIMORE, MARYLAND

It was a cool, crisp morning as Patrick rolled his wheelchair down the middle of Sharecroppers Lane. Laney had left late yesterday with David.

Patrick tried to tell himself it would be a simple trip. During the day, he'd done an admirable job of distracting himself, but once night fell, there'd been no more distractions. His sleep had been piecemeal at best. Most of the time, he'd simply lain in bed as a torrent of worry rushed through his mind. Finally, he'd given up and headed to the kitchen to make some banana bread. Baking had turned into a solace of sorts these last few years.

The baking had been enjoyable and the bread delicious, but now he found himself still burdened by his worries. He wasn't sure what to think about Laney's trip.

She'd sent a text just a short while ago to say they were on the way back and that she would explain everything when she arrived. He was looking forward to that explanation.

Over the years, he'd seen a lot of remarkable things and met people he never imagined he would meet. But this latest revelation and what it could mean, he couldn't quite wrap his mind around it.

In fact, ever since Cain had mentioned the End of Days to him, he'd worried about what the future had in store for all of them. The End of Days was something that he, of course, was familiar with. There wasn't a priest out there who wasn't familiar with the Book of Revelation.

If he was being honest, though, he'd never put much stock in it. He'd always thought it was more of a cautionary tale of what could happen if people didn't hold the line against evil in their daily lives. Or, as many scholars suggested, a discussion on the role of the Roman rule in Israel. He never thought about it as an actual prophecy of the future. But events of the last century in particular seemed to indicate that his dismissal may have been naive.

Patrick looked up in surprise, realizing that he'd already reached the main gate of the estate. These early morning journeys weren't unusual for him. In fact, once he'd started to come back from the depression that Delaney's absence had pushed him into, he'd started these morning trips as a form of exercise.

But soon he realized that they were more than that. They were a form of meditation, or perhaps a promise to the day that he would make it count. That he would give his best and try his hardest to stay in the moment.

Those first few weeks when Laney had disappeared had been hard. But then the weeks that followed had been even harder. Patrick had not been able to wrap his head around the idea that Laney was truly gone.

Perhaps it was because she'd disappeared before.

But as the weeks turned into months and the months turned into years, there was no denying that she was well and truly gone.

And with her, a part of his heart had seemed to shut down entirely. For so long, it had been just the two of them against the world. He'd been a priest in the Roman Catholic Church, but the reality was, it was him and Laney that he thought of as family. She was his first thought in the morning and his last thought at night. She was all he had left of his sister.

And even years later, when he learned the truth that she was not his sister's biological daughter, but Lilith's, it didn't change the connection he felt with Laney or with his sister. He saw his sister's fierceness in Laney's protective nature. He saw his brother-in-law's seriousness in Laney's determination to do the right thing. So while biologically they may not be related, she was his family and always would be. Blood didn't change that.

The thought of blood brought him up short. It always came down to blood, didn't it? Laney had made that statement more than once. And she wasn't wrong. Laney's blood had been the catalyst that had removed the ability of the Fallen across the globe. Blood and the spilling of it was part of the ritual in the church at every mass. The blood of the Fallen could be used to turn someone without those abilities into someone with abilities.

And now it looked like the blood of Jesus was once again coming into play, or at least Gedeon believed that his blood would come into play. And allow him to what? Destroy an archangel?

The only reasonable target for such a weapon would be Michael. Michael was by far the most powerful of the archangels. And he was supposed to play a role in the End of Days. In fact, according to the Book of Revelation, it was Michael who led God's armies in Heaven against the evildoers, eventually succeeding in casting them down to Earth.

But if that were the case, why would he be the target of Gedeon?

Gedeon, or Samael as he was known in the Bible, was a dutiful soldier of God. God surely couldn't want the death of Michael, could he?

But then again, Drake was as far from the vision of Michael depicted in the Bible as one could get. Michael was always the most stalwart, the most determined in his conviction to do right

THE BELIAL BLOOD

by God's orders. Drake was not exactly what Patrick would call godly. In fact, Drake seemed to be focused on having a good time and looking for a laugh.

He was awfully Scottish that way.

But there was a loyalty in Drake that could not be doubted. Drake loved Laney. That was clear to anyone who saw them together. And he'd seen Drake when Michael had taken over. It had been a completely different person. Drake's time spent on Earth had changed him. His time being around humans had changed him. And if Patrick was being honest, he had to say that change was for the better.

As much as Drake was not the person Patrick would have picked for Laney, in the end he was exactly who Laney needed. Drake did not question her. He did not doubt her when she felt the need to do the things that only she could do. No, Drake simply stood by her side and supported her and helped her where he could. Patrick couldn't ask for more from Laney's partner than that.

Laney had been devastated when Drake died, when she'd had to kill him. Patrick had worried that she would not be able to recover from that. But slowly, she'd come back to life. But he'd noticed a sadness that always seemed to float in the air around her, even as she tried to hide it. He'd been relieved when she'd started to date again, but it soon became clear that she was only doing so to make the rest of them feel better.

The truth was, after Egypt, all of their lives were better. In fact, the world was a better place because of Delaney's actions.

But the reality was that for Laney, her life was greatly diminished without Drake in it. And after all she'd been through, after all she'd sacrificed, it seemed so cruel to not have that one piece of her soul returned to her.

He rolled up the main path and looped around the fountain in front of the main headquarters of the Chandler Group. His gaze strayed toward the back of the estate where Henry and Jen lived with their children. Of course, Laney could have taken that piece of her soul back. When Ralph had appeared to her in Colorado, she could have chosen to have Drake returned to her.

But instead, she chose to allow Henry to come back. She chose to allow Tori to have a father and Jen to have a husband rather than putting her own happiness first. Patrick got choked up just thinking about it. There were many characteristics that could be used to describe his niece, but unselfish was at the top of the list.

He blew out a breath. His heart started to pound harder at the incline in the drive. This was always the toughest part of the morning routine. He leaned into the hill, his arms straining as he crested it and then smiled at the achievement. When he'd first started this, it had been impossible for him to reach the top. But now he could do it with a little effort.

He put the brake on his wheelchair and reached down for the water bottle he always brought on his morning outings. He took a long drink of the cool liquid and then recapped the bottle, slipping it into the bag at the side of his chair. Birds twittered loudly in the trees, surrounding him, and he sat there for a moment just breathing in nature.

The sound of the birds, the slight breeze, along with the sight of the trees and the flowers filled him up, and he felt the rightness of the moment. It bolstered him.

Laney had been through more trials than most, but she'd always come out on the other side. And now was not the time to be worried about her. Now was the time to be happy for her. Because if Drake was out there, Delaney would find him. There was no doubt in his mind.

CHAPTER 26

MASSA, ITALY

Across the room, the scene on the monitor shifted to a picture of the front gates of the Chandler Estate as Gedeon strode in. The house was quieter today, with five of his new recruits over in the United States.

Gedeon had wanted to go himself, but this mission was too critical for him to chance someone catching sight of him on some random cell phone. He had no doubt that Delaney McPhearson had put an iron cage around the people she loved. And all eyes, electronic and otherwise, would be on the lookout for Gedeon.

Which meant he would have to settle for a bird's-eye view of this particular endeavor.

He found he didn't mind it so much. Anything that would help achieve this particular goal was well worth it. Sacrifice and discipline were the hallmarks of Gedeon's character, after all.

"Any problems?" he asked as he pulled out a chair and took a seat in front of the video feed.

Lucius shook his head, pulling his gaze from the monitors in front of him. "No, nothing."

"McPhearson is in the air?"

"Yes, she just left."

Gedeon frowned. He'd been disturbed to learn she was in Italy. For a moment, fear had lanced through him at the thought that she'd somehow found him. But instead of heading for Tuscany, she headed to Rome and an old orphanage. They had waited to see if she changed course, but she then took off for Greece before returning once again.

Now she was heading back to the States. He wasn't sure what that was all about. But her being on this side of the ocean was beneficial to their current plan.

"What about the estate?"

"We've been running the security checks all night. We've managed to get into just about every aspect of their system. And their response time has been rather slow, although it's been increasing. We should we are ready to go now."

"What's the response time?"

"Two minutes and twenty-eight seconds. That's the fastest they've been able to boot us out of the network."

Gedeon nodded. A lot could happen in two minutes and twenty-eight seconds. "Are our people ready to go?"

"They're just waiting for your order."

Gedeon flicked a gaze across the screens. "Where is she now?"

"She was spied going out for an early morning run with her father."

Perfect. Gedeon nodded. "Then let's begin."

CHAPTER 27

BALTIMORE, MARYLAND

A SWEAT HAD BROKEN OUT ALONG PATRICK'S BROW AS HE HEADED back toward the main gate. He would loop past there and then head back to Sharecroppers Lane. It had been a good outing this morning, and he was feeling better. He was still stressed and worried about Laney, but she could handle what could come. After all, she'd already handled everything that had come before.

A car honked from behind him. Patrick glanced over his shoulder as Jen pulled up next to him and rolled down her window. She smiled. "Morning, Patrick. How's your run today?"

He grinned back at her. "Pretty good. I think I got up that hill in my best time yet."

"I told you that you need to start training for one of those half marathons. I'd be happy to help you."

Patrick chuckled. Jen was a fitness fanatic. She was always training in her personal time for some marathon or triathlon somewhere. And she was always trying to get other people to join her. But most weren't as excited by the idea of running, or in Patrick's case, wheeling twenty-six miles.

"I don't think I'm quite ready for that yet."

"Well, there is a 5K in two months. That's just 3.2 miles. And the proceeds go to a children's cancer charity."

Patrick rolled his eyes. "You are incorrigible."

She smiled. "That's not a no. I'll get the race information and email it to you. Let me know if you want to do some early morning training together."

Before Patrick could talk his way out of it, she'd rolled up the window and headed down the drive. He shook his head, watching her go. She really was relentless. It was what made her so good at her job and made her such a good friend.

And perhaps it wasn't the worst idea. Besides, she was right: 3.2 miles wasn't exactly a marathon. Maybe he could see if Nyssa wanted to do it with him and Delaney. They could walk along with him for the 3.2 miles.

He smiled, picturing it, his excitement beginning to grow. Actually, that might be kind of a nice family activity. Maybe he could talk Cain into it as well. He was humming to himself, imagining it as he headed toward the main gate. Up ahead, Jen waved at the guard house as she drove through the gates, using her remote to open them.

Up ahead, two individuals stood inside the guard hut next to the main entrance. As Patrick rolled closer, he was surprised to see that one of them was Dylan Jenkins, one of the co-heads of the estate security. Usually, Patrick stopped by and chatted with the guards on his outings, but it was unusual to see a director there this early in the morning. He rolled to a stop as Dylan stepped outside.

Dylan gave him a nod. "Patrick. Morning."

"Morning, Dylan. Everything all right?"

Dylan flicked a glance over his shoulder, a frown marring his face. "Not sure. We've had some computer issues this morning."

"Computer issues? What kind of computer issues?"

"The system's been acting up. Different security grids going offline before they come back online again."

"Is there a pattern to the issues?"

Dylan shook his head. "Not that I can tell. It seems to be random. And the system's only gone down for five seconds at most. We called in one of the techs, and they're working on the problem, but I don't know ..."

"You're worried."

Dylan started to shake his head and then stopped. "After what happened recently with all of you having to hide out, I don't like the timing of this. We've never had an issue like this before, and I don't like it."

"Should I take Nyssa down to Dom's bunker?"

Dylan paused. "I don't think we're there yet. But maybe just have yourselves ready to head there if we give the yell."

Patrick nodded. "Will do. In fact, I'll head home now and make sure that Nyssa is where she needs to be so that we can take off. Actually, we'll just go down and have some breakfast with Dom this morning."

"That's not a bad idea. Maybe you should see if the McAdamses want to join you."

Patrick studied Dylan. He'd known the man for years. A former Navy SEAL, he and his co-head, Mark Fricano, had served with Jake. The two heads were easygoing and always quick with a laugh. But both of them took their jobs very seriously. And if Dylan was suggesting that they head for Dom's, then he was a lot more worried than he was letting on.

"Okay, I'll do that. Let me know if you find out anything," Patrick said.

"Will do."

Patrick rolled past the main gate, turning once again down the main drive. *It's all right. It's just a computer glitch,* he told himself. But Patrick found himself picking up his speed nonetheless.

CHAPTER 28

Worry rolled through Patrick's mind as he hurried down the quiet avenue of Sharecroppers Lane. No one seemed to be up, or at least, no one seemed to be stirring outside.

But then again, it was still before seven. He hurried down the sidewalk and rolled into the path and up the small ramp to the front door. Opening it up, he let himself in and called out, "Cain? Nyssa?"

Silence greeted him. A quick glance to his right showed that Cain's and Nyssa's running shoes were missing, which meant they would be out for at least the next thirty minutes.

Shutting the door behind him, Patrick wheeled himself forward, debating what to do. Dylan had said that he wasn't sure that there was anything to the security lapses. But Patrick didn't like the idea of their computers going wonky right now either, especially with Laney being away.

A nervous gnawing that began in his gut was slowly creeping up his chest. *I'm overreacting. Dylan would put out a warning to the whole estate if there was a problem.*

The thoughts did nothing to calm his fears.

Well, if I'm overreacting, I might as well completely overreact, he thought as he wheeled himself into his bedroom. He headed to the closet and pulled open the door, pushing his clothes aside and revealing the gun safe tucked back there. He quickly input the password, and the door sprung open. Yanking on it, he pulled it fully open and glanced at the contents inside. A shotgun, two boxes of shotgun pellets, a Beretta, and a Glock, as well as an M4, along with ammunition for all of it.

He reached in and pulled the shotgun out. He grabbed the box of shells as well and quickly loaded two before dumping the rest of the box into the bag on the side of his wheelchair. He tossed the bottle of water that had been in there on the bed.

Grabbing the Glock, he loaded it. Slamming the magazine into place, he chambered a round. He slipped it into the holster on the side of his wheelchair.

The holster had been put on at his request years ago. He'd found it helpful when he went to the gun range, but this would be the first time he'd used it outside of that activity. He grabbed two more magazines and slipped them into the same bag as the shotgun pellets.

This is overkill. I'm being ridiculous, he told himself.

But his heart had started to race when speaking with Dylan and had failed to slow down even when he returned home. So while it might seem like overkill to some, with everything that he and the others had been through, he needed to listen to the warning that was blaring away in his mind.

CHAPTER 29

HER BREATH EVENING OUT AS HER LEGS CAUGHT THE RHYTHM, Nyssa fell into the ease of the run. When her father had first started insisting she go on these morning runs with him, Nyssa had not been a fan. The last thing she wanted to do was get up early and go running around the estate.

But then the nightmares had started, and sleeping in was no longer an option. So she'd grudgingly started the runs with her dad. And she'd been shocked to find that she actually enjoyed them.

Each time it was the same: When the run first started, her mind would be going in a million different directions, worried and stressed about everything else. But as the run progressed, she would slowly but surely forget about everything, her mind going blank and just focusing on breathing in and breathing out.

Her father said that it was his form of meditation, and she could understand the argument now because that was what it felt like. He ran next to her, tall and strong. He flicked a glance down at her and grinned before his attention returned to the ground in front of them.

Nyssa smiled, doing the same. She liked this early time with him. A lot of her friends from school complained about their parents, but Nyssa had never felt that way about her father and Uncle Patrick. There were definitely times where they were overprotective. But she liked spending time with them. She liked just being around them.

And lately that had been even more true. They both knew about her nightmares. But she tried to keep the worst of them from her dad at least. He seemed overly worried about them. But her uncle, he just made her breakfast and listened. He seemed to think that everything could be solved by a good cup of tea.

And she had to admit she definitely felt better after those morning breaks, although she really wished she could figure out why she was having those stupid dreams. Susie never had any dreams like that. No one from her school ever had nightmares like that. She knew that Molly sometimes had nightmares, but it wasn't every night. And Molly wasn't an older version of herself in her dreamscape.

That was the part that bothered her so much. It wasn't that the people in the dream were unfamiliar. It was that they were both complete strangers and somehow familiar to her at the same time. She didn't know how to explain that. How was it that she couldn't recognize their faces and yet somehow down deep had this sense that she did know them?

She didn't know how to explain that to her uncle or her father. She could already tell that they were worried about her. And she didn't want to give them more to worry about.

They still wouldn't explain to her why they insisted she head off with Laney when they had been down at Luis's place. Her father had been downright frantic, insisting that she go with Laney, even though the rest of them would be following in just a few hours.

And since that point, she'd been basically under estate arrest. She hadn't been allowed to leave the estate at all. Not that her uncle or father left very often, but still. It seemed like she always had someone watching her every move.

Nyssa rolled her shoulders, trying to push away the dark thoughts. She wasn't sure what exactly was going on, and no one wanted to tell her.

"You okay?" her father asked, looking down at her with his blue eyes.

"Yeah, I'm fine," she said, wondering once again at how she'd come to live with her father and Uncle Patrick. Years ago, they'd explained that neither of them was her biological father. And Nyssa had no problem with that. They were her fathers in every sense of the word. So the fact that she was adopted really didn't bother her at all. One day, she'd track down her birth parents, but right now that wasn't really important.

But she was curious as to how her uncle and father had ended up adopting her. They weren't a couple. So why would two bachelors who weren't in a romantic relationship adopt a young girl? And Uncle Patrick was a retired priest. It seemed an unusual choice for someone at that stage of their life.

But every time she tried to find out a little bit more about how she came to be part of this family, they said that they would explain everything to her once she turned thirteen.

Nyssa both welcomed and dreaded the beginning of her teenage years.

She loved the idea of being a teenager. She and Susie talked all the time about all the things that they would do when they finally reached that milestone.

But part of her was worried, and she couldn't even say why. There was just this niggling little fear that when she became a teenager, things were going to change, and in her life, change rarely happened for the better.

CHAPTER 30

Nyssa finished the trail with her dad and headed down the path toward Sharecroppers Lane.

She loved this part of the run. The path was lined with bushes and tall flowers. There was something almost magical about it. All the bright colors and the close confines of the path made her feel like she was running through a fairy tale.

In many ways, she supposed her life was a bit fantastical, like a fairy tale. She had her super-powered friends. Dom, who lived underground. The incredible cats that wandered through the estate.

But all fairy tales also had one critical character: the villain. That one evil individual looking to destroy the happiness of the good people in the fairy tale.

Snow White had the Evil Queen. Sleeping Beauty had Maleficent, Shrek had Lord Farquaad, although she supposed that last one was kind of fun to watch.

The others, though, if you took away the cartoons and the Disney approach, were actually kind of terrifying. In *Snow White*, a stepmother tries to kill her stepdaughter. In *Sleeping Beauty*, an evil woman tried to destroy a young woman's life by basically putting her in a coma.

Nyssa frowned again, wondering why Disney always seemed to make women the villains. Cruella, Maleficent, the evil stepmothers, Ursula, the list went on and on. Back at the time when most of those were created, women didn't exactly have equal rights, so the likelihood of them being the villain was incredibly low. But she supposed that Hollywood wasn't exactly known for its uplifting portrayal of female empowerment.

"What has you looking so serious?" her dad asked. "Are you thinking about the dreams again?"

Nyssa looked up at him in surprise. "No, actually, I was thinking about how unfair it is that in Disney films they always seem to make a female the villain."

Her dad's eyes widened, and a chuckle burst from his lips. "You never cease to surprise me, daughter. And yes, you are completely right. Females often were made out to be the villains."

"Yeah, and how come they are always just a witness to their own story? I mean, Snow White and Sleeping Beauty are asleep for a good portion of their tales. And in *The Little Mermaid*, it's the prince who finally defeats Ursula, not Ariel. It's really kind of gross and a horrible message to send to girls."

"Well, I assure you that you will be front and center in your own story." His smile faded as the words left his mouth.

Now it was her turn to look at him in concern. "What's the matter?"

He quickly plastered a smile on his face. "Nothing. Just thinking about my plans for the day."

He was lying. That was blatantly obvious. But pressing him wouldn't get her any answers. If there was one thing her dad was, it was stubborn. And she supposed even though they weren't biologically related, it was a trait that she'd picked up from him as well.

THE BELIAL BLOOD

Or maybe she got it from Uncle Patrick. He was like an oak tree when he set his mind to something.

They reached the end of the path and jogged out onto Sharecroppers Lane, slowly shifting from a run into a walk.

Her dad glanced at his watch and nodded. "Not bad, not bad. We're definitely improving our time."

"Olympics, here we come," Nyssa joked.

"Hey, I wouldn't mind having a daughter in the Olympics if that's your desire."

"That's most definitely not in the cards for me, but I appreciate the support."

"Well, that's what I'm here for. To support you in all things."

"Cain! Nyssa!" The two of them turned as Mary Jane walked down the sidewalk from Dom's shelter toward them.

"Morning," her dad called out. They waited until Mary Jane joined them.

Mary Jane wrapped an arm around Nyssa's shoulders. "Morning you two."

"Oh, don't, I'm sweaty," Nyssa said, trying to squirm away.

"I don't care. I'll take my morning hugs," Mary Jane said.

Nyssa slipped into the hug. She loved that about Susie's mom. She was always hugging people. Cain and Patrick hugged her all the time, but Mary Jane, she was kind of Nyssa's unofficial mother. When Laney had gone missing, a giant hole in Nyssa's life had opened up. And Mary Jane, she'd stepped up to take over the role of dominant female figure in Nyssa's life.

And Nyssa had to admit, it was awfully nice to have someone who was so concerned about you. Mary Jane, she had this way about her that just kind of made you feel like you belonged. And when you felt like you belonged with Mary Jane, life just seemed better.

"Where are you coming from?" her dad asked, glancing back at Dom's.

"Oh, I'm trying to get some exercise too, although I'm starting with a good walk." She nodded in the direction of the main gate. "Molly and JW went off for a run a little while ago too."

"Is Susie still sleeping?"

Mary Jane grinned. "Of course. That girl definitely likes her sleep. We won't be seeing her for at least another two or three hours."

Her father looked at Mary Jane, and something was exchanged silently between the two of them. Forcing a smile to his face, he turned to Nyssa. "Why don't you go grab a shower and see if Patrick's got breakfast started? I could use some pancakes."

"You always can use some pancakes," Nyssa said, rolling her eyes. But she received the message that was sent: Mary Jane and her father wanted to speak without her listening in.

"I'll see you guys later." She started to jog down the sidewalk toward their cottage.

"Feel free to go wake up my lazy daughter," Mary Jane called out behind her.

Nyssa laughed, knowing that Mary Jane meant it jokingly. Although Nyssa might head over to drag Susie out of bed after breakfast.

Up ahead, the front door of their cottage opened, and Patrick rolled himself out onto the front porch.

Nyssa grinned at the sight of him, and then her grin faded as she noted the shotgun attached to the back of his wheelchair and the rifle in his hand. Her jog stuttered to a walk, her mouth falling open. What on earth was he up to?

She opened her mouth to ask when wind out of nowhere blew her hair in front of her face. Her head jerked back as her eyes shut for a moment against the onslaught.

And when they opened, a man stood in front of her.

CHAPTER 31

After debating internally, Patrick had gone back to the gun safe and grabbed the rifle. The handgun and shotgun were good, but with the rifle he'd have better aim at a distance.

And if someone was coming, distance was always better.

He rolled out onto the front porch, relieved to see Nyssa making her way down the sidewalk. A few feet behind her, Cain and Mary Jane were speaking quietly.

Patrick's chest released some of the tension at the sight of them and the normality of the scene. No one looked alarmed, although Cain and Mary Jane were having a hushed conversation. He frowned, watching the two of them, trying to figure out what exactly it was they were worried about, but he saw nothing behind them that would indicate a problem.

His focus returned to Nyssa. Her cheeks were bright from the morning run, and he could see how relaxed the exercise had made her.

It was amazing how much she looked like Laney. Nyssa had even commented on it once when they'd been going through some old pictures that he'd found of Laney when she was a kid.

It had taken everything in him not to explain why it was that the two of them looked so similar. But he and Cain had agreed—not until she was older. But he supposed when she turned thirteen, there wouldn't be any need for that conversation at all. Years ago, when he and Cain had first taken on the care of Nyssa, he'd thought it would be impossible to forget who she truly was and just love her as a little girl.

But that had not been the case. He rarely thought about her destiny and the deadline that was looming above them until the last few years.

And even now, as he stared at her, it was hard to imagine that this beautiful young girl that he truly loved would in essence disappear in a few months when she realized what her destiny was.

He hated that for her. He understood why it had to happen, but much like he felt about Cain's punishment, it seemed too harsh, especially being her decision, in his opinion, was better for the entire world.

But no one asked him. And he was well aware that he held no power in this current situation. So he would just do what he'd tried to do for the entirety of her life: be there for her in whatever way possible, in whatever way she needed.

Now as he watched her walk toward him, he caught the shift in her face as she spotted the weapons attached to him. He winced. If this all turned out to be a mistake, then he'd unnecessarily worried her. He and Cain had been clear that for the next few months, they wanted to keep her worry to an absolute minimum.

Of course, the appearance of Gedeon on the scene had truly made that all but impossible. But Patrick being well armed, sitting on the porch waiting for her to return from a run, certainly wasn't going to ease her mind any.

Movement from the corner of his eyes pulled Patrick's attention. The movement was so fast that by the time he'd turned, it had shifted.

Nyssa screamed as the man appeared in front of her.

Patrick fumbled with the rifle, pulling it into his shoulder, his heart pounding as Cain took off at a run toward Nyssa.

Mary Jane bolted up the nearest path, knocking on the door and bursting inside, no doubt to call for reinforcements.

Nyssa screamed again as Patrick settled the rifle. He blocked out everything else, focused on the man who held Nyssa, and prayed that his aim was true.

CHAPTER 32

Nyssa took a stumbling step back. The man was in his thirties with dark-brown hair and pale brown eyes. Where had he come from? She didn't know him. She'd never seen him before.

Even as her mind stumbled to make sense of the man directly in front of her, she knew what he was: one of the Fallen.

Nyssa tried to run but the man was too fast. They were all too fast. Before she could even take a step, he reached out and grabbed her by the front of the shirt, hauling her up toward him. "Well, hello there, Lilith. Lovely to see you again."

Nyssa shook her head, trying to pull away from the man, but he was way too strong. "I'm not Lilith. My name's Nyssa."

The man chuckled. "Yes, the curse. I didn't think it was true. But we'll take care of that."

A hot, wet liquid splashed across Nyssa's face. The man released her and crashed to the ground. Nyssa stumbled back. Her mouth gaped open.

Blood pooled underneath the man's head from where he'd fallen.

"Nyssa, run!" her uncle yelled, already barreling down the cottage path toward her.

THE BELIAL BLOOD

The sound of running feet reached her from behind as her father sprinted up the path toward her.

But Patrick was closer. She ran for him, her heart pounding.

Lilith. Why did he call her Lilith? She didn't know anyone by that name. Why would he think that was her? And why was he looking for her here?

Patrick reached the end of the path and rolled onto the sidewalk. Nyssa was ten feet away. Patrick's face was full of worry his gaze focused on her steady. *Just get to Uncle Patrick. If I get to Uncle Patrick, I'll be okay.*

Movement behind her uncle stirred. Her heart soared into her throat as the events unfolded in slow motion, even though the person who caused them moved incredibly fast.

A man sprinted down the sidewalk and slammed into her uncle's wheelchair. Patrick went flying out of the chair and slammed his head into the side of the rock wall.

Nyssa screamed as he crumpled to the ground, blood pooling around him just the way it had for the other man.

CHAPTER 33

This couldn't be happening. This could not be happening.

"No!" Nysa screamed as she sprinted for Patrick. Gunshots rang out as Nyssa reached his side.

The man that was coming for her turned with a growl toward the security jeeps that appeared at the end of the street.

"Nyssa!" Her dad raced toward her, but the man near her bolted toward him. With horror, she watched as her dad went flying across the yard and into the door of their neighbor's house. He crumpled to the ground on their porch.

The man turned toward Nyssa, but before he could take a step, someone darted from the other side of the street and tackled him. All Nyssa could make out was a flash of long bright red hair.

The two rolled onto the ground, and her rescuer rolled to her feet. Molly stood between Nyssa and the man. "Stay away from her."

The man charged, and Nyssa couldn't see exactly what was happening as they fought and moved farther down the road.

Nyssa turned her attention back to her uncle. His eyes were closed, his face incredibly pale. Blood poured from his head unabated. This was bad. Really, really bad.

"No, Uncle Patrick. No." Nyssa placed one hand on his chest and the other over his wound, as if she could somehow keep the blood from pumping out.

"No. You can't do this. You can't leave me," she said because she knew in her heart of hearts that her uncle couldn't survive a hit like that. He'd been always there for her. But she'd seen him grow weaker in the last few years. The damage to his spine had weakened other parts of his body as well.

And now he lay in front of her and she could barely feel a pulse. His chest and heart rate seemed to be slowing down.

"No. You are not allowed to die. Do you hear me? You are not allowed to die." Warmth rolled through her, heating her from the inside out as she stared at her uncle, her father, and willed him to open his eyes. She could not let him die. She could not.

The sounds of the fight behind her all but disappeared as she focused entirely on him. "Stay with me. You have to stay with me," she said, her eyes filled with tears, her throat tightening.

Her whole body seemed to be overheating as she stared at him. "Please don't go. I can't do this without you," she begged.

Hands grabbed her shoulders. With a cry of surprise, she looked up into the face of a woman with short dark hair. "Time to go," the woman said with a sneer.

Nyssa barely had time to brace herself before she was yanked from her uncle's side and thrown over the woman's shoulder.

CHAPTER 34

IN THE STREET, MOLLY DUCKED THE HOOK AIMED AT HER HEAD AND slammed her fist into the man's ribs and then another one into his kidneys. She reached underneath his extended arm and slammed an uppercut into his chin before yanking on the back of his hair and slamming his face into her knee. Stomping on the back of his knee, she gripped the man's chin and then the back of his head and twisted.

The light slipped from his eyes as he dropped to the ground. But he wasn't dead. A Fallen could survive a broken neck. She just needed him out of commission so that she could keep everybody else safe.

She whirled around, looking for Nyssa.

"Molly, get in!" JW screeched to a halt next to her in one of the Chandler security jeeps.

"Nyssa. Where's Nyssa?" she yelled frantically, scanning the street for her. Patrick was down, an ominous amount of blood surrounding him. Nyssa had been right there.

"One of them grabbed her. Get in!" JW yelled.

Molly dove in the passenger door. JW was moving before she had the door closed. She and JW had been out for a run. It had

THE BELIAL BLOOD

been a nice run, peaceful. She'd even been thinking about how lucky they'd been that after all that craziness down in South America and Greece that things seemed to have calmed down.

It was like she had dared fate and lost.

She and JW had just made it back through the gates of the estate when she'd felt something was wrong. Without even a word to JW, she'd bolted to Sharecroppers Lane in time to see the man reaching for Nyssa. She didn't hesitate, just darted forward. Her only goal was to keep Nyssa safe.

And she'd failed.

"Do you have a signal on her?" she asked as she hung onto the bar above the door as JW burst out of Sharecroppers Lane toward the front gate.

JW nodded toward the dashboard. "On my phone."

After everything had happened in England, Cain had pulled Molly aside one night and asked her to keep an eye on Nyssa. Molly wasn't sure what all was going on with Nyssa, but she knew that there was something special about the girl. Something special about who she was.

She'd overheard enough conversations to know that Nyssa wasn't a Fallen or anything like that. She wouldn't have abilities, but for some reason she was critical to the belial world.

Molly hadn't asked Cain many questions. She'd learned long ago that answers from him were often long, involved, and many times few and far between.

Besides, the truth was she didn't need to know why Nyssa was special. She'd known Nyssa since she was a baby. Nyssa had been in and out of their house since that time. Molly had spent as much time with Nyssa as she'd spent with her own sister. And as far as she was concerned, Nyssa was her sister as much as Susie was.

She grabbed JW's phone and watched the dot on it. All of them, unbeknownst to Nyssa, had an app on their phones that allowed them to track her. Thank God whoever grabbed her hadn't gotten rid of her phone. "They're heading southeast. What's over there?"

"A couple of things, but there's a private airport. I bet they're heading there."

Molly nodded, knowing the one he was talking about. She grabbed her phone and dialed Lou.

Lou was groggy when she answered. "Hey, what's up? It's early."

"There's been an attack on the estate. They grabbed Nyssa. They're heading out to Martin's Airfield, over by you. You and Rolly are closer than I am. I need you to get there."

All sleep was gone from Lou's voice. "We're on it."

Molly disconnected the call and turned to JW. "They're going to head there. I can move faster than you can."

JW pulled over to the side of the road in a screech of brakes. "Go."

With one last look at him, she sprinted out of the car and prayed that they were able to get to Nyssa in time.

CHAPTER 35

HER RIBS ACHING, NYSSA SLAMMED HER EYES SHUT AS THE WOMAN continued to run nauseatingly fast. When the woman grabbed her and threw her over her shoulder, she hadn't had time to do anything except gasp. They'd sprinted across the estate and leapt over the estate walls in a speed that seemed too impossible to be real.

And the whole time, Nyssa pictured Patrick. He was dying. She knew he was dying. She needed to be with him. She slammed her fists into the woman's back. "Let me go. Let me go."

The woman let out a snarl. "Shut up or I'll knock you out."

The venom in the woman's voice made it clear that she would do exactly that. And Nyssa was no match for the woman's abilities. Still, quieting down felt like a cowardly move. "Let me go," she insisted.

The woman shrugged her shoulder, and Nyssa went flying through the air.

Her breath left her in a gasp, and she didn't even have time to scream before another set of strong arms caught her. It was a bone-jarring catch that would no doubt leave her with bruises.

"You take her. I don't want to deal with her," the woman snarled.

The man said nothing as he held her cradled in his arms and took off at a run.

In this position, she didn't have a shoulder jabbing into her ribs, but the man's grip was like iron. She'd have bruises along her arms and legs from where he held her. She turned her head toward his chest to avoid the wind blowing straight in her face. It was so strong, she couldn't even open her eyes.

The man said nothing as he ran. Nyssa couldn't seem to find words either.

And really, what would words do anyway? It wasn't like she was going to be able to talk them into letting her go. No, they had her, and now she just had to wait and find out why.

They ran for what felt like forever, but Nyssa knew it probably had only been a few minutes. Her head pounded and her stomach rolled. Finally, the man slowed and then stopped, placing Nyssa on the ground.

She only managed to stay upright for half a second before she crumpled to the ground, her legs unable to sustain her. She pictured Patrick and her father back at the estate and turned on her side and threw up.

The woman who'd initially grabbed her sneered as she walked by. "Pathetic."

Nyssa's cheeks flamed at the comment, even though she knew she shouldn't care what a kidnapper thought of her. But she was thinking the same thing. It was pathetic how she'd been unable to fight back or help Patrick.

"Why did you take me?" she asked, her voice trembling.

The man who grabbed her crouched down in front of her. He waited until she looked up.

"I'm no one," she said.

"See, that's where you're wrong. You're incredibly important. And it's time you learned who you really are." The man opened his

THE BELIAL BLOOD

mouth, but then his head jerked up, and he narrowed his eyes, turning to his left.

Two blurs appeared on the horizon.

The man vaulted to his feet. But the blurs didn't slow. They crashed into the man as three more individuals stepped out of the hangar.

From her spot on the ground, Nyssa wasn't sure what was happening. Nonetheless, she prayed the new arrivals won, even though she couldn't see who they were. But if they were fighting these guys, she was Team New People all the way. And she had to think that they were a better shot for her than these other ones.

The woman who had grabbed her was slammed into the side of a truck. Nyssa looked on as Rolly slowed enough for her to get a glimpse of him. Relief washed over her as she caught a quick glance of Lou fighting the others.

Emotion crawled up her throat. They'd come for her. They hadn't even been on the estate last night, but they'd come for her.

Rolly tossed the woman like he was throwing a shot put. She went sailing across the runway, landing with a heavy thud and then rolling and not getting back up. Then he dashed over to Nyssa. "You okay, Nyssa?"

She nodded. "Yeah, I'm—"

A blur careened into Rolly. He went flying in a tangle of legs and arms.

Nyssa crab-walked back to keep from getting hit but still got the glancing blow of a kick to her thigh that stung. She continued back until she crashed into a truck. Fighting seemed to be all around her.

Which meant she had only one option: to hide.

CHAPTER 36

MOLLY HAD NEVER RUN SO FAST IN HER LIFE. THE IDEA OF SOMEONE taking Nyssa brought back all the memories of when Susie had been taken. Which, of course, brought with it the memories of when she herself had been taken. She didn't know what this Gedeon wanted with Nyssa, but whatever it was, it couldn't be good for the young girl.

And as fearful as she felt right at this moment, she didn't slow her steps. If anything, it made her move faster. Because if she was feeling this scared, then Nyssa's fear must be ten times worse. She was just a little kid, even though she acted at times like she was a grown woman, the same way Susie did.

But she wasn't. She was only twelve. Twelve was not old enough to be considered full grown by any stretch of the human imagination, no matter what Nyssa and Susie thought and argued at times.

Up ahead, Molly saw the entrance to the airfield. As she got closer, she heard the sounds of a fight. Her heart raced, and she hoped that Lou and Rolly had arrived before her.

She slowed, not wanting to get grabbed before she could see

what was going on. Ahead, Lou leapt off the front of a truck and slammed the heel of her boot into the side of a man's face.

Molly couldn't help but wince at the move. The man's face shook, and she was pretty sure his jaw was dislodged as he slumped to the ground.

A hundred yards away, Rolly squared off against two individuals. They faced off for the barest of seconds before the one of the individuals charged.

Waiting until the last possible second, Rolly grabbed the man's outstretched arms and twirled, holding onto his arm and continuing the man's movement. With a cry, the man went flying across the space, slamming into the side of the airport hangar.

The second man didn't wait for the first to recover. He was already crossing the space toward Rolly.

The man reached out as if to kick. But Rolly turned around, yanked on the man's leg, and pulled the man forward. Off balance, the man didn't have a chance as Rolly slammed his elbow into the man's knee and dislocated it.

The man let out a cry, but Rolly merely grabbed his ankle and swung him in the same direction as his pal.

That was all the time Molly had to watch because a woman with long blonde hair caught sight of her. With a scream, she headed toward Molly.

Molly waited, timing it so that she didn't spin until the woman was only a few feet away, and then she launched a spinning side kick right into the woman's chest. She could feel the bones in the woman's rib cage crack as her foot made contact, sending the woman launching into the air and slamming into the side of a truck.

Molly scanned the area for Nyssa.

It was a small airport, smaller than the one that the Chandler Group used. There were only two runways. One had a small plane already idling.

Molly had no doubt that was the one that these people were

going to use to take Nyssa away. But not on her watch. But she couldn't see Nyssa anywhere. Where was she?

Lou caught sight of her and yelled, "Find Nyssa. She's hiding!"

Molly nodded, following the direction that Lou pointed. But some of the individuals that they'd taken down were already getting up. These guys, whoever they were, seemed to be recuperating awfully fast.

Which meant she needed to find Nyssa immediately. There was no time to waste. She took off in the direction that Lou had pointed and prayed that she found her before these other people did.

CHAPTER 37

THE HANGAR WAS EMPTY AS NYSSA SLIPPED INSIDE. SHE COULD still hear the sounds of the fight continuing outside. In her mind, she pictured Lou and Rolly. How had they found her? And did that mean others were coming as well?

Nyssa really hoped it did.

At the same time, she felt like a coward for hiding while Lou and Rolly were out there fighting for her. But she was no match for the people out there. She wasn't even sure if Lou and Rolly were.

But why on earth had they grabbed her of all people? She wasn't this Lilith person. There was nothing special about her. Her thoughts stilled for a moment as a voice deep in the back of her mind spoke: *Yes, there is.*

She wanted to shove the thought away, but she knew that it would be no use. And she wasn't stupid. She knew she had something to do with the Fallen. From the small snippets of conversation she'd caught, she had a feeling it had to do with her birth parents.

Neither her dad nor uncle wanted to discuss her biological parents. All they said was they were good people who loved her very much. But Nyssa was pretty sure that they were Fallen or a Nephilim, which meant that she'd probably have powers one day.

Was that what this was all about? Were these people somehow related to her biological parents?

And if so, were they trying to get her back? Because it didn't seem like they were trying to kill her. They could have killed her forever ago if that were the case.

But they took her instead. And she couldn't think of any other reason why someone would want her.

She scrambled behind a tool tower as she heard voices coming from the office up ahead. It sounded like the voices were getting closer, and the tool tower wasn't much of a hiding place. Her mind scrambling, she searched the space. It was pretty open. There. A space behind some lockers—if she squeezed, she could fit.

The door of the office started to open. With a squeak, she dashed across the open space. Holding her breath, she squeezed behind a series of lockers.

Peeking from her hiding spot, she had a better view of the door. She watched as a man stepped out, a phone to his ear. "No, it's not McPhearson. It's two of her people: Lou Thomas and Rolly Escabi."

The man was silent as he listened to the person on the other end of the line.

"Yes, our people have engaged them, but they're proving surprisingly adept at fighting them off."

He paused again to listen.

"Yes, sir, of course. I'll make sure that she is on the plane personally." The man disconnected the call and strode toward the door.

Holding her breath again, Nyssa flattened further back against the wall.

The man opened the door. With a cry, he went flying back, twisting in midair and landing on his chest with a thud.

THE BELIAL BLOOD

And then Molly was standing in the doorway. In a blur, she crossed the space and slammed the man's head into the concrete. Gripping him by the hair, she yanked his head up. "Where is she? Where is Nyssa?"

The man managed to twist his body and wrap his legs around Molly. She slammed her elbow into his face, but he got her down to the ground and straddled her.

Even as his nose bled into his mouth, he grinned down at her. "Stupid girl. You should have killed me."

He aimed a punch right for Molly's face. Molly managed to twist to the side and slammed her fist into the man's throat. His eyes bulged. She followed it up with an eye poke to those bulging eyes. He let out a garbled scream.

Managing to break one of her legs free from underneath him, she cocked her leg and slammed him in the chin with her heel. Then she wrapped the leg around his throat and yanked him to the side.

At this point, Nyssa's jaw was practically on the floor. Molly was so soft-spoken, so quiet and unassuming. If Nyssa weren't watching it right now, she would never believe that Molly was capable of it. And she felt so much better knowing that Molly was here.

"Where is she?" Molly demanded again, keeping her leg wrapped around his throat.

"I'll never—" Molly shifted so that she grabbed the man by the back of the head and chin and then broke his neck. She crawled from off of him and stared at him for a moment. And that was when Nyssa saw the Molly that she knew. Her eyes were full of horror at what she'd just done.

Molly looked around, and Nyssa realized she was looking for her. She slipped out from behind the lockers.

"Nyssa!" Molly blurred across the space and wrapped Nyssa it in a hug before stepping back and studying her from head to toe. "Are you hurt? Did they hurt you?"

157

Nyssa shook her head numbly, even as some of the hurt that she'd been pushing off rolled through her. Her ribs ached, as did her back and her thigh, but it was nothing that required a doctor, just a lot of ice. Her voice shook when she spoke. "No, no. I'm okay. How did you find me?"

"We can talk about that later. We need to get you out of here."

They headed to the door.

The door burst open, and Rolly flew through it. He hit the ground and rolled before getting to his feet with a wince. He flicked a glance over at the two of them. "Oh, good, you found her. Although all things considered, it might be better if you guys were still hiding."

Before Nyssa could ask what he meant by that, four attackers zipped into the room, spreading out in front of them.

Molly yanked Nyssa back behind her. "As soon as you have a chance, you run," she ordered Nyssa, not taking her eyes off the threat in front of them.

Nyssa nodded, even though Molly couldn't see it and even though she had a feeling that running was no longer going to be an option.

CHAPTER 38

THE POWER RADIATING OFF THE FOUR IN FRONT OF MOLLY, ROLLY, and Nyssa was practically a palpable thing.

Molly swallowed as she stared at them. They didn't look any different than some of the Fallen that she'd fought with in the past, yet she knew they were much more powerful. In Greece, she'd been so focused that she hadn't had time to really take in their essence. But here, there was enough of a pause for her to see just how terrifying these people were.

The man that she'd taken down earlier, he should have been down and out from the blow she'd given him. But he'd just shook it off. So these were not regular Fallen, not by a long shot. She'd heard Laney and Jen talking about angels. But these guys couldn't be angels. Angels were the good guys, right?

Regardless, now she and Rolly were outnumbered two to one. Nyssa couldn't be part of this fight.

Molly rolled her shoulders and took a breath, loosening up her stance and getting on the balls of her feet. She needed to be ready. And if she was too stiff, she wouldn't react be able to quickly respond.

Rolly cracked his neck next to her and smiled at the group

assembled across from them. "Welcome to the rumble in the hangar. Step up, step up. No need to wait on ceremony."

Two of the men growled and darted toward Rolly.

One of the men made a beeline for Molly. She saw his punch coming from a mile away. She dodged it easily, latching onto his wrist and twisting it into a wrist lock. She moved so fast and his force was so great that his wrist snapped, sounded like a gunshot. He let out a cry as he dropped to the ground.

Molly shifted him, still keeping a hold of his wrist, and flipped him onto his chest. Placing her foot on his shoulder, she yanked his arm back and then yanked on his shoulder, wincing inside as she heard the shoulder pop as well. Then she leaned down and stomped on the back of the man's neck.

"Molly!"

Nyssa's terrified scream yanked Molly's head up. Her eyes narrowed as the woman grabbed Nyssa and start to blur with her out the back door of the hangar.

Molly was right after them, sprinting for everything she was worth. A second blur moved in on them from around the corner.

Molly got a quick glance at long dark hair and a blue sweatshirt and knew that it was Lou.

Lou dove, wrapping the woman in her arms and slamming her into the concrete as Molly dove and grabbed Nyssa, rolling so that her arms and legs protected the girl from the impact of the fall. They landed twenty feet away from where Lou was now battling the other woman.

A shot rang out. A gun in her hand, Lou stood with blood sprayed across her shirt. Her chest heaved she looked at Molly. "They're going to keep coming for Nyssa. You need to get her out of here."

JW's jeep appeared from the side of the building. Lou took aim. "No. It's JW," Molly cried.

Lou lowered the gun. She nodded at Nyssa, her eyes intent. "Get her out of here."

THE BELIAL BLOOD

Molly flicked a glance back at the hangar. Lou shook her head. "I don't know what this is, but it's clear they want her. So you two get her out of here. Get her far away from here and keep her safe. Rolly and I will finish this up, and as soon as you guys are clear, we'll take off."

JW screeched to a stop next to them. He leaned out the window with a long gun in his arms and fired as Lou did the same.

Molly's eyes widened as she saw the two individuals now down from around the side of the building. She hadn't even seen or heard them coming. And she hadn't sensed them at all. In fact, she hadn't sensed any of these people. How was that possible?

"Go. Get Nyssa safe. It's the only way." Before Molly could say a word, Lou disappeared back inside the hangar.

Nyssa looked dazed. Molly grabbed her and practically carried her over to the jeep.

"Incoming!" JW let out a burst of gunfire as the two they'd shot started to get up.

Flinging open the back door, Molly dropped Nyssa in the backseat and slammed it shut.

She slid over the roof of the car and jumped into the passenger seat as JW switched his attention to the two individuals who appeared in the doorway. One of them dropped. Rolly appeared behind the other one and yanked him back into the hangar.

"Go, go, go!" Molly said.

JW hit the gas and tore onto the runway. He turned toward the airport exit and kept his foot firmly placed on the gas.

Molly kept her eyes focused on the area behind them, but nobody was giving chase. Lou and Rolly must be keeping them busy. Her stomach dropped at the thought of it.

Nyssa sat curled up on the backseat, her legs pulled to her chest, her arms wrapped them.

"Keep going," Molly said as she climbed into the back.

Molly arranged herself on the seat next to Nyssa and wrapped her arms around her, pulling her toward her. "Nyssa," she said softly.

Nyssa didn't say anything, but her whole body shook.

"There's a blanket in the back," JW said, flicking a glance at them in the rearview mirror. And that single glance was enough for Molly to see the worry in his eyes.

Molly leaned across the backseat and into the storage area of the jeep. She flicked open the emergency case and pulled out a stiff blue blanket. She quickly wrapped it around Nyssa as tears silently slipped down the girl's cheeks.

"Where am I going?" JW asked.

Molly shook her head, her mind a complete blank. They couldn't go back to the estate. It wasn't safe. In fact, anywhere she could think of, she was pretty sure it would be unsafe.

"I don't know."

Words burst out of Nyssa in a torrent. "We can't go back. They're coming after me. I can't go anywhere that people know me. You guys need to get away from me. If you're with me, you'll get hurt."

Molly wrapped her arms tighter around the trembling girl and pulled her into her side. "Shh, quiet. It's okay. And no, we're not leaving you, Nyssa. But you're right. We can't go back to the estate."

She pulled out her phone and called Jake. He answered quickly. "Molly?"

"We have her."

"Thank God. Where are you?"

"Outside the airport in Talbot County. Lou and Rolly are still there fighting. They're going to need some help."

Voices sounded in the back of the room where Jake was, and then Danny's voice came across the line. "Molly, you need to ditch your phones."

"What's going on?"

"They're in the system. I can't guarantee they can't access your phones. Get rid of all of them."

"Hold on." She placed the phone down and then turned to Nyssa. "Nyssa, honey, I need your phone."

Nyssa frowned but reached into her back pocket and pulled it out. Picking it up, Molly said, "Got them."

Jake answered. "Okay, honey, do what Danny said. Lose the phones."

"Where should we go, though?"

"Somewhere safe. But don't tell me. We're not sure if the system is secure yet."

Fear bubbled up in Molly's chest as she swallowed hard. "Jake?"

"I will find you, Molly. Don't doubt that."

And she knew he would. She pictured Jake appearing in that god-awful facility. He'd found her then. He'd find her now. "Okay."

"Stay safe. I love you, Molls."

"I love you too, Jake." She disconnected the call and then rolled down the window and tossed the phones out. JW did the same with his from the front seat. "Their system's compromised?"

Molly nodded. "Yeah. We have to find a place to hide out. We have to go somewhere that people don't know us."

JW met Molly's gaze in the rearview mirror. "I know a place."

"Is it safe?"

JW paused for a second. "Yeah, for this threat it is."

CHAPTER 39

OVER THE ATLANTIC OCEAN

JOLTING AWAKE, LANEY STARED AROUND THE CABIN OF THE JET. SHE blinked hard, then wiped at her eyes. She'd fallen asleep shortly after takeoff, the sleepless nights since Greece finally catching up with her.

David was in the cockpit, and she thought about going up to see him, but she really needed a moment. Although she'd slept, her dreams had been strange, filled with images of temples and people buried for centuries.

Pulling over her travel bag, she reached inside and pulled out the box where'd they secured the jug they'd taken from the cave, but she didn't unlatch it. David had assured her that the box would survive a plane wreck. And being Laney had been attacked on a plane a few times, she really didn't feel like tempting fate just to ease her curiosity.

And she was curious. There was obviously something in the jar. She could hear it sloshing around. Was it possible this was what Gedeon had used on Drake? But where was Gedeon getting his supply? They had stopped at the site of the original well to

THE BELIAL BLOOD

check, but it was bone dry. That wasn't the source. Had another well popped up?

The thought brought up mental images of the markings of that room back at Ephraim's. If she had been thinking straight, she would have shown them to Cristela to see if she understood them. She'd have to make sure she did when they got home. She had a feeling there was a whole other layer of knowledge that Gedeon had and was using.

She nearly snorted at the thought. Of course there was an untapped reservoir of knowledge out there. Wasn't that what these years involving the Fallen had proven time and time again?

Carefully, Laney placed the box back in her bag. Dom would analyze it when she got back. Hopefully, he'd be able to replicate it. But she had feeling that would take some time, and she wasn't sure time was something they had.

Each minute that passed, she felt the ticking of the clock. Drake was out there somewhere, being put through God knew what at Gedeon's hands. She needed to get him back. And she'd go without the Inceptus if they needed to.

She just really hoped that they wouldn't.

She ran her hands over her face. *Okay, enough thinking about what could or should or might happen. Time to focus on the here and now.*

Her gaze flicked toward the front of the plane. David seemed to be taking everything in stride, but Laney had no doubt that he'd been shocked to his core. After all, Sister Cristela had been constant presence in his life since he was ten years old. It would be like Laney learning her uncle was immortal. It would cause her to pause for more than a second or two.

After all, how did one wrap their head around the idea that one of the people that helped raise them couldn't die?

The thought brought her up short as she realized that one day that was going to be Nyssa's experience as well. How would she feel knowing that Cain was immortal, or at least used to be?

And she realized that it was a good thing they hadn't said anything about Cain's history to Nyssa before.

But truth be told, Nyssa didn't seem too curious about Cain's long history. She'd asked questions about his family and things like that, but they were normal questions that someone would ask. Nothing in them indicated she thought he had a much longer history than a normal human.

Laney sank back against the seat, picturing the young girl. She was also a type of immortal, she supposed. If Ralph had been speaking truthfully—and there was no reason to think he wasn't—this would be her last existence.

But Laney couldn't help but wish that that existence meant that she didn't have to play the role of mother of all. She wanted her to have one existence where she just got to be a normal person, or at least a normal child. Thirteen seemed such an incredibly young age to take on the burden of all that responsibility.

But Laney supposed that fairness hadn't exactly been a prominent characteristic of her life. She'd seen more than her share of unfairness not the least of which was her own life. She'd suffered, bled, and sacrificed, and yet for some people she was still the personification of evil. She'd finally found the love of her life—or more accurately, of lifetimes—and he'd been pulled away from her.

But now he was back too. Urgency burned within her. She needed to find him. And finding Gedeon was the way to do that.

Maybe Danny had been able to discover something that might lead them a little closer to his location. She pulled out her phone to check, surprised to see that there were a bunch of missed calls and texts that she hadn't heard when she'd fallen asleep. She hit voicemail as she checked her texts. Multiple had arrived from Henry, Jake, and Jen telling her she needed to call home now.

Laney's gut tightened as she stared at all of the messages before she quickly called Jen.

THE BELIAL BLOOD

Jen answered as soon as the call connected. "Laney. Where are you?"

Laney, who'd already been walking toward the cockpit, slid open the door. "David, where are we?"

"We're going to land in about thirty minutes," he said, his voice somber.

Laney met his gaze for a minute before he turned back to the controls.

"That's good," Jen said, overhearing David's reply.

"What's going on?" Laney asked.

Jen let out a deep sigh. "There's been an incident on the estate. Someone shut down the security system."

Laney slunk into the copilots chair. "Oh my God. What happened? Who's hurt?"

"Your uncle and Cain. But they weren't the target."

Laney felt lightheaded and had to force the words past her lips even as she knew the answer. "Who was?"

"Nyssa."

CHAPTER 40

NORTHERN MARYLAND

The car rocked gently as JW sped down the highway. They had switched cars with a friend of JW's and then taken off again. This car was an older Toyota sedan.

Nyssa sat in the back again, the blue blanket, still wrapped around her shoulders, but even with it around her, she couldn't seem to get warm. All she could picture was Patrick lying on the ground and then her dad going flying into that wall.

As the image flashed through her mind again, she closed her eyes, as if somehow by closing her eyes, she could force the image away from her mind. But if anything, it just brought it out in starker relief.

They had come for her. All of that violence, all of that horribleness had been because of her. What if her uncle was dead?

She gripped her knees tighter. He couldn't be dead. He was getting on in years, and his health was fading, but she couldn't imagine him not being there. And if he died because of her, she would never be able to forgive herself.

Her mind shifted from the violent images of Patrick to the

THE BELIAL BLOOD

violent images of Lou, Rolly, and Molly at the hangar. She pictured Molly once again fighting that man on the hangar floor.

It had been so unlike her.

And then JW had shown up and shot those people. He'd actually shot them. In fact, when they'd changed cars, he'd grabbed a bunch of guns from his friend as well.

Nyssa shook her head. All of this violence was swirling around her. And it was all because of her. She was to blame for all of this. Somehow she was to blame for it. Her stomach heaved.

"Stop the car," she said softly.

Molly turned around and looked at her. "What was that?"

Swallowing hard as she felt the bile rising, Nyssa lifted her head. "Stop the car."

"Are you feeling all right? Do you need to go to the bathroom?" Molly asked.

"Stop the car!" Nyssa screamed.

JW flicked a glance back at her before quickly pulling over on the side of the road. Nyssa scrambled for the door handle and lumbered outside.

Molly got out and stood staring at her. "Nyssa, what's wrong?"

Nyssa backed away, shaking her head, tears rolling down her cheeks. "Stay away from me."

Her brow furrowed, Molly took a step forward, her hand extending toward Nyssa. "What's going on? What happened?"

Nyssa shook her head, backing away, keeping one hand out in front of her, the other clutching the blanket to her shoulders. "Stay away from me. It's not safe. You need to stay away from me."

She turned as if to run, but Molly blurred and appeared right in front of her. Her eyes wide, she stared down at Nyssa, concern in her eyes. "Nyssa, what are you doing?"

Shaking her head, Nyssa backed away from her. "It's not safe! Don't you understand? If you stay with me, you'll get hurt just like Uncle Patrick, just like my dad."

"That's not your fault."

"But it is! They came for me. They were hurt because of me."

Nyssa started to back away again, but Molly took her gently by the shoulders. "I know it feels like that. Trust me, I *know* it feels like that. After I was kidnapped I thought of the people that had been hurt..." Molly swallowed hard before blowing out a shaky breath and continuing. "But it's not the fault of the person targeted. It's never their fault. They didn't cause anyone else to behave that way. When people do violence, it's their fault, no one else's."

"But you'll get hurt." Nyssa's voice broke when she said it.

Molly frowned. "Don't you get it? If you get grabbed, if you get hurt, then I get hurt. The reality is there is no way to avoid that in this situation. Don't you know that if something were to happen to you that it would tear all of us apart?

"There's nothing you can do that will keep me from helping you. You are my sister, Nyssa. You might not have been born into my family, but you *are* my family, nonetheless. And I cannot and will not let you face this alone. I don't know what's going on. I don't know why these people are after you. But I do know that I will keep you as safe as I can manage. So if you run, I will just follow you. You are not on your own, Nyssa. I will not let you face this on your own."

Nyssa looked up into Molly's face. She wanted to argue that Molly should go, that it would be safer for her to go. But she was just so scared. She didn't want to do this on her own. She didn't even know what this was. "But—"

"No buts. We're in this together. And we'll figure it out together. JW knows a place that we can go that'll keep us safe. And we'll stay there until everybody else figures out what is going on. Because even though JW and I are the ones who are with you now, you know we're not the only ones trying to keep you safe. Jake, Laney, Jen, Henry, and all of the Chandler Group are going to be working to figure this out. And while they do that, we're going to hide away. You're not alone in this, Nyssa."

Before she knew it, Nyssa had wrapped her arms around Molly and was sobbing for everything she was worth. Her legs gave out, and she sank to the ground.

Molly dropped down with her and held her tight. "You're not alone," she whispered in Nyssa's ear. "I won't let you be."

CHAPTER 41

OVER THE ATLANTIC OCEAN

The remainder of the short flight was excruciating. Her uncle was in the hospital. He'd been hurt bad. Cain had been hurt as well. And Nyssa was in hiding.

Laney sat on the edge of the copilot's seat as if by somehow leaning forward, she could make the plane go faster. It was stupid and nonsensical, and yet she couldn't make herself sit back.

"Did you know?" she asked David.

"Yes. They reached me when we were about halfway across the Atlantic. You were sleeping, and there didn't seem any reason to wake you up just to tell you that things had gone badly back home. And there was no news to deliver."

Laney ran a hand through her hair. She struggled to accept the fact that Nyssa was safe. Because no one knew exactly where Molly and JW were. They'd dumped their phones.

She knew that Molly would do everything in her power to keep Nyssa safe. But if Gedeon was after Nyssa, and after her in such a bold and violent way, they were still in danger.

THE BELIAL BLOOD

She needed to be on the ground. She needed to be able to do something to help. She pulled up her phone and flicked a glance at the screen. No new messages.

Her uncle was at the hospital and getting X-rays and a CAT scan. He hadn't regained consciousness by the time they'd reached the hospital, and he'd lost a lot of blood.

Laney started to tremble as she pictured him. He'd done so well after his injury years ago. But it had weakened him. And she wasn't sure his body could handle this kind of shock.

"Almost there, Lanes," David said as he nodded toward the runway up ahead.

Laney finally sat back as David started the descent.

Her uncle and Cain were in the hospital and Nyssa was missing. Everything had gone so horrible so fast.

Walking along the front of the porch, Gedeon flicked a glance at his phone. They had grabbed Nyssa from the estate just as planned. It was amazing how well the plan had gone. The Chandler Group had relied too much on their technological security, and Gedeon had been able to exploit that and slip right in before they were even aware of what was happening.

But his people were supposed to call once they were in the air. And they had not yet done so. He paced along the length of the porch one more time before pulling out his phone and calling.

It rang a few times and then went to voicemail. Disconnecting the call, he shoved the phone back in his pocket. What was going on?

He growled as he stared out over the land. In all the time he'd been on this planet, he'd never had the problems like he'd had with McPhearson and her people.

When he'd first started on these missions, he'd been sent to speak with different humans to see if they gave in to the temptation. Sometimes it was something as simple as food: taking it from a neighbor who desperately needed it. Other times it was money or sex that tempted these humans to the dark side. But it never took longer than a few days to pull people into that darkness. Humans were such weak creatures.

This mission was different. And it was so much more important. But these people were so much more difficult. Delaney McPhearson should simply get out of Gedeon's way, and then she and her people would be safe. But that was not how she operated. The safest route would be for all of them to simply hand over Nyssa. But instead of doing that, they fought.

He shook his head. He didn't have much experience with people like this. He was used to the people who, after only a little coaxing, were happy to give in to the temptations that Gedeon presented to them.

But these people couldn't be tempted by the usual things. He'd need to give some thought to what would change that perspective. There had to be something. There was price for everyone.

He pictured Delaney McPhearson when they had been in that alley in Greece. He'd held Drake in front of her, the man she loved. But instead of saving him as she should have, as any other human would have, she'd gone and saved that other boy.

He'd been confounded by her action, not that he'd let it slow him down. As soon as she turned to the boy, he'd taken Drake away. But her actions had thrown him.

Why had she not saved Drake instead? She'd known that he was weaker than the boy. And there was a chance that the boy might have survived. But nonetheless, she'd saved him instead of Drake.

But that little action had led to Arturo being added to their household. Perhaps the care for a child would make Michael similarly weak. His phone rang, and Gedeon yanked it up. Finally. "Status report. Are you in the air?"

"No, sir. There's been a complication."

THE BELIAL BLOOD

Gedeon rolled his hand into a fist. "*What* complication?"

They had intentionally waited until Delaney McPhearson was in the air before they moved in on the estate. She should have been unable to reach her people back in the States. They had also waited until Jennifer Witt was off the estate and Henry Chandler was in the bomb shelter. That left largely human security. It should have been easy.

"Three of McPhearson's people followed us to the airfield. During the skirmish, they managed to get the girl away."

"And you followed and caught her again?"

There was a pause on the other end of the line. "No, sir. Two of them took the girl while the other two held us at bay long enough for them to get away."

Gedeon stared up at the sky, trying to pull back the wave of anger rolling through him. "Who took her?"

"It was the woman known as Molly McAdams and a man that we have yet to identify."

Gedeon frowned. The name was vaguely familiar, but he couldn't pull up an image in his mind's eye. "Who is Molly McAdams?"

"She's the stepdaughter of Jake Rogan."

Gedeon stepped back, stunned for a moment at the statement. Molly McAdams had been the one who the United States government had experimented on. From all reports, she'd been traumatized by the experience. She was quiet and hadn't been involved in any of the Chandler projects that Gedeon's people could find. Categorized as an incredibly low risk of violence toward them. In fact, she was viewed as one of the weaker chains in the Chandler Group. "How is that possible? She's not strong enough for this."

"She took down Octavius."

Gedeon's eyebrows rose at that statement. He was not easy to take down. Gedeon would have to reevaluate the threat of the McAdams woman. "What are you doing to find her?

175

"We have our people out searching, and we have all electronics under surveillance."

Gedeon shook his head. They would no doubt ditch all of their electronics. His people now were making the same mistake as the Chandler Group: relying too much on technological equipment. "They'll have ditched all of that. Search all known locations that Molly McAdams might go, and find out who this man with her is."

"Yes, sir, I will."

Gedeon disconnected the call. He stared out over the yard. Molly McAdams. The young woman looked a lot like Delaney McPhearson. And apparently she was a lot like her as well.

She shouldn't have been a risk. She shouldn't have been a barrier to anything. What was wrong with these humans? They did not fit into the categories they were supposed to.

Gedeon knew that he'd underestimated McPhearson's feelings for the people in her group. That was no doubt why she'd chosen that boy rather than save Drake. It turned out that he was a boy she'd helped raise for a number of years when he was younger.

And from the report, Molly McAdams had known Nyssa since she was young as well. Perhaps there was something to the human nature that when they knew someone since they were a child, it made them care more for them, even as they got older. Even to the point that they would place their own wants and desires behind the need to keep that individual safe.

Gedeon would have to think on this a while longer. Sacrificing one's own desires to help another was not an aspect of human nature he was familiar with. Over his long time on the planet, it was not something that he'd been exposed to much.

But apparently the willingness to sacrifice for someone else gave humans unknown strength.

Molly McAdams shouldn't have been able to get Nyssa away from his people. She certainly shouldn't have been able to take down Octavius. He was a phenomenal fighter.

Gedeon had underestimated the McAdams woman just like he'd underestimated Delaney McPhearson. He frowned, realizing that he was making the same mistakes over and over again.

If he didn't know any better, he would swear he was becoming more human.

CHAPTER 42

The trip from the airfield to the hospital was fast. They got a police escort, and other police officers had actually driven ahead, cordoning off roads to allow them clear passage straight through.

Normally Laney didn't like taking advantage of any perks that came with the ring bearer experience. But right now with her uncle lying in a hospital gravely ill, she would take advantage of whatever perk she could to get to his side as fast as possible.

David pulled up right in front of the hospital. "Go. I'll park the car, then I'll come in and find you."

Laney stepped from the car but leaned back in. "No. Get the Inceptus to Dom. It needs to be a priority now. And make sure Dom's place has extra protection. The Inceptus is our best chance at defeating Gedeon."

David nodded. "Okay. But I'll be back once it's safely delivered."

Nodding her thanks, Laney strode for the hospital doors. Before she reached them, the doors slid open and Jen stepped outside. Laney fell in step with her.

The two headed right for the doors as Jen spoke. "He was

taken in for CAT scan. They managed to stop the bleeding, but Laney, you're going to have to prepare yourself. He lost a lot of blood."

"How? How did this happen?"

"We're still figuring out exactly how they got into our system. But they must have had a team of hackers working with them. From what Danny can tell, they started breaking in last night, testing different aspects of the estate's security system. And then when they were ready, they shut down all of our security. We had no communications. We had no cameras. We had no ability to control any of the anti-terrorist enhancements that Henry arranged. They completely shut us down."

"How is that possible? Gedeon has shown no technological ability of that level at all. So how did he manage this?"

"That is the question. You're right. Gedeon hasn't shown this ability before. He has to be paying someone to get them to do this because this is way above his skill set. Danny said that it would take a highly experienced group of hackers to pull this off. Apparently they did it in such a way that it wasn't detectable until it was too late. That's not easy to do, especially with all the protocols we have in place. Danny and Dom are both helping with the analysis, but it's going to take a while to find out who's behind it, if we do it at all."

Laney wasn't sure whether that truly mattered. The damage had been done. "What about now? Are the systems safe?"

"Not entirely. They're still flushing some of the code from the system."

"So we can't trust our own technology."

"Not yet. They're building firewalls as they go through it and have initiated a whole set of protocols I can't even begin to understand to keep this from happening again."

Damn it. They didn't need this, not right now. Not when they needed to find Nyssa and Drake. "What about Nyssa? Any word?"

"Last we know, she was with Molly and JW. They've

completely dropped off the grid. We haven't seen them since the airfield. JW's trained in this. He'll have ditched the car and taken them somewhere no one will find them. We haven't heard a peep since then."

"So no news is good news."

"Yes."

"And you trust JW?" Laney hadn't had a chance to get to know him, so she would have to go with Jen's impression.

Jen didn't hesitate. "Yes. He won't let anything happen to Molly or Nyssa. He'll keep them hidden. And Molly won't let anyone hurt Nyssa. She'll keep her safe."

Laney met Jen's gaze and heard the rest of the statement that Jen didn't want to say out loud.

Or die trying.

CHAPTER 43

After the events of the day, Molly felt completely drained. They'd managed to get Nyssa back into the car after her breakdown, but Molly was worried about the young girl.

She knew from experience and from her research how difficult trauma on a young person could be. And Nyssa was most definitely traumatized.

Even the quick look at Patrick and Cain that Molly had gotten, the injuries, at least to Patrick, were going to be life changing if not life ending.

His body wasn't going to respond to them as easily as someone who was much younger. A friend who was in med school explained one day that it didn't matter how athletic or healthy an individual was as they aged. When they experienced a trauma, even if they ran marathons, their body would still respond like a seventy-year-old rather than a thirty-year-old.

There was no way to change that response through exercise or healthy diet. Bodies aged; that was just how it worked. Which meant that Patrick was in for a long recovery. *If* he managed to recover.

Molly didn't like to think about Patrick being hurt. He'd

become the grandfatherly presence in her life. He was such a calm and logical man, and he had a wicked sense of humor. And he always seemed to have tea and biscuits available whenever anybody needed to talk.

She flicked a glance in the back of the car where Nyssa had fallen asleep about an hour ago. She couldn't imagine how Nyssa was going to handle it if Patrick didn't make it. And she well knew the guilt that Nyssa would feel.

As much as what Molly had said to Nyssa was true about the blame being solely on the aggressor, Molly still felt guilty about Zane's death. Even though he'd been a genetically modified panther, he'd been such a true friend. The word "friend" didn't really capture the bond that the two of them had shared. Imagining his lifeless body on that lab table still brought her to tears.

How was Nyssa going to be able to handle the memories of what had happened to Patrick? She prayed that she wouldn't have to, and that Patrick would fully recover, but it was a long shot. And while there had been many miracles that seemed to pop up around the Chandler Group, that seemed like one that was too great to even hope for.

Pulling her attention from the decidedly dour tone her thoughts were now taking, Molly focused on the landscape zipping past her through the car window. The area around them had slowly grown less and less familiar as JW drove.

He sat behind the wheel, quiet, his focus on the area surrounding them. He occasionally flicked a glance in the rearview mirror and switched lanes often.

Molly couldn't help but wonder at the fact that she felt safe with him. The truth was she'd felt safe from the moment she'd met him, which was not normal for her.

But she was also amazed that he hadn't even blinked when she'd mentioned that they needed to get Nyssa away. He'd merely come up with a plan and started driving. There was no questioning. There was no doubt of whether or not he could step away from his life. He simply did it.

And she was so completely grateful for that.

She stifled a yawn and blinked, focusing on the road up ahead.

"You should get some sleep," JW said.

Molly shook her head. "No, I'm fine."

He gave her that smile that made her stomach tremble. "Liar. But you really should get some sleep. I'll have you take over the driving for a little bit down the road and it'll be better if at least one of us was a little more awake."

Molly searched his face. "Are you sure?"

"I'm sure. Get some sleep. I'll wake you when we get close."

His words seem to be a command to her eyelids because they were already starting to droop. She snuggled into the seat, trying to get a little more comfortable. "Maybe for just a few minutes," she murmured.

CHAPTER 44

THE HOSPITAL WAS ABUZZ, AND LANEY NOTED THE EXTRA SECURITY Henry had brought in from the estate. Jen, noting Laney's attention, nodded toward the familiar faces. "Henry called in all our security, and I've called in some people from Homeland to have them secure the estate. Until we know exactly what's going on, we're going to have to rely more on human security to make sure that things are safe."

That idea made Laney nervous. As much as she didn't like to rely on technology, especially when it was proven that it could be so easily hacked, humans could also be compromised.

Plus, as well trained as their people and Homeland's people were, they were no match for the force that had come to the estate. But here was one group that could stand a chance against them. "What about the other Fallen?"

"They're already making their way back here," Jen said.

Everyone had dispersed after the events in Greece, heading back to their homes. But they had promised to return as soon as they were needed. Laney had hoped they would be able to spend more time with their families before they were called up again.

THE BELIAL BLOOD

But unfortunately, it looked they were going to be needed sooner rather than later.

"How did all of this happen, Jen? How are we back here again?"

"Gedeon," Jen growled. "We need to take that guy down and make sure he stays down. Did you have any luck in Italy?"

The journey with Cristela seemed like it had happened a lifetime ago. "Yeah, at least I think so. We know what the source of the fluid that he used on Drake is."

"That's great."

Laney lowered her voice. "I have a sample on the way to Dom. There's not much ,but I'm hoping he can replicate it."

Jen raised an eyebrow. "And how exactly did you find it? Let me guess, some sort of ancient mystery hidden within some sort of impossible-to-decipher puzzle?"

Despite the fear and worry racing through her, Laney had to smile at Jen's description. "Actually, a little old nun showed us the way."

Jen grunted. "Well, that's easier than most of our recoveries."

Visualizing the story Cristela had told them about how she'd destroyed the well and hidden the vial, Laney knew that wasn't entirely true.

As they reached the third-floor landing, all thoughts of the Inceptus slipped away, as did all the light-heartedness. Jen pulled open the door, and they stepped out onto the floor.

Henry, who'd been leaning against the wall, stepped away from it and hurried over. He wrapped Laney in a big hug. Laney leaned into her brother, her head against his chest, listening to the steady beat of his heart.

"How are you?" she asked.

The growl started in Henry's chest as he spoke. "Annoyed. I was down in Dom's shelter when everything began. By the time I got back to the surface, everything was over. Cain and Patrick were down and Nyssa was missing."

"And Nyssa? Is there any word?"

"Jake's heading up the search. We're waiting for them to make contact. Although it might be better if they didn't do that for a little while."

Laney nodded, a gnawing feeling in her gut. If they couldn't trust the technology around them, it definitely would be better if Molly didn't contact them for a while. Hopefully she and JW would be able to keep their and Nyssa's heads down long enough for the rest of them to figure out everything else.

"And my uncle?" Laney leaned back to look up at Henry's face.

He met her gaze for only a moment, but that was more than enough for Laney to read the fear there. "We're waiting on the results. The doctor should be up any minute with them."

Letting out a slow, measured breath, Laney closed her eyes. It would be okay. He had to be okay. "What about Cain?"

"He's banged up, and he has a concussion, but he'll heal." Henry nodded to the door just down to his left. "He's in there if you want to go see him."

Laney didn't rush for the door, and she felt like a coward for her hesitation. But she didn't want to see the look on Cain's face when they talked about Nyssa.

But she hadn't gotten to this point in her life by staying away from unpleasant conversations. So she straightened her shoulders and moved down the hallway.

"We'll wait for you out here," Jen said softly.

Laney nodded at the two of them and slipped in the door.

The blinds were drawn and the light was dim. There was a single bed in the room, and Cain lay upon it, a large bandage across his forehead. Scrapes and bruises dotted his face and arms.

Laney stood for a moment against the wall, steadying herself. Her heart broke at the sight of the injuries. He'd been through so much in his life. But this loss, this danger to Nyssa might be the most difficult thing he'd ever faced.

Cain slowly opened his eyes and gave her a small sad smile, reaching a hand out for her. "Laney."

She hurried across the room and gripped his hand. He squeezed it tightly, staring at her with his blue eyes. "Any word on Nyssa?"

Laney shook her head. "No. They've gone to ground."

Cain's face fell.

Laney hurried to speak. "But that's probably a good thing. We can't trust our communications right now, and so them not getting in touch keeps them safer."

Cain closed his eyes, leaning his head back against the pillow. "I know part of you believes that."

Yeah, and the other part is trying really hard to believe it as well. She squeezed his hand. "How are you feeling?"

"Like an impotent old fool." He opened his eyes to study her. "If I'd still been cursed, maybe Nyssa would be safe."

Cain had been cursed when he'd killed his brother, Abel, back at the beginning of humanity's reign on this planet. At that point, his eyes had turned to pure black. Anyone who saw him would think he was a demon and run away.

And they would be the better for it. Because anyone who tried to harm him would have whatever harm they tried to inflict on Cain sent back at them sevenfold. Anyone who stabbed him would result in seven stabs along their body, each one deeper than the one before. One broken bone would result in seven, each one more brutal than the one before.

So the fallen angel who'd thrown Cain into a wall would have been practically pulverized by the same punishment being meted out against them.

Laney wasn't sure what to say to Cain's claim. She didn't think it was true. But no one was completely rational in moments like these.

Cain had lost his abilities when Laney had taken the Fallen's abilities. He'd embraced the fact that he was no longer cursed with a gusto that often made her smile and sometimes made her laugh out loud. This was the first time she could remember he'd ever regretted that the curse had been lifted.

"You don't know that. And from what I understand, Uncle Patrick was hurt before you could reach them."

Cain sighed. "I suppose that's true. But it doesn't change the fact that I wish I could have done things differently. I wish there were something more that I could do."

"Unfortunately, I know that feeling well."

Cain shook his head. "These thoughts aren't getting us anywhere. Tell me, how did your trip to Italy go?"

"I'm not sure this is a time for that discussion."

"Please, Laney. I need something to distract me or I'm going to go crazy."

She studied him, weighing the pros and cons of talking about what she'd learned and finally turned and pulled up a chair. "Well, we met Cristela. You knew all this time she was at the orphanage?"

Cain nodded. "I've kept track of her over the years. We've crossed paths a time or two. She actually ..." He paused. "She was a bright spot in a rather long existence. There was never any judgment on her face, just understanding and peace. And being she was able to provide that to me, I figured it was only fair if I kept her identity protected as well. It seemed the least I could do. How is she?"

Picturing the old nun, Laney tried to capture in words what she felt about the woman. "Mysterious. She's aging. I mean, she's immortal like you, I suppose, but while you stayed the same age, she has been aging all this time."

Cain nodded slowly. "Yes, she is not quite like me. She's an angel, although not technically a Fallen. But like Fallen, she ages, albeit at a microscopic pace. I'm not sure what will happen in another few hundred years."

Laney sat back hard at the thought of that. Would Cristela truly still be around hundreds of years from now? That seemed impossible, and yet she'd already been here for thousands of years.

"She explained that the Inceptus, the liquid that Gedeon used to weaken Drake, was most likely from a well that hasn't been seen in thousands of years. It used to be guarded by the angels, by her. It no longer exists. But she hid a small portion away."

"Did she give you any idea where the well might be?"

"Better than that. She led us to it. The sample's on the way to Dom as we speak. But I'm not sure that's the most important thing right now. We need to find Gedeon. We need to keep him from going after Nyssa."

Cain stared at her for a long moment before shaking his head. "No, that Inceptus is the most important thing right now."

Laney's mouth fell open. "What? How can you say that? The longer Gedeon's out there, the longer Nyssa is in danger."

"Yes, that's true. But what happens when you catch him? How will you be able to stop him?"

Laney crossed her arms over her chest. "Well, I haven't tried decapitation yet, but I'm pretty sure that'll at least slow him down."

Cain chuckled lightly and then winced, bringing a hand to his head. "Don't make me laugh. And yes, that would probably work, at least for a little while, but are you sure you're going to be able to decapitate an angel of his strength?"

Laney wasn't sure how to answer that.

"Besides, you don't know where he is. And until you do, you need to find a way to weaken him. You need a weapon to take him down."

The Inceptus could be that weapon, but it wasn't the only one. "We need the Arma Christi."

Cain nodded slowly. "Yes, but he already has some of the parts. Which means this Inceptus is your best chance right now for taking him down. You need to replicate it, or at least save enough for one shot at Gedeon. It's the weapon that will enable you to take him off the board. And until you do that, Nyssa won't be safe. Finding Gedeon and taking him down with this new weapon is your priority."

Laney sighed, not wanting to face the truth in his words. She wanted to rush out and find Nyssa and wrap her up, keeping her safe. But she also needed to do all those other things too.

Nevertheless, she wanted to tell him that he was wrong and that she could keep Nyssa safe while tracking down Gedeon, but the reality was she couldn't. As powerful as she was, she was still one person. And trying to keep Nyssa safe while doing all of those other things would be impossible. Cain was right: until Gedeon was gone, none of the others would be safe.

"I hate this. I hate that this has all fallen on Nyssa's head. She doesn't deserve this at all," she murmured.

"No, she doesn't. But it seems oftentimes that the people least deserving of painful experiences are the ones most likely to be exposed to them." Cain took a deep breath. "Take Gedeon off the board. I need you to make Nyssa safe."

Laney turned back and looked into his eyes. The depth of the pain in them was heartbreaking to see. And she could not allow herself to fail him. "I'll find a way."

"I have no doubt you will," he said.

CHAPTER 45

MASSA, ITALY

THE BOULDER SAILED ACROSS THE OPEN SPACE AND SLAMMED INTO the side of an old tree. It crashed through the wall, landing inside in a shower of wood and dust.

His chest heaving, Gedeon stared after it as if he could destroy the boulder itself with just a glare. They had lost Lilith. His people had given him an update just a few minutes ago. They had no sign of her. They'd found the car, but it had been ditched along the side of a road.

There was no indication of what kind of car they had taken in its place. And nothing in the car itself indicated where they had gone.

Gedeon was beyond incensed. How had she slipped through their fingers? They literally had the girl in their grasp, and they had let her escape.

He grabbed another rock and sent it sailing through another tree.

All his planning, all his preparation, and he'd been foiled yet again. And Delaney McPhearson couldn't even be blamed for this one.

How was it possible that he kept running into walls like this?

Blood pounded in his ears as he shook his head. The sound of it brought him up short. He straightened, his breaths coming out in pants. He'd never felt like this before. He'd never felt this angry before. He'd never felt *any* emotion like this before.

That was what was making him fail. He took a step back, breathing deep. That was it. Somehow his emotions had gotten caught up in everything that was happening.

And he knew exactly why that was: because he'd seen Lilith. For some reason, she crawled under his skin like no one else had been able to.

He hadn't expected to see her. And to see her looking so innocent, so young, it had been jarring to his system and thrown him off his game.

He'd watched her from afar for eons. But she'd been around longer. She'd been here since the very beginning. God's chosen creation, the mother of them all. Blessed and beautiful in his sight.

With awe and wonder, he'd watched her journey through lifetime after lifetime, and slowly his attention had shifted from idle curiosity to something more. It had taken him a while to recognize that there was a connection between the two of them, even though, at that point, they'd never met face-to-face.

He knew in his soul that when they met, she would understand that connection. When they met, she would fully embrace the rightness of the two of them together. He had no doubt of that.

But he'd had to bide his time. His primary duty was, of course, to his missions. But then one fated day, his mission had brought her within striking distance. He'd grabbed her as she'd made her way home from the village and taken her away to a home he knew was vacant. There he'd spoken to her for the first time.

A frown marred his face as he thought of the fear he'd seen in her eyes that first day. She hadn't known who he was, but she'd known what he was. And it hadn't just been fear in her eyes but revulsion as well.

She'd glared up at him, her hands on her hips, the fear slowly replaced with anger. "I will not change my mind. Humans need to be mortal. You and your brethren can stop hounding me."

Gedeon had been surprised at her words. Some of his brothers had been trying to get her to take back that fateful decision. "That is not why I have come to speak with you. I thought it would be wise for us to get to know one another."

Lilith narrowed her eyes at him. "What is your name?"

"Samael."

Her eyes widened in response, and she took a step back. "The angel of death."

Gedeon shrugged, even though part of him was thrilled that she knew who he was. "Some call me that. But there is more to me than that. Besides, are you not also the mother of death? You have brought more souls to their end than I ever could."

He took a step forward, reaching for her. "I would like to share with you—"

Arrows rained in from the window next to him, piercing his side as they found their mark. He hissed out in pain as the door behind him flew open. Four women, all armed, all muscular, burst into the room. The one in the lead, a tall dark-haired woman, threw a spear that caught him in the back.

Another sprinted forward, slashing out at the back of his knees as the two other women grabbed Lilith and lowered her out the window to others waiting below.

Gedeon roared, grabbing one of the women as she attempted to slash his neck. He held her up with one hand. "You will not keep her from me."

The woman glared back at him, her eyes full of determination. "Oh, yes we will."

Pain pierced through his back as two spears impaled him. He snapped the neck of the woman he held and tried to whirl around, but the pain from the spears and the cuts at the back of his knees dropped him to the ground.

The women didn't even hesitate as they circled him, slashing and stabbing. "You cannot kill me," he spat as blood dribbled down his chin.

The women didn't slow their attacks as one spoke on their behalf, slicing open the cuts along the back of his knees that had healed over. "No, but we can make you wish you were dead."

Gedeon growled at the memory. The women had been true to their word and had slashed and hacked at him for hours. They'd managed to remove his arm and one of his legs from below the knee. When the blood loss was enough that he lost consciousness, they left him lying there on the ground.

When he'd awoken, it had taken time for him to recover, and by that time there'd been no sign of Lilith.

It took him lifetimes to find her again. That next time, the fear he'd seen in her eyes and the disgust had made him do things that he did not think he was capable of.

Her followers had found him again and left him in much the same state as they had the first time. He curled his hands into fists. Those women. Always women.

But this time, it would be different. This time she was so young, she did not have any memories from her past lives yet. Which meant she would not remember him.

It was an opening, one he would exploit. He would grab her. He would find her and show her that they were meant to be together. And once her memories returned, it would not matter because he would already have established a bond between them.

He took a deep breath, closing his eyes and focusing on his breathing in and out, in and out. Slowly, his heart rate began to return to normal. He breathed in for ten minutes, waiting until his heart was calm, his breathing unencumbered.

Then he opened his eyes.

Lilith was important, but not as important as she would be in the future. He still needed to find her and bring her to their side, but he had some time for that. But there was another step that needed to be taken, and soon. Because without the Arma Christi, everything else would be lost.

He turned and strode back to the building. Lucius slipped out the front door before he could speak.

Gedeon looked at his second in command and nodded. "We need to head to Rome."

Lucius, his tablet already in his hands, nodded. "Do you want me to reach out to our contact?"

"Yes, tell him we're coming to town. Tell him what we need him to do. He will not give you any trouble."

"Yes, sir. And how many people am I taking with us?"

Gedeon thought for a moment. "Michael is still on the drip?"

"Yes, sir. We have enough for at least a few days."

He paused for another, longer moment, then shook his head. "There will only be three of us. Everyone else must stay here. There must be at least two individuals in the room with Michael at any given time. I am not taking the chance of him escaping again."

"Yes, sir. When do you want to leave?"

"Immediately."

CHAPTER 46

BALTIMORE, MARYLAND

A knock sounded at Cain's hospital room door just before Jen peeked her head in. "The doctor's here. She wants to talk to you about the results of the CAT scan."

Laney stepped closer to the bed, gripping Cain's hand. "Send her in."

The door opened, and a slim woman in her early forties with long black hair pulled back in a headband stepped inside. She had the copper complexion of someone who had Indian or maybe Pakistani roots somewhere back in their family tree.

"Good morning," she said. "I'm Dr. Rachel Abidi."

Laney nodded. "I'm Delaney McPhearson."

The doctor gave her a smile. "Yes, I know who you are. Cain, how are you feeling?"

"Anxious," he said.

"How's my uncle?" Laney asked.

The doctor nodded at Cain. "I assume it's all right to speak here?"

"He's family," Laney said firmly.

THE BELIAL BLOOD

"Very well. I actually have some questions before we discuss your uncle's condition. I was hoping you could answer them."

Frustration rolled through Laney, but she tried to hold it back.

Before the doctor could get to the first question, the door opened again. An African American woman with a familiar face stepped inside: Gina Carstairs, the secretary of Health and Human Services and a good friend. Her eyes were full of worry and a doctor's gaze as she scanned both Cain and Laney. "I'm so sorry."

Dr. Abidi stepped aside, her eyes widening at the appearance of the secretary. Laney was sure visits from the President's inner circle were not a common occurrence for Dr. Abidi's patients.

Gina crossed the room quickly and engulfed Laney in a big hug before moving next to the bed. Kissing Cain on the cheek, she took a hold of his other hand and faced the doctor.

Laney noted the look of concern on her face as she studied Cain. And it wasn't a clinical look. Her and Cain had grown closer over the years, and Laney kept hoping that maybe they'd take the next step, although it had never happened.

"Forgive the interruption. I was out of town and just got back." Gina looked at the doctor and the chart in her hand before glancing back at Laney and Cain. "Should I wait outside?"

Cain kept a grip on her hand. "I think perhaps your medical knowledge could be beneficial to us at this point."

Gina nodded. "Of course."

Laney turned back to the doctor. "You were saying, Doctor?"

"Yes, I was wondering about your uncle's previous injury."

Laney had explained her uncle's injury to dozens of doctors, but Cain was the one who gave the explanation this time. During Laney's absence these last few years, he'd been the one who accompanied her uncle on those doctor's visits. Anger at Azazael yanking her away from her life reared up in her, but she tamped it back down, even as she made a mental note to see if there had been any leads on his location.

She couldn't help but think back to that horrible day. Samyaza had engaged in a multi-pronged attack: the cats at the preserve, the estate, and the cabin in the woods where Patrick was hiding with Cain and Nyssa. Jen had lost her first pregnancy that day, and Patrick had lost the use of his legs to a bullet in the back.

Cain finished up with the most recent outreaches. "Henry Chandler has had every specialist across the globe examine him, and they've all said the same: nothing can be done."

A wrinkle appeared on the doctor's brow as she nodded. "Yes, I had some of his older X-rays brought in for a comparison."

Laney frowned. "Why are you asking about his spinal injury? Was his spine further injured today? I thought it was the head injury that was the concern?"

Consulting her chart again, the doctor nodded. "The head injury was reported as the greatest concern when he was brought in, but there were some inconsistencies that I've been struggling to understand."

"Inconsistencies? Like what?" Gina asked.

The doctor looked at the three and then closed her chart. "When your uncle presented, we were informed that there had been massive blood loss from a head wound. That is, of course, always a concern, especially for someone of his advanced age. While the body might survive until well into your hundreds, it grows more fragile as the years go on. And a head injury with the amount of blood loss that was reported could be life-threatening."

Laney's heart started to pound. The doctor would have said if he had passed. But she did not like the direction the conversation was heading.

The doctor continued. "When he arrived here, he was unconscious. Which seemed to support the notion that the head injury was in fact dire."

Laney frowned. "*Seemed* to support?"

The doctor opened her mouth and then closed it as if struggling to find the words. "We can find no evidence of the head injury."

Laney looked at Cain and then back at the doctor. Cain looked just as confused as her. "I don't understand. What do you mean you can't find any evidence of the head injury?" Laney asked.

"When your uncle arrived, he was covered in blood. We feared the worst. When we cleaned the blood off of him, however, while we could find a small swelling—and I do mean small, perhaps a bump one centimeter across on his left temple—there was no cut. There was nowhere for the blood to have escaped. The blood couldn't have been his."

Laney frowned. "But that doesn't make any sense. I mean, everyone said it was his blood. He was the only one it could have come from."

The doctor looked just as baffled as Laney felt. "That was what we were told as well. His head was covered in blood. His shirt was soaked in it. However, we can't find a wound that links up with that type of injury. We are struggling to figure out exactly what happened. There was some initial swelling of the brain, but even that has gone back to normal levels."

"Is he awake, then?" Cain asked.

"No, not yet. And we can't explain that either. He shouldn't be asleep with that kind of injury, or lack thereof."

Laney wasn't sure what to make of the doctor's words. She hadn't been there for the fight, but she doubted that people could get her uncle's injury so wrong.

As if hearing her thoughts, Cain shook his head, sitting up a little straighter in bed. "No, I saw Patrick go flying into that rock wall. And Jen, she reported all of the blood."

The doctor nodded. "Like we said, there was a great deal of blood on him. But at this point, we're not even sure if the blood is his."

"Well, let's get this settled." Laney pulled out her phone and texted Jen.

A moment later, she stepped into the room, closing the door behind her. "Hey, what's going on?"

"We need to know about Patrick's injury," Laney said.

Jen frowned. "What do you mean? Isn't that what the doctor's here for?"

"What did you see when you first found him?" Laney asked.

Jen blanched. "He was lying on the sidewalk in front of the cottage. There was so much blood."

"Did you see a wound?" Gina asked.

"A wound? Um, no, but all that blood. Why are you asking this?" Jen asked.

"There seems to be some doubt about whether the blood was Patrick's," Cain said, looking completely bewildered.

"What?" Jen asked.

"There's no wound, Jen," Laney explained.

Jen's mouth opened and then closed as she stared at the three of them. "Okay, well, we'll take a sample of blood from his clothes or the scene and match it."

"That will take some time," the doctor said.

Laney looked at Jen, who nodded, slipping out the door. Jen would make sure that the blood from the estate was tested ASAP.

But Laney had no idea what to think about the fact that her uncle didn't seem to have a wound that would bleed. And then her eyes widened as she thought of one possibility. "Was Nyssa injured?"

Cain paled, shaking his head. "No, no, I don't think so."

"But she was near Uncle Patrick, right?"

Cain nodded. "Yes, she was only a few feet away when he got hit. She ran to him, and then I got hit, and I don't know what happened after that."

Laney felt faint. Had Nyssa actually been hurt during the attack? But then why wouldn't Molly, Lou, or Rolly have said something about it?

"Hold on a second, Doctor." Laney pulled out her phone. She quickly dialed Lou.

Lou answered after only two rings. "Laney? Are you back in the States?"

"Yes, I'm back."

"Thank God. You heard?"

"I heard. I'm at the hospital now. I need to ask you about Nyssa. Was she hurt when you saw her?"

There was a pause on the other end of the line. "You mean emotionally?"

"No, physically. Was she cut at all during the attack before she got to the airfield?"

"If she was, I didn't see anything. And she was wearing that pale-blue sweatshirt of hers. I would have noticed the blood. There was some blood on her hands, but it was dried. So no, I don't think she was hurt."

"Okay, thanks, Lou."

"Laney," Lou said quickly before Laney could hang up the phone.

"Yeah?"

"When you find Nyssa or Gedeon, Rolly and I are in. Whatever you need, we're in."

The events of the time travel had really shaken Lou, so she knew that statement was well thought and determined. "You're in. As soon as we get any info, I'll make sure you're involved."

Lou let out a breath. "Good. They shouldn't have gone for Nyssa. Kids are supposed to be off limits."

"Yeah, they are." Aware of the eyeballs watching them, Laney spoke quickly. "I've got to go. We'll talk later."

"Okay." Lou disconnected the call.

Laney turned to the others in the room. "Nyssa wasn't hurt during the attack. The blood's not hers."

The room went quiet as everybody tried to figure out exactly what was going on.

Gina finally broke it. "Why were you asking about his spinal injury? Was there additional damage done to his spine?"

Another frown marred the doctor's face. "No, in fact, the opposite. His spinal injury, it seems to be healing."

It took a moment for the doctor's words to register. "That's not possible," Laney said.

Dr. Abidi inclined her head. "If you had spoken with me a few hours ago, I would have said that you were right. It should be impossible. But I've compared his old X-rays to the ones we took today. And there is definitely improvement. I'm at a loss as to how to explain it, just like I can't explain where all that blood came from. Nothing about your uncle's case makes sense."

"So what does that mean?" Cain asked.

The doctor let out a long breath. "Your uncle's in much better condition than a man of his age with the injury that was reported when he came in should be. And I honestly have no way to explain it."

CHAPTER 47

THE DOCTOR AND HER TEAM WANTED PATRICK TO GO THROUGH another battery of tests, so Laney wasn't able to see him yet. That only seemed to add to the worry growing inside her, despite the doctor's assurance that he was doing extraordinarily well for someone who'd been through what he'd been through, although Laney could tell the doctor would feel much better if he regained consciousness.

As the doctor left, Henry stepped into the room, and Laney gave him a quick rundown of what the doctor had said.

Henry frowned. "How's that possible? I saw Patrick. The blood was absolutely everywhere. And I could have sworn I saw the wound on his head." Henry pulled out his phone. "Let me call Jake. I think he installed one of those doorbell cameras a few months back. Maybe they got some of what happened on the street."

"That camera wasn't taken over like the others?"

Henry shook his head. "No. It's a closed circuit. It goes directly to a file in Jake's home. Honestly, I totally forgot about it until right this moment. I'm not even sure if Jake ever got it up and running." He took a step away from Laney. "Hey, Jake. Did you ever get that doorbell camera set up?"

Laney moved back to the bed. Gina had left to go over the results with the doctor to see if she could help or speed things along.

Laney leaned against the edge of the bed. "What do you think?"

Cain's face was lined with worry. "What I think is, well, what I think I hope is wrong."

Laney frowned. "What do you mean?"

Cain shook his head. "I can only come up with one explanation. But I'm just not sure if it's possible."

Henry disconnected the call from across the room. "Jake forgot about the camera as well. He's having Mary Jane go through the footage to see if the camera caught anything."

Laney nodded, hoping that something might come of it. At the very least she hoped they could figure out the source of the blood. She turned back to Cain to ask him what he'd been referring to when the door opened again.

A nurse stepped in. "Oh, I see we have a packed room," she said. "I'm afraid I need to take the patient's vitals."

Laney stepped away from the bed. "We'll give you some privacy." She and Henry crossed the room and stepped outside into the hall.

Jen was just stepping off the elevator and strode down the hall toward them. She nodded at Laney and Henry. "D'Artist was at the estate. He had already taken samples of the blood. He's rushing them down to Dom. We should have an answer shortly."

Dom had blood profiles for everyone on the estate, an unfortunate necessity. Laney nodded, leaning back against the wall. She looked around and then frowned. "Where's David?"

"I ran into him while I was downstairs. I told him what was happening, and he decided he'd be of more use back at the estate with Jake. So he was calling some of his contacts, trying to get a lead on Gedeon and his hideout."

That was probably for the best. Here, David wouldn't be able to do anything but offer more moral support, although Laney could admit that right now she could use a little moral support. Her uncle was actually doing much better than any of them expected, and yet somehow that didn't ease her mind.

"How much blood was on the scene around my uncle?" Laney asked.

Henry let out a breath. "Laney, it was a lot. I'm glad you weren't there to see it. The whole side of his head was covered, and his clothes were soaked in it. To be perfectly honest, I don't know how he even made it to the hospital."

Laney's stomach dropped at his words. She took a shuddering breath, her knees weakening for a moment. She could not lose her uncle, not like this.

And even as she thought it, she knew she had no control over that. One day he would leave her. But a violent attack was not what should bring that about. He deserved to just slip away in his sleep, quietly, on a night far in the future.

Henry's phone beeped, and he flicked a glance down in it. "Mary Jane sent the video." He frowned. "My phone's not going to be a big enough screen."

"There's a lounge down the hall with a large screen. We can watch it in there." Jen led the way.

Laney trailed behind her and Henry, her mind whirling. Nyssa was still somewhere, and Lou was right—they needed to find her. And Gedeon was out there doing God knew what. And then there was Drake, who was probably the one Gedeon was doing things to.

It felt like she was the last person in this race, being lapped by the other runners. Gedeon was making all of these moves, and Laney and her people were only reacting to them. After Greece, they'd felt a small surge of victory because they had managed to turn the tables on Gedeon.

But that victory had been incredibly short-lived. Because he'd most definitely caught them unaware. And whatever he was doing right now, they were completely unprepared for.

CHAPTER 48

ROME, ITALY

THE PLANE TOUCHED DOWN WITH A SHORT HOP. THE METAL BEAST raced down the runway for a little bit before the brakes were applied.

Gedeon sat at a window, staring out at the rushing landscape. His knuckles were white as they gripped the armrest. Slowly, he released them.

Flying was not natural. Only the animals with wings were supposed to be up in the air. But humans had subverted that nature and overcome that weakness to create planes.

Gedeon curled his lip.

Humans were always taking things that did not belong to them. The air did not belong to them, and yet they had conquered it. The same with the sea, and now they had even shifted into space.

And each time they moved into one of these areas, they left an ecological disaster, each turned into a human garbage dump. The seas were perhaps the most egregious case. There were 5.25 trillion pieces of trash in the ocean, with one to two millions tons being added every year. Only 269,000 tons floated on the surface while the rest were pieces of plastic microfibers.

Humans had created a practically invisible poison to choke out sea life. But they also created large eyesores, testaments to their careless disregard for nature, such as the five large garbage patches strewn across the globe. Rather than specifically created, they had been formed by the currents of the ocean gathering all the trash carelessly tossed in, grouping it together en masse. The largest garbage patch was the Great Pacific Garbage Patch, which was twice the size of Texas.

The carbon dioxide levels made it clear that the skies were no better. Those levels were higher today than at any point in at least the past 800,000 years. Over the past 171 years, humans had raised the level of CO_2 by 48% since 1850, a greater amount than what was seen in the previous 20,000 years.

And now space was a junkyard, with different countries just leaving their space junk up there to the point where it now endangered satellites and space stations that orbited the earth.

Humans were a plague of locusts destroying everything they touched. Thanks to humanity, the extinction rate was anywhere between hundreds, if not thousands, above the natural base extinction rate. This was not the first extinction period that the Earth had gone through, but humanity had urged on the death of millions of creatures at a much faster rate than before, even to their own detriment.

As the number of creatures on Earth was reduced, humans pushed more and more into habitats where they did not belong. As a result, humans became exposed to more and more diseases.

The creatures that would provide a buffer to protect humanity were among the first to go extinct, while those that spread disease proliferated and survived. It was in humanity's interest to protect these creatures, yet it was those chasing the mighty dollar and the short-term gains they brought that held the most sway.

Gedeon pictured humans when they had first crawled out of

the muck. They were little more than animals. But modern humans were not the only hominids that had existed on this planet. There were many varied branches of the human tree that had been snipped off throughout time. But *Homo sapiens* were the only ones that managed to adapt and survive.

But that cunning and that ability to survive may doom their very existence if they didn't change the way they treated the planet.

Of course, none of that would matter when Gedeon's plan came to fruition. The humans that survived would deserve the hellscape they had created for themselves.

The plane taxied for a little longer and then finally came to a stop. Gedeon released his hold on his armrests, shaking out his hands. There was not much that frightened Gedeon, but trusting his physical body to this metal coffin was not something that he would ever grow accustomed to.

He looked back at Sandra, Simone, and Yael. Yael stood up and headed for the door. He unlocked it and slipped outside. Simone was right behind him. As Sandra stood, she gave him a small bow. "I will make sure the car is ready, sir."

Gedeon said nothing as he watched her walk down the aisle and slip outside as well. When they were both gone, he finally stood, his legs feeling a little weak. He growled his frustration.

Leave it to the humans to create something that made him feel weak. Another black mark against them as far as he was concerned.

They had populated every inch of the globe and had created ways to get there that were unnatural, which required this stupid means of transport.

He preferred the days of ships and carts. Where you actually had to take time to get to your destination. Where you had to actually put some thought into whether or not it would be worth the trip. Humans now hopped on trains, buses, subways, and even planes on a lark.

The strength finally returning to his legs, he strode down the aisle of the plane. It was all right. Soon he would show them the error of their ways.

And besides, those errors had made sure that this was all possible.

CHAPTER 49

BALTIMORE, MARYLAND

THE HOSPITAL LOUNGE WAS JUST AT THE END OF THE HALL. There were two couches that faced one another, a couple of round tables, each with four chairs around it, and a counter with a refrigerator. And against the side wall facing the couches was an eighty-inch TV. Henry headed over to it and started connecting his phone.

Jen pulled Laney toward the kitchen area. "When's the last time you ate?"

Laney opened her mouth to argue that she wasn't hungry, but then she stopped herself. She couldn't actually remember the last time she'd eaten. It had to have been before she and David headed to Italy. And then she shook her head. "Actually, I had a few cookies at the orphanage."

Rolling her eyes, Jen grabbed a bowl and quickly filled it with some cereal from a canister and then poured in some milk and handed her a plastic spoon. "Well, believe it or not, that is not enough food to sustain a body. Here."

Laney looked down at the bowl and then raised an eyebrow.

Jen looked back at her. "You're going to eat every spoonful."

Laney grinned. "You're using your mom voice."

"Well, apparently you need to hear my mom voice. Go. Sit. Eat."

"Yes, ma'am." Laney took the bowl and sat at one of the tables. She ate without really tasting it, knowing that Jen was right and that she just needed to get something in her stomach.

Jen made coffee for the three of them and brought the mugs to the table. Laney took a sip and let out a sigh. "Caffeine really is a gift to humanity."

Raising her cup in salute, Jen chuckled. "Yes, it is." She took a sip and then placed her mug on the table. "How did Italy go?"

Laney pictured Cristela's face. "It went well. It was unexpected, though."

Jen raised an eyebrow as Henry joined them. "Unexpected how?"

Laney looked at Henry, who nodded. "I'll explain after. It's a bit of an involved story. Maybe we could just see if this video has anything?"

"Sure."

As Laney finished up her cereal, the door opened. A pale Cain was being pushed inside by Dylan, who gave Laney a shrug at her raised eyebrows. "He insisted on seeing the recording after the nurse left. I'll be right outside if you need me."

"I need to see if it's what I fear," Cain said.

Laney pushed Cain's chair closer to the TV, setting the brake.

"What do you think happened?" Jen asked.

Cain just shook his head, and none of them pressed him further.

"It's ready." Henry turned to the screen and set the video playing.

Laney and Jen stood up and walked closer to it. The recording from the doorbell camera was aimed at the front door and walkway of Jake and Mary Jane's home. But there was also a good view of the sidewalk across the street in front of Patrick and Cain's home.

"Mary Jane cut it to just a few minutes before the attack. I'll fast-forward," Henry said. There was no one on the street as the scene shifted subtly.

But then the front door of her cottage opened, and her uncle wheeled himself out. Laney frowned, leaning forward. "What does he have in his hands?"

Stopping the recording, Henry zoomed in. Laney let out a gasp as she noted the weaponry that he held. "He knew something was coming."

Henry nodded. "He spoke with Dylan at the main gate when he was out for his morning constitutional. Dylan explained about the security concerns the night before. It must have made Patrick nervous, so he apparently went home and emptied the gun safe. We reclaimed most of the weapons after he'd been taken to the hospital."

Laney's stomach tightened. "Keep playing."

Henry started the recording again. Her uncle looked to the right as Nyssa came into the frame. Once again, Laney's stomach bottomed out as she tensed for what was to come.

It didn't take long. A man zoomed into view, stopping right in front of Nyssa. Patrick raised the rifle to his shoulder, and the man fell back. Her uncle wheeled forward, still shooting, and then a second man slammed into the side of Patrick's wheelchair. Heart in her throat, Laney watched as her uncle flew out of the wheelchair and crashed into the rock wall, his head hitting first.

All the air seemed to leave Laney's lungs in one gasp. Spots appeared around the edges of her vision. He hit the wall so hard. He couldn't have survived that kind of hit, few could.

Jen wrapped an arm around Laney's shoulders, helping keep her steady as the recording continued. Laney glanced over at Jen, the look of horror on Jen's face no doubt identical to the one on her own.

Then Nyssa was beside her uncle. Dropping to her knees, she reached down to him, her back to the camera.

Laney frowned, stepping closer to the screen. She couldn't see what Nyssa was doing, but she could see the blood pooling around her uncle.

A body blurred into the frame, a woman with short dark hair. She said something to Nyssa, then grabbed her. The two of them disappeared out of the frame. Her uncle lay still on the sidewalk.

Henry zoomed in on Patrick. The blood on him was clear. Laney sucked in a breath at the macabre display. The blood was all his. Nyssa and the Fallen who'd been nearby hadn't been injured.

The next person on scene was Mary Jane. She rushed over to Patrick just before some of the Chandler guards arrived and they all began doing first aid on him. The crowd made it difficult to see what was going on.

Laney stepped back from the TV, frowning. "It *was* my uncle who got hurt. It wasn't Nyssa, right?"

"I didn't see Nyssa get hurt at all," Jen said.

"And Lou said that she wasn't injured, at least not physically, at the airfield the last time she saw her," Laney said.

"So what's going on with Patrick?" Henry asked.

Laney turned back to Cain, who sat staring at the screen, his face paler than it was when they had started. He hadn't made a sound during the whole replay. "What do you know?"

Cain's hand was at his mouth. He slowly lowered it. "I'd hoped I was wrong."

"Wrong about what?" Laney asked.

He met Laney's gaze. "It was Nyssa."

"What was Nyssa?" Jen asked.

Cain took a deep breath. "Your uncle, he was hurt severely. But the reason his back is healing, the reason that his head injury isn't what it should be, the reason that he is still asleep, is because he's in a healing sleep."

The truth behind his words slammed into Laney, and she let out a gasp.

Jen looked between the two of them. "I don't understand. What do you mean he's in a healing sleep?"

Cain's hands were shaking, and Laney knew he wouldn't be able to answer her. He didn't want to say the words out loud. So it was up to Laney. "My uncle was gravely wounded, but Nyssa healed him."

"She can do that?" Jen asked.

Laney shook her head. "Nyssa can't. But Lilith can."

CHAPTER 50

ROME, ITALY

The streets of Rome were busy as Gedeon sat in the backseat of the older model Mercedes, Simone next to him. Packed end to end, he glanced at the cars moving at what he considered to be a glacial pace.

The city of Rome. He'd been to it many times. In fact, he'd been to it when it had first been created. He'd even watched Romulus and Remus as they fought over its origins.

Born to a vestal virgin, the paternity of Romulus and Remus remained cloaked in mystery. Some fools claimed the god of war, Mars, had fathered the twins, while others maintained it had been Hercules. Still others maintained the pregnancy was forced upon Rhea by an unknown attacker.

According to the legend, the twins had been sent down a river in a basket before being saved first by a she-wolf and then a shepherd and his wife. Eventually they became shepherds themselves before fate brought them to the court of King Amulius, who they then killed.

While refusing the crown they were then offered, the brothers set out to create their own city. Their travels brought them to the current location of Rome. Yet they could not agree which hill to begin the construction on: Palatine or Aventine.

After a long standstill, Romulus simply began digging around Palatine. In true brotherly fashion, Remus mocked Romulus's wall. Eventually fed up with the mockery, Romulus killed his brother. Others claimed he was killed by a supporter of Romulus, and others that he died by jumping over the wall. In all versions, though, one fact remained constant: the formation of Rome began with death.

But all cities did, at least the great ones. Someone needed to conquer in order to build and expand. All of Earth was truly dripping in blood.

The newer cities with their monuments of steel were cold and callous structures. But Gedeon had an affinity for the buildings that had stood the test of time. He had visited many of them: the Pantheon, the Acropolis, the complex at Angkor Wat, the Great Pyramid, and a multitude of others. He'd been inside many of them when they were brand new. And it was good to see that consistency, that holding on to the past, that appreciation for the things that came before.

Finally, the traffic broke, and Sandra quickly took advantage of an opening. As they slipped down a side street, Gedeon could see the top of the obelisk in St. Peter's Square.

The Vatican was their destination. It had six entrances, but only three were open to the public: St. Peter's Square, the Arch of the Bells, and the north wall entrance for the Vatican museums and galleries.

The Vatican itself was a sprawling complex that included St. Peter's Square, the Vatican Palace, the Sistine Chapel, St. Peter's Basilica, the Vatican Apostolic Library, and an array of other palaces, sacristy, a radio station, and the massive museum complex.

Gedeon shook his head as he passed a street kiosk selling trinkets emblazoned with an image of the Pope to commemorate an individual's visit to the holy site. They had turned the seat of the Catholicism into a massive tourist trap. On the flight, he had read that over five million people visited each year, which worked out to about 20,000 per day.

Sandra pulled up to one of the private Vatican entrances. The guard, in his colorful uniform, waved the car through after the driver showed the proper identification. Gedeon smiled. They put so much stock in these little papers and files on their computers. All of it could easily be forged, and yet they still maintained their trust in it.

Back when Earth was new, and humans were small in number, everyone knew who belonged and who did not. It was easy to tell who should be allowed in and who should be kept out.

This reliance on technology and files and information would be the downfall of humanity.

And he did mean that quite literally.

CHAPTER 51

BALTIMORE, MARYLAND

Nyssa had healed Patrick. They had watched the recording one more time, but there was no denying it: Patrick had been fatally injured, and Nyssa had healed him. Now Laney sat in the chair next to Cain's bed, needing the support.

Sitting in the chair on the opposite side of the bed, Jen shook her head. "I don't understand. How was Nyssa able to heal Patrick?"

Henry, who stood leaning against the wall near the window, was the one who answered. "It's what she did for Jake in Egypt," he said softly.

Laney nodded numbly. "Yes."

Years ago, back at the beginning of all of this, they had been in a tough spot in Egypt. Jake had actually been shot in the head. He'd been dead. Laney knew in her gut he'd been dead. But Victoria, her mother, had been there and had been able to bring him back.

She couldn't raise the dead, exactly, but Lilith had the ability to heal. She only did it on rare occasions, but mostly she tried not to

THE BELIAL BLOOD

do it at all. And yet she'd saved Jake back then because she couldn't bear to watch her daughter's heart break. They hadn't mentioned what had happened to anyone. No one knew about it other than those who had been there: her uncle Henry, Jake, and Laney.

And none of them had told anyone. They said Jake had been injured, but no one mentioned Victoria's role in his recovery. And now that same ability had appeared in Nyssa—*before* her memories had returned.

"What does this mean?" Laney asked.

Cain shook his head. "I don't think she did it intentionally. I don't think her memories have returned yet. We still have a few months. But I think when she saw Patrick lying there, she must have opened the door to those abilities somehow, and when she leaned down to help him, she healed him."

Laney wasn't sure what to think or to feel. Her uncle was going to be all right. That was without a doubt a blessing. But none of them wanted Nyssa to be robbed of the last few months of her childhood. Of course, Gedeon was doing a fine job of stealing any joy from those months at the moment.

"Does this mean she'll recover her memories sooner?" Jen asked.

"I have no idea," Cain said. "It is safe to say that this is new ground that we are treading upon. I don't know if she's ever been awoken early. I hope to God she hasn't. Her childhood is short enough."

Laney agreed with the sentiment.

But perhaps in this situation, it would be better if she knew about her past lives. Because the alternative was that she was simply a terrified twelve-year-old girl who felt completely and utterly powerless.

CHAPTER 52

ROME, ITALY

THE SCENT OF INCENSE LINGERED IN THE AIR AS GEDEON STEPPED from the car. He looked around the portico at the thick stone bricks that lined the building in front of him.

He had always been a fan of these types of buildings. They looked solid, as if they could withstand an assault. Of course, they would not stand the test of him, but barring his or one of his brethren's interaction with them, the building should make it just fine.

The doors opened, and a priest in his mid-forties hurried out in a flurry of movement. His light-brown hair was already graying. His brown eyes sat above a hawkish nose and below a large forehead.

The priest swallowed nervously, but a smile graced his face. "Oh, you honor us greatly with your presence here today," he said.

The guards at the door flicked a glance toward Gedeon, narrowing their eyes as they studied him.

Gedeon stepped toward Father Jonathan Scarf and lowered his voice. "You need to be more cautious with your words."

THE BELIAL BLOOD

Alarm flashed across the priest's face, his mouth dropping open and his eyes widening. He lowered his voice, leaning toward Gedeon. "I'm so sorry. I'm just so excited. But yes, you are right, of course." The man's British accent came through clearly as he spoke.

"Remember I am merely a friend of the family that you are showing around. Nothing more than that," Gedeon said.

"Yes, of course." The priest stepped back. "I'm so glad that you were able to join us today. I hope your flight was all right?" the man asked loud enough for the guards to hear.

Gedeon nodded at Simone, who would stay with the car, before he answered the priest. "Yes. There were no problems."

"Excellent. Well, if you will follow me?" The priest gestured to the doors.

Gedeon indicated that the priest should go first, and after a moment's hesitation, he headed toward the doors. The guards pulled the doors open once again, giving Gedeon and his companions close scrutiny.

Gedeon paid them no heed.

Father Jonathan led them down a long hall, pointing out various items of interest as they traveled. He stopped in front of a large painting. "This portrait was done by an abbot in England in the 1400s. Notice how it depicts the Devil's temptation of Christ in the desert."

Gedeon, who'd been barely paying attention to any of the priest's ramblings, stopped, cocking his head to study the picture. The Devil floated above Jesus, his frame gaunt and cast in black.

Jesus himself was thin and scrawny, but there was a beatific smile upon his face.

Gedeon shook his head. Neither of them had looked like that during the encounter.

It had been one of Gedeon's only failures. For forty days and forty nights, he'd tested Jesus to get him to give in to temptation, to turn his back on what he was supposed to do. But the man had not wavered. He'd stayed true to his mission and his calling.

Gedeon curled his lip at the thought of it. And now that man had spawned a legion of followers across the globe.

Catching Gedeon's interest in the piece, the priest nodded toward it. "Have you seen this before? It's from a private collection. I don't think it's been made public."

Gedeon turned his back on the portrait. "No."

The excitement on the priest's face faded. "Yes, well, I believe there is something much more interesting up ahead. Uh, if you will follow me this way."

The priest pointed out a few more objects and artifacts as they followed but he'd picked up his pace and didn't stop at any of them.

As they turned down one hall the priest nodded toward a doorway up ahead. It was an old door with a rounded frame.

The priest pulled some keys from his pocket and unlocked the door ushering, everyone through and then closing it behind him. He leaned against the door after he locked it. "From here on out, there are no cameras."

Gedeon nodded. While the public spaces of the Vatican were covered in cameras, there were isolated spots inside the Vatican itself that were free from any type of surveillance. In fact, the Vatican itself was a sprawling complex. He had no doubt that there were small parts of it that hadn't been visited by humans in person or technologically in years, if not centuries.

Father Jonathan pushed himself off the wall. "We need to hurry. I don't want anyone to worry about my absence."

"You have not taken care of that?" Gedeon asked.

The priest winced. "I have, sir. But there is a new priest from Canada who has taken to stopping by my office at various times. I cannot control his enthusiasm for his work. I've told him I will be busy all afternoon, but sometimes he stops by anyway. It shouldn't be a problem, but the sooner that we complete this, the better for everyone, yes?"

Gedeon inclined his head, agreeing with the point.

Looking relieved at the gesture, the priest gestured to the hallway that spanned to the right. "This way."

This part of the Vatican was less well lighted than the more public spaces that they had been walking through. The stones here were darker. In fact, there were no windows along this hallway and only dim incandescent lights to lead the way.

The priest hustled down the hall and then turned down a second hall and then a third before stopping in front of a door. His breathing was a little erratic from the pace that he'd set. "I had the piece moved here."

"And did that raise any alarms?"

The priest shook his head. "No. They trust my recommendations when it comes to the ancient artifacts and their security. I suggested that this would be a safer location being it was just above the necropolis entrance and farther away from the public sphere."

Gedeon nodded. "Then open the door."

The priest did just that, and they stepped into what looked like a stone cell. There were no windows, and the priest reached in, flicking on a light switch by the door. Standing in the center of the room was a wooden pallet, and upon it was a rock pillar.

Gedeon stepped forward and stared at the structure. "This is the original?"

The priest nodded, his eyes focused on the artifact with feverish devotion. "Yes. It is the Column of Flagellation. There is no doubt this is the pillar that Jesus was scourged upon at the command of Pontius Pilate."

Gedeon smiled. "And there are still drops of his blood embedded within the stone?"

"There is much blood embedded within the stones. Not all of

it, of course, will be His, but some undeniably will be. The Column of Flagellation was held at the Basilica of St. Praxedes in Rome since the early thirteenth century. The column was discovered by St. Helena in the fourth century."

Gedeon stepped forward and could almost feel a small glimmer of energy wafting off the pillar. The priest was right. This was the original.

He nodded to Yael, who slipped the backpack off his shoulders. He and Sandra took the drop cloth from inside and lay it on the ground.

The priest stepped forward with a look of alarm. "What are you doing?"

Gedeon looked down at the priest. "Nothing for you to be concerned about."

Yael and Sandra moved to the pillar, each standing on a side before they lifted it up and placed it on the drop cloth.

The priest started forward. "No. You can't move it. You're not supposed to even touch it."

Gedeon reached forward and grabbed the priest by the back of the neck. He yanked him back.

The man stumbled, unable to get his feet underneath him. Straining to straighten himself, he looked up at Gedeon in fear. "What are you doing?"

"What needs to be done."

He punched the priest in the side of the head. The man's eyes rolled to the back of his head as his body went limp. Gedeon dropped him to the ground as Yael and Sandra centered the pillar in the middle of the drop cloth.

Yael looked back at Gedeon.

Gedeon stood with his arms crossed across his chest. "Begin. And make sure that you don't miss a piece."

Yael smiled and then slammed his fist into the pillar as Sandra did the same from the other side. Wherever they punched, the pillar turned to rocks and dust cascading to the drop cloth below.

THE BELIAL BLOOD

The more they punched, the more the pillar was destroyed, and the greater the satisfaction within Gedeon grew.

CHAPTER 53

MASSA, ROME

Drake hadn't seen the boy in three full days. And he was growing worried. He had no idea where he was. He didn't even know if Arturo was still alive.

Gedeon was not known for his patience, but he was known for his temper. The boy could easily have been the recipient of his anger, and Gedeon would think no more of it than he would swatting at a fly.

Drake stood up, stretching his back, his limbs feeling weak as he started his exercise regime.

They were keeping him weak through the Inceptus, but he still needed to maintain what little strength he could.

The prison of Gedeon's making was small, not leaving him a lot of room to do much. So he started with jump squats, lowering himself and then leaping upward. He did a set of ten, shook out his legs, and started the next set.

He'd reached number eight on the fourth set when the door opened. The boy was pushed in. But it wasn't Gedeon who brought him in but another angel, one whom Drake recognized.

THE BELIAL BLOOD

Drake had met him eons ago. And he was surprised he would be part of this. "Lucius?"

The angel shoved the boy toward the corner. Arturo let out a little cry as he stumbled, tripping over his feet and landing in a heap.

Drake darted forward but then jumped back as an electrical charge filled the air in front of him.

Lucius smirked. The smirk was so out of character for the angel that Drake knew that it caused him to pause for a second. "Lucius, what are you doing? You are part of this?"

Lucius looked down his nose at Drake. "Yes, Michael. Of course I am part of this."

"Of course? What do you mean of course? You can't possibly believe that Gedeon is following orders."

"He says he is, and I am honor bound to obey him. Besides, he's right."

"Right? Right about what?"

"All of it. Humans have always been the favored ones. And that role has always been undeserved. As time has gone on, it has become more and more clear. Why should we play second fiddle to these cockroaches? They have no strength. They have no honor. It's time to go back to the way things were."

A chill rolled over Drake. "What do you mean back to the way things were?"

Cold laced the angel's words. "Their time is over, Michael. It's our time now. This planet, all its beauty, they've destroyed it. They don't deserve it. But we have been loyal. We deserve our own paradise."

"You can't mean that. That can't happen. We are not meant for this world."

Lucius raised his eyebrows. "*You* are the one telling me that we are not meant for this world? How long have you spent in this world, Michael? How long has it been since you've done your duty? You don't get to tell me what we are owed anymore. You're not really even Michael anymore, are you? You're Drake, the consort of the ring bearer."

The old Michael would have lashed out at Lucius and put him in his place, but Drake just stared at the man, trying to figure out how he could have changed so much. "What's happened to you? This is not you. You've always studied the humans, watched them, been intrigued by them, but you're never cruel or judgmental of them."

"Yes, because that was my job. But now my job is to help Gedeon. And my eyes have been opened. Besides, by helping Gedeon, I am helping myself and my brothers and sisters."

That wasn't true, and Drake knew it. "You know that not all of them will agree with you. You know this will lead to war."

"Better a war than the existence we had before this. It's coming, Drake. And you have an important role to play in it."

Drake stared at Lucius. "Whatever you think I'm going to do for you, I'm not."

Lucius smiled. "But you see, you already are."

CHAPTER 54

BALTIMORE, MARYLAND

THE TESTS FOR HER UNCLE WERE GOING TO TAKE ANOTHER HOUR, SO Laney let Cain rest for a little bit. Dom had gotten back to them and confirmed that the blood on the sidewalk was Patrick's, which meant Nyssa had, in fact, done something to heal him.

Dom also said he was working on the Inceptus, although he did not provide a timeline for when he might be able to replicate it. As for Nyssa, there wasn't much to report. The airport the attackers had flown into still held their plane. They'd managed to track that down.

Jen had people staking it out, although Laney doubted they'd return to it. They must know it would be found by now. But the fact that it was still there gave her hope that they were still looking for Nyssa. She supposed that was a good thing.

But there was still no word from Molly or JW. Laney was trying not to let that upset her. They had been told to go radio silent. It was just hard believing that no news was good news.

Jake was running down leads and had people searching for

Molly, Nyssa, and JW. But so far he'd found nothing really to go on. Danny was scouring cameras looking for any sign of them.

Laney shifted between wishing Molly would contact someone at the Chandler Group and worrying that if they did, the communications would be intercepted. She wanted to go back to the estate and help with the search, but she wasn't sure what exactly she would be doing there. She didn't have the computer skills to track them down online. The only other thing she could offer was driving aimlessly around hoping to catch sight of them.

So as much as she wanted to be out there looking for Nyssa, she knew that right now she needed to leave it to the others.

But she couldn't just sit here and twiddle her thumbs. So she turned her attention to the meeting that she'd had with Cristela. It was beyond strange to think that she'd been around for so long and had lived such an incredible life. Yet she'd seemed perfectly content to be helping kids decorate cookies.

She wondered what her official forms at the orphanage listed her age as. Which led to her wondering how long she'd actually been there. If she'd been there since David was a child, it had to be at least thirty years.

She pulled open the note that Cristela had slipped her just before she left. It had directions about how to combine the Arma Christi. Essentially, each of the pieces of the Arma Christi had to be melted down and combined at a high heat. She'd expected that much. What she hadn't expected was the need for some sort of harmonic resonance to complete the process.

Although she supposed she shouldn't be surprised. Harmonic resonance was what had activated the belial stone in Montana years and years ago.

In the modern world, harmonic resonance as a power form wasn't well understood and was rarely used. But back in history, there were always reports of songs and chants and tones that were used to elicit certain responses. The most well-known were the

THE BELIAL BLOOD

walls of Jericho, which fell after the blowing of trumpets by the Israelites.

Laney ran a general Google search, trying to find something that might indicate the type of harmonic resonance that would be needed for creating the Arma Christi, but she had to quickly admit she was woefully out of her depth.

She shot off an email to Dom to see if he had any ideas of what would be needed and winced at how much she was putting on his plate: replicating the Inceptus, an autopsy on the angel, a report on sound energy, and that was on top of all the other projects he had running. But there was no helping it. She thought for a moment about having Danny do the research, but he was focused on the search for Gedeon and Nyssa.

Henry popped his head in the door after she'd just hit send. "They've brought Patrick back to his room."

She quickly got to her feet and looked over at Jen. Jen waved her on. "It's probably best if he doesn't have too many visitors at once. You go on. I'll keep working here."

Laney didn't need to be told twice. She hustled down the hall next to Henry, and he led her to the room next to Cain.

Stepping inside, Laney was unsurprised to see Cain in a wheelchair next to the bed. Lying in the bed was her uncle. She hurried over to his side. Patrick lay still his eyes closed. She glanced over at Cain.

"He's still unconscious, but the doctors say his vital signs are in the normal range." Cain's words drifted off.

"And his back?"

Cain shook his head in wonder. "It seems to have healed. His head injury as well. They're not sure why he's still unconscious. But doesn't he look better?"

Laney peered at her uncle's face, surprised at the change in his appearance. It was still most definitely her uncle, but his face looked healthier, younger.

Her eyes widened as she looked at Cain. "She did it. She really did it. She healed him."

Laney reached down and took her uncle's hand as she pulled up a chair and took a seat. She squeezed his hand. "I'm here, Uncle Patrick. I'm right here."

The slightest pressure squeezed her hand back. Her gaze flew to his face. "Uncle Patrick?"

His eyes flickered open for a moment. "I'm here, Laney."

Tears welled up in Laney's eyes, and she realized how desperately she'd needed to hear those words. She'd needed to know that he was still here.

Across from her, relief was splashed across Cain's face as well.

Laney stood up and kissed him on the forehead. "It's going to be all right, Patrick. Everything's going to be all right."

He nodded, squeezing her hand one more time before he fell back to sleep. Her uncle dozed for another hour before he fully awakened.

And when he did, he wanted some tea. Henry quickly arranged to have some delivered along with some food. While he arranged for that, Patrick looked between Cain and Laney. "Where's Nyssa? Is she all right?"

Laney and Cain had already discussed what they would share with Patrick at this point. And even though the doctor said that he was exceptionally well, they wanted to tread lightly into those waters. "She's with Molly and JW."

Patrick let out a sigh. "Good. That's good. Those were Gedeon's people, weren't they?"

"Yes. But it's all right. They grabbed Nyssa, but Molly, Lou, Rolly, and JW were able to get her back from them. And now Molly and JW are keeping her somewhere safe."

Patrick closed his eyes. "Thank God. When I saw them on the street, I knew they were coming for her. I should have said something sooner. I should have—"

"You did everything right, Uncle Patrick. You didn't do

anything wrong," Laney said. "And it's going to be just fine. In fact, there's something you need to know. You're back it's healed. With therapy, you'll be able to walk again."

Patrick's mouth fell open and he looked between the two of them. "What?"

Cain nodded as he stepped forward. "It was Nyssa, Lilith," he said softly. "When she realized you were hurt, she tapped into those abilities and healed you."

After a long quiet moment, tears sprang to her uncle's eyes. One rolled down his cheek. He wiped it away. "I'd given up. I never thought that would be possible."

Laney squeezed his hand. "You'll be up and running in no time."

Patrick held onto her hand with a nod. "And Nyssa? She's really safe?"

"Gedeon is still looking for her. It's why she can't come back just yet," Cain said.

Patrick took a shuddering breath. "It never gets easier when someone you love is in danger."

"No, it doesn't," Laney said softly, picturing first Nyssa and then Drake.

Patrick opened his eyes, shaking his head. "Okay. I need a distraction or I'm going to go stir crazy. Tell me about your trip to Italy. How did it go with Cristela?"

Glad for the distraction herself, Laney quickly told him about what had occurred with the ancient nun.

Patrick asked a ton of questions, most of which Laney didn't have an answer for. At some point, she would have to get her uncle over to Italy so he could sit down with Cristela and question her to his heart's content.

"So the Arma Christi as a weapon, it can be done?" he asked.

Laney nodded. "Yes. But there's a harmonic resonance component to the creation of it that I don't understand."

It was now just the two of them in the room. Cain had gone

back to his room. Unlike Patrick, who seemed to be perfectly fine, Cain was still suffering the effects of his injuries.

Idly taking a bite of the lemon pound cake that Henry had dropped off with the tea, Patrick nodded. "Harmonic resonance is a critical component of a number of religious and ritual ceremonies, especially in the long-forgotten past. In fact, there are even a series of buildings that have been created to maximize the harmonic resonance of the structure."

Laney's head jolted up at that. "Harmonic architecture?"

Patrick smiled. "I suppose that's as good a term as any. Anyway, they were constructed so that when certain tones were played, the structure itself would vibrate and be amplified. For some of them, even the structure itself can be used as a method of sound."

The idea was intriguing, but Laney wasn't sure how that got her closer to figuring out what was necessary for the Arma Christi.

"What about Drake? Have you been able to find any sign of him?" her uncle asked.

Laney shook her head, the unsettled feeling returning in her gut. "No. Wherever Gedeon is, I'm sure that's where Drake is. But we haven't been able to find Gedeon at all. There's no trace of him. I don't understand how he's able to cover his tracks so well. I mean, most of the angels that come down, they don't exactly excel at modern technology, at least not like this. Yet Gedeon is somehow eluding us."

Patrick leaned back against the pillow, closing his eyes. "He's probably paying someone, bribing someone, or threatening someone to cover them. That does seem to be the way these ones get things done."

Laney nodded. She was about to agree with him out loud when she realized that he'd actually fallen asleep.

She pulled the tray away so he didn't accidentally knock it over while he was sleeping and then turned off the light next to the bed, adjusting the blankets around him. She kissed him on the cheek and then pulled out her cell phone and quickly called Danny. She moved to the far side of the room and kept her voice low as he answered. "Laney?"

"Hey, Danny. Any word on Nyssa?"

"No, I'm sorry. Not yet."

Laney nodded. She'd expected as much. Someone would have called to let her know if they had found anything.

"What about the attack on the Chandler security system? Have you been able to trace that at all?"

Frustration rolled through Danny's voice as he answered. "Not exactly. We know that it was an outside group. But I haven't been able to trace it directly back to them. The group, whoever they are, are good, really good. That helps narrow down who it could possibly be. There are only a few groups that could manage such an undertaking.

"And the coding that's used, some of the analysts think they recognize it. They think there's a group out of Belarus that could be behind it, but we can't say that conclusively yet."

Laney frowned. Belarus was a former Russian state that had declared its independence in 1990. It was overflowing with civil rights abuses that ranged from cracking down on journalists and torturing protestors. It was not known as an area that embraced individual freedoms and an egalitarian society.

"So, it's a group for hire?"

"That's what it's looking like."

"Have you been able to shore up the weaknesses in the system?"

"The system's secure now, but we're going to have to keep an eye on it and make sure that they don't find any other ways in. This group is good, and they're fast."

"Okay."

Danny was quiet for a moment as Laney's thoughts tried to work a Belarus hacking group into the scenario.

"How's Patrick?"

Laney looked over at the bed. "Doing surprisingly well. In fact, I think he's doing better than Cain is."

"That's good. From the description of his injury, well, I was pretty worried. It's a miracle."

Yes, it is, she thought, but out loud she said, "Is there anything I can do to help look for Nyssa? I feel helpless just sitting here. There's got to be something I can do or somewhere I can go."

"Laney, I wish there was. But until we hear from Molly and JW, there's nothing for anyone to do. I mean, we're basically just spinning our wheels hoping that something pops up."

"Do you think they'll get in touch?"

"I'm sure they will. We just need to wait."

CHAPTER 55

SOUTHERN PENNSYLVANIA

A FEW MINUTES TURNED OUT TO BE MUCH LONGER. WHEN MOLLY finally opened her eyes, it was pitch black out. She sat up, stared at the sky, and then looked back at JW. "You were supposed to wake me."

He shrugged. "I wasn't tired. And you did more fighting than I did back there, so I figured you needed your sleep. Besides, I'm used to not getting a lot of sleep. It's one of the things they train us for."

Before he'd gone to work for the Angel Force at Jen's request, JW had been a Marine. In fact, he had been the assistant to the head of the Angel Force, Scott Decker.

Molly idly wondered what Decker was up to these days. She hadn't heard much about the Angel Force since the courts had ruled their registration unconstitutional. But she had no doubt that that little man, still full of hatred, was behind the scenes plotting. She shook her head, not wanting to go down that path. She flicked a glance in the back and lowered her voice. "Did Nyssa wake up at all?"

JW shook his head. "No. She's been out the whole time. And she hasn't made a peep. So I'm hoping that's a good thing, and maybe her mind just shut down, not letting her think about everything that's happened."

Molly hoped that was true as well. The mind could wall off and protect itself at times, and she hoped that it had done so for Nyssa, allowing her at least a few hours of peace from all of the craziness that was now her life.

Molly glanced through the car windows. It was all completely unrecognizable. The area was a lot more rugged and rural than the highway they had been on when she'd fallen asleep.

"Where are we?"

"We're just crossed out of West Virginia into southern Pennsylvania."

Molly looked at JW in surprise. He was from West Virginia. Danny, JW, and his brother had grown up there with their parents. Their mother had died when they were young, and their father … well, 'violent alcoholic' seemed to be an understatement to the man's character.

"Where are we heading?" Molly just realized she hadn't asked in all this time where JW was taking them. She just trusted that he'd known a place.

"I had a friend when I was growing up that had a hunting cabin. It's in a really remote area. No one will be able to find us there."

"Will they be able to trace you to it?"

JW shook his head. "No. Rick enlisted in the Marines as well. He's over in Kabul right now. He's the only one in his family left. His dad's in a home. And I know that Rick doesn't come up here very often, even when he's in the country. It's going to be pretty rustic and hasn't been taken care of well over the years. But it'll have a roof and some walls. I figure we can stop somewhere pick up some supplies, then head out there."

THE BELIAL BLOOD

Molly nodded. "Okay, but how are we going to get the supplies? We can't use any of our cards."

"I keep an emergency stash on me. It was in my jeep, and I transferred it over when we switched cars. We'll have enough to get what we need."

"You're quite the Boy Scout."

"Marine, actually," he said with a grin.

And Molly smiled back at him, feeling like maybe, just maybe, this was all going to work out.

CHAPTER 56

ROME, ITALY

The pillar that was once used to brace the body of Jesus Christ was now a pile of dust in the middle of the drop cloth.

Carefully, Gedeon's people wrapped the dust up, securing it so that not a single speck of dust would escape. Once it was all secure, it was placed within the duffel bag.

Yael handed the duffel bag to Gedeon. Gedeon took it, not bothered by the weight of it.

The destruction of the priceless relic didn't bother him either. It was going to have to be destroyed for the next stage anyway. And this would make it much less cumbersome to move.

"You are clear on the next step?" Gedeon asked.

Sandra nodded. "Yes, sir."

"Explain it to me," he demanded, knowing it needed to be done carefully.

"We will take the priest with us down into the necropolis. We will stay hidden there until you call us to let us know it is time. At that point, we will kill the priest and arrange him the way we discussed."

THE BELIAL BLOOD

Gedeon grunted, satisfied with the response. "And if anyone should discover you in the necropolis?"

Yael didn't blink as he answered. "We kill them."

CHAPTER 57

BALTIMORE, MARYLAND

THE HOSPITAL WAS QUIET. HER UNCLE WAS ASLEEP ON THE BED across the room, and Laney sat at the desk that Henry had had brought in a few hours ago. He and Jen had finally headed back to the estate, leaving a contingent of security guards at the hospital.

Cain was asleep next door.

Laney rubbed her eyes as she looked away from the screen and stifled a yawn. She should get some sleep as well. But while her body was tired, her mind wasn't quite ready to shut down yet.

It had been a long night at the hospital. Laney had researched the Arma Christi but hadn't gotten any closer to figuring out how the harmonic resonance component factored in. She was learning a lot more information about early Christian beliefs and pre-Christian beliefs, though.

And some of them weren't exactly supportive of the Church. She'd already known about the similarities between Christianity and other religions of the time, Mithraism in particular.

But it was the historical Jesus and his link to Egypt that was really making her mind go into hyperdrive. Jesus allegedly went to Egypt and learned a secret knowledge, which he brought back and taught from. Yet, the most secret of rituals was one very few were allowed to partake in.

There was also the rather striking arguments that Jesus was no poor man but actually a wealthy son, even a man who had a claim to the throne. Back then, religion and politics were intertwined. If you ruled, it was because God deemed it so. There was no separation. So all the talk about God was also political.

She wasn't sure how her uncle felt about those arguments. But it did make her wonder about Herod, who had slaughter all the firstborn sons around the time of Jesus's birth. Had that really been to kill Jesus? Was it a religious action or just a political one?

And did that have anything to do with the Arma Christi? And why Nyssa was being hunted, or was she just grasping at very disparate straws?

Even if it was a rabbit hole, it was an intriguing one. It kept her attention well into the night. She finally fell off to sleep just before dawn. She didn't even hear the nursing staff when they came in to check his vitals every hour and finally woke up just before eleven.

Rubbing her eyes, she winced as her back twinged from sleeping on uncomfortable hospital furniture all night. Henry sat at the chair over by the window and smiled when he caught her eye. "So, you finally decided to join us."

Laney stretched from the small love seat that she'd been curled up on. "Yeah, I was really out. Is there anything to report?"

Henry shook his head. "No. Nothing on Nyssa, nothing on Gedeon. We are at a standstill."

Laney sighed, pushing off the blanket and placing her feet on the floor, her head in her hands. She was still trying to believe that no news was good news, but it was still an effort. Gedeon was somewhere, doing something that they probably should know about. The fact that they had no clues as to what did not make her feel better.

R.D. BRADY

"I brought you some coffee." Henry nudged his chin toward the side table.

Laney leaned over and grabbed the mug, which was still warm. "You are my favorite brother."

Henry chuckled. "I don't believe there's a lot of competition for that position."

"Even if there were, you would still be my favorite brother."

She took a sip and sat back, her brain not fully functioning quite yet. And she was fine with that. In fact, it was kind of nice for her brain to be quiet for a change. It was like one of those early mornings when you stepped outside, and the world was silent and at peace.

A nurse stepped in the room and walked over to her uncle, who was just opening his eyes. The man smiled down at him. "Good morning, Father Patrick."

Her uncle mumbled. "Morning." His eyes searched the room and met Laney's. He gave her a small smile.

The nurse bustled around checking vitals and then nodded. "The doctor said that you could be discharged so long as you have medical personnel to oversee you."

Patrick nodded. "Excellent. How soon can I get out of here?"

The nurse laughed good-naturedly. "I hope it's not the company."

"No, no. I'm just anxious to get home."

The nurse made a notation on his chart, hanging it back up at the end of the bed. "I'll go see about the paperwork."

With a nod at Henry and Laney, the nurse slipped back out the door. Laney turned to Henry. "He's getting discharged? Is that safe?"

Henry met Patrick's eyes and then gave his attention to Laney. "You fell asleep last night before I returned. I stopped back to check on you. He was awake, and we agreed that it would be best if we move him and Cain back to the estate. They're going to be set up in Dom's shelter, and Gina is going to oversee their care.

THE BELIAL BLOOD

Plus, we'll have a physical therapist come in and work with Patrick. I just felt it would be safer for all involved."

Laney nodded, knowing he was probably right. But she didn't like the idea of the two of them heading back to the estate where Nyssa had been grabbed. But Dom's bomb shelter hadn't been breached, Which meant it was probably safer for them there than at the hospital. "Okay. Besides I think I need to talk to Dom."

Henry frowned. "About what?"

"The Inceptus. I haven't heard anything yet, and I'd like an update."

"Then let's get this show on the road," Henry said.

CHAPTER 58

URSINA, PENNSYLVANIA

The taste of salt water was still on Nyssa's tongue as she opened her eyes.

Her breaths came out in small pants. She covered her mouth with her hand to muzzle them. She didn't want to let Molly or JW know that she'd had another nightmare. They'd been decidedly freaked out last night when she'd had her first one and woke up screaming.

They thought it was about the attack at the estate. She supposed that might have spurred it on, but she didn't explain about how she'd had the nightmares for months on end, although she was pretty sure Molly already knew. She'd spent enough nights over at Susie's house that Molly had been around for a few of the nightmares.

Nyssa now stared up at the hunting cabin's ceiling. It was a dark brown, and many of the boards were warped from age and weather. The walls were rough to the touch, a few worn through so the night air rushed in. There was an old linoleum metal table up by the front door and a small kitchen that contained only two cabinets and a wash sink. There was no electricity. There was a hot plate for cooking that ran on propane. The bathroom was little more than an outhouse with a basin of water on a table.

"Rustic" seemed almost too luxurious a description for this place, but it definitely was not somewhere easily found.

There were two queen-sized beds, one set on each side of the room, and one old futon set near the wood stove. Nyssa and Molly shared one of the beds while JW took the other.

JW had set up a bunch of security cameras around the place and alarms to let them know if anybody was coming. He'd been awake when she and Molly had crawled into the bed after wiping off the sheets they found in the one closet the best they could. Nyssa had awoken a few times, and each time JW had been awake, quietly watching the monitor he'd set up on the kitchen table. He seemed a lot like Jake and didn't seem to need much sleep. Now he was finally asleep, though, and lay quietly in the bed across the way.

Molly was asleep next to her. But for Nyssa, that was no longer an option. None of them had gotten much sleep last night, and her waking up screaming hadn't helped with that. She didn't want to wake them, but she also couldn't stay in bed much longer.

Slowly, she pushed back the blanket and sat at the edge of the bed before slipping on her sneakers. She grabbed a blanket off the back of the futon and walked quietly to the front door.

She glanced back over her shoulder, but neither JW nor Molly stirred. Opening the door a crack, she paused. But it didn't make any noise, which was a miracle, and then she slipped through, closing it silently behind her.

She wasn't trying to get away. She just needed some fresh air. She walked over to the old rusted metal swing and curled up in it, pulling the blanket around herself.

The images from the dream flooded through her mind. This time she'd been on a ship. It almost looked like a Viking ship with the outfits that everybody wore. There'd been a storm, and the ship was going down.

Nyssa rested her chin on her knees as she stared off into the woods. She longed to sit in the kitchen with her uncle Patrick and have him make her some tea.

An image of him from the attack slipped through her mind. She winced, closing her eyes once again, as if she could shut the image away. But all she seemed to accomplish was to bring it into starker relief.

All that blood.

She prayed that he was all right, but she wasn't entirely sure that there was anyone on the other end of her prayers listening. Her family and friends had been through so much. She envied the other people she went to school with, who just kind of flitted through life without any seeming worries. They went home. They watched TV. They complained about their parents. It was an easy life.

None of them had to go into a bomb shelter to hide away from people attacking their home. None of them had to flee the country when even the bomb shelter wasn't strong enough to keep them safe. None of them had to worry about people they loved disappearing for years on end. And none of them had to watch the man that treated her like a daughter bleed out on the sidewalk in front of her home.

It was all too much.

And it seemed like the events were increasing in speed and intensity. Nyssa knew that it was building to something. She wasn't sure what because everyone got very quiet whenever she walked into one of those conversations. But something was coming, and soon, in the next couple of months. Or maybe it wasn't the next couple of months. Maybe the schedule had been bumped up by that horrible man's actions.

A chill rolled up Nyssa's spine, and she wrapped her arms tighter around her knees.

THE BELIAL BLOOD

But why did they want her? Was she just a way to get back at Laney? But then why not take Patrick? Of course, she was smaller, so she was easier to move, but that these people already had Drake. Threatening to hurt Drake would be enough to make Laney do whatever was necessary. So why take her as well if it was just as some sort of bargaining chip?

No, she had a feeling it had something to do with her specifically, or this Lilith person. Why couldn't they understand she wasn't Lilith? Maybe that was the name her birth parents gave her, and maybe this all had to do with them? She didn't know. But she needed to find out.

"Nyssa!" Molly's voice called out, fear lacing it.

"I'm okay. I'm just outside," she yelled back.

The door opened, and Molly's face appeared, framed by the darkness behind her. "Hey. You can't leave without telling us."

"Sorry. You guys were sleeping, and I just wanted to get some fresh air."

Molly slipped outside and took a seat on the swing beside her. "More bad dreams?"

Nyssa nodded. Molly sighed, running a hand through her hair. "I wish I could tell you that they'll go away. But I think we both know that's not true. It's going to take a while for things to go back to normal."

"Do you think things *will* go back to normal?" Nyssa asked.

"I hope so."

Footsteps from inside the cabin indicated that JW was up as well.

Molly stood up. "You know what always makes me feel better? Pancakes. How about some pancakes?"

"How?" Nyssa asked picturing the non-existent kitchen.

"I have no idea. JW insists it's possible."

Nyssa forced a smile to her lips. "That sounds great. I'm just going to stay out here for a little bit. Can you call me when they're ready?"

A look of concern crossed Molly's face before she nodded. "Of course." She headed back inside, leaving the door ajar behind her.

Nyssa looked back out at the woods.

Molly was a good person. Susie was lucky to have such a sister. And Nyssa could see something was happening between JW and Molly, even though it seemed like neither of them was brave enough to say anything.

Nyssa once again leaned her head on her knees, her arms wrapped around both legs as she stared off into the woods. All of these people around her who cared about her. They were all trying to protect her.

But she knew deep inside that they wouldn't be able to protect her from what was coming. They were only prolonging the inevitable. And she couldn't do that to them.

Besides, she wanted to find out what was going on. She wanted to find out why she was in the middle of this. And she wanted to keep the people around her safe.

After all, that seemed to be what everybody was always trying to do. Cain had taken her in to protect her. Patrick had gotten hurt trying to protect her. Jake, Laney, and Henry back when she was a baby had rushed in to protect her.

Laney was always trying to protect everybody.

And now it was Nyssa's turn. Which meant she needed to find a way to get away from Molly and JW.

Because the only way she'd be able to protect them was to leave them.

CHAPTER 59

BALTIMORE, MARYLAND

GETTING THE SHOW ON THE ROAD WASN'T QUITE AS QUICK AS ALL OF them had hoped. It took an hour to get her uncle and Cain together and out of the hospital. The trip back to the estate was blessedly quiet. Even the traffic seemed to have eased to allow them an unencumbered trip.

Laney sat in the front of the SUV with Henry, Patrick, and Cain in the back. No one spoke much. At the hospital, it was easier not to imagine Nyssa. But once they got back to the estate, it would be hard not to think about what she was going through. And wonder where she was.

Laney and Henry pulled up to the bomb shelter, where Jake was waiting along with Mary Jane and Gina.

Mary Jane hurried forward, hugging Patrick and Cain and bustling about, getting them situated into wheelchairs and talking with them. She had everyone organized and moving into the shelter before Henry and Laney could really do anything.

Laney leaned against the hood of the car, watching Mary Jane

R.D. BRADY

take charge with a smile of gratitude. "She really has this mom thing down, doesn't she?"

Jake walked over and leaned against the car next to her. "That she does. That woman can organize anyone."

"Any word?" she asked, even though she knew he would say something if there had been.

Jake shook his head. "No. But we'll find them."

Laney nodded. And the three of them followed the others into the shelter. Dom's shelter had been created decades ago when Henry had first brought Dom into the Chandler Group. A brilliant agoraphobe, he could not deal with the stresses of the outside world, and the bomb shelter made it possible for him to have a life.

There were three blast doors that a person had to go through just to get to the shelter, and from there it was a twenty-minute walk.

By the time Laney and Henry and Jake reached the front foyer of the shelter, they could hear Mary Jane ordering people to set things up in the two guest rooms. Laney stepped into the main room, which had a kitchen along the left-hand side and a large sectional on the right for all of Dom's guests. The light above his lab door was green, indicating that Dom was inside.

Without a word, Henry, Jake, and Laney headed over to the kitchen island, which was overflowing with platters of food.

Laney looked at the display with mock horror. "How many people are we expecting here?"

Jake chuckled. "Mary Jane has been feeling a little out of sorts since Molly has been gone, so she started baking, and then she got up early and started cooking. Molly better come back soon or else everyone on the estate is going to be stuffed to the gills and in need of new wardrobes."

Jake's tone was joking, but Laney knew how worried he was about Molly.

252

THE BELIAL BLOOD

She grabbed a plate and started filling up before heading over to the long dining table. Henry and Jake did the same, joining her.

None of them spoke as they ate, and then a few minutes later the light above Dom's door switched to red, and the door popped open.

Dom stepped out, wearing his usual oxford shirt in desperate need of an iron along with khaki shorts. Today he was also wearing dark-brown moose slippers, and his hair, which was normally a crazy halo around his head, had been neatly styled. His cat Tiger slipped out the door, as did Cleo.

The two cats came over to greet the newcomers. Laney reached down and ran a hand through each of their coats before grinning at Dom. "I like the haircut, Dom."

Dom placed a self-conscious hand on his head. "Mary Jane came over early this morning and said I needed a haircut."

Laney tried not to laugh. That sounded exactly like Mary Jane. And the last time she'd seen Dom, he'd definitely been in need of a haircut. "Well, it looks really good."

"Thanks," Dom mumbled as he headed to the kitchen, grabbing a plate and a large mug of coffee for himself.

Cleo bumped against Laney.

Okay?

Trying, Laney thought back at her. *Can you two go stay with Uncle Patrick and Cain? I think they need you.*

Cleo bumped against her again before she and Tiger disappeared down the hall toward the guest rooms.

Dom settled in at the table across from Laney. "I've been reviewing that list you sent me about the Arma Christi. It's interesting."

Laney had sent a copy of the list that Cristela had written out for her to get Dom's thoughts on it. "What do you think? Is it possible?"

"I think it's possible. But you have to understand that sound energy in the modern age is in its infancy. We know that sound can move objects. In fact, we've even created handheld objects that can be used to move small objects. But theoretically, the idea that they could be used to combine elements together, it is possible. We just haven't done it yet."

"Or just not recently," Jake muttered. He wasn't wrong. Although the comment revealed that Jake had come a long way from the skeptic she had first met.

As for Dom's comments, Laney knew that the science was there. She'd read about the recent attempts at using sound energy last night.

But it was Jake's comment that pulled her attention. For eons, there had been reports about megalithic structures being created through the use of sound. It had been laughed out of archaeology for so long, dismissed as merely primitive people's simplistic storytelling. But recent years had demonstrated that sound waves could be a powerful force when it came to affecting physical objects. In fact, research indicated that different tones could even go as far as to create different symbols from sand. The shapes got more complex the higher the tone that was used.

"Any idea where or how such a process could happen?"

Dom shook his head. "There's nothing happening in any of the labs across the globe that could do anything along these lines. No one is that advanced. Unless there's someone who is leaps and bounds ahead of what I'm aware is out there."

Laney sank back against her chair. That seemed highly unlikely. Dom tended to keep up on what was happening across the globe.

"But shouldn't that be a good thing? If no one is capable of putting this thing together, then shouldn't we be relieved?" Jake asked.

Henry shook his head. "No. Gedeon wouldn't go to all this trouble if he didn't have a way to put the Arma Christi together. He knows something. We just don't know what that is."

Jake's comment from earlier rattled around her head as Laney

THE BELIAL BLOOD

spoke. "What if we're looking in the wrong place? Or at least the wrong time?"

"What do you mean?" Henry asked.

"What if we're not looking for technology that comes from a modern-day lab? What if we're supposed to be looking back in time at an ancient site? Many of them were created to elicit certain sounds."

"Sounds?" Jake asked, a bit of the old skeptic rearing its head.

Laney leaned forward, placing her elbows on the table as she warmed to the idea. "Yeah. It's intriguing. Many of these sites, they vibrate when certain tones are created. And they all vibrate at about the same level."

"What level?" Henry asks.

"Around 110 hertz," Dom said.

The three of them turned to Dom.

He shrugged. "Research on humans has found that that level also can generate what is considered an out-of-body experience."

Laney grunted, rolling the information through her mind. She'd read about it last night, but she'd been too tired to truly take it in. But now she had to wonder if these ancient sites could vibrate at a certain level and that the level was responsible for creating these out-of-body experiences. Was it possible that these were what the ancient stargates did? Was this what people experienced when they reported seeing beings from other dimensions or going to other locations? Was it merely their minds that had been impacted by the sound around them? And was Gedeon going to use one of these sites for the sound energy needed to compile the weapon?

Dom scraped the last few pieces of eggs off of his plate and then bit into an apple Danish, wiping his mouth before he spoke. "I can generate a list of archaeological sites that seem to employ some sort of sound energy."

"That would be very helpful. Thanks, Dom," Laney said.

He took a big drink of his coffee and then stood. "I'll go take care of it now."

As he stood, Laney spoke. "What about the Inceptus?"

His cup and plate in hand, Dom paused. "I'm finishing up one last batch of tests. I'd like to wait until I have those results before I say anything. I should have something for you in about thirty minutes."

Laney wanted to push him on it, make him take a guess. But the Inceptus had been hiding for thousands of years. Thirty more minutes wasn't too long to wait. Dom placed his dish and cup in the sink before he hustled back to his lab.

"Anyone else feel like we're going back to the beginning?" Jake asked softly.

Laney turned to him. "What do you mean?"

"Sound energy. It's what Azazael used to initiate the belial stone."

Henry stared at him in shock. And Laney realized it was just occurring to him. But Laney knew it wasn't the only repeating event. "That's not all," she said. "Lilith brought Patrick back, just like she did Jake."

Jake nodded. "It's like everything is happening all over again."

"Yeah, but what does that mean? What comes next?" Laney asked.

His shoulders hunched, Henry shook his head. "I don't know. But I have the feeling it's not going to be good."

The talk about the past repeating itself was not something the triad wanted to delve into further. Luckily, her phone rang, offering a distraction. She pulled it from her pocket, glancing at the screen.

"Everything all right?" Henry asked.

Laney nodded. "Yeah. It's from David. Professor Peretz has found something. David is bringing him to the estate."

"That's the professor that Gedeon grabbed, right?" Jake asked. "The one doing the research on Jesus's bloodline?"

Laney nodded. "Yeah. Gedeon was trying to track down the ancestors of Jesus."

Jake started ripping apart a croissant, popping a piece in his mouth as he did so. "I don't understand that. I mean, if we take out the religious component of all of this, Jesus was alive 2,000 years ago. Any blood of us would have been diluted by the generations in between. So why is his blood so important?"

Laney shook her head. "I don't know. But Gedeon was trying to figure it out. Which means that we need to try and figure out why."

CHAPTER 60

Mary Jane had gotten Patrick and Cain settled into the guest rooms. Now the two of them had had something to eat and were sitting watching a movie in Cain's room.

The rest of the staff had headed back to the surface. Gina was staying with them, watching the movie and keeping an eye on them. Mary Jane had headed back to her cottage to get some sleep.

It was only Laney, Henry, and Jake in the main room when David arrived via the back entrance of the bomb shelter. David stepped inside, ushering a small man behind him.

Laney had explained to Henry and Jake about Moeshe's research under Gedeon's orders. And that Moeshe had relayed all of that information to Gedeon and then apparently had claimed that he could find the actual lineage of Jesus Christ.

Laney was skeptical of that last claim. She figured that the professor had been stalling, just trying to keep himself alive. But the fact that he had something to reveal suggested that he had, in fact, found something.

The professor walked in, his shoulders hunched, his frame gaunt.

THE BELIAL BLOOD

Henry walked over. "Professor Peretz. It's nice to meet you. I'm Henry Chandler. I'm sorry for what you've been through."

Moeshe's mouth dropped open as he looked up, up, and up at Henry. Laney had forgotten how shocking her brother's height was to people who didn't know him. The professor's small hand was all but swallowed up in Henry's large one.

Laney hid her smile as Henry led the professor over to the table. "Professor, it's good to see you again."

The man looked over at her, blinking hard behind his thick glasses. "Dr. McPhearson. It's good to see you again as well. I heard what happened to your uncle. How is he faring?"

"Surprisingly well. He's actually here. Perhaps after we speak, you'd like to visit with him?"

"I would like that very much."

Laney led him over to the dining room table. As she settled him in and introduced him to Jake, Henry brought over some coffee, a croissant, and some jam as David had said that that was his favorite.

Moeshe's eyes lit up at the sight of the snack. "Oh, delightful."

The man started to eat, and although Laney was anxious to hear what he had to say, she didn't feel like she should rush him. He'd been through a lot in the last few weeks, and if a croissant made him happy, then he deserved to eat it in peace. Two cups of coffee and an apple Danish later, he sat back, patting his stomach. "Oh, that was delicious. I do love an apple Danish."

"Me too," Laney said. It was one of her weaknesses.

"You have been most patient with me when I'm sure you're anxious to hear what I've found," Moeshe said as he pushed away his plate.

Jake leaned forward. "Gedeon was interested in the lineage of Jesus Christ?"

Moeshe nodded, pushing his glasses up his nose as he opened up his bag and started pulling out papers. "Yes. When I first arrived, he wanted to trace the Merovingians. I was able to do that, but then he was interested in modern-day ancestors. As you can imagine that wasn't quite as easy."

Laney had no doubt about that. It's not as if there were complete records from 700 years ago that they could easily trace. And going back even further, the records were even more scarce.

"You were able to find an ancestor?" Henry asked.

"Ancestors. As was expected, there are many that could be considered part of Christ's lineage. With so many generations in between, it's impossible for there to be just one or two. It's interesting because Jesus was said to have had quite a large family."

"What?" Jake asked.

"Oh, yes," Moeshe said, his eyes twinkling and reminding Laney of her uncle when he got excited by a topic. "In fact, I found five main family lines that seem to have the most direct link to Jesus." He slid a piece of paper across the table.

Laney picked it up and glanced at the names.

They didn't mean anything specific to her. Two of them appeared to be political families, but it was entirely possible that that was a different branch than the ones directly related to Jesus.

Laney handed the paper over to Jake and Henry, who glanced at it and then placed it in the center of the table.

"Do you have anything more specific than family names?" Jake asked.

Moeshe nodded. He pulled out four folders and placed them on the table, a list on the top one. "These are the genealogies that I was able to find. It links the names back through their ancestry. Two of them can be found in the United States, one is in France, and one is in India."

Laney glanced at the rest as Henry and Jake leaned forward as well.

"There are only four families here. I thought you said there were five?" Jake asked.

Moeshe nodded, pulling out another folder from his bag, but this one he held on the table in front of him, his hand upon it.

"There is one more family. But I thought it best to provide the other four first."

A gnawing started in Delaney's gut. "Why?"

"Because this last family is someone you know."

Laney's eyebrows rose at that. "Who is it? Who's the last family? Who are the last descendants?"

Moeshe looked at Jake and then turned his attention to Henry and Laney. "You two."

CHAPTER 61

Something akin to surprise rolled through Laney, but it wasn't pure surprise. Somewhere deep down she'd been waiting for a revelation like this. Because wasn't that how it always worked? As soon as they figured out what was happening, the rug got pulled out from underneath them.

Henry, however, did not look like he'd been prepared at all. "What? No, that can't be right."

Moeshe pushed the file toward Henry, who grabbed it and anxiously flipped it open.

"The link is through the maternal line. Your mother was a descendant."

Lilith was reborn over and over again but always to different families. But the fact that she might be born into the Jesus line, well, that that couldn't be a coincidence.

David, who'd been silently leaning against the kitchen island with a mug of coffee, placed the coffee down on the countertop. "Well, Moeshe, I think that you have completely blown everyone's mind for a moment. How about if we go check in on Patrick?"

The professor looked around the table, no doubt taking in the varying levels of shock splashed on the faces across from him and spoke quickly. "Yes, yes, that would be lovely."

Laney nodded toward the hallway off the main room. "He's down in the guest room."

David helped pull out the professor's chair and escorted him from the room.

Silence fell across the table as Laney, Jake, and Henry tried to accept what had just been presented to them.

"It can't be true," Henry said.

And apparently acceptance was going to take a little bit longer for her brother.

"Why not?" Laney asked.

"Because ... I mean, because it just can't," Henry said.

Jake shook his head. "I really think we all need to just take that series of words out of our vocabulary."

Henry turned to him. "You can't think that this is true. There's no chance that ..."

Jake spoke softly. "That what? That you're a Nephilim? She's the ring bearer? Your mother's Lilith? We're the triad? You came back to life? I came back to life? What can't I believe, Henry?"

Henry's face paled. "But this just seems so ... it just seems like a lot."

She stood up. "I'll be back in just a second, okay?"

Henry and Jake looked at her but nodded. Laney hurried out of the room, heading in the direction David and the professor had gone. They had only just reached the guest room when Laney appeared in the door.

Patrick looked up with a smile. Cleo was curled up at his feet. "Laney. Are you going to join us?"

Laney shook her head. "No, um, not just yet. I need to borrow Cain for a moment."

Cain's eyebrows rose in surprise, but he stood swiftly and then winced, realizing he should have taken a little more care. "If you'll excuse me for a moment."

263

R.D. BRADY

Laney tilted her head, and they walked farther down the hall, away from the room so no one could overhear them.

Cain followed, a frown on his face. "Is everything all right?"

Laney opened her mouth and then shut it. She wasn't really sure how to answer that. "I don't know. But I need to talk to you about something."

He nodded. While Cain had known Lilith almost his entire life, he had also lost track of her at times, as she was reborn time and time again. But he'd also read the Followers' compendium on Lilith's former lives. He and Patrick had both scoured it over the years.

"I have a question about Lilith."

Cain grabbed her arm. "Have they found her? Is there news?"

Laney cursed herself for her thoughtless phrasing. "No, no, it's nothing like that. I'm sorry."

Cain's shoulders dropped. "I just ... I keep hoping that they'll reach out. I know it's not safe, but I can't help but want to hear from her."

"I know the feeling. But it's actually one of Lilith's past lives that I'm wondering about."

Cain raised an eyebrow. "Her past lives? Well, I'll answer you if I can, although I don't see how that's relevant to what's going on right now."

"During the time of Jesus, where were you?"

Cain's surprise was evident at the topic. "I was in northern Africa. But you have to recall that at the time, no one viewed Jesus as the son of God. In fact, there were multiple messiahs during that time. He was just one of them. The fact that he resulted in such a following that exists to this day is rather shocking. I always thought it would be John the Baptist who had more of an impact."

Laney knew that that was true. In fact, Jesus's divine nature hadn't been decreed by the Church until three centuries after his death. At the Council of Nicaea, they proclaimed him to be the son of God. And a lot of people argued that was done for political purposes. Many argued Constantine embraced Christianity as a means to bring together his fractured empire. In reality, he was a follower of Sol Invictus, the sun god cult, right up until his death, when he converted to Christianity.

"Where was Lilith at the time of Jesus's life?"

Cain met her gaze for a long moment. "Why do you want to know that?"

"I just ... I need to know."

"Lilith was there at the time of Jesus's life. She was, in fact, his most important apostle."

Laney leaned back against the wall. Moeshe had been right. But she needed to hear the name. "What was her name?"

Cain spoke softly. "Mary Magdalene."

CHAPTER 62

MARY MAGDALENE. THE CHURCH HAD CALLED HER A PROSTITUTE, but in the early Church, she'd been anything but. She'd been Jesus's most loyal disciple. So loyal, in fact, that the other disciples had been jealous of the relationship Jesus had with her. They'd even asked him why he treated her so much better than the rest of them. There were even claims that Jesus had kissed her on the mouth.

Laney had long ago accepted that Mary Magdalene had been married to Jesus. It hadn't been what she'd been taught by the Catholic Church growing up, but the evidence was there for anyone willing to look.

Jesus had been in his thirties when he'd been put to death. It would have been extremely unusual for him not to be married. In fact, it would have been so unusual that it would undeniably have been mentioned by one of the gospels writers. Yet no one did. And the term rabbi that was used to address him could only be used when referring to a married man.

There was so much about Jesus that was cloaked in mystery, but over the last few decades, more and more scholars had started to look into the historical side of Jesus to see what they could find about the man's actual physical life.

The more research that was done, the more clear it became that the legend of Jesus as the poor son of a carpenter wasn't entirely accurate. It seemed that Jesus actually came from the house of David, and that he had a claim to the throne.

Mary Magdalene as his wife was another factor. The Church, and Peter in particular, had tried to distance themselves from her. Jesus had wanted Mary to continue his movement. But Peter was the one who had taken up the gauntlet after Mary had disappeared.

Now they knew that Mary had fled in fear for her life and the life of her unborn child. Her brother, Lazarus, had accompanied her along with Joseph of Arimathea.

It had never occurred to Laney that Lilith might have been Mary Magdalene, though.

"Laney? Why is this troubling you so much? You know Lilith has had countless lives."

Laney studied the man in front of her. He'd been an immortal and had been alive and seen so many things.

But right now she could see the worry on his face, and this worry was for her. He was already so stressed and worried about Nyssa and Patrick that she didn't want to add more to his plate.

"It's not. I'm just surprised I didn't put it together sooner. It's just another piece in the puzzle. Nothing to worry about."

He frowned. "Are you sure?"

She forced the worry from her face. She leaned up and kissed him on the cheek. "Yes. Thank you for your help."

The look on his face remained skeptical, but Laney simply linked her arm through his and led him back down the hall. "How are you feeling?"

"Good. It's good to be back on the estate. I have a little headache, but nothing that Tylenol can't handle."

"That's good. But don't try to do too much too soon," Laney said.

Cain laughed. "You of all people are telling me not to do too much?"

Laney smiled. "As they say, do as I say, don't do as I do."

"I don't think that's the exact phrasing," Cain deadpanned.

"It's been a long few days. Humor me." She stopped at the door where her uncle was speaking with Moeshe.

The good-natured smile slipped from Cain's face as he looked down at her, replaced with lines of worry along his forehead. "Are you sure you're all right?" Cain asked.

Laney nodded, patting his arm. "I'm fine. Just lots of thoughts going around this head of mine."

"All right. But if there's something I can do to help …"

"I'll be sure to let you know. Now go. Enjoy Gina's company."

Cain smiled at her and then slipped back into the room.

Laney walked a little farther down the hall, but she wasn't quite ready to join the others, so she found herself leaning back against the wall. Lilith had been Mary Magdalene. Laney was a descendant of Jesus, and then Lilith had been put back in Jesus's ancestral line again in order to bring Henry and Laney into this world.

There was something there. Something they weren't seeing.

Laney stared down at her hands, thinking about the fact that Jesus's blood, at least part of it, rolled through her hands.

Once again, it came back to blood.

Her head jolted up, a thought murmuring at her from the back of her mind. Jesus's divinity hadn't been determined until the third century AD. Blood. Lilith born over and over again. Mary Magdalene and then Victoria Chandler.

And now Nyssa.

What if …

Laney straightened up from the wall, her hand going to her mouth. No, it wasn't possible.

But Jake was right. How many times had she thought that and been proven wrong?

Laney hurried into the main room. David had joined Henry and Jake at the table. The three of them looked up.

Henry stood, his face showing his concern. "Laney? What's wrong?"

She waved him back down to his seat and then stood at the end of the table. "What if we're looking at this wrong?"

"What do you mean?"

"We keep looking at this, or at least Moeshe is looking at this, as the descendants of Jesus. What if that's not what we're actually looking for?"

"I don't understand," David said. "Moeshe's research is on the descendants of Jesus."

"No, Moeshe's research is on the descendants of Jesus *and* Mary Magdalene. And Lilith was Mary Magdalene. What if it's not the descendants of Jesus that Gedeon is looking for? As Jake said before, that blood was going to be so degraded. But what if he's looking for the descendants of Mary Magdalene, or more accurately, Lilith *and* Jesus?"

"You think he's looking for Lilith?"

"No." Laney shook her head, then looked Henry in the eyes. "I think he's looking for us."

"But that doesn't make any sense. All of the items from the Arma Christi have the blood of Jesus on them, not the blood of Mary Magdalene."

Laney slumped into the chair. She'd forgotten about that. Maybe she was wrong, but something in her gut told her that she wasn't. "True, but those have the actual blood of Jesus on them, not blood that's been degraded across 2,000 years. What if they need both? The blood from the passion of Christ and some sort of descendant of Mary Magdalene?"

"Are you sure you're not reaching? I mean, Jesus is the bigger name," Jake said.

That was true. But was he actually the one with the greater impact? She knew it was sacrilege to say that or even think that, but Lilith had been the one who had had the power to make humans mortal. Jesus was the one who had, in essence, made them immortal by saying that they would live after death. Weren't they just two sides of the same coin? And then if those two bloodlines came together ...

"No, I think it has to be both. He's not just looking for Jesus's bloodline. He's looking for Lilith as well. And the strongest bloodline linked to Lilith ..."

"It's us," Henry said softly.

CHAPTER 63

LANEY'S HEAD SWAM, BUT SHE FELT LIKE SHE WAS ON THE RIGHT path. Gedeon wasn't just after the descendants of Jesus—it was the combination of Mary Magdalene and Jesus.

Henry's face paled. "Oh my God. Tori, Witt." He blurred for the door. Laney watched him go, knowing he was going to place his kids in an armored box. Because while Laney and Henry were the closest link, Henry's children were the second closest.

"We know that from history and from what Cain told us that Gedeon was obsessed with Lilith," Laney said. "We thought that meant in some sort of romantic way. Some sort of stalker way. But what if it wasn't that? Or wasn't just that? What if he needed her for some other reason?"

David looked around at the three of them. "I feel like I'm missing something here."

Laney took a deep breath. "Lilith is reborn time and time again. She has been ever since she decided that humanity should be made mortal."

Impatience laced David's words. "Yes. I know that. But we don't know where she is right now, do we?"

David had been raised as a Follower of the Great Mother. He

knew about her reincarnations. And he also knew that she was very rarely found before she was well into adulthood. Laney didn't think she'd ever been found when she'd been a child. There would be no reason for anyone to know who she was. After all, she wouldn't have her memories. Even Lilith wouldn't know who she was.

"We know where Lilith is," Laney said slowly.

David frowned.

"But Victoria died not thirteen years ago," he said, giving Laney an apologetic look. "How could you possibly know where she is? She doesn't have her memories yet."

"No, she doesn't. But about twelve years ago, Samyaza started looking for her. She started grabbing newborn children shortly after Victoria died. She was going through their blood work, trying to find signs of Lilith."

Laney could see the wheels turning in David's head. "And she found her," he said.

Laney nodded.

He looked around the table. "And that little girl has been raised here on this estate."

Jake nodded. "It's not that we didn't trust you, David. But Nyssa had been through so much and *is* going to go through so much. We just wanted her to have as normal a childhood as possible without people staring at her and wondering."

David stood up from the table and then paced along the island. Neither Laney nor Jake said a word until he returned to the table. "Okay, I'm not going to say I'm not a little angry. I do feel like I could have been brought into the circle of trust, but I'm going to shove that aside for the moment. Because I think we have a bigger problem. We need to get Nyssa back now. If Gedeon is really looking for Lilith, then he's going to be pulling out all the stops to find her. We need to track her down. We need to double and redouble our efforts."

David's urgency got through to Laney. "He's right. We can't

THE BELIAL BLOOD

wait for them to make contact. We have to find a way to reach out to them first. We have to get Lilith back. We have to keep her safe."

"But how? We've tried everything. The analysts are running every camera in the country. We've got everybody looking for her. There are no other strings to pull."

David scoffed. "Oh, please. You people have more supernatural tricks than an Eric Kripke production. So why don't you find something unnatural that we can use to track her down?"

Laney shook his head. "Our powers don't work like that. We can't just have a vision. Nephilim don't have visions. We can't track her down that way."

Jake cleared his throat. "Actually, there *is* one Nephilim that has visions."

CHAPTER 64

FINDING NYSSA WAS NOW OF CRITICAL IMPORTANCE. David and Jake headed up to the main house while Laney headed to Sharecroppers Lane.

Jen, who they'd called once they had figured out the next step, had met them outside the bomb shelter and now accompanied Laney.

Laney stared at her, noting the pallor of her skin. "You spoke with Henry?"

Jen nodded. "Yeah. He's got the kids in the panic room while he and my parents get their stuff together. They're all moving in with Dom."

Laney sighed. Dom's shelter had once been a quiet place. Now, it needed to be expanded to accommodate all those who needed its protection. "Are you sure you don't want to be with them?"

Jen shook her head. "Henry is many things. Calm when his children are in danger is not one of them. And I just get annoyed at how irrational he is. It's better for all of us if we separate right now. Besides, I need something to do."

"I'm not sure this will provide much of a distraction."

Jen gave her a grim smile. "I'll take what I can get. Do you really think this is going to work?"

Laney shook her head. "I have no idea. I don't think this has been done before. But I figure we need to at least give it a shot."

Jen nodded. "I agree. Anything's worth a shot at this point."

Laney could feel Jen's gaze on her. "What?"

"I'm just wondering how you're feeling. That's a lot to take in. I can tell Henry has shoved it in the back of his mind until he gets the kids safe. But what about you?"

Laney didn't slow down, but she did give herself a moment of pause to contemplate her answer. And the truth was it wasn't a lot to take in. "I'm actually kind of okay with it. I mean, with everything that we know about Henry and my past, believe it or not, it's not that big a deal."

Jen raised her eyebrows at that.

Laney shrugged. "The truth is, learning about Victoria being my actual mother was more mind-blowing than this. This just feels so far removed. So, yeah, I guess I'm not bothered too much about it. Right now. I'm just really worried about Nyssa. We have to find her."

"Then we'll do just that," Jen said as they turned up the path toward Lou and Rolly's cottage.

Laney raised her hand to knock on the door, but the door swung open before she could make contact. Lou stood framed in the doorway. "What's happened? Have they found Nyssa?"

Jen shook her head. "No. Not yet. We actually need to speak with Max."

Max had been staying at Lou and Rolly's place for the last few weeks.

Lou stepped back, swinging the door wide. "He's still sleeping. He was up late last night working with Danny at the main house."

Laney stepped inside. "I'm afraid we're going to have to wake him. There's something we need him to do."

Lou frowned. "What?"

"Find Nyssa," Jen said.

CHAPTER 65

Max had been asleep on the couch in the living room. Although Laney had a feeling he needed the sleep, they needed his help more.

But they weren't complete ogres. After waking him, they gave him some time to grab a shower and get a bite to eat before they pressed him to see if he could do anything to find Nyssa.

Now he sat back on the couch in the living room. Lou and Rolly had gone up to the main building to give them a little privacy. Laney was grateful for the consideration. The less people staring at Max, the better.

Max sat across from the two of them, shaking his head. "I've never done that before."

They had just explained that they wanted him to essentially force a vision to see where Nyssa was.

"I understand that," Laney said. "But you have the same abilities that Edgar Cayce did. And he used to be able to go into trances. And in the trance he could see things. I'm hoping maybe we could try the same thing with you."

A renowned twentieth-century psychic, Edgar Cayce would slip into trances and answer questions put to him. He would often provide readings that highlighted an individual's past lives, health diagnoses, and prophecies of the future. His readings were touched upon today, and many of the health remedies he suggested while under a trance were eventually accepted as protocols.

Max looked between the two of them. "I don't know if that's going to work."

Jen shrugged. "Neither do we. But we need to at least try."

Max was a quiet for a moment. "I'll try. So what do I do?"

Jen nodded to the couch behind him. "Why don't you lie back and close your eyes. Get yourself comfortable. You've been working on meditation, right?"

Max nodded as he grabbed a pillow and pushed it to the end of the couch and then lay down. "Yeah. It's actually been going pretty well. I can slip under pretty quickly."

Laney wasn't surprised. Max had had visions on and off since he was a child. As the reincarnation of Edgar Cayce, it was entirely possible his brain was tuned in to that ability. He just hadn't tried it before intentionally.

Jen leaned forward, keeping her voice soft as Max closed his eyes. "Okay, Max, I want you to start meditating, but this time instead of just focusing on your breath, I want you to think of Nyssa. Picture her and where you think she is. Just keep her in your mind as you start to go under."

Max nodded, his eyes still closed. "Okay."

The room was quiet with only the sound of Max's breathing. Laney gripped the sides of her armchair and stared at him, waiting for something.

Max cracked open an eyelid. "You know, why don't you two go for a walk around the neighborhood or something? Staring at me is not exactly helping me relax."

Jen chuckled as she stood. "Yeah, okay. That's fair." She grabbed Laney's arm and hauled her up. "Come on. Let's leave him to it."

Laney let Jen guide her outside. Jen started for the road, but Laney shook her head. She didn't want to be too far away in case Max came up with anything. "Why don't we just go sit out back?"

Laney led the way to the back of the house. There were a couple of Adirondack chairs set up around a firepit back there, and Laney and Jen each took a seat.

Neither of them spoke, and Laney was comfortable in the silence. She needed the quiet to give her mind a little time to consider everything that they had learned.

If she and Henry were descendants of Jesus and Mary Magdalene, then their blood might be critical. She'd have to make sure that Henry was safe, the same way he'd have to make sure that she was. And Tori's and Witt's safety would take precedence over either of theirs.

But when it came to Gedeon, there would be no hiding, at least not for her. She would be the one leading the charge. Of course, she currently had no idea where to charge into. How had he managed to hide himself so well?

Danny said that the eastern European group they believed were behind the attack was available to the highest bidder, which meant that Gedeon had deep pockets. And maybe he'd used that group to keep him hidden.

But if they were still keeping him hidden, then how were they going to track him down? He had most of the pieces that he needed for the Arma Christi—except for the spear, which Laney still had.

She realized then that she hadn't thought about the other objects associated with the passion of Christ. She'd been so focused on the most famous ones that she forgot there were probably other items related. She quickly pulled out her phone and sent off a text to David.

We need to check on all the items associated with the passion of Christ and make sure that they're secure. If they're not, we need to secure them.

David responded quickly. *I already reached out to the Vatican when all this first started. They removed all of the items from the passion from their original locations and took them to the Vatican vaults to keep them safe.*

Laney let out a breath. Thank God at least someone was thinking. *Thanks*, she typed back. And David sent her a smiley face emoji. Laney grinned at it before shoving her phone back in her pocket.

Jen flicked a glance at the house. "How long do you think we should wait before we go check on him?"

"I don't know. I know that Cayce could be in a trance for up to an hour."

"Do you really think he can do this?"

"Probably. But whether or not he can do it right now for us? I'm not sure. We probably should have been training him to do this, but we just never really thought of it."

"Well, you have an excuse. You were actually sucked out of the timeline for a little bit."

Laney grinned her. "You're right. *You* should have thought of it."

Jen laughed. "Just add it to the list."

The two of them smiled and then went quiet. Laney stared up at the sky, feeling the warm sunlight on her skin. She closed her eyes, telling herself she'd only close them for a moment. But before she knew it, Jen was shaking her shoulder. "Laney?" she said softly.

Laney's eyes flew open, and she stared into her friend's face. Jen nodded back toward the house. "Max wants us to come in."

Laney roused herself, wiping at her eyes. "How long was I out?"

"A little over an hour. Come on, let's go see. I think he's found something."

Laney and Jen made their way in through the back door. Max was standing at the kitchen island drinking a tall glass of water.

He placed it on the counter as they stepped inside, wiping his mouth at the back of his hand.

"Well?" Jen asked.

Max nodded to the kitchen table. "Let's take a seat."

He made his way around the island and plopped into a chair. Jen and Laney sat across from him.

Max pushed his phone toward the center of the table. "I wasn't sure whether or not this was going to work. But I figured I should probably record it just in case. I seemed to remember reading somewhere that Edgar Cayce didn't recall what he said during his trances. So I set my phone up to record."

"And there's something on there?" Laney asked.

Max gave a stiff nod. "I queued it up." He pressed play, and Max's voice burst out into the kitchen.

"A house, old, made of wood. Trees surrounding it. A brook babbles in the distance. Tall conifer trees and a smell of coal in the air."

Max stopped the recording.

"Is that everything?" Jen asked.

"All that's relevant to Nyssa. I don't remember what I saw, but from what I can tell, it's a cabin in the woods. I didn't provide any street names or critical markers, just that it's a cabin in the woods and that there's the scent of coal in the air."

Laney sat back, her mind racing. It wasn't a lot to go on.

"Well, Nyssa wouldn't know of a place like that," Jen said. "She spent her entire life on the estate. Anywhere she knows of, the rest of us know too."

Laney nodded. "And the same is almost entirely true for Molly. There are a few places that Jake took them on vacations over the years, but they've already checked those out and had no luck."

"Which means that it has to be somewhere that JW knows," Max said.

Laney pulled out her phone and dialed Danny.

"Hey," he said. "Did Max tell you anything?"

THE BELIAL BLOOD

"A little. He thinks Nyssa is in a cabin somewhere in the woods. There's a smell of coal in the air. That's about all we've got. But we think it might be related to JW."

Danny paused. "Where we grew up, there was always the scent of coal in the air."

Laney's heart began to race. "Did you guys have some sort of family cabin?"

"No, nothing like that. But there were some hunting cabins in the woods around us. Let me do a little research. I'll check on JW's friends from childhood, see if any of them had cabins. Then I'll expand it to his other known acquaintances and see if any of them have any property holdings in the woods. It'll take a while, but at least it's something."

"Okay. Let me know if you find out anything."

"Will do." Danny disconnected the call.

Laney looked at Jen and Max. "I guess we just need to wait."

Jen leaned back in her chair. "I hate waiting," she grumbled as she stood. "I'm going to go see how I can help back at HQ."

Laney started to stand as well. "I'll join you."

Placing a hand over hers, Max spoke. "Uh, Laney, could you wait a minute? I need to speak with you about something."

Stopping halfway up, Laney retook her seat with a frown. "Everything okay?"

"Yeah, sure," Max said in a tone that made it clear he was a horrible liar.

Jen looked between the two of them. "Okay, obviously Max thinks this is for your ears only. I'll go light a fire under people. See you two later."

Laney waited until the front door had opened and closed before she spoke. "What's going on?"

He grabbed his phone, holding it in his hand. "Um, well, I played for you the part about Nyssa. And I thought that was all there was. But I kept it playing when I grabbed a drink, just to make sure. And there was one more part."

281

R.D. BRADY

Nervous ripples stirred through Laney's stomach. "You're not exactly putting me at ease."

He just gave her a nervous smile before he looked down at his phone. "You need to hear this." Taking a breath, he pressed play and then placed the phone in the middle of the table.

It took everything in Laney not to push her chair back from the table. But whatever was on that phone, she needed to hear it. So instead of backing away, she leaned forward.

For the first few seconds, there was nothing, just the sound of Max breathing. And then his voice broke through.

"The time is at hand.

Old enemies will reappear.

The angels will rise up.

War will split the world apart.

The ringbearer will determine the world's fate once again."

CHAPTER 66

THE RINGBEARER WILL DETERMINE THE WORLD'S FATE ONCE AGAIN. Laney had no idea what to do with Max's prophecy. Angels rising up? Was that the Fallen, or were there others that were going to jump into the fight? And the world splitting apart—that had almost happened once. She couldn't let it get to that point again. But how exactly was she supposed to stop it?

Max's prophecy was detailed enough to worry her but not detailed enough to give her any ideas on what she could do to keep it from happening.

And right now, as worrying as it was, getting Nyssa back was a greater worry. So she shoved it to the back of her mind so she could focus on something more concrete: locating Nyssa and the others. Unfortunately, there wasn't much for her to do there.

So after only an hour, she found herself heading back to her cottage to wait for some news. Unfortunately, patiently waiting had never been Laney's strong suit. Luckily Dom had started to send her lists of places that had used sound energy in their construction.

The first one he sent was the Newgrange structure in Ireland.

Laney had heard about the prehistoric monument, but she'd

never been there. In appearance, it was less impressive than some of the other ancient sites. From a distance, it looked like a grass-covered mound. But the structure had been created so that during the winter and summer solstice, light illuminated the interior.

That, however, wasn't what intrigued Laney. Apparently, visitors reported that you could feel the vibrations within the site in your chest at certain times of the year.

And the research indicated that the site vibrated at about 110 hertz.

Another site that Dom sent over was from India. In Hampi, there was a Hindu site that had an unusual creation called the stage pavilion. Within the pavilion were fifty-six columns. Each column was created from pure granite. Yet when striking the columns, they sounded exactly like the notes created from musical instruments, percussion, woodwinds and so on.

When the British discovered the site in the nineteenth century, they cut down one of the columns to try and figure out how they had created such extraordinary music. But the column was simply granite. There is nothing magical or unusual within it, at least that the British could see.

More recent research, however, had indicated that there was some sort of geopolymer blended within the granite that helped create their unique sounds. The problem was that polymers hadn't been created until the 1950s, and the Indian site dated back to at least the 1400s. So yet again, there was a site more technologically advanced than should have been possible.

Laney shook her head as she read the description.

All of these sites indicated that there was some higher knowledge that had been lost long ago. And she couldn't help but think of how much cleaner the world had been back then. Humans had made an absolute disaster of the world today, in large part through its technology. Fossil fuels were a huge polluter of the world. In fact, the creation of many of the goods and services that were used these days polluted lakes and streams and the lands surrounding them.

In Florida, there was even a toxic waste dump surrounded by even more toxic mounds. An old fertilizer plant manufacturing phosphate took the radioactive waste left behind during the manufacturing process, which they would simply stack up. And then in between the stacks were huge lagoons of highly acidic and radioactive water. Every once in a while, the toxic water threatened to overrun the mounds, creating an Armageddon-like natural disaster.

Laney shook her head. Yet back in time, humans had incredible technology, and without the earth paying the price for them. Somewhere along the way humans had lost that knowledge, knowledge that could have not only benefited mankind but the planet as well.

Cleo walked in and rubbed against Laney's legs. Laney reached down and ran a hand through her fur.

Worried?

Laney nodded. "Yeah. I can't find Nyssa. We have no idea where Gedeon is or what he's up to. I just don't know what to do."

Run?

Laney laughed. "You think a run is the answer for everything."

Cleo just looked up at her expectantly.

And suddenly the idea of going for a run sounded perfect.

"Give me a minute." She dashed up the stairs to get changed. And only about five minutes later, she was back down the stairs and stretching on the front porch. Then her and Cleo took off through Sharecroppers Lane and into the field.

Laney's breath lined up with her footfalls, and she relaxed into the run.

She didn't know what it was about running, but she always felt powerful after and during a run. There was also something so incredibly freeing about it. Perhaps that was what she liked the most. She felt unencumbered when she ran.

R.D. BRADY

She lost herself in the rhythm of the run and managed to do a full hour before returning to her cottage.

Cleo had been right. A run had been a good call. The worry and stress had diminished. And after she took her shower and threw on some clean clothes, she felt even better. She padded downstairs, grabbed a bowl of grapes from the fridge, and started munching on them as her phone rang.

Swallowing, she grabbed the phone glancing at the screen. It was Jake. "Laney, we think we might have a location."

CHAPTER 67

WITH CLEO BY HER SIDE, LANEY WASTED NO TIME HEADING UP TO the main headquarters. She burst in the front doors and took the steps up to the third floor two at a time. She hurried into Henry's office, which was directly across from the stairs.

Jen, Danny, and David were there along with a handful of other analysts. The left-hand side of the room had become the search center.

Jake's office down the hall was the search center for Gedeon. Laney's office had turned into the sleep center, where analysts would go and just take a quick cat nap before returning to work. "What have you found?" she asked.

David nodded to the computer, turning it around so Laney could see it. "JW had a friend in grade school. His name was Travis Wall. His family has an old hunting lodge just over the West Virginia border in Pennsylvania. It's two towns over from where JW and Danny grew up."

Danny took over the tale. "The hunting lodge was left to Travis after his grandfather passed away. Travis's mother is deceased, and his father is in a home. Travis is in the Marines and is currently stationed overseas. But I ran an analysis of JW's phone and electronic correspondence, and he kept in touch with Travis over the years just every now and then. But it's the clearest link to a place where JW might feel safe. Plus, him and Travis were close growing up."

"Sounds good to me. Do we have a team ready to go?" Laney asked.

Jake strode in the door. "I have them suiting up right now. I assume you want to go?"

Laney nodded. "You assume correctly."

Jake looked at the others. "I'm going to take two choppers. We'll let you guys know as soon as we hear anything."

David looked like he wanted to join them, but he nodded. "All right. Let us know when you get her."

"We will."

Laney turned and followed Jake out the door.

This was good. Getting Nyssa back was good. But part of her worried that maybe, just maybe, they should have let Nyssa stay hidden.

CHAPTER 68

ROME, ITALY

WITH MORE THAN A LITTLE TREPIDATION, GEDEON GLARED AT THE plane on the runway as the car pulled to a stop. But the heat of his glare was less than usual. Even this metal coffin could not fully dim the good mood the initiation of his plan had brought.

Lucius, who sat next to him on the computer, made no move to get out of the car.

Gedeon opened his door and stepped outside, stretching his back. Cars were not meant for men of his size. He stepped toward the plane when Lucius called out to him. "Sir, I think we found her."

Gedeon turned back and leaned into the car doorway. "You think or you know?"

"The Chandler Group is moving out. We've intercepted their location. They're heading to a place in southern Pennsylvania. Laney McPhearson and Jake Rogan are among those in the group."

"Where are our people?"

"A few hours away in northern Virginia."

"Can they beat McPhearson's team to the site?"

"It'll be close. I think they might be a few minutes behind them."

"Then tell them to hurry. I want Lilith in our control."

"Yes, sir." Lucius turned back to his computer.

Gedeon watched him for a moment. The man's fingers flew over the keyboard in a blur of movement. He did not understand exactly how the computers worked, sending messages through the air. But they were a critical tool in this modern world, and Lucius was incredibly adept at them.

He turned away, staring out into the air as if he could see the message being sent.

They had a location on Nyssa. His people knew that getting her was the top priority. And they knew the cost of failing him again.

Which meant they would not fail. Lilith would be his shortly, and then the next step in the process could begin.

CHAPTER 69

URSINA, PENNSYLVANIA

Nyssa's eyes flew open. Her heart raced, and she covered her mouth with her hand, trying to keep the sound of her haggard breathing from being too loud in the quiet cabin.

Sunlight streamed in from the windows. She'd lain down and didn't remember closing her eyes.

Molly, who'd been reading a book next to her, turned toward her. "Nyssa? What is it?"

Struggling to keep her voice even, Nyssa shook her head. "Just a leg cramp. I'm fine. Go back to sleep." She blinked, realizing she must have fallen asleep when she'd tried to read.

Molly studied her for a long moment. "You want to go take a walk or something?"

"Uh, no, um, not right now. I, uh, need to use the bathroom." Feeling Molly's gaze on her, she was careful to keep her movements unhurried as she bit her lip.

Closing the bathroom door as quietly as she could behind her, she slipped down to the floor, leaning her head back against the door. Then she curled her legs up to her chest as she wrapped her arms around them.

Another dream. You'd think by now she'd be used to them, but she never seemed to get used to them. Each time there was more horror, and most importantly, loss.

In fact, loss seemed to be the pattern that connected the majority of the dreams.

Long ago, she'd realized somewhere in the back of her mind that they weren't simply figments of her imagination or her subconscious throwing together a smorgasbord of imagery. They were, in fact, memories from her past lives.

She'd overheard her uncle and Cain talking about Laney's past lives. They didn't know she'd overheard them. But apparently the ring bearer had been around time and time again.

But Laney's past lives were nothing compared to Laney's biological mother's. Apparently, she lived time and time again for what seemed like forever. Reincarnation was therefore not a foreign concept to her. Her and Susie had even spent hours talking about who they might have been in previous lives. A princess? A soldier? They wondered if they had always been the same gender or if sometimes they had lived life as a man or even an animal. Susie was sure she had previously been a wolf. It had been fun thinking about the possibilities.

But these dreams were not fun. These images were not fun. And these past lives, if that's what they were, were not fun.

And they offered no clue how the past lives would make those horrible people come after her now. Nyssa wasn't sure what exactly her role in all of this was. She wasn't sure if she was anyone important like Laney. She doubted it. After all, she was just a girl. But she was convinced now that these were images from her own lives.

More importantly, she had a feeling that these memories were trying to tell her something.

And what they seemed to be telling her was that the people she loved, the people that were close to her, died because they were close to her.

Her chin resting on her knees, Nyssa stared at the wall, not seeing it. Instead, she saw Cain, her uncle, Susie, Laney, Jen, Henry, Danny, Max, and everybody else from the estate.

Her uncle had already been hurt, as had Cain. And Nyssa knew without a shadow of a doubt that the others would place themselves right in front of danger to protect her.

They already had.

Even now, they were still doing it. Molly and JW had risked everything to take her away and hide her. Lou and Rolly had appeared at that airport, and she didn't even know if they were okay. They'd left them behind.

And the people that were after her were so incredibly powerful. Molly was powerful now, but she was just one person. JW was a soldier, and she'd seen the guns that he'd loaded into the car, but when it was only guns against the Fallen, the Fallen tended to win.

So that meant it would be up to Molly.

And again, Molly was just one person.

Tears formed at the back of her eyes as Nyssa shook her head. Molly wouldn't be able to win. She would be hurt or worse, and Nyssa would be taken anyway. The question was only how many people were going to be hurt before that happened.

And Nyssa couldn't let that happen.

In order to keep people safe she needed to leave. It might not be safe for her, but at least those around her would be. To keep the others safe, she needed to stay as far away from them as possible.

CHAPTER 70

THE TWO SIKORSKY S-92 CHOPPERS CUT THROUGH THE EVENING air. Laney sat in the back of one with Max and Jen. Hans and Jake were in the front. Laney drummed her fingers on her thigh, staring out the window and wishing they could go faster.

Jen reached over and placed a hand over Laney's. "We're almost there."

Laney nodded but didn't say anything. She couldn't seem to manage words right now. And with the noise of the chopper, she certainly wasn't up for yelling.

They'd left the estate shortly after they had figured out where Nyssa and the others could be. In the other chopper were the other Fallen. Jake was the only non-Fallen on this trip, and his presence was non-negotiable.

Even with the firepower they all held, and the extra skills that came from their Fallen natures, niggling worms of worry crowded Laney's mind. She tried to tell herself that her fear was irrational. They had no indication that Gedeon knew where Nyssa was.

Still, those thoughts did nothing to tamp down the worry crawling up her skin and overtaking her mind.

At every point of this process, Gedeon seemed to be one step ahead of them. And Laney worried that that would be the case here as well.

She took a deep breath, staring out the window at the sky rushing by. How many times had she done this? Rushed to someone's rescue, her heart in her throat, imagining all the things that could go wrong?

She was sure she couldn't even remember all the times. Back when the world had been targeting Fallen, she and Drake had rushed around the world on the regular, pulling people out of different countries just in the nick of time.

And sometimes they arrived too late.

The thought of Drake made her heart beat faster and her stomach bottom out. They had no clues as to where Gedeon had disappeared with him. They had no idea if he was still alive.

But Laney had to believe he was. Gedeon had him for a reason. Laney didn't know what it was, but once they got Nyssa back safely, finding Drake would be her top priority.

It had to be. Once again, she replayed seeing him in Greece. It had become her favorite and worst memory all in one. Would things be different now if she had gone for Drake rather than Max? Would Max have survived anyway without her intervention? Would she have been killed taking on Gedeon alone?

But choosing Drake felt like choosing herself. And she couldn't do that, not when Max was at risk. She didn't regret that choice the same way she didn't regret choosing Henry to come back rather than Drake.

But as soon as Nyssa was safe, she was choosing herself. She was choosing Drake.

And God help anyone who got in her way.

CHAPTER 71

HEADING TO ROME

Frustration and impatience rolled through Gedeon. He sat back in his chair on the plane, staring out the window. His knuckles were white as they gripped the chair's armrest. This infernal contraption would be the death of him.

He wasn't sure if he could survive plunging from this high a height. He supposed he probably would although the healing would be a long, drawn-out process.

He took a deep breath, trying to get his focus back. Being up here, it always made him uncomfortable. It robbed him of his ability to think rationally. It was a weakness he didn't share with anyone. In fact, no one was allowed to even look at him when he was on a plane.

Simone sat toward the front, unconcerned with their means of travel. She had acclimated to this world better than Gedeon had. Gedeon did not like this modern world. He did not like this reliance on technology. It all felt so false.

Humans were supposed to be these great creations, and the reason they were great was because of their connection to one another. Their ability to feel and emote. But technology cut them off from those emotions. And then technology manipulated and enhanced certain emotions, such as rage and anger, while leaving other ones muted.

All of these humans crawling all over this planet, and yet most of them felt alone. What a waste. Yet they were the chosen people.

Gedeon could acknowledge that the angels were alone as well, but none of them were bothered by it. They were created to be alone. They were created to follow orders and not think about themselves and what they wanted.

Humans were selfish creatures. They cared more about themselves than they did their fellow man. Their history of wars was a testament to that.

It was also a testament to how easily they could be encouraged to violence. Throughout history, men had been able to harness their power and force thousands of soldiers to battle to the death.

These were certainly not the chosen people.

Gedeon grunted. Force. That wasn't quite the right word. Most of them had gone to war willingly. A few pretty words, and they thought nothing of taking another human's life, in direct violation of the Commandments.

The plane rumbled and then dipped for a few heart-racing seconds. Gedeon sucked in a breath, gripping the armrest so tightly that he squeezed the metal. The plane leveled out as the pilot managed to slip around the turbulence.

Gedeon gritted his teeth. *I hate this.* He stared at his watch and then pulled out his phone.

His second-in-command in the field answered quickly. Gedeon didn't give the man a chance to speak. "Report."

"We're almost at the site. We should have her in our custody within the next twenty minutes."

A thousand orders rolled through Gedeon's minds. There were so many things that he could tell them to do and how to do it.

But he settled for one simple order. "See that it is done."

CHAPTER 72

URSINA, PENNSYLVANIA

The forested area that surrounded the cabin of Travis Wall was just up ahead. Laney leaned forward as Jake directed them to a small clearing not too far from the cabin.

Jen was out of the chopper in a flash, and Laney was right behind her. They moved away from the whirling blades as Jake shut the chopper down.

Laney waited until everyone had disembarked from the second chopper and joined her before she spoke. "Anybody sense anything?"

Even though Laney's senses were more attuned, she needed to make sure she wasn't alone in what she was feeling.

"I only feel one, and it's faint," Jen said.

Laney nodded her agreement. That was most definitely Molly.

Jake stepped forward. "We're going to spread out. We're looking for Molly, Nyssa, and JW. If you see any hostiles, take them out immediately. Do not wait. This group is incredibly dangerous."

"Do we know if they're even here?" Mateo asked.

THE BELIAL BLOOD

Jake shook his head. "No. But we can't trust that they don't know about this location. So act as if they're about to jump out of a tree at any moment, all right?"

Everyone nodded back at him. He flicked a glance at Laney, who scanned the group before she nodded. "Let's go."

They headed into the trees, spreading out. Laney went straight for where she could feel Molly. After five minutes of walking, the signal was stronger. She stopped in the middle of a group of trees.

Next to her, Jake paused too, looking around. "You got something?"

Laney smiled. "Molly, come on out. It's us."

Molly slipped from behind the tree. Her red hair was in a long braid over her shoulder, and though her eyes looked tired, she looked unharmed. Her shoulders sagged in relief. "I was really hoping it was you. I knew you guys would find us."

Jake bustled across the space and wrapped her into a hug, careful to keep his M-4 to the side. "You okay? You're not hurt?"

Molly hugged him back with a smile. "We're all good."

"Where are JW and Nyssa?" Laney asked.

"When I sensed the Fallen, I sent them into the woods."

Jake looked down at her with a frown. "And you were going to face a group of Fallen on your own?"

Molly shrugged. "Well, I was hoping it was you guys. And so I figured I'd check first."

"Molly, they can sense you," Jake said. "It would have just been you against all of them. You can't take those kinds of chances."

Molly raised her eyebrows. "I can't take those kinds of chances? Have you looked at your history?"

Laney chuckled. She understood Jake's concern, but the reality was that by keeping Nyssa safe, Molly was placing herself in harm's way. There was no way around that. And she'd done a good job. "Where are the others?"

"Back this way. Follow me." Molly jogged a little down through the trees. There'd been a path there at one point, but it was massively overgrown, showing that no one had been here in a while.

"Hippopotamus!" Molly yelled into the trees.

Laney grinned at the code word.

And she looked around, waiting for Nyssa to appear.

CHAPTER 73

The woods were quiet as Nyssa hunkered down behind a tree with JW next to her. Molly had sensed multiple Fallen in the area. She was pretty sure it wasn't Gedeon because she couldn't actually sense them. But they weren't taking any chances. JW and Nyssa took off for the trees while Molly went to go check it out.

Nyssa's heart pounded as she imagined Molly coming across the same people from the airport. She hated this. She hated that she was sitting here hiding while Molly was going off to face danger on her behalf.

It couldn't continue like this. She couldn't just sit back and let the people she cared about place themselves in danger for her.

"Hippopotamus!" The word rolled through the air.

JW, who'd been standing next to her, relaxed his posture as he grinned down at her. "Looks like it's your friends."

Nyssa didn't return the smile.

With a machine gun over his shoulder, JW frowned down at her. "You okay? What's wrong? Is it Molly? Because that's the code word. It's not the bad guys."

Nyssa shook her head as frustration rolled up inside of her. "It's just ... Have you ever felt like something bad was about to happen? Like you knew something bad was about to happen and you just didn't know how to stop it?"

JW dropped down to one knee so that he could be at her eye level. "I've felt like that before."

Nyssa met his gaze. "And what happened?"

JW flicked his gaze away before he looked back at her. "Bad things happened. But I survived it. And you, you'll survive it as well. Besides, when it happened to me, I didn't have people looking out for me. I was basically on my own. But you have dozens of people keeping you safe. And that's what they're going to do. They're going to keep you safe."

He stood up. "Now come on. Some people are going to be very happy to see you."

Nyssa followed him back to the cabin, his words rolling through her mind. She knew Danny and JW had had a pretty rough childhood. And she had no doubt that was what JW was referring to. They hadn't had anybody to protect them.

And he was right: Nyssa had lots of people to protect her. She had lots of people that would step in front of danger to keep her safe.

But that was the problem. She had lots of people that would stand between her and danger. Which meant she had lots of people to lose.

CHAPTER 74

THE OLD HUNTING CABIN WAS A SINGLE-STORY BUILDING WITH cedar shake siding. Dull and drab and definitely looking like it could use a little TLC.

But Laney could imagine the possibilities. Rundown little cabins tucked away in the woods held a special place in her heart. Something about them always seemed so peaceful.

The thought brought her up short.

It was a little cabin in the woods where she'd first learned that Victoria Chandler was her biological mother and that her life until that point had been a lie. It was also a cabin in the woods where the government had finally tracked her down and tried to kill her.

Maybe she needed to rethink her idea of cabins as being a tranquil oasis that kept her away from the horrors of the rest of the world.

She looked around but didn't see JW or Nyssa anywhere. The rest of their group started to filter out of the woods on either side. A few stayed a little farther back, forming a perimeter.

Movement from across the clearing on the other side of the

cabin pulled her gaze. JW stepped out wearing jeans and a green shirt that helped him blend into the woods.

And right behind him was Nyssa.

Her blue-and-white tie-dyed sweatshirt was lined with dirt. And her hair was pulled back in a messy bun.

Her face was drawn. She looked tired, and she looked older than Laney had seen her ever look before. But physically, she looked uninjured. And right now, that would do.

The weight that had been pressing against Laney's chest lightened at the sight of her. *Thank God.*

She took a step forward. Tingles, sharp and painful, rolled over her skin. She whirled around, reaching for the gun at her hip. "They're here."

CHAPTER 75

"They're here!" Laney repeated with a yell, bringing her weapon up.

Jake's was already in his hand and pulled to his shoulder. As she turned, she saw JW grab Nyssa and pull her behind him.

From what she could tell, the threat was coming from behind Laney and the others. Nyssa and JW were on the far side of the clearing, the farthest away. Not that it made much difference when you were talking about people who could move with speeds that the angels could.

The team that had come with Laney looked around, keeping their eyes peeled, their bodies tense, waiting.

Jake moved closer to Laney. "Priority is getting Nyssa to the chopper and out of here," Laney said, not taking her eyes off the woods.

Jake relayed the message to the others through their earpieces, not taking his eyes from the trees surrounding them either.

Laney frowned as the signal grew stronger. They should be able to see them by now. What was going on?

The slightest rustle of leaves was all the warning they had before three of the angels dropped from the treetops.

R.D. BRADY

One of them landed near Hans, but Hans managed to sidestep so he didn't get pummeled. He grabbed the angel and slammed his fist into the man's head before he was able to lash out at him.

But the man took the blow like it was nothing.

Max, who'd been nearby, pulled his handgun and managed to get two shots off, only one of which managed to embed itself in the side of the angel.

Laney called on the wind, her hair flying out behind her as the storm clouds rolled in up above. Lightning crashed into the angel that Hans had just kicked off of himself.

Molly stood watching, her eyes going large and catching Laney's gaze.

"I'm going for Nyssa," Molly said, turning and darting across the clearing.

Laney turned, watching her blur across the space, but then a second blur collided with her, and the two of them went rolling in a heap.

CHAPTER 76

THEY FOUND THEM.

Nyssa backed up, her eyes widening as the people fell out of the trees.

There were four of them, but there seemed to be so many more. They moved so fast. And even though the group that had come with Laney were Fallen—or at least Nyssa assumed they were Fallen—they seemed to be completely outmatched.

"Stay behind me," JW ordered, pulling Nyssa over to a tree as he lined his gun up along the side of it. He let out a burst of gunfire, and Nyssa stood behind him, her hands over her ears.

Molly sprinted toward them but was tackled.

Max came out of nowhere and caught Nyssa's gaze. Determination in his eyes, he bolted for her. But he, too, was tackled and flung out of the way.

A blur appeared and then stopped about ten feet away. The man glanced around the area. Nyssa recognized him from the estate. He was the one who had grabbed her initially.

She ducked back behind the tree but not before she caught the man's eyes. And saw his smile.

JW let out a nonstop stream of gunfire. "Hide, Nyssa, hide!"

Stumbling back, Nyssa bolted into the woods. But she didn't go in a straight line. She knew that that would be too easy to track. She turned to her right, making her way around the side of the cabin.

Behind her, she could hear someone tearing through the woods, but then the sound grew more distant.

She let out a small sliver of a breath, feeling relief, but it only lasted a moment. He'd no doubt realize that she hadn't gone straight back, and any second now he'd be back looking for her.

Nyssa picked up her pace, trying hard not to make any noise at the same time. But the two seem mutually exclusive. She could either go fast or she could go silent. She couldn't do both.

She decided silent was better. Speed right now was nothing. She was a turtle compared to these guys. So she slowly picked her way around the side, trying to keep her breath from giving her away.

She felt a small measure of pride as she managed to make it to the other side of the cabin without seeing anyone or being seen.

But she could hear them. Bursts of gunfire rang out, punctuated by screams and cries of pain. All those people were fighting and getting hurt, maybe worse, to protect her and here she was hiding away.

The fact that they had tracked her down to the middle of nowhere meant that they were not going to give up. They were going to keep coming. More people were going to get hurt as they tried to stop them.

And Nyssa didn't think there was any way that they could stop them. They weren't just Fallen. They were something else entirely. Which meant that they were more powerful.

A vision of her uncle Patrick lying on the ground slipped through her mind.

People had already gotten hurt. How many more was she going to let that happen to? Wasn't she just putting off the inevitable? There would come a point when there would be no one left between her and those who wanted her.

She managed to get to the other side of the cabin and stop for a moment behind a large oak tree. She peered around and saw Jen.

An angel bolted toward her, but Jen moved incredibly fast. She grabbed the woman's outstretched hand and flipped her over her shoulder, pulling her weapon from her holster at the same time. She shot the woman five times in the chest, and the woman lay still.

Nyssa blanched from the violence but knew that there was no helping it.

Movement from the cabin caught her eye as another one came around the side. She didn't recognize this one, which meant they had more people than she'd seen at the airport.

The individual grabbed a log from the pile at the side of the cabin and tossed it toward Jen. Her back toward the individual, Jen didn't see it coming.

Nyssa stepped out from behind the tree. "Jen, look out!"

Jen dove for the ground, barely missing getting slammed by the log. She rolled on the ground, shooting at the attacker.

But the attacker seemed to know where the bullets were going to land and dodged them, heading straight for Jen.

Nyssa stared in horror as the man reached Jen, swinging for her face. Jen dodged, tackling the man around the waist. Then they were moving too fast for Nyssa to make out the moves. Nyssa just watched the blur of activity, feeling completely helpless.

But she wasn't helpless. There was one thing she could do that would stop all of this.

CHAPTER 77

It all went bad so quickly.

Laney was still amazed by the speed of these individuals. Besides Greece, which was just a blur, it had been so long since she'd fought the people in this group that she had forgotten how fast they all moved. It was like fighting in a tornado, with people whipping around.

She watched as more and more angels appeared. She counted eight so far. Which meant they had even numbers, which was not good for them at all.

The one saving grace seemed to be that Gedeon wasn't here. But that was a small comfort in the current situation.

Laney tracked an angel toward the left and managed to get off a single shot before he moved out of range. Damn it. She needed to be faster.

A flash of blue appeared from the corner of her eyes. Laney turned, her heart nearly stopping as Nyssa stepped out of the trees. "I'm here! I'm over here!"

Then Nyssa stopped, not moving, not hiding, not getting out of the way.

"Nyssa, no! Run!" Laney yelled.

But Nyssa just looked back at her, a clear look of apology on her face.

Laney's heart dropped. She hadn't been calling to Laney or any of the others who'd come to rescue her. She was giving herself up. She was sacrificing herself so that the rest of them would be safe.

Molly let out a scream. "No!"

Laney sprinted across the space toward Nyssa as she sent lightning raining around the young girl, a cage to keep anyone from getting near her.

She couldn't let her do this. She wouldn't let her do this. Nyssa could not give herself over to them. That was not an option.

A body slammed into Laney's side. Pain roared through her ribs as she went airborne.

"Laney!" someone screamed, but she didn't know who.

Preparing herself for the pain of the impact, Laney was surprised when she felt arms wrap around her. She hit the ground, but the arms surrounding her kept her safe. She looked up into Hans's face.

He looked down at her and gave her an abrupt nod. "Okay?"

"I'm okay."

She scrambled off of him, her side screaming at her, but she managed to straighten just in time to see an angel grab Nyssa and take off into the trees. "They've got her! Follow them!"

Max and Jen were already giving chase.

Laney's heart was in her throat as she started to follow as well. But with her stinging ribs, she was moving even slower than before.

But it didn't stop her. Ignoring the pain, she continued on and prayed that they would get to Nyssa in time.

CHAPTER 78

For twenty minutes, they searched the woods but found no sign of Nyssa. In fact, all of the angels had disappeared as soon as she had been grabbed. Finally, Jake called it. "We're not going to find her this way."

Laney knew he was right, but it was a hard pill to swallow. They had gotten her back for just a moment before she was taken from them.

Nyssa's disappearance wasn't the only bad news.

Somewhere during or before the fight, the choppers had been taken out. They were completely disabled.

Jake had put in a call to the headquarters, and they were sending new choppers to come get them, but it would take a little while.

Now Laney sat on a log near the useless helicopters. Jen touched Laney's ribs, and Laney winced. Tutting, Jen dug into the first-aid kit and pulled out a roll of tape. "Pull up your shirt. Let me see the damage."

Laney did as she was ordered.

Jen sucked in a breath. "Laney."

Laney glanced down at the bright red that now scarred the

THE BELIAL BLOOD

side of her rib cage. She was going to be in for a world of bruises in the not-too-distant future.

"Just tape them up, please," Laney said softly.

Thankfully, Jen did so without another word. Laney didn't think she could handle any empty platitudes or comforting words right now. Her one job had been to keep Nyssa safe, and she'd failed. How had this gone so badly so quickly?

It took Laney a moment to realize she'd asked the question out loud.

"Because we still have a rat?" Jen said.

Laney's head jolted up. "What?"

Jen finished taping Laney's ribs. She cut off the remainder of the bandage and dropped it back into the first-aid kit. "They followed us here, Laney. We led them here."

"How?"

Jen shook her head. "I don't know. But I already contacted Henry and Danny to figure it out. Because something isn't right. They shouldn't have been able to find Nyssa. I mean, we barely found Nyssa, and the only reason we did is because we know JW and Danny. They don't have that information. Which means they had to have gotten it from us."

Jen was right. God, they'd been so stupid. But had they really been stupid, or had they just trusted the people around them?

"Danny and Henry are doing a complete overhaul of the system again and going through all of the personnel to see where the information could have slipped out."

"They managed to follow us here. They managed to get through our defenses. I mean, we've dealt with this stuff before, but not like this. Whoever they've got running their tech is years beyond us. And I'm just worried that we can't trust our technology or our communications."

"And if we can't trust that ..." Jen's words dwindled off.

But Laney finished the statement for her. "Then we're in a lot of trouble."

CHAPTER 79

MASSA, ITALY

THEY WERE ONLY TWENTY MINUTES FROM LANDING. THE PILOT HAD just called back to let them know.

Gedeon stared out the window. Time seemed to be moving at a snail's pace, even as they hurtled recklessly through the air.

They should have reached Nyssa by now. They should have called by now.

More than anything, Gedeon wanted to find out where they were at. But if they were at a critical point of the mission, he couldn't risk giving them away. He couldn't risk them being distracted or pulling attention toward him at an inopportune time.

Which meant he needed to sit and wait.

He hated waiting.

Waiting had never been something that had been required of him. He was always the one leading the charge or being in charge. He did not have to wait for other people to get back to him. He did not have to wait for people to finish what they were doing to give him attention. He always went first and called the shots.

THE BELIAL BLOOD

But right now there were so many things that were happening that he could not do all of them by himself. He needed to delegate. It was a new endeavor for him and not one that he liked.

Simone walked back from the front of the plane. "I'm sorry to interrupt you, sir. But I wanted to let you know that we have heard from the ground team, and everything is set for our arrival."

Gedeon grunted. "Good. I want to hit the ground running as soon as we land."

Simone bowed low. "Of course, sir." She turned and headed back down the aisle.

Gedeon watched her go.

Simone had been a recent addition to his ranks. He'd had to refill them after the debacle in Greece. And now he was thinking he would have to fill them even more.

It wasn't that he expected his people to fail him. Quite the opposite. He had nothing but expectations of success.

But once this stage was complete, they were going to need more bodies.

More bodies, though, were never a problem. He had millions of angels to command at his fingertips. It came with his position.

Humans tended to group all angels together, but there was a hierarchy within which the angels existed. Not all angels were created equal. There were nine orders of angels, set in concentric zones out from God. The closest to him were the seraphim followed by the cherubim. These were the ones least like humans. In the next grouping were the thrones, dominions, and virtues. Then the powers, principalities, and the archangels followed by the angels. Michael, of course, existed outside of the hierarchy.

Gedeon curled his lip.

But Michael wasn't exactly the angel he'd always been. Gedeon, however, was fully coming into the powers he'd always had.

Before now, he'd often come to Earth, but his missions had been smaller. They had therefore involved fewer angels, usually

315

R.D. BRADY

just himself. But the lack of a need for a large team didn't change the fact that he had legions at his command ready to do his bidding.

And soon it would be the time for him to finally make use of them. Soon he would fulfill his reason for existing. He embraced the coming of that moment. He'd grown tired of humans and their weaknesses.

He still didn't understand why they were held in such high regard. They were so easily tempted. One after the another, they had fallen for his words and been condemned because of it.

Even now, he had humans that he'd been visiting since they were children, crafting them, molding them, bringing them over to his side. Like that priest over at the Vatican. He'd been perfectly placed to provide them with what they needed. Gedeon had first visited him when he was a child. A few visits here and there pushing him in this direction or that, and he had a priest exactly where he needed him to be. The man had been perfectly manipulated.

So simple, so weak.

Gedeon growled, pulling out his phone. He needed to know what was going on with his other team.

He quickly dialed.

Afriel's voice was breathy when he answered. "Yes, sir?" he said.

"What is your status?"

It took a moment for Afriel to answer, and Gedeon could picture him trying to get a breath. "We've got the girl. We are making our way back to the other airport. We'll be in the air within thirty minutes."

Gedeon sat back, contentment rolling through him. Finally. Of course, they had had the girl before and lost her at the airport. "Be sure that nothing goes wrong this time. I will not suffer any problems again."

"Yes, sir. Of course, sir."

Gedeon disconnected the call. He knew things could still go wrong. But he felt it in his bones: Lilith was his.

And now they could truly begin.

CHAPTER 80

URSINA, PENNSYLVANIA

It was a solemn group that sat in the clearing waiting for the Chandler helicopters to retrieve them.

Laney didn't feel like talking to anyone, and everyone seemed to be in the same mood.

Molly's eyes were bloodshot from crying. She blamed herself for not keeping Nyssa safe, which was crazy, because it wasn't her fault. If anything, it was Laney and the others who were to blame. If they had stayed away, Nyssa might have still been safe.

Jake walked over and sat down next to Laney.

"How did they find us?" Laney asked.

Jake dropped his voice. "Danny still doesn't know. Either someone's still in our system or we've got a mole."

Laney preferred to think that someone had hacked into their system. She certainly didn't want to think that someone had betrayed them. They had been very careful with who had been hired for years after one experience of having been betrayed. But she'd been out of the game for a while, and she couldn't swear that everyone was loyal to them.

THE BELIAL BLOOD

"What do you think?" She asked Jake.

"If someone betrayed us, I have to think it's because they got to their family or threatened them in some other way. The people we have now, they're loyal, Laney. And I'm not just saying that because I helped hire a bunch of them.

"We do checks all the time. We analyze their financials. We look if there's any areas of their life where they're starting to have problems that could come back to us. And there hasn't been anything. So I don't think that's the answer. Maybe someone got into our system again."

She shook her head. "Or maybe they never left. We need to find out who's been behind all of this. Not some shadowy group. We need to get them. We need to put them out of commission."

"I agree."

Dark shapes appeared in the sky in the distance, drawing Laney's attention. "But first we need to get Nyssa back."

"You know that's the top priority. As soon as we get any leads, we'll be right on that."

Laney nodded, although she wondered if it would do any good. Leads were something they were in short supply of. And even then, they were outclassed. She prayed that Dom would figure something out with the Inceptus.

Because if he didn't, then the next time they brushed up against these individuals, the result would be the same. Which meant that whatever Gedeon had planned, there'd be no one who could stop him.

CHAPTER 81

IT HAD BEEN HER IDEA. NYSSA KNEW THAT. SHE'D BEEN THE ONE who had stepped out of the trees and let them see her. No, she'd actually called them to her.

So why was she so terrified?

The trees had flashed by in a blur as she was yanked into someone's arms and thrown over a shoulder.

With every step, the man's shoulder dug into her ribs. By the time they stopped an hour later, she was barely conscious from all the jostling. Or maybe it was just the fear rolling through her.

She'd been thrown into the back of a plane with little ceremony. No one had said a word to her.

She had scrambled toward the back of the plane as the others climbed on board. No one even looked at her. They ignored her as they got themselves into seats.

Nyssa scrambled for a seat at the back of the plane and put on her seat belt as the plane began to move. It took off just minutes later.

At the front of the plane, she heard someone on the phone. "We have her."

THE BELIAL BLOOD

Nyssa blood's was pounding so heavily in her ears she couldn't hear any more of the conversation. She stared out the window, her whole body shaking.

What have I done?

CHAPTER 82

MASSA, ITALY

FINALLY.

They had her in possession. And they were in the air. McPhearson wouldn't be able to touch them.

He sat back as contentment rolled through him. It had taken too long to retrieve Lilith, but she was finally where she needed to be.

Now he just needed the spear, but that would be an easier acquisition. He gave himself a moment to enjoy the moment before he pulled out his cell phone and dialed the team at the Vatican.

Philip answered quickly. "Yes, sir?"

"We're good. Send the message."

He closed the phone and sat back, picturing where they were heading and what the next steps would be. Soon it would all truly begin.

At least for him. For many others this was the beginning of the end.

CHAPTER 83

URSINA, PENNSYLVANIA

In the chopper, Laney sat in the copilot seat with David at the stick. He didn't ask any questions, just waited until everyone was bundled into the chopper and took off into the air.

Henry had brought two people with him in the second chopper, who would stay with the downed choppers and make the necessary repairs.

Laney stared out into the sky, picturing Nyssa's face. There was no doubt in her mind that Nyssa had intentionally called the angels to her. And Laney knew why. It was something she would have done. To keep the others safe, she had sacrificed herself.

Laney leaned her head against the glass. Was this what it was going to be? One of them sacrificing themselves after the next, until there were none left?

Part of her knew that it was a sign of the high moral character and courage of the people she was with that so many were willing to take such a step. But she was also so angry that it was always her people who were having to sacrifice.

Right now, they were on the precipice of something incredibly dangerous. Whatever threat was on the horizon was larger than even the threat Samyaza posed years ago.

But instead of having a worldwide coalition defending against this threat, it was just Laney and the former fallen angels, along with the people of the Chandler Group, leading the fight.

She couldn't help but think about the irony of that. The fallen angels who had longed for freedom and had fallen in order to achieve it now were the ones who were caught up in another war and had been for years. The fallen angels, the demons of the Old Testament, were now the saviors of the world.

At least that's what she hoped.

But part of her knew that they were outclassed, that *she* was outclassed. And she couldn't help but wonder if she could do more, be more.

Dom said the Omni had been relegated to a non-factor after the events in Egypt. But now that there were Fallen out there, at least a small group, it could be reconstituted.

Dom was working on it in the lab right now.

Should she take the Omni? After all, the taking of the Omni removed her ability to sense the Fallen. But she had a feeling that because of the strength of the signal from the angels that she would at least get a small warning from them.

Her current strength and speed were absolutely no match against them. Besides which, she couldn't command anyone besides a fallen angel. Which meant that that those abilities weren't very helpful right now.

In fact, she was feeling generally useless. She couldn't find Drake. She had no idea where Nyssa was.

She was spiraling in a cycle of self-doubt, but she couldn't seem to pull herself out of it. They just couldn't seem to get a handle on Gedeon. It felt like they were always scrambling and always losing.

Even when they won, it seemed as if it was a hollow victory.

They technically won in Antarctica but destroyed an ancient

THE BELIAL BLOOD

city in order to do so. In Greece, it would have been a win except that they had lost Drake. They managed to save Nyssa back at the airport, but only to put her into hiding and then lose her again.

No, they weren't winning, not by any stretch.

Drake. Laney tried not to think of him too much. It was too painful to think he was out there somewhere and that she couldn't reach him.

She had no doubt that Gedeon had him nearby. But still she didn't have Gedeon. He was moving around this world without anyone seeming to know where he was.

She frowned, thinking about that. How was he able to move so easily? He had to have more than this one hacker group keeping him hidden. Other people had to be working for him.

Or maybe countries.

Unfortunately, many countries around the globe were still working on developing the powers of the Fallen. And Gedeon was the only game in town as far as that was concerned. Was there some country out there helping hide him in exchange for Gedeon providing them with some sort of abilities or the promise of them?

Although it made her sick to her stomach, she couldn't rule it out.

The chopper set down just behind Chandler HQ, but Laney stayed where she was as everyone disembarked, just staring out the windows, lost in thought.

"Laney?"

Her head jolted up and looked over at David. The chopper had shut down, the blades moving slowly and just about to completely stop.

"You okay?" he asked.

She let out a breath. "I don't know. This one is hard."

"We'll get her back, Laney."

Everybody kept saying that, but no one knew that for sure, so Laney just gave David a nod and opened the chopper door as his phone beeped. She slipped outside and looked toward the path that led to Sharecroppers Lane. She needed to go tell her uncle and Cain. She was not looking forward to that conversation.

David walked around the chopper toward her, holding his phone out. "There's something on the news you need to see."

Laney shook her head. "What is it?"

"There's been a murder at the Vatican."

Laney frowned. "That's horrible, David, but I think we have enough on our plate right now."

"Well, I'm afraid this is something that's being added to our plate."

Laney took the phone from David's outstretched hand. "Why?"

David's mouth was a thin line. "Because the body has your name on it."

CHAPTER 84

FROM THE GRAINY PICTURE ON DAVID'S PHONE LANEY COULD TELL the priest had been stripped to the waist. Something had been written on his chest in blood, and an envelope had been attached there. She didn't want to think about how it was staying in place.

But that was not the most disturbing part of the display. The priest had been raised up high in front of St. Peter's Square and hung from an obelisk that had been brought from Egypt by Caligula. It was the only obelisk still standing since the time of the Romans. Originally situated in Caligula's garden, it was moved to its present location in 1500.

The millions of tourists who walked by it every year probably didn't know the history of the towering relic. But now as Laney stared at the macabre display in horror, she couldn't help but think this was not the first abomination the relic had seen. After all, Caligula was known for his cruelty. Apparently he was often quoted as saying, "Remember that I have the right to do anything to anybody."

And he did. He would make his senators run for miles in front of his chariot. He raped his sisters and the wives of his men. He thought nothing of ordering executions and took great pleasure

R.D. BRADY

in watching torture. He even went so far as to have himself declared a god.

His reign lasted four years, and he was arguably the cruelest of Romans leaders. He was also the first leader assassinated.

Those cruelties and Caligula's fate rolled through Laney mind as she stared at the priest pinned to the obelisk. "Who is this?"

"His name is Father Jonathan Scarf. There's not much known about him yet. I'll contact Bas and see what he knows. But it looks as if he was strung up in St. Peter's Square. And your name is written in blood on his chest."

Laney blanched at the idea. "Was it one of those cult groups?"

A number of cult and fringe groups had sprung up after the events in Egypt. Some of them were harmless, just fans of the Fallen, almost in a cosplay kind of way. But others had a much darker element to them. There'd been a few run-ins with the police and some attempts at blood drinking. But usually that was voluntary. Crossing the line to murder—and such a public murder —that was a new step.

"Don't know yet. But I don't think so. Whoever managed to get that body up there did so quickly. Only someone with certain abilities would be capable of that."

Laney closed her eyes. *Oh crap. What new hell is this?*

"I'll let you know as soon as I get more information." David paused. "Do you want me to go with you to talk to your uncle and Cain?"

Laney's gut churned. The cowardly part of her wanted someone else to break the bad news to them. But she couldn't do that. They deserved more than that.

She shook her head and turned toward the path. "No, I've got this."

CHAPTER 85

Laney walked up to the cottage from the back. Both her uncle and Cain had insisted on returning to the cottage to get it set up for Nyssa. They said they would sleep down at Dom's, but they wanted her homecoming to be here. Security ringed the cottage. Laney nodded at them as she passed.

Approaching the back gate, she could see the lights were on in the kitchen, and there was movement, which she assumed was Cain.

Laney wanted to turn tail and run. To go for a nice long run around the estate with Cleo.

But the rest of the team was back on the estate, and she didn't want Cain and Patrick finding out from anyone other than her. So she steeled her shoulders after she hopped the back fence and walked toward the door.

It was flung open before she reached it.

Cain darted outside, his eyes scanning the ground behind her. "Do you have her? Is she with you? Is she okay?"

A lump formed in Laney's throat, and it took her a moment to speak past it. "Let's head inside."

Cain's whole body went still. "Laney," he said, a word of warning in his tone.

"Inside, Cain," she said gently.

He backed into the room, keeping his gaze on her.

Patrick was just to the side of the door, and Cain stopped when he reached him blindly reaching for Patrick's hand.

Laney swallowed hard. "The directions were accurate. Molly, JW, and Nyssa were at the cabin. When we arrived, we found Molly almost immediately. She'd sent JW and Nyssa into the woods to hide. By the time we reached the cabin, they had returned as well."

Cain's shoulders sagged with relief.

And Laney hated that she had to tell the next part. She took a deep breath. "But then the angels appeared. We fought them off, but we were outnumbered. Nyssa, she darted into the trees, but she returned. And instead of running away, she called them to her."

Patrick was shaking his head. "What? Why would she do that?"

"I think she did it to protect the rest of us. As soon as they grabbed her, they took off. We gave chase, but we weren't able to catch them."

Cain shook his head too. "No. No. What are you saying?"

"I'm sorry, Cain. They have her."

Cain stared at Laney, his mouth falling open, his face crumpling before he dropped to the ground.

Laney dashed forward and managed to catch him as sobs racked his frame.

Tears rolling down his cheeks, Patrick wheeled closer and placed a hand on Cain's shuddering shoulders. Laney wanted to say something to make it better. She wanted to do something to make it better.

But all she could do was be there.

CHAPTER 86

AN HOUR LATER, LANEY SAT IN AN ADIRONDACK CHAIR IN THE backyard of her uncle and Cain's cottage. It was a quiet night, and stars filled the sky.

Cleo had just wandered off for a run with some of the other cats.

And Laney was glad. She wanted to be alone.

It had been rough with Cain and her uncle. To see Cain just collapse like that was worse than she'd imagined. She wrapped her arms around herself, wishing she could go back in time and do things differently.

A shape emerged from the darkness, and Henry walked down the path toward her.

Laney watched him approach without saying a word.

He hopped over the fence and pulled up a chair next to her. He flicked a glance at the cottage before he spoke. "How are they?"

The scene from earlier rolled through her mind again. "Devastated, terrified, angry, without hope. It was so awful, Henry."

He didn't give her the empty platitudes that everybody else had been sharing about how they'd get her back. He simply took her hand and gave it a squeeze.

And she held on to him, needing his strength right now.

Because right now she wasn't a ring bearer, and he wasn't the CEO of a billionaire corporation. They were just a brother and sister offering each other the only comfort they could. They sat quietly for a few minutes before Laney spoke. "Do you have any news?"

"Yes. We translated the message on the priest's chest."

Laney blinked. It took her a moment before she realized what he was talking about. With everything that had happened in the cottage and being so caught up in the emotion, she'd forgotten about the priest who'd been suspended above St. Peter's Square. "Translated?"

Henry nodded. "Your name was written in English. But the rest of the message was in an envelope with the body. It was a series of symbols. It was very difficult. We couldn't align them with anything or any known language.

"Finally, Danny suggested that we look at the old languages and see if anything popped up. And it did. Both he and Jen agree that the message seems to point to the Hypogeum."

The Hypogeum. Laney knew it. In fact, she'd even visited there with her uncle when she was younger. It was an ancient site in Malta. It was a 6,000-year-old burial chamber located on the island of Malta in the Mediterranean. Construction of the site had begun around 4,000 BC. The builders had been the people of Malta and Gozo, whose purpose was to ritualize life and death. Six thousand people were buried at the site, and archaeologists had found beads, amulets, intricate pottery, and carved figurines alongside the bones.

For thousands of years, aboveground structures mirrored those under the ground. By 2500, it had fallen out of use and been buried by time. It wasn't rediscovered until 1902, when construction workers burst through the ruins.

The Hypogeum even predated the Great Pyramids, at least if you went by mainstream archaeology. It was part of a series of heritage sites on the archipelago of Malta. The Hypogeum was probably the best known of all of them.

And it was also a spot that was built not just to be impressive but with special acoustic qualities. "That's where Gedeon is going to put the Arma Christi together."

"We all agree that's the most likely scenario."

Laney paused, looking at Henry. "There's more to the message, isn't there?"

Henry nodded. "He wants you to bring the spear. You can trade it for the life of Lilith."

Laney shook her head. "He's never going to give her up."

"No, he's not. It's a trap."

Laney slunk down farther in her chair. "Of course it is."

CHAPTER 87

MASSA, ITALY

GEDEON WANTED THEM IN MALTA, AND HE WANTED THE SPEAR. They all agreed he was going to get at least one of those things.

"I've got the staff working double time. We'll be wheels up in the morning. Where are we?" Jake asked as he walked into the conference room.

Laney blew out a breath. "I've got the flight plan worked out."

"But we can't agree on the spear," Henry said.

It was just the three of them in Henry's office. The estate was pulling things together for the trip. There were a few people they were waiting for that would be flying in tonight. Laney wanted to rush there right now, but she knew that would be stupid. They needed intelligence. They needed a plan. Going in unprepared would do Nyssa no good.

Jake sat down next to Henry. "Yes, the spear. We can't hand it over to him. He can want it all he likes; he can't have it."

"But it's the price for Nyssa," Henry said.

No one believed that Gedeon was going to give up Nyssa. It was simply a ploy to get Laney to bring the spearhead with her.

But that wasn't the only reason she couldn't hand it over. Legend had it that the person who possessed the spear would be victorious in battle. It was probably untrue, but Laney couldn't take that chance. "I have Danny creating a copy of the spearhead. We'll bring that. The real spear will stay in the States."

"Is that wise?" Henry asked.

Running a hand through her hair, Laney blew out a breath. "I don't know. But my gut tells me we can't hand it over. And right now my logic is tripping over itself with all the things that could happen, so I'm going with my gut."

"I think it's the right call," Jake said as his phone rang. "Speaking of which ..." He stood up, answering the phone as he headed for the door. "Go for Rogan."

"Okay, I have some levers to pull." Henry stood up and glanced out the window at the darkening sky. "I hope you're going to head home in a little bit and get some sleep."

"Oh, of course. That was next in my list," Laney said.

Henry chuckled as he headed for the door. "Well, I tried."

Laney turned and shifted her gaze to the windows. She hoped she was making the right decision about the spear. If she wasn't, Nyssa would pay the price.

A knock sounded behind her. "Are we interrupting?" David asked as he stepped in with a man who could still easily walk the catwalks of Milan if he wanted to with his lithe build and Scandinavian features.

Laney stood up, walked over, and hugged Gerard Thompson tight. "It's good to see you again, but I had hoped it was under better circumstances."

Gerard hugged her tight before looking down at her. His blue eyes were filled with concern. "Me as well. How are Cain and Patrick holding up?"

She pictured them as she'd last seen them. "They're ... holding."

"Sometimes that's all you can hope for."

"I have some more news about the Vatican murder," David said.

Laney gestured to the table. "Well, take a seat and fill me in."

"I can come back," Gerard said, stepping toward the door.

"No, actually, stay. You might be able to offer a little insight," David said.

Gerard raised his eyebrows at that but took a seat. Laney quickly recounted what little she knew of the incident and then turned to David. "What do we know about this priest?"

"From all reports, he was a good man. He joined the priesthood as soon as he was able to." David paused.

"What is it?" Laney asked.

David flicked a glance at Gerard. "I'm not sure how much stock to put into this, but he reportedly to have claimed to have been visited by an angel since he was a child."

"An angel?" Gerard asked.

David nodded. "Yes. It started when he was young, maybe five or six. His parents knew he was destined for the priesthood, his faith was so great. And they believed his visitations to be real."

"Did they ever see this angel?" Laney asked.

"No, but they say the visits changed their son."

"It was Samael, or Gedeon, as you call him," Gerard said softly.

Laney and David turned to him. "What?" Laney asked.

Gerard sat back, a pensive look on his face. "It was Gedeon who visited him. It's a technique of his. He'll visit children to mold them so he can place them in positions where he can make use of them when they're adults. I'm betting this Father Jonathan was one of his kids."

Disgust rolled through Laney, along with anger that a child would be groomed in such a way. "That's … that's immoral."

Gerard shrugged. "I thought you would have given up your view of angels as the good guys by now."

Laney thought she had too. But she supposed somewhere down deep, she still clung to the notion that there were rules the angels needed to follow. That there were lines they would not, could not cross.

But apparently she was naive.

David pushed the folder he had over to her. "That's everything I've learned so far. On that horrible note, I need to run. I promised Rahim and the kids I would be home for a family dinner tonight. And being Malta is tomorrow, I cannot disappoint them." He stood and kissed Laney on the cheek. "Try and get some sleep."

"Oh, I plan on a full eight hours."

"Liar," he said, before shaking Gerard's hand. "Good to see you again, Gerard. I'm glad you'll be with us tomorrow."

"Wouldn't be anywhere else," he replied.

Laney waited until David was out of earshot before she turned to Gerard. "Actually, there might be someplace else for you to be tomorrow instead."

CHAPTER 88

BALTIMORE, MARYLAND

"Somewhere else? Where else is more important?" Gerard asked, an eyebrow raised.

Laney had expected such a response, and part of her was still questioning whether or not it was the right one. So instead of answering his question, Laney asked her own. "How much do you remember of your time as an angel, before the fall?"

His eyes widening, Gerard sat back. "Uh, some. Flashes of things, but no full memories, the same with my past lives. Although, I have to say that the memories, they've increased some since I've been with Noriko."

"Really? You've never mentioned that."

"It's not something I talk of with anyone but her. But her, I knew her before. I was married to her before. That reconnection, I think it's the catalyst." He frowned. "Why are you asking?"

"Do you remember Gedeon?"

"I've never met him. I was what was known as a dominion. I was tasked with delivering justice in unjust situations."

"You remember that?"

THE BELIAL BLOOD

"I do. I've actually thought about the different hierarchies a lot lately. Some from each group fell. It was one-third of all the angels that fell after all. But the ones that embraced the lighter sides of humanity, they were from the powers, the virtues, the dominions, and even the thrones. The others, they were from the remaining hierarchies."

Struck by Gerard's words, Laney sat back hard, thinking them over. Was it possible that certain hierarchies were predisposed to turn against humanity while others were predisposed to help them? "Why do you think that is?"

"I've been giving that some thought as well. The seraphim and cherubim are the least human. There are a few of them who fell, but the ones who did, they do not consider humanity their equal or even worthy of their time. They came to Earth to dominate, not dwell amongst humans."

"Samyaza and Azazael."

Samyaza, yes, but Azazael, no. He was a principality. He had command over the lower angels. Like the archangels, but not to be confused with the archangels who exist outside the hierarchies. They really should have come up with a separate name. They also had limited interactions with humans. Archangels interacted long enough to deliver a message. But the powers, the virtues, the dominions, and even the thrones, our jobs were to observe, to protect. It required more interaction."

"You were infected by humanity."

Gerard smiled. "Yes, I suppose we were. Why all this interest now? What does this have to do with Gedeon?"

Max's words drifted through her mind. *The time is at hand. Old enemies will reappear. The angels will rise up. War will split the world apart. The ringbearer will determine the world's fate once again.* She swallowed. "I need an accounting of the Fallen. I need to know who is still out there and what side you think they are on. Do you know where some of them are?"

He nodded slowly. "Yes. I've been keeping track. I've lost sight of a few but not many."

"Good. And there's one in particular I need you to track down."

"Who?"

"In this lifetime, he goes by Damien Swann, but you know him as—"

"Azazael. He was the one responsible for your disappearance."

Laney nodded. "Yes. We brought him back, but the Angel Force interrupted us, and I have no idea where he went. And I haven't been able to search for him since."

"Well, you have been a little busy."

A small smile crept across Laney's face. "I always seem to be a little busy."

"You really need to strike a better work-life balance."

"Tell me about it." She rolled her eyes with a smile but then it dropped from her face. "But I need you to find him."

Gerard frowned. "Do you think he's a danger? He's just human, isn't he?"

"He is. But I still need to know where he is. And I need to make sure he's not linking up with any of the others."

Gerard frowned. "I understand your worry about Azazael, but is that really important at this moment? Can't it wait?"

It was a reasonable question. Objectively, it shouldn't matter right now. But Laney had this feeling, and it had started before Gedeon had even appeared. It had started just before she had met Azazael again.

And the feeling told her that things were heating up. Now with Max's warning, she needed to get a better lay of the land. She had been gone for five years. She didn't know where all the players were anymore. But she had a feeling Gerard did. He'd been on both sides of the fight with Samyaza. If anyone could find out what the others were up to and where they were, it was him.

"Yes. I'm afraid it's going to be very important."

CHAPTER 89

MASSA, ITALY

Lucius hurried into the kitchen as Gedeon was finishing up his lunch. "Gedeon, I think I have something."

Gedeon looked up, wiping the remains of his panini from the edges of his mouth. "What is it?"

"I sent the copies of the research from the professor to a graduate student."

Professor Peretz had absconded before he had been able to finish his work. But at the end of each work day, Lucius would take copies of everything that he had done. Which meant that while they had lost the professor, they still had the bulk of his work.

Lucius had suggested that there was enough there that someone else would be able to complete the research. Apparently in this day and age, anything could be bought for the right price. Although if he was being honest, it wasn't different from any other day and age.

"And?"

"And he's done well. He said that it took him a little while to

R.D. BRADY

understand what Peretz was getting at, but once he understood, he realized he was trying to track those blood types to specific families in the modern day. He came up with a list of twelve families that could possibly be linked."

"Twelve? That's too many." That had to be at least forty or more people, assuming there were at least four in each family. He wanted a smaller sample than that. He wanted to know who exactly was the heir.

Gedeon growled. "Tell him to keep working. We need him to narrow that down even further."

"I don't think that will be necessary." Lucius handed over a sheet of paper. "Look five names down."

Gedeon scanned the sheet, his eyes falling upon the name, and he inhaled sharply. "Victoria Chandler."

Lucius smiled. "It's Lilith."

That was true. Victoria Chandler was one of her former identities. But the name was more important than that. "That means her children are the heirs."

"Yes."

A sense of rightness rolled through Gedeon. All this time he'd been planning for this moment. He'd been setting things up, arranging them even as doubts plagued him. Had he been doing the right thing? Was this the right time?

But this was exactly the right time. Because the two bloodlines had mixed and created not just two offspring but one who was the ring bearer. If there was any confirmation he needed that his mission was righteous, this was it.

Gedeon stood up. "Prepare everyone. We'll be heading to Malta shortly."

"Yes, of course."

Then Lucius paused, turning back. "What about our guest?"

Gedeon smiled. "Those plans have already been set in motion."

CHAPTER 90

BALTIMORE, MARYLAND

SLEEP WASN'T SOMETHING THAT LANEY HAD GOTTEN MUCH OF LAST night. As she made her way down through the blast doors of Dom's bomb shelter, she blinked hard before yawning wide enough to crack her jaw.

Thank God Malta was going to be a long plane ride. She was definitely going to need to get some sleep or she was going to be useless to everyone.

I'm already useless.

She shook her head at the errant thought. Thinking that way wasn't going to help anyone. In fact, thinking that way was going to be a problem for everyone. She needed to slip out of this negative thinking trajectory she'd gotten herself on.

And she was hoping that this trip to Dom's might help do that.

Pushing through the last blast door, she walked inside. She sniffed the air and smelled bacon. Stepping into the main room, she found Dom standing next to the kitchen island, a breakfast spread next to him.

Touched by the effort he'd gone to, she smiled as she made her way over. "When did you have time to do this?"

Dom shrugged, shifting nervously. "I couldn't sleep, so I had plenty of time."

Laney peered closely at him and could see the stress around his eyes. She gently took his arm. "Are you okay, Dom? Should I call Gina?"

Dom shook his head. "I already did. She's going to come and stay while you guys are away."

Dom had made incredible strides in the last decade or so. But the re-emergence of the angels had definitely caused him to backtrack a little bit. But it was a good sign that he was the one who'd called Gina to ask for help.

"That's good."

She didn't say that everything would be all right or that they'd be back before he knew it because both of them knew those were hollow words. So instead she sniffed the air like a bloodhound. "Is that coffee?"

"Hazelnut."

One of her favorites, which Dom well knew. She grinned and walked over to the coffee pot and poured them each a mug before she sat down at the island. "And I'm starving."

Dom grinned as he grabbed plates. "Well, I can take care of that."

The two of them sat and ate, keeping the conversation light for a good ten minutes. But finally, Laney's stomach was filled, and there was no putting off the reason she had come. Wiping the edges of her mouth, she placed the napkin next to her plate and asked, "How did it go with the Inceptus?"

"I managed to replicate it. I only managed to make about four doses. If I had more time ..."

Laney shook her head. More time was not a luxury they had. Each minute that Nyssa was in Gedeon's clutches, the more worried Laney became.

The more worried all of them became.

It had been an effort not to rush right out of the estate last night and head to the airport. But cooler heads had prevailed, and they had all agreed that they needed to be prepared and not just rush in. So they'd be leaving in one hour's time.

"Four doses. That's good. How effective is it?"

"Incredibly. Think of it like the Omni on steroids. It will remove an archangel's powers."

"I know. I've seen it," she said softly, picturing Drake yet again.

She still couldn't believe that she'd seen him and that she'd been unable to find him. Knowing he was out there was killing her. But Drake could take care of himself. Or at least he used to be able to.

Nyssa, though, she was just a child. And even more than that, she was a child who would only be one for a short while longer. She needed to be the priority.

At the same time, she was hoping that when they found Gedeon and Nyssa, Drake would be there as well. That she could scoop them all up in one mission.

But she was beginning to doubt that. Gedeon was smart. He wouldn't put Drake close to them again, not after what had happened last time. That didn't mean that finding Drake wasn't important and wasn't something that she was going to make sure happened.

"I already had the samples sent up to the main house. But I would advise you to try it on someone else before you go after Gedeon, just to make sure. I'm 99.9% sure I got the chemical composition correct," Dom said.

"That won't be a problem," Laney said, picturing the individuals that Gedeon had surrounded himself with. "I'm more than happy to find a guinea pig."

CHAPTER 91

AFTER BREAKFAST WITH DOM, LANEY STOPPED BY HER UNCLE AND Cain's cottage. Although she had wanted them to stay down at Dom's, that hadn't been an argument she wanted to take up with them last night. Gina had stayed over to make sure they were fine and left early in the morning to pack a bag to stay with Dom for a few days.

Now Laney sat with Cain and her uncle at the kitchen table. Neither of them touched their food, which was quickly growing cold.

"The physical therapist is coming by today," Cain finally said. While her uncle's back had healed, it would take time and therapy before he had full use of his legs again.

"I don't want a physical therapist," her uncle argued. "Especially not today."

Laney reached out and gripped his hand. "I know you guys are worried. But there's nothing you can do right now. And you need something to help pass the time. It's going to take hours just to reach Malta. So see the physical therapist. It'll be good for you. And Nyssa would want it as well."

Patrick met her gaze and then stared down at the tabletop. "What if she's not Nyssa anymore? What if she's Lilith?"

"She's always going to be Nyssa, even when she gets her memories back. This time it's different for her. She's got all of us. She's got you two. But she wasn't Lilith at the cottage. We still have time."

"The idea of her near that man …" Cain ran a hand through his hair before tugging at its ends.

From the state of his hair, it was clear that he'd been doing that a lot over the last few hours. His eyes were also bloodshot and had bags underneath them. He hadn't even gotten out of his pajamas, which was not his way at all.

Laney didn't know what to say to either of them to make them feel better. She didn't think that there were any magic words at this particular moment. A glance at the clock made it clear that she didn't have time to find them. She stood up. "I have to get to the main house."

Cain stood up as well, but Laney walked over to her uncle and hugged him tight. Once again, she struggled with trying to come up with the right words to say. Nothing came to mind, so she simply went with what was in her heart. "I love you, Uncle Patrick."

He gripped her tightly. "I love you too."

Cain walked her out of the kitchen and down the hall.

They stopped at the front door, and Cain let out a shaky breath. "I know you've been through a lot. I know you've done a lot. But please, Laney, bring her back. Please."

Laney had no answer to that. So she just hugged him tight as well—and silently promised that she was coming back with Nyssa or she wasn't coming back at all.

CHAPTER 92

SOMEWHERE OVER EUROPE

THE PLANE STOPPED TWICE. BOTH TIMES, NYSSA TENSED, READY TO be grabbed and thrown in the back of a car. But neither time did they get off the plane. Apparently, they were just refueling stops.

In fact, no one paid any attention to her at all.

The only time one of them spoke with her was when she was brought a bag of food. The woman dropped it on the chair next to her. "Eat."

Then she'd walked away.

Nyssa was starving, so she'd dug into the food while wondering if it was even safe. She'd seen some movies and read some books where people had drugged the food they'd given their captive. But Nyssa's hunger ran over that concern.

She'd stayed awake for hours and only dozed a little here and there. But after the second fuel stop and her stomach being full, the movement of the aircraft once they had taken off again lulled her into sleep.

She jolted awake when the aircraft touched down again. Her eyes shot open as soon as she became aware of her surroundings.

Her heart began to race.

I shouldn't have done this. The thought rolled through her mind. She pictured Laney's face again just before she'd been grabbed. She'd been shocked, devastated.

Nyssa's stomach curled at the memory. At the same time, Nyssa knew that there had been no other choice.

All those people had come to help her, to save her, and they were getting hurt. Some of them could have been killed for all she knew.

There had been no other choice. She'd done what needed to be done.

Her uncle Patrick and father had already been hurt because these people had come after her. That wasn't going to change.

The door to the aircraft opened, and Nyssa could swear the whole craft shuddered as a man stepped on board.

In fact, 'man' didn't seem like the right word. He was huge, like some sort of Greek god stepping out of a book. He walked down the aisle of the plane toward her, his shoulders almost wider than the aisle.

Nyssa sat up straighter, pushing herself back in her seat as if she could somehow disappear into it.

The man kept his gaze straight on her, making it clear he wasn't going to let her disappear. He walked toward her, and Nyssa couldn't pull her gaze away, even though everything inside of her was screaming that she needed to run.

But there was nowhere to run to.

Her mouth went dry as he stopped in the aisle next to her chair and stared down at her. She had to crane her neck to look up at him.

"Lilith," he said softly.

Nyssa swallowed hard, trying to get a little moisture back in her mouth. Why did they keep calling her that? She wasn't Lilith. Then another darker thought rolled through her mind. What would happen when he realized she wasn't this Lilith? Nevertheless, she took the chance to clear this all up.

"I'm not Lilith. My name's Nyssa."

The man shook his head. "You don't know yet who you are." He leaned down, and Nyssa leaned farther away. "But I'm going to help you remember."

CHAPTER 93

BALTIMORE, MARYLAND

A QUICK STOP BACK AT HER COTTAGE TO GRAB THE BAG SHE'D PUT together late last night and then she was heading up to the main cottage.

Cleo joined her when she was halfway up the long flowered path. She slipped in from between two Douglas firs and brushed up against her for a moment as she started in the same direction.

Laney glanced down at her. "You ready for this?"

A sense of excitement ran through Cleo. *Yes.*

Laney understood the feeling. Cleo had been out of the action for a while now. And she wanted a taste of it again.

They didn't have a lot of soldiers that they could bring with them. So they were bringing as many cats as possible.

Perhaps it would give them an edge. After all, she doubted Gedeon was planning on a feline force. There'd be six of them joining them.

Laney reached the top of the path, and the back of the estate spread out in front of her.

A few people milled around on the veranda, but Laney just cut around the side toward the front.

She spied Max standing, talking to Mateo and his daughter over by one of the vans. Quickly scanning the group, she saw the other members of the Fallen Force, as they'd taken to calling themselves.

Jen and Henry were arranging people over by another of the vans. Jake was talking quietly to Mary Jane. Molly and JW were just coming up the main drive from Sharecroppers Lane.

Henry caught sight of her and headed over. "Hey. Come to see us off?" she asked.

"No." Henry's cool blue eyes focused on her green ones. "I'm going with you."

Laney was already shaking her head before he finished speaking. "No. Jen's coming. And you both can't—"

Henry took a step forward, his large frame towering over Laney, forcing her to look up at him.

"This is not up for debate, Laney. I've been sitting on the sidelines, and I have no intention of doing that again. You, me, and Jake, we started this together. It doesn't feel right for one member of the triad to not be part of this. Maybe that's why we're struggling. But I'm not sitting this one out. I'm going with you."

Determination was stamped across his face, and Laney knew that there was no talking him out of it. They may not look a lot alike but they both had that streak of stubbornness.

He continued. "My kids are in danger, Laney. I need to do everything in my considerable power to keep them safe."

Henry obviously was not going to be swayed from his decision. "I could order you to stay back," she said softly. She'd never used that ability on Henry.

"You could. But that would only last as long as you could see me. And as soon as it wore off, I'd be coming after you. It's not right me sitting out, Laney."

THE BELIAL BLOOD

"But what about Tori and Witt? Wouldn't it be better for you to stay here and keep them safe?"

"Along with Jen, they are the loves of my life. And I would do anything to protect them. And this is part of protecting them. We need to get a handle on this situation. And we need as many bodies as we can. And right now we don't have a lot of powered individuals. You need me, Laney. You know you do."

More than anything, she wanted to argue with him. She wanted to keep him back. She wanted to keep him safe.

But he was right. She was worried that the small force they had wouldn't be enough. And every extra soldier would make a difference. She was also worried that even with all of this, they still would fail.

And she worried about what that could mean for the world.

Placing her hands on her hips, she craned her neck to look her brother fully in the face. "Don't you dare get killed ... again."

He reached down and hugged her tight. "You either, little sister."

CHAPTER 94

A DIRECT ROUTE TO MALTA WASN'T GOING TO WORK WITH THEIR plan. They needed to do at least one stopover to refuel. They could wait until Malta, but Laney and the others all agreed that it would be better if they were able to leave Malta as quickly as possible if that became necessary. So they didn't want to have to waste time refueling the plane if they could avoid it.

Where to stop had been a matter that was greatly debated. They didn't have any sort of authorization from any world government for what they were about to do. Of course, in the past, they never got authorization for the things they were about to do. It took too long to explain to bureaucracies what needed to be done. By the time information ran up the levels of command, windows of opportunity had closed.

Besides, Laney often viewed the acts of the Fallen as something that sat outside of country borders. Countries, she'd come to realize, were just artificial lines created on a map. In reality, they didn't really mean anything, especially not to the Fallen. So as she still wasn't clear on who was friendly toward them and who was against them, they all agreed it was better to work under the

THE BELIAL BLOOD

assumption that it was better to beg forgiveness than ask permission.

There was a slight bump as the plane touched down at Lausanne Airport. It was located on the middle of the northern end of Lake Geneva in Switzerland. Most people had been asleep when they touched down, and the cabin stirred restlessly.

Laney stood up, and Cleo did the same, raising her butt in the air and doing the panther version of downward dog. "Come on, girl. You can go have a run. But stay away from the building, and stay in the shadows, okay? Keep the others in the shadows as well."

I will, Cleo said before heading down the aisle.

Most people looked like they needed to stretch their legs as well. But there wasn't much conversation. Everyone was subdued, and the cabin was quiet.

Laney skirted around the few people who'd stood and nodded at David as she slipped out the door with Cleo. The two of them moved to the far end of the runway and waited for the rest of the cats. Laney looked across the group. There were six of them, including Cleo and Zaria. Most had come from the estate. In fact, there was only one cat left on the estate: Tiger, Dom's cat. Tiger had become an emotional support cat, and it was too much to ask Dom to let Tiger go.

Her gut clenched at the idea of them being put in harm's way, especially Cleo. They were the last of their kind. And the world would be lost without them. But Amar Patel had tried to play God. And she wouldn't do the same. When these wonderful creatures passed on from this world, their kind would be no more. And she would have to accept that.

Another item on the long line of things she must accept.

Laney looked out at the cats now. "You stay in the shadows. Don't go near any humans. They don't know we're here, and we don't want to let them know we're here, okay?"

She knew they all understood what she was saying.

Cleo turned to each of them, giving them a look much like a mother warning her kids to behave. And then she darted toward the grass. The rest of the cats fell in line behind her.

Laney watched them go until they slipped into the shadows and she couldn't see them.

Henry, Jen, and David stepped out of the plane and were talking quietly. Jake stepped out of the other plane and headed over toward them, but there was no urgency or concern on his face. It looked like he was just looking for a little companionship.

Laney, however, wasn't. Stuffing her hands into the pockets of her jacket, she walked along the runway. Her gaze drifted toward the eastern end of Lake Geneva. The city of Geneva was located there. She and Drake had spent two nights there once, a lifetime ago. Laney had had meetings with some people from both the Red Cross and the UN, both of which were headquartered in the beautiful city.

She loved the look of Geneva. It was surrounded by the Alps on one side and the Jura Mountains on the other. It sat in the valley in between the two. It was a financial center and held an array of international organizations.

The UN should have been a place that Laney could have gone for help throughout the years. But like many other large and unwieldy organizations, it had become mired down in bureaucratic red tape. The good it could do was hampered by restrictions, by guidelines, and by the public perception of its actions.

Laney understood how these organizations could have their original intent subverted by the realities of modern life. It only made it clear that for certain endeavors, it was best to play it close to the chest and not invite in all of these others.

Speaking of which ...

Laney turned and headed back toward the hangar, a light breeze ruffling her hair.

Jake jogged toward her from the plane. "We've got headlights."

Laney looked in the direction he was pointing. Sure enough, there was a set of three vehicles heading toward them.

"Any problems?" Laney asked.

Jake shook his head. "No. They have the proper verifications. It's them."

"Let's get everyone back in the plane. I don't want them knowing who we've got until we're sure."

Jake paused for a moment. "I'm going to move half into the hangar just in case."

Laney smiled. "Always so trusting Jake."

Jake snorted. "Yeah, well, our best laid plans have a habit of going sideways," he said before he jogged back to the others.

You're not wrong, my friend, she thought as she turned toward the grass. *Cleo, keep the cats away. We've got company.*

We'll be watching, Cleo responded.

Laney smiled. Then she turned and headed toward the lights.

As she approached, she could better make out the type of vehicles heading toward them. One was a Mercedes SUV; the other two were large military trucks.

Laney stopped on the runway, her arms crossed over her chest, her legs braced as the vehicles headed toward her. Above her, clouds shifted as she prepared just in case Jake was right and this plan went sideways.

The vehicles stopped when they were twenty feet away.

One of the occupants slipped out of the back of the Mercedes. They stepped forward into the spotlight.

Nancy Harrigan, former secretary of state and current secretary general of the United Nations, smiled at Laney. "It's good to see you again, Dr. McPhearson."

CHAPTER 95

Laney walked with Nancy along the edge of the runway, away from the trucks and from Laney's group after she gave the all-clear to Jake.

Neither Laney nor Nancy spoke for a moment as they walked. Nancy had been the first person Laney had seen after she'd woken up from the events in Egypt. The two of them had kept in touch over the years, barring Laney's little trip through time.

Nancy broke the silence. "I saw that you were back. I don't suppose you'd care to share where you've been?"

"I'm afraid that's a longer story than what we have time for."

"I had a feeling it might be. I brought you some presents."

"Gifts?"

"Of a sort."

Nancy raised her hand, and uniformed soldiers started pouring out of the back of the trucks.

"How many?"

"Twenty. But they are the best of the best."

Laney had contacted Nancy to see if there was any information she could provide her on Gedeon. The two of them had talked on and off over the last couple of days, although she hadn't shared that with anyone except Jake.

The soldiers that disembarked from the trucks looked fit and ready for battle. But this would be a battle unlike any they had ever experienced. "And you sure they're up for this?"

"As much as anyone is. After the events in Egypt, the world has been trying to find the Omni, but not all of us are focused on that. We know that even without the Omni, we're going to need fighters who can protect the world should the threat of the Fallen rise again."

She paused for a moment. "And it has risen again, hasn't it?"

"Not exactly, but it looks the same."

Nancy met her gaze and then nodded, accepting the answer, at least for now. "They've been trained to fight the Fallen. We use robots and drones to simulate the Fallen's moves. They are good and fast, but this will be their first field exercise. I assure you, though, if there's anyone that has the capability to take on the Fallen, it's this group."

Henry and Jake were organizing the soldiers, divvying them up into different planes. Laney watched for a moment, assessing each of the their soldiers. They looked strong, capable. "Do they know what they're heading into?"

"We've all watched the recordings of Gedeon. They've been asking to do something."

Enthusiasm was good, but it also could be a problem. "And the command structure?"

"Captain Lindsay Graf is in charge, but she understands that you are the one calling the shots. She will follow your orders, and so will the others. They've been taught about you. They know who you are. I'm afraid some of them might even have a little bit of hero worship going on."

Laney cringed at the idea, but at the same time, she recognized that that might come handy. "I wouldn't have asked for the help if we didn't need it."

"I know. And the fact that you asked makes me concerned that this problem is bigger than we realize."

"Not yet. But it will be if we don't nip it in the bud. We need to stop Gedeon, and we need to stop him now."

"And can you do that?"

Laney thought of the Inceptus carefully contained in the small container in her pocket. "I hope so."

CHAPTER 96

VALETTA, MALTA

THE COTTAGE WAS SET ALONG A CLIFF SIDE THAT OVERLOOKED THE bluest water Nyssa had ever seen. Her window was right along the cliff's edge, overlooking the water below.

Nyssa was pretty sure they weren't doing it to give her an awesome view but because the drop outside her window was about 300 feet straight down to the rocks below.

Being able to look out at the water, though, did make her feel a little bit better. She wasn't sure where they were. No one had given her the tour.

After the terrifying meeting on the plane, the man called Gedeon had turned his back on her and ordered the others to bring her. She'd been carted out of the plane and taken to a waiting SUV.

Then they'd driven through the quiet streets to this cottage. She'd been brought inside last night and shown to her room, and then no one had come back to see her.

She'd paced along the edge of the room for hours, waiting for what she was sure was going to be something horrible, but no one came. Eventually she fell asleep curled up in the corner of the room with some blankets.

The dawn light had awoken her.

And now she could hear footsteps heading toward the room. She tensed as the door opened. A man walked in carrying a tray and placed it on the table over by the window. Then he stepped back outside.

Gedeon immediately took his place in the doorway, making it seem tiny in comparison. He even had to turn slightly sideways to fit through.

Nyssa swallowed hard, backing up against the wall.

Gedeon smiled. "You have nothing to fear from me, child. Come have breakfast."

Nyssa looked around for an escape, but all that was behind her was the rough stone wall.

"I am trying to be polite. Do not test me."

Nyssa swallowed, jamming her hands behind her back so the man couldn't see how badly they were shaking as she walked over to the table.

Gedeon smiled as he held out a chair for her.

Nyssa stepped into her place, and as he pushed it forward, she nodded. "Thank you."

"You are most welcome, Lilith." He took his seat across from her.

Despite her fear, the breakfast looked delicious. It was simple: just eggs, croissants, and fruit, but her stomach growled in response. She hadn't eaten since the plane, and that had been hours and hours ago.

"Please don't wait on me. I know you must be hungry." Gedeon placed his napkin in his lap.

Nyssa hesitated as the same worries that she'd had about drugged food flashed through her mind, but once again, her stomach overrode her concerns. She started to eat.

The raspberries were absolutely delicious. They practically melted in her mouth. Her uncle would absolutely love them.

The thought of Uncle Patrick turned her stomach a little bit, and she slowed down her consumption. God, she hoped she was all right. He had to be all right.

"Do you remember me?" Gedeon asked.

Nyssa shook her head. "No."

The man sighed. "I had heard that this was what became of you each lifetime. But we have never met when you've been in your child state. It is unusual."

Nyssa wasn't sure what to say to that. She had absolutely no idea what the man was talking about. So, she simply continued to eat.

"Do you really not remember anything of your former lives?"

The hand that she'd been raising to her mouth paused in midair before Nyssa continued its journey toward her mouth. "No."

Gedeon leaned forward. "Your hesitation suggests that is not true. I think it is clear that we are not equal in power. Do not make me threaten you to get you to answer my question."

The words were said in an almost conversational tone, but they were terrifying nonetheless. Because he was right. There was no competition between the two of them. It would be like competition between an ant and a human.

"I have dreams. I don't know what they're about, but I think they might be about me from different times."

Gedeon sat back in his chair, nodding. "Yes, that makes sense. As you get closer to your awakening, the memories are beginning to seep through."

As much as the man terrified her, Nyssa also got the feeling he knew a great deal about who she was. Her father and uncle knew a great deal as well. But they were keeping it from her. Gedeon here looked like he didn't want to keep anything back. "Who do you think I am?"

"I do not merely think. I *know* who you are. You are Lilith, the mother of all. You have been on this planet longer than anyone. You are reborn time and time again. But for the first thirteen years, you have no memory of those past lives, a small gift from the Creator. And then when you turn thirteen, your memories return."

Nyssa reared back in her chair. "Lilith? But she's a demon."

Gedeon chuckled. "No, Lilith is no demon. That is what the humans told one another to create a fear of her. She is a human, and quite a resilient one. She determined that humans would become mortal rather than the immortal beings they were originally created to be. And for that decision, she must live each life over and over again with the knowledge of all the lives that came before."

Nyssa stared at him, wanting to believe he was crazy. Reincarnation, she knew, was real. But she couldn't possibly be this Lilith. She was just Nyssa, boring plain Nyssa.

"You're trying hard not to believe me. But somewhere down deep you know I'm telling the truth."

Nyssa stared at the man across from her.

Even though he was being polite, she could feel the edge of violence that surrounded him. She also got the feeling that he knew her very well. "And did you know this Lilith, I mean, I guess, me?"

Gedeon nodded. "Yes. We have crossed paths many times in your former lives. It is almost as if destiny keeps pushing us together."

The tone of his voice sent chills down Nyssa back. That was crazy creepy. "I don't remember any of that."

"Yes, unfortunately I believe that. But somewhere down deep you know that what I speak is true."

Nyssa didn't want to think about it because she had the feeling he was right. "What do you want from me?"

"Oh, a great deal, but that is a conversation for another time. Once you have grown. For now, I will settle for this."

Before Nyssa could even move, he snatched her hand, pulling her forward. Knife in his hand, he sliced a cut just below her wrist. She cried out in pain as blood welled up and dripped from her arm.

Before any of it could splash on the table, Gedeon slid a glass underneath it, catching all of the bright red liquid.

He smiled. "Your blood is more precious than gold. And I intend to grow rich from it."

Nyssa stared at her blood dripping into the cup. And then looked at the man sitting across from her.

A combination of desire and crazy seemed to roll through his eyes, and she knew she'd made a horrible mistake.

CHAPTER 97

When they were thirty minutes outside of Malta, Danny announced that Gedeon was already there. Laney had figured that was the case, but she had hoped to beat him there. As a result, they discussed the plans in flight and hit the ground running.

This was not Laney's first trip to Malta. She'd been here as a child, two years after her parents had passed away. Her uncle was visiting a colleague who was aiding in a dig there. She didn't recall much of it except for the incredible blue of the water. It was like a land carved out of time. She remembered sitting high up on a cliff, and looking out over the water, she'd felt a peace that had been missing for a long time.

She also remembered the people being incredibly warm and welcoming. In fact, the island's reputation for hospitality extended back to St. Paul, who'd been shipwrecked on the island back in the first century of the Common Era. Unsurprisingly, Roman Catholicism was a large influence on the island.

Malta was an island in the Maltese archipelago in the Mediterranean. It was made up of five islands: Malta, Gozo, Comino, and the two uninhabited islands of Cominotto and Filfla. EU's smallest member state was located ninety miles south of Sicily and 186 miles east of the African continent.

The island chain that constituted Malta was a critical location, and its governance had changed hands many times over its history. The Phoenicians, Romans, Greeks, Arabs, Normans, Sicilians, Swabians, Hospitallers, French, and British had all claimed the archipelago at one point or another. The last was Britain. The Maltese people were recognized for their incredible bravery under the onslaught of both Germany and Italian bombardments in World War II. The island was devastated. In 1962, it declared its independence and joined the Commonwealth.

Valetta, the capital city of Malta, sat on the eastern end of the main island, in between Marsamxett Harbor and Grand Harbor. It was the first modern planned city in all of Europe, and one of the smallest. It had been created by a Catholic order, the Knights of St. John, back in the 1500s. The city was littered with museums, palaces, and ornate churches. The baroque style was apparent in the city architecture.

The Hypogeum's series of underground alcoves and corridors were carved into soft limestone just three miles from Valetta. The builders expanded existing caves, and over the centuries excavated deeper, creating a temple, cemetery, and funeral hall.

The closeness of the site to a heavily populated area gave Laney more than a little pause. With the speed of the Fallen, that meant that the battle could rage for miles in an instant. The entire city center could be affected.

But there was no help for it. If they evacuated the city, it would let Gedeon know they were there.

Nonetheless, she'd sent ahead some of their people to start quietly emptying out some of the closest businesses and homes. It was a small comfort to know that they would be out of their way, but she had to at least try.

Laney stood now on a cliff with binoculars to her eyes as she looked toward the Hypogeum. There were two individuals standing at the door. They had to be Gedeon's people.

She was too far away to sense them, but she knew from Danny's retrieval of the airport recordings that they could have at least six people with them plus Nyssa. Her stomach clenched as she pictured Nyssa on the film. She'd looked so scared.

She lowered the binoculars, and Jen did the same next to her.

"Two guards. No others have been spotted yet. Danny's till trying to track down where they're holed up. Is there any chance they don't know we're here?" Jen asked.

Laney shook her head. "No. Gedeon sent us a damn invitation. He's expecting us. Which means there's got to be more than six. They're somewhere spread out, probably looking for us."

"So what's the plan?" Jen asked.

Laney stared over at the Hypogeum. Gedeon was waiting for her. He wanted her there. Best not to disappoint the man.

"I guess we're going straight in. But first we have to conduct a little experiment."

David had caught sight of one of Gedeon's men doing a patrol a little farther out from the Hypogeum.

Laney had her people spread out, creating a loose net around the man, although they kept their distance so as to not let him know where they were.

She patted the pocket where she held the Inceptus. She needed to know before she faced Gedeon whether or not it worked. She couldn't chance going in there and using it and having it fail.

The existence of the Inceptus made her wonder. Why did Gedeon need the Arma Christi if he already had the Inceptus? Could the Inceptus kill an angel? Or just weaken them? She supposed the fact that Cristela was still alive answered that question. Gedeon wanted more than a long life for someone.

THE BELIAL BLOOD

"He's heading toward you." Mateo's voice was quiet over the earpiece.

"Roger. Move forward, but stay out of range," Laney ordered.

"Will do," came the quick reply.

Jen stood twenty yards away and gave Laney a nod.

Laney tapped the mic at her throat. "Jen and I are going in. The rest of you start to move the circle in slowly. But whatever happens, do not let him escape. He cannot let Gedeon know we're here yet."

The rest of the team clicked their mics to show they understood.

Laney blew out a breath and then emerged from her hiding spot. She kept her pace, unhurried as she strode forward. Jen kept parallel to her. They crested a small hill together as Laney felt the tingles of recognition roll over her.

The man walking up the ancient path stopped, narrowing his eyes. He was a small man, only about five foot six with dark hair and sun-touched skin. But despite his small stature, Laney could feel the power radiating off him.

In a flash, he burst from his spot toward her. Laney tensed and then called on the wind. The gale force shoved against him, pushing him back and back again as Jen burst in from the side and slammed into him, throwing him up in the air.

Henry burst in from the other side, grabbed hold of the man, and slammed him into the dirt.

Jen rushed to Henry's side, holding the man down as well. Lou burst out of nowhere and added her strength.

Laney darted forward, pulling the syringe from her pocket as she did. She slid to a stop at the man's side and jabbed the needle into the back of his thigh.

"Let go of me!" He bucked, writhing under their grips.

"Keep a hold of him!" Jen yelled.

Laney called on the wind again, shoving it down against the man and helping hold him in place.

The man grunted, still struggling. But Laney could feel that those struggles were weakening. Her gaze jolted to Jen, whose eyes widened, and then she grinned. But none of them released their hold.

It was only seconds before the man's movement became practically nonexistent. The hold of the others was keeping him firmly in place.

Laney tensed, knowing this was the moment of truth. She released the wind first and then nodded at Lou. "Back away."

Lou hesitated for a second and then lifted her arms, stepping back. Jake, who'd run over while they'd been holding the man down, kept his gun aimed at the prone figure.

Laney turned to Henry and Jen. "Your turn, Henry."

He released the man as Jen grabbed the man's arm and bent it behind his back. The man let out a cry. Laney took that as a good sign.

Jen hauled the man up. He winced as his arm was held behind his back painfully.

"Well, how do you want to test this?" Jen asked.

"Like this." Laney threw a hook at the man's chin.

His head jolted to the side from the blow, and Jen had to support him to keep him standing up. When his head turned back to Laney, blood seeped from the corner of his mouth.

In the fights with the other angels, none of them had made them bleed. She looked at Jen and smiled slowly. "It worked."

CHAPTER 98

NYSSA SAT IN THE CORNER ROCKING, HER ARM CURLED UP TO HER chest. The white bandage stood out against her pale skin, and she stared at it again, a shudder running through her as she remembered that man taking her blood.

After he had enough, he'd carefully placed a cloth napkin over the wound, holding it until it had stopped bleeding. He'd had one of the others come in and bandage it up. Then he'd left without a word.

She stared at her arm, wondering what kind of craziness was going through the man's head. Why on earth would he want her blood?

He had to be insane. There was no other explanation.

That would be a change. The Fallen were always powerful, but she'd never got the sense that they were unstable. But this guy, he was straight-up nuts. Even though part of her thought that it was possible about the past lives, she couldn't possibly be Lilith.

When she'd first been taken and that man had first called her Lilith, she never made the connection. After all, why would she? Lilith was a demon, at least that was what she found when she did her research.

R.D. BRADY

She'd overheard her dad and uncle talking about her one day, and they'd clammed up as soon as she walked into the room. So as soon as she'd a moment, she'd gone and looked her up. She was supposed to have been the first wife of Adam, before Eve. Nyssa had never heard that before. But then Lilith had refused to stay married to Adam, and Adam had taken on Eve.

Lilith had then been cast out and was the demon who crept into baby's rooms at night and killed them. How on earth could anyone think that she was Lilith?

Her legs ached, as did her arm, although the legs were from staying crouched in the corner for so long. She stood up, stretching them out. Pins and needles shot down her thighs as the blood rushed through them.

She needed to get out of here. She couldn't just stay and wait for the others. This had been such a colossal mistake.

The door opened, and she whirled, her hand going to her throat.

"Ah, good," Gedeon said, "you're awake. You need to come with me."

For a brief moment, Nyssa thought about arguing and resisting. But one look at the size of Gedeon and it was clear that all that would do was anger him. Being he'd already bled her when he *wasn't* angry at her, she didn't want to find out what he would do when he was, so she crossed the room toward him.

With a nod, he stepped outside into the hall, and she followed him through. She hadn't gotten a good look at where they were staying the night before. She'd been rushed into the room, and then the door had been closed behind her.

Now she could tell the cottage was bigger than she realized. It had another three bedrooms that they passed. The walls were still that rough stone, suggesting that it was incredibly old.

Gedeon stepped out into the main room. Through a doorway, she could see a small quaint kitchen that overlooked the cliff.

The living room had only two small windows that looked out

THE BELIAL BLOOD

onto a barren rock face. There were no neighbors or other houses anywhere to be seen. Her hopes plummeted. She'd had a vague plan of maybe yelling and attracting attention. But she wouldn't be able to yell loud enough to attract anyone's attention way out here.

Her shoulders slumped as the direness of her situation hit home again.

Gedeon was unaware of the thoughts in her head, or perhaps unconcerned about them, as he moved to a long table across the room. He waved Nyssa over, as she'd stopped at the entrance of the room. "Come here. You need to touch these."

Nyssa frowned as she made her way over, worried about what she would see on the tabletop. But there was nothing gross there. There was a huge box of sand. A couple of branches, plus a couple of other small metal pieces. She frowned, looking between each of them. "Why?"

"Because I want to see if you can sense their power."

Nyssa had no idea what he was talking about. And Gedeon apparently was done waiting for her because he grabbed her arm, his hand squeezing the injury from earlier, and she winced in pain. But he didn't notice or didn't care. He plunged her hand into the sand.

She tensed, waiting for something, but there was nothing. Her hand was completely submerged in the sand, and it felt like any other sand. She shook her head. "It doesn't feel like anything."

Gedeon frowned. He pointed at the small pieces of wood. "Try that."

Not wanting him to grab her again, she gripped the wood and waited for a beat. But just like with the sand, there was nothing. "No."

With a growl he indicated the nails and then some small slivers of wood.

Nyssa went through each of them, picking them up and holding them for a long moment, concentrating, but she got nothing off of them. She wasn't even sure what exactly she was supposed to be sensing, feeling, or looking for. They felt like the inanimate objects they were.

She took a tentative step back from the table after she'd touched the last object. "I don't know what you want. But I don't feel anything in any of those."

Gedeon sighed. "I was afraid of that. Until you come into your memories, I think those senses are blocked off. I had hoped that perhaps exposing you to them might bring them to light. But that is not to be. Which means you are of no use to me."

Nyssa's eyes widened, and she took another step back.

But Gedeon ignored her. He turned to the two individuals who had followed them into the room. "Take her back to the room and keep her there. We'll be leaving for the site immediately."

CHAPTER 99

The Inceptus had worked. The man was no more powerful than a regular human now.

Jen trussed him up and carted him back to the jeep, where she secured him with chains in the back of it. They had tried to ask him questions, but he'd refused to answer.

And they didn't have the time that it would take to get answers out of him. Besides, no one had a yearning for torture, so they were just going to make sure he couldn't alert Gedeon.

But Laney couldn't help the feeling of exultation that rolled through her. They had this. If she could just get close enough to Gedeon to stab him, then all of this could be over.

Because while she might not be willing to kill the man that was now wrapped in chains, she had no such reservations when it came to Gedeon. That man needed to be wiped from the earth. Nothing good could come from his continued existence.

Even in her own mind, it sounded bloodthirsty. But she couldn't help but remember all of the damage that Samyaza had done. If they had managed to take Samyaza off the board earlier, they would have avoided a lot of heartache and possibly a lot of international conflict.

The international community was just starting to become aware of Gedeon. And the sooner she nipped this in the bud the better. That was no doubt what had spurred Nancy into providing her with the troops with few questions asked.

Two of them would stay behind with their new prisoner while the rest would join them in taking on Gedeon. So far, Laney hadn't gotten any pushback from any of them. They all seemed to be willing to follow her orders. Some even seemed to appreciate being able to follow her orders.

Now she had the rest of the UN people and her own people positioned around the Hypogeum, along with the cats. There had been no sign of Gedeon. And they weren't sure where exactly on the island he was.

But she had no doubt he would be heading here soon.

She worried for a moment about him sensing them, but the reality was he'd invited her here. Surprise wasn't really an option in this particular situation. The best she could do was have her people stay aware and notify her as soon as something happened.

But there was one piece of the puzzle that she hadn't been able to figure out yet. She tapped the mic at her throat. "Has anyone seen any sign of Drake?"

Danny answered. "Nothing yet, Laney. But I've got all the cameras on the island at my disposal, and I've even managed to tap into quite a few cell phones. I'm constantly running surveillance to see where Gedeon and his people are. When I find them, I'll let you know."

Laney nodded. "Okay. Thanks."

She released the button and stared out over the bright blue waters. *Where are you, Drake?*

CHAPTER 100

MASSA, ITALY

Hours after Lucius had left, their fight rang through Drake's mind. If Lucius was right, the angels were heading for a civil war. What was Gedeon thinking? He was basically leading a rebellion, the same rebellion that Samyaza had led. Had it really come to this?

The scuffle of a shoe pulled his attention back to the here and now. The boy sat in the corner of the room, his arms wrapped around his knees. His knees were scuffed and there was more dirt along his calves. He'd been so quiet while Drake got lost in thought.

"I have been horrible company today." Titling his head to the side, Drake studied the boy's body. He wasn't sure if he was imagining it or not, but he seemed to look even thinner. "Are they feeding you?"

The boy sniffed. "A little."

Rolling his hands into fists, Drake pictured plunging one of them through Gedeon's face. Why would they go to all this trouble just to hurt a child? It was inhuman.

Although he supposed so was Gedeon.

In the Bible, in most religions, and even in just popular culture, angels had taken on a sweet, caring persona. Drake had laughed out loud the first time he'd seen what Michelangelo thought Nephilim looked like. They were the ones closest to God and were the least "cuddly" of all the angels, which was saying something.

But that perception of angels as helpers persisted. But that wasn't who they truly were. They were the soldiers of God carrying out his orders and dictates. There was little laughter in that life, little caring. And Drake, at one point, had been the top soldier.

He wasn't sure what his role was anymore. He wasn't sure what any of their roles truly were anymore. Gedeon certainly seemed to be going off script by a wide margin.

Drake wished he had some food to give the boy, but he wasn't given much either. Occasionally they remembered. He supposed they hoped that it would help keep him even weaker, and if he was being honest, it was helping.

But they had to allow him a little bit of strength or else the sigils would have no effect. It was a delicate balance, one he hoped he would be able to exploit at some point to his benefit. "I'm sorry you're going through all of this. I wish I could help you."

Arturo shrugged, not meeting his gaze. "It's not your fault. It's that big man's. He's horrible."

"Yes, he is."

"But at least he's gone for a little while."

Drake's eyes narrowed, his whole body going still. "What do you mean he's gone? I thought he was supposed to return."

Arturo nudged his chin toward the door. "He did, but then he left again. And some of the others, they left too."

Drake frowned. "Did you hear them say anything? Where they were going or anything like that?"

Arturo shook his head. "No, nothing like that."

Drake frowned. What was going on? He hadn't seen Gedeon in days, but that seemed normal.

But he'd expected Gedeon to keep him close at all times. He was surprised he would leave him entrusted in the care of the others, especially given what had happened last time he'd done so.

Which meant whatever had called him away was important.

Drake walked to the very edge of his circle, careful to stay within its boundaries. He crouched down so he was eye level with the boy. "You must have overheard something. A country, a city, some word that they used to describe what was happening. Maybe a name?"

His face lit up at the last question. "A name. I did hear a name. It was um, Lizette. Or Lily. Something like that. Yeah, he was going to get someone named Lily."

"Was it Lilith?"

"Oh yeah, that was it."

Drake's mouth fell open. Lilith. Gedeon had always been obsessed with Lilith. He'd forgotten about that, and it was only Arturo's mentioning of her name that brought it back.

But she wasn't Lilith. Not yet. She was too young. She was still a child.

The small amount of food in his stomach rose into his throat at the thought of Gedeon getting his clutches on Nyssa. He could still picture her as a beautiful little baby.

He'd never really cared much for babies. But there had been something about Nyssa that had just pulled him in. It was spending time with her that made him wonder about whether or not a child might actually be something he'd want at some point in the future.

"Did they say anything else?"

The boy reared back, and Drake forced himself to lighten his tone. "Anything would help. Did they say where they were going or whether they would be coming back?"

Arturo shook his head slowly. "No, but I got the impression

that they already had Lilith and that Gedeon was going to meet them somewhere. And then there was something about ... I mean, I don't know if this is right, but I think they were talking about Delaney McPhearson."

Drake forced himself to stay calm. "What did they say about her?"

"That they were going to use Lilith or something to get her to come to them? I'm not really sure. But they seemed to think that it would be something that would draw her out."

Drake's heart raced. They were going after Laney. He couldn't let that happen. He looked toward the door, knowing that they would be coming in soon to give him his injection. Drake leaned forward. "Arturo, I'm going to need your help. Do you think you could help me?"

Arturo glanced at the door and then nodded slowly.

Drake smiled. "Good. Here's what we're going to do."

CHAPTER 101

VALETTA, MALTA

Danny's voice broke through the headset. "We've got movement."

Laney's head jolted up. She'd nearly fallen asleep waiting.

Gedeon must have known one of his people had been grabbed, and yet he'd made no move. He'd stayed hidden. But it looked like that time was now over.

"Where?"

"Heading to the Hypogeum at a fast clip," Danny replied. "They're not even trying to hide what they are."

Worry gnawed at Laney's gut. This was all so out in the open. She worried about what that meant, but she supposed she was just used to the fallen angels, who for eons had kept their existence relegated to the shadows. Apparently, Gedeon felt no such compunction.

"Nyssa or Drake? Is there any sign of them?"

"No sign of Drake yet. And Nyssa isn't with them. They stopped long enough for me to see that. They're not bringing her to the Hypogeum."

No. Laney closed her eyes. They had planned on getting Nyssa at the Hypogeum, but if they didn't bring her, then what should they do? Were they holding her back as some sort of leverage?

"Hold on a sec," Danny said.

Vague muttering from Danny was all she heard for another minute or two. "Okay. I've checked the direction from where they were coming. There are six houses up that way, five are grouped together, and one is set far off on its own, right at the cliff's edge. That has to be where they're keeping Nyssa."

Laney nodded. It was a guess but a pretty good one. And they needed to get Nyssa safe. And maybe Drake was there too.

Right now, her priority had to be getting Nyssa back and stopping Gedeon. Which meant they needed to check it out.

"Any way to tell if Nyssa's inside the cottage?"

"No. But that seems to be the only place they could have been. We've already checked out their plane at the airport."

Laney frowned. She turned to David. "Looks like you're up."

David grinned. "About time. I don't like sitting on the bench."

"Just get her back."

"We will."

"You know the plan?" she asked.

"Get Nyssa out and then hightail it to the airport with Molly and JW. Grab the first plane and get the heck out of dodge."

Laney grinned. "That's about it. Think you can handle it?"

David scoffed. "I'm going to pretend you didn't say that. I'll call you when we have her." David headed over to the cars.

JW, Molly, and Mateo broke away from the group and climbed into the jeep with him. They would head over to the cottage and retrieve Nyssa. Henry was behind the wheel.

Laney's gut clenched as she watched the jeep disappear. *Please let this go all right.* But that was all the time she could let worry have. She shoved the fears from her mind. Her people were capable. They could handle this. And she had to keep her eye on the ball.

THE BELIAL BLOOD

Laney tapped her throat sending out her message to everyone. "They're heading to the Hypogeum. I need everyone in position. We'll move on my mark."

CHAPTER 102

Gedeon had left. Nyssa didn't know where, but he was gone. She'd been shoved back in her room, and she'd listened through the door as most of them left. She could still hear footsteps so she knew at least one was still here.

She paced along the window, glancing outside every time she passed by. Now she moved over to the window and peered down. The cliff face was uneven, and part of her wondered if maybe she'd be able to climb it. She'd gone climbing a bunch of times with Jen, and she was pretty good at it.

But even the thought of climbing down there without a rope made her lightheaded, and she pushed away from the window. She wasn't getting out that way. But she needed to somehow.

She had no doubt that Laney and the others were coming to find her. And once again, she railed against herself for slipping away from them. She'd thought she was helping. She'd thought that she was keeping them safe.

But from what she'd overheard, they'd arrived here, coming for her yet again. She hadn't protected them at all. She'd only postponed what was going to happen.

THE BELIAL BLOOD

And now she needed to at least get herself out of this stupid cottage so she couldn't be used as a bargaining chip.

At the same time, she couldn't understand why all of this was happening. That guy Gedeon had to be crazy with all his Lilith talk. Yet he had convinced all these others to help.

Which meant they were insane too.

She looked up as the door opened. The man who'd grabbed her from the cabin stepped inside and placed a plate of food and a tall glass of milk on the table. "You need to eat," he said gruffly.

Nyssa just stayed against the wall, not saying a word.

He shrugged and just walked back out the door, closing it behind him.

She walked over to the table and uncovered the dish. Some sort of sandwich with some potato chips.

Grabbing the bag, she ripped it open and ate one of the chips before taking a sip of the milk. She needed to get out of this. She just had no idea how to do it.

CHAPTER 103

THE JEEP ROLLED ALONG THE OLD DIRT ROAD. THE WATER WAS ON their right, and Molly glanced over at it. It really was beautiful. She'd seen the movie *Troy* years ago, and she couldn't help but be reminded of it when she stared out at the incredible landscape.

Malta had been inhabited for thousands and thousands of years. And its coastline looked completely untouched by the modern world even though she knew that was impossible. But even with the beautiful calming scenery, her knee jiggled, stress and worry rolling through her.

JW placed a hand on her leg. "It's going to be okay. We'll get her back," he said softly.

Molly looked up to into his eyes and saw the commitment and determination there, but she also knew how easily these things could go badly. And Nyssa was just a kid, with a fragile little body that could be easily hurt if not killed by a careless move of any of the people that held her.

"I hope so," Molly said as she looked at the other inhabitants of the car.

Henry sat behind the steering wheel, his large fame frame barely fitting in the SUV. When she'd first met Henry, she'd been a little frightened of him. He was just so large. But he truly was a gentle giant. She just really hoped that he was more giant than gentle when they met these people.

David was always quick with a laugh and a smile, but she could sense the ruthlessness underneath him. Mateo she didn't really know at all, but she knew he was a Fallen and that he was committed to getting Nyssa back.

Had they brought enough people with them? Still, she wasn't sure how she was going to keep all of them safe.

"It's just around this next bend," Henry said.

Molly sucked in a breath and then looked at Mateo, who nodded back at her. The two of them opened the car doors on either side and slipped out, rolling for a second before they sprinted up ahead.

The ground all but disappeared under her feet as she lengthened her stride. *We're coming, Nyssa. We're coming.*

CHAPTER 104

The potato chips were quickly finished, as was the milk. Nyssa wasn't interested in the sandwich. She walked to the bathroom and splashed water on her face, staring at her reflection in the mirror. *Come on, Nyssa. Think. There's got to be something you can do.*

But nothing came to mind. A yell sounded from outside her room.

Nyssa peeked her head out of the bathroom doorway and then ducked her head back in, locking the door.

She looked around the room for something, anything she could use as a weapon, but there was nothing there.

The door to her bedroom crashed open.

Nyssa's body tensed as she scrunched up back against the wall.

The door to the bathroom flew open. The man who'd brought her food stepped inside. He dashed across the room toward her. Nyssa slipped to the side, somehow avoiding his grip.

The man growled. "You're coming with me."

"No, I'm not." Nyssa aimed her kick right in between his legs. The great equalizer, as Laney had called it when she'd taught it to her years and years ago.

THE BELIAL BLOOD

And this man, this incredibly powerful man, dropped to his knees, holding his crotch.

Nyssa bolted out of the room past him. Her heart pounding, she knew she had mere seconds, if that, before he recovered.

A growl behind her made it clear she had overestimated her time. She sprinted toward the open doorway, praying the whole way. With a yell, she felt the ground shudder as the man tore after her.

She tensed, knowing that this was going to hurt. She was almost at the doorway.

A blur burst through the doorway and slammed into the man, sending him sailing out through the window and down to the cliff below.

Nyssa looked on in shock as Molly spun around and searched her from head to toe. "Nyssa, are you all right?"

Nyssa sprinted across the space, wrapped her arms around Molly, and burst into tears.

CHAPTER 105

"We have Nyssa."

David's voice broke through Laney's earpiece. A smile burst across her face as her shoulders slumped in relief. *Thank God.* She tapped the mic at her throat. "Is she all right? Is she hurt?"

"She's fine. We're almost at the airport."

"Are you being followed?"

A laugh was in David's voice. "No, and it seems unlikely we will be. There were only two of them at the cottage, and Molly and Henry tossed them both off a 300-foot cliff."

Laney winced, but at the same time she couldn't help but grin. "Good. Get her on the plane and get it in the air."

"Will do. I'll meet you at the rendezvous."

Laney let out a breath and turned to Jen, who grinned at her. "Stage one complete."

"Yes, it is. Now we move on to the tougher part."

Laney wanted to wait until David was in the air, but Gedeon had already arrived at the Hypogeum. They couldn't let him get too far into the ceremony before they moved. Because if they did, it was entirely possible they'd be too late.

So they needed to go now.

Taking a deep breath, Laney tapped the mic at her throat. "All right, people, it's show time. Everybody check in."

One by one, every member of her team clicked their mic. She nodded, glad that none of them had gone against the original plan. When they had seen Gedeon and his forces heading toward the Hypogeum, her instinct had been to stop him.

But until they had Nyssa safe they couldn't do that. So she'd told everyone to stay back, stay hidden, and let them get through. And all her people had done exactly that and they were all still in position.

"Okay, we're moving in. Take out the guards around the outskirts first, Jen and I will head into the Hypogeum itself. When you take out the guards, do not hesitate. You are required to be as brutal as possible. Unfortunately, even that may not kill them. So I want two people on each one of theirs. And watch out for the cats. Remember they are on our side. Help them if they need it. And do not assume because Gedeon's men are down they are out. They will not be. Let's go."

Laney called on the wind and the clouds, feeling the lightning in the air. Wind blew back against her hair as she strode forward. It was time to end this.

CHAPTER 106

The fight did not go as planned. Almost as soon as Gedeon's forces appeared, Laney's people engaged them. There were fifteen in Gedeon's forces, including Gedeon.

The cats, the UN force, the Fallen Force all worked in tandem. The fighting was furious. The plan had been to separate them and take them out one by one.

But instead of spreading out, they all grouped around Gedeon.

Despite the strange tactic, Laney and her people attacked. Weapons were used first, forcing Gedeon's people to break away from him to defend themselves.

As soon as they did, the cats lunged for them. Caught unaware, a few of them stumbled. That stumble was enough for the cats and the Fallen Force to engage.

Even with that, the others stayed around Gedeon, making sure he was protected. As one, the group made it toward the Hypogeum, and Gedeon slipped inside. His forces then stayed outside, keeping anyone else from entering.

We need to get in there, Laney thought as she called on lightning again.

CHAPTER 107

Tuning out the sounds of the battle outside, Gedeon stepped into the Hypogeum's first chamber. The Hypogeum had three levels. The first two were open to the public, the third was dangerous and restricted.

The open space was part natural and part the result of hard work to cut out the spaces. Completely protected from the humidity and humanity that afflicted the aboveground structures, the structure had stood for thousands and thousands of years.

Intricate honeycomb designs had been scrawled into the rock walls. A few red ochre symbols had similarly been created along the walls, but otherwise, it was blank.

A sense of calm and rightness fell over him as he moved farther in. This was where he was supposed to be. This was his duty. This was what he'd been created for.

Not that he'd had doubts. If there was one thing that Gedeon was good at, it was being assured of his place. He knew who he was and what he was supposed to do.

He made his way down the slight ramp leading to the Oracle Room. It was an oblong chamber about fifteen feet long. Small, it could not hold many individuals, but that was by design. The

Oracle Room was created for sound. Niches had been carefully crafted into the wall to amplify and echo sound waves.

A portion of the room had been cordoned off with yellow tape. Plywood covered a hole in the ground. But it wasn't near the spot Gedeon was headed.

He crossed the room to the back and toward a rock altar. Slipping the bag from his shoulder, he placed it on the altar and breathed in deep. This was how structures should be created. Not those steel and metal monstrosities that littered the humans' cities. These types of structures stood the test of time and were one with the goals of the Creator.

This particular structure had been created not just for its beauty but to emphasize critical tones, a science that had been long lost to the modern world. They placed no importance on words or tones. They looked at the old ways of chanting as primitive and superstitious beliefs.

Such fools.

Carefully, Gedeon undid the bag and pulled out the objects. He uncovered the bowls with each of the objects from the Passion ground down to their smallest parts.

Then he pulled out Nyssa's blood, uncapping it and placing it at the center of the altar.

He smiled. Almost everything he needed was here. Now he just needed one last part.

Letting the power of this moment roll through him, he raised his hands and began to chant.

CHAPTER 108

LANEY'S PEOPLE WERE TRYING TO WHITTLE GEDEON'S people down, but they would drop them and then bounce right back up a few minutes later.

It was proving impossible to keep them down completely. Each time Laney tried to engage with one of them, they slipped away from her.

She wasn't sure what to make of that.

Bringing down the lightning and using the wind to push them away, she managed to shove some away from the entrance. But each time she did so, others stepped into their place.

It was clear they had been told to allow no one to enter.

"Do you get the feeling they don't want us going in there?" Jen yelled as she slammed a side kick and then a round kick into one of the Gedeon's people before following up with an uppercut that sent the man flying.

"Yeah, I do," Laney said as she used the wind to toss the man even farther.

The hairs along Laney's neck began to rise. She strained and could hear a low hum coming from inside the Hypogeum.

Jen dashed over to her, breathing hard. "He started something. We need to get in there."

Laney nodded.

A sense of familiarity rolled over her. She couldn't hear the chant, but the way it made the hair on her body stand on end and the feeling that coursed through her was reminiscent of when Azazel had activated the belial stone so long ago.

Laney swallowed hard, wondering what it was exactly that Gedeon was unleashing inside the Hypogeum.

"I'll clear the way and then come in after you," Jen said.

We will help, Cleo said.

Laney nodded. "Let's do this."

She stood up and sprinted for the Hypogeum as Jen, Cleo, and two other cats bolted ahead of her, yanking Gedeon's people out of the way.

Laney called on the wind, ready to shove the next one out of her way, but he simply stepped aside.

Laney frowned. What in the world?

Continuing toward the Hypogeum, each time she reached one of Gedeon's people, they simply stepped out of her way, allowing her passage.

As soon as she was past them, they stepped back into place, blocking anyone else from following her. In fact, Laney made it right to the door of the Hypogeum without incident.

A glance over her shoulder showed that no one else had made it in.

Laney swallowed as she could hear the chanting more clearly. And the hairs all over her body were practically vibrating in response.

She swallowed for a moment, gripping her gun. *Well, that's not ominous*, she thought just before she stepped inside.

CHAPTER 109

A WALL OF ENERGY SEEMED TO ENVELOP LANEY AS SHE STEPPED inside the Hypogeum. There were three levels of the Hypogeum, but in her gut, Laney knew where he would be: the Oracle Room. It was named after the Oracle of Delphi, which Laney would take as a coincidence, but she didn't believe in those. She wondered what Cristela knew of the site. *If I live, I'll have to sit down and talk to her about that and a lot of other things.*

In fact, she'd been drafting a mental list of all the things she needed to ask Cristela. Writing those things down was going to have to happen sooner rather than later because the list was getting awfully long.

But she shoved those thoughts aside. That was a conversation for another day. Today was reserved for Gedeon. Quietly, she made her way down the ramp to the Oracle Room. The closer she got, the louder the chanting sounded and the more electric the air felt.

It had been years since she'd been here. And like many things viewed as an adult, it looked much smaller than it had in her memories. The alcoves she remembered being deep and dark were much more shallow. The honeycomb designs she'd pictured on every surface were only seen in a few spots.

Gedeon though looked exactly as he had the last time she'd seen him: huge and frightening. He stood at the other side of the room near an altar, his hands up in the air, chants emitting from deep in his throat. Laney didn't recognize any of the words.

And she was glad for the recorder on her chest that would get at least some of this for her uncle and Cain to hopefully be able to figure out when she got back home.

Assuming she managed to get back home.

Gedeon's back was to her, yet she had the feeling he knew she was there. For a moment, she didn't move, and she stared at the spectacle unraveling above the altar.

Small particles of dust and dirt swirled in a small vortex. She watched, her eyes widening as drops of blood rose in the air from a small container on the altar and joined the mix.

In her gut, she knew that was Nyssa's blood.

Gedeon flicked a glance over his shoulder at her and smiled. "Just in time."

CHAPTER 110

LANEY HAD NO IDEA WHAT GEDEON THOUGHT SHE WAS JUST IN TIME for, but as far as she was concerned she was just in time to stop him. She pulled the trigger. Three bullets slammed into his back.

"No!" He flung himself away from the altar and bolted across the space too fast for Laney to even see. He knocked the gun out of her hands. It went sliding across the room, coming to a stop near a cordoned-off area with orange cones and yellow caution tape, which looked strikingly out of place in the ancient site.

"A gun! You brought a *gun* into this sacred site?" Gedeon grabbed Laney by the front of the shirt yanking her off her feet.

She brought her knee up, but Gedeon shifted to the side, and she only caught him in the thigh.

"That won't work on me twice." He flung her across the space.

Laney's arms and legs pinwheeled, but there was no purchase as time seemed to slow down. She crashed into the back wall, her head cracking against it with a skull-splitting thud.

Stars danced in front of her eyes as she hit the ground. She propped herself up on her arms, blinking hard as her thoughts seemed to slow.

She was thinking about standing up but her brain seemed to

be working slow, and her body was even slower. Before either of them could catch up, Gedeon was there in front of her, hauling her up and slamming her back against the wall.

More stars burst in front of her eyes, and she knew she was on the verge of passing out.

"I don't understand how you've survived this long. You have gone against Samyaza and the other Fallen, and look at you: just a weak pitiful human. You should have been wiped out eons ago."

Laney didn't necessarily disagree with him. The fact that she'd survived to this point was honestly a miracle in more ways than one. Fighting through the darkness that seemed to be seeping in at the corners of her vision, Laney glared up at him. "Where's Drake?"

Surprise flitted across Gedeon's face before he laughed. "So, you do still care about the man. I honestly thought that you were done with him. After all, he did try to kill you."

"No, he didn't. Michael did."

Gedeon leaned his face closer to her. "Drake *is* Michael. He just can't remember it."

Cold fear washed over Laney. So that was his plan. To pull Michael to the forefront. "Where is he? What have you done with him?"

Gedeon smiled. "Oh, he's somewhere safe. Safe from you, that is. But don't worry, you'll see him again."

Then Gedeon frowned, tilting his head. "Or maybe you won't."

Before Laney could so much as breathe, Gedeon lashed out with a knife that he'd had hidden in the folds of his shirt. Blood bloomed across Laney's wrist. With a gasp, her eyes widened, and her knees buckled.

Gedeon slid his arm around her waist, holding her up as he stared down at her.

"This won't work. I didn't bring the spear."

He smiled down at her again. "I never needed the spear. I only needed you."

CHAPTER 111

I ONLY NEEDED YOU. THE WORDS ROARED THROUGH LANEY'S MIND, chasing back the darkness. Her blood. He needed her blood to finish the ceremony.

The spear had been a ruse. It probably could have been used, but once he'd gotten the pillar from the Vatican, he no longer needed just a small, tiny spearhead.

God, she'd been so stupid.

Gedeon dropped her to the ground and then dashed back to the altar, returning with a small glass. He held her wrist above it and squeezed. Blood poured into the cup. He only filled it about a quarter of the way and then dropped her arm.

"Now, don't bleed out on me. I think this is enough, but if not, I'll come back for some more." He headed back to the altar.

Laney slumped to the ground, her whole body feeling like it wanted to give up.

Across the way, Gedeon placed the glass of her blood on the altar, raised his hands in the air, and resumed his chanting. The cadence of his voice sent the vibrations in the Hypogeum into overdrive. Laney could feel the pulses pounding through her body.

Once again, the small vortex swirled together in the air up above him, slowly coalescing into what would be the weapon that Gedeon needed. This time, her own blood joined the aerial dance.

She couldn't let that happen.

Staring at his back, she could still see where the three bullet holes that had since healed. She frowned, picturing how quickly he'd flung himself away from the table.

Why?

Then it hit her: He didn't want his blood to mix with the other elements of the Arma Christi. Which meant she needed to find a way to get his blood in there.

Even as the blackness encroached on the edge of her visions, she shook her head, widening her eyes trying to keep herself awake.

She grabbed the edge of her shirt and slipped it over the cut on her wrist. Then she grabbed it with her other hand, squeezing tight as she scanned the room.

There. Her gun was across the room next to the cordoned-off section.

An idea began to form. It would take luck and almost perfect timing, neither of which seemed to be on the menu at the moment, but she had to at least try.

Gedeon was completely focused on his task as Laney crawled across the room.

The effort seemed gargantuan at this point. But she dragged herself across the floor, shaking her head every time the spots appeared in front of her eyes.

You can do this. You have to do this.

She didn't know what was happening with the battle outside. But if they could, her friends would already be in here to help her. So this was on her. She managed to get across the room, only having to stop twice.

Finally, relief flowed through her as she gripped the cold metal of the gun, even though she knew that this was only one small step in the process. She raised the weapon, still keeping her other hand on her wrist to keep the blood at bay, but also to help brace herself.

Her vision wavered. Blinking hard, she flicked the weapon to automatic. It didn't matter if her aim wasn't perfect. Gedeon was a big enough target that she should be able to get him with a spray of bullets.

She flicked a glance up to the ceiling, not sure who exactly she was talking to. *Please help me*, she begged.

And then she returned her focus to Gedeon and pulled the trigger.

CHAPTER 112

THE BULLETS SPRAYED ACROSS THE ROOM, CHIPPING AWAY AT THE altar and then through Gedeon's thighs and back.

Once again, he screamed. He turned from the altar and blasted across the room.

Laney tossed the gun away, as the magazine was empty anyway. As Gedeon reached her, it took all of her focus to do what needed to be done.

As soon as he grabbed her, she grabbed the front of his shirt and flung herself back, pulling him with her, his momentum already heading in that direction anyway.

With a surprise cry, he fell toward her. The two of them crashed through the yellow tape and into the plywood on the ground. The plywood split apart, and then they were falling.

Laney wrapped her legs around Gedeon's hips and twisted. Unprepared for the move, Gedeon showed no resistance to it, and Laney ended up sprawled on top of him just before they slammed into the stalactites below.

As soon as they hit, Laney rolled off. The stalactites pierced through Gedeon's back. And although Laney moved as quick as she could, part of a stalactite cut into her ribs.

She fell to the ground with a thud, pain lancing through her side, the same side she had hurt at the cabin. The ribs were well and truly broken this time. And blood still poured from the wound at her wrist.

The world began to slip in and out as her blood pooled on the floor around her. Laney wanted to close her eyes and rest for just a moment, but she knew if she did, she wouldn't be opening them again.

Next to her, Gedeon let out a scream of rage as he slowly pulled himself off the stalagmite. It protruded a foot above his chest. It was a long, slow painful process to yank himself free.

He cut off the top half and then pulled himself upright, heaving as he stayed on the ground on all fours, breathing deep.

Laney knew she needed to move away, but she simply didn't have the energy.

Gedeon's head jolted up, his eyes narrowed as he focused on Laney. "You. What do you think you've accomplished? All you've done is kill yourself. And I'm still going to finish the ceremony."

That was probably true. But Laney was hoping that maybe she'd bought her friends enough time to get inside and stop Gedeon.

He crawled toward her on all fours and then reached over with one hand and dragged her toward him. "I was going to leave you alive so that you could see what was to come. So that you could see how you have failed. But now I don't think I will."

The darkness that had been encroaching on her moved swiftly across her brain.

She smiled as her eyes closed. *You're too late,* she thought as the darkness swept through.

CHAPTER 113

MASSA, ITALY

THE HOURS SEEMED TO DRAG BY. DRAKE WASN'T SURE HE WOULD BE able to keep himself from screaming in frustration. No one came in.

Apparently, they were putting off his dose for a little while. On the one hand, it seemed unwise. On the other hand, it seemed like maybe they knew something. Once again, he scanned his cell, looking for any sign of cameras.

Nothing. He paced along the confines of his cell, aware of Arturo's eyes upon him.

He knew he had to be making the boy more nervous, but he couldn't seem to get himself to calm down. They had Nyssa and were going to use her to draw out Laney. He needed to get out of here. He needed to warn her. He needed to help her.

The rational side of his brain knew that Laney no doubt would be aware that it was a trap. But the irrational side of his brain felt like he needed to get to her.

When he'd first started watching humanity, he often shook his head over their foolishness. How they would rush into a burning hut to save a child when there was no chance the child could be saved and no chance that they themselves would even be able to escape the flames. Yet in they would run. It took him eons to understand that feeling.

And now that feeling was crawling just under his skin.

The desperate urge to do something to help her, to keep her safe, even while he knew that he wouldn't be able to get to her in time. But those arguments did nothing to tamp down his need.

Finally, the door opened. He looked on as Mario walked in carrying the dart gun with the Inceptus darts. The name had finally come to him a few nights ago. He had no idea where they had found the stuff. That well must have long since gone dry.

Mario stayed along the back wall, nowhere near Drake. They had long ago given up trying to grab him to shoot him with the liquid. Even in his weakened state, it hadn't gone well for them, so they had shifted to shooting him.

Drake growled as he caught sight of the gun, keeping his gaze away from Arturo.

Mario grinned in response. "This is my favorite part of the day."

Drake had never met Mario in his life as Michael. But he'd come to know him through their unfortunate encounters as of late. He was a sadist at heart. And a true believer in Gedeon. Even though he couldn't sense the man's level, he had no doubt he was a power.

Much like in the human military, within the angel forces, all sorts of personalities were required. The sadists were responsible for some of the darkest duties. Two angels destroyed the cities of Sodom and Gomorrah. Angels had destroyed a 185,000-person army from Assyria. And, of course, there was Gedeon's starring role in the Passover, bringing death to all the firstborn sons.

But those times and those missions were long in the past.

R.D. BRADY

Those missions had been relegated to the dustbin, and the angels called upon for that had been set in the back of the angel forces, not destroyed, but simply never called upon again.

It looked like Gedeon had found a use for them again, however. And from the few interactions he'd had with Mario, it was clear that he took a great deal of joy in his work.

Mario lined up his shot, but Drake shifted, forcing Mario to move closer to Arturo's corner. Mario growled. "Why do you always make this harder than it has to be?"

He pulled the trigger, but Drake managed to slip to the side. The dart sailed harmlessly past him.

Unnoticed by Mario, whose focus was entirely on Drake, who'd moved again, Arturo slipped along the wall and grabbed a dart from the floor, gripping it in his hand as he stood against the back wall.

Letting out another growl, Mario shot at Drake in quick succession. He managed to dodge one dart, but the other found its mark. He could feel the weakness flowing over him.

Mario stepped toward the edge of the circle. "I don't understand why you fight. You know it's inevitable."

Drake kept his head down and mumbled. From the corner of his eye, he saw Mario frown.

"What?" Mario leaned forward.

Drake mumbled again, hunching his shoulders as if too weak to look up.

"What?" Mario asked, leaning forward even more. And his upper body crossed over the edge of the circle.

Drake darted to his feet and yanked him forward into the prison.

Mario let out a yell.

"Now, Arturo." Drake ordered.

Arturo rolled the dart toward him.

Drake snatched it up and plunged it into Mario's upper arm.

THE BELIAL BLOOD

Mario let out a yell, dropping the gun. Then his eyes widened when he realized what had happened. "No. No, you can't—"

Grabbing the dart gun, Drake shot Mario in the thigh. Tossing the gun aside, he grabbed Mario by the hair and slammed his face into the concrete floor. The force wasn't strong enough to knock him out, so Drake did it again.

Mario's eyes rolled up in his head, and he passed out.

Drake took the man's face and slid it along the rough floor. Blood soaked into the concrete, distorting the symbols below.

The symbols were written in angel blood. The only way to undo them was to distort them with more angel blood, and not Drake's—he'd already tried that.

As soon as the blood soaked into the ground, Drake felt the change in the room. His ears popped as if a barrier was releasing, and that was exactly what had happened.

Hurrying across the room to the door, Drake peeked outside. There was no noise, no sound of alarm. His worries about a camera in the room appeared unfounded. He closed the door softly and then waved toward Arturo. "Come. We must go quickly."

Arturo shook his head, backing up against the wall.

Drake flicked a glance at the door but knew he couldn't leave the boy behind. He hurried across the room. Out of habit, he kept away from the circle. He knelt down in front of Arturo.

"I know you're scared. You have every right to be. You would be crazy if you weren't. But this is our chance to get out of here. And we have to take it. If we don't, there won't be another one. And I think you know that your chances are better out there with me than they are in here with the rest of them."

Arturo looked at where Mario lay still unconscious in the circle. "You'll take me home to my mom?"

"I'll get you somewhere safe," he promised.

The seconds were ticking away, and it took everything in

Drake not to shake the boy into hurrying, but if he did that, he would lose him.

And he could not leave him behind.

Finally, Arturo nodded. Drake stood, grasping the boy and pulling him behind him. "Good. We need to go now."

CHAPTER 114

VALLETTA, MALTA

Watching Laney disappear into the Hypogeum as Gedeon's people cleared out of her way sent bolts of terror through Jen. If Gedeon wanted Laney in there, then that was exactly where she should not be.

Slinging one of the men who'd grabbed her and given her a punch that would have broken more than a few ribs, Jen gritted her teeth as she tapped her mic. "Laney's in the Hypogeum. We need to get in there now."

Cleo let out a roar, which Jen took as complete agreement.

Despite the urgency that she and the others felt to get inside, the minutes ticked away as they fought Gedeon's people to get to the entrance.

And all Jen could do was picture the horrors that were happening to Laney inside.

Laney had been through some incredible things and achieved some impossible feats. But Jen hadn't seen a single burst of lightning appear inside the Hypogeum. Not a single gust of air.

And those were Laney's strongest weapons. She'd heard

gunfire, but neither Laney nor Gedeon had reappeared, and in her heart of hearts, Jen feared the worst. Terror and panic were starting to crawl over her.

"Where is she?" Jake asked as he appeared at Jen's side, blasting one of Gedeon's people who was trying to come up behind her.

Jake must have been using a 50-cal because Jen could see right through the man with the hole that he'd created.

Jen wiped her brow as sweat rolled down into her eyes. "She went inside at least three minutes ago. I haven't heard anything, Jake, at least nothing good." Jen tapped her mic. "Danny, do you still have eyes on Laney?"

"Yeah, and it's bad, Jen. You need to get in there. You need to help her."

Jen heard the fear in Danny's voice. And all it did was ratchet up her own fear, but it wasn't helping her get in. These guys didn't seem to care what happened to them so long as no one else got into the Hypogeum.

"She fell!" Danny cried. "I couldn't see exactly where, but she fell."

Jake's face was set in a grim line. But before either of them could say anything, a blur appeared from the Hypogeum, running through the fighting groups, and disappeared out of sight.

After only a moment's hesitation, the rest of Gedeon's men took flight as well.

Jen and Jake exchanged a glance and then sprinted for the Hypogeum door. "Laney!" Jen yelled as she burst into the room.

CHAPTER 115

MASSA, ITALY

THERE WERE VOICES DOWN THE HALL, BUT NONE OF THEM WERE raised in alarm. Drake waved Arturo behind him and led them away from the voices. Hopefully there were stairs this way.

His choice proved to be the right one, and he quickly started up the stairs with Arturo right behind him.

Once again, he was being held in a subterranean level. The first level they reached looked as if it might be a garage level. They had just stepped onto the tile floor when voices came from down the hall.

Grabbing Arturo by the shirt, he yanked him into the closest door, closing it behind them. It was some sort of storage room. Drake put a finger to his lips. Arturo flattened himself against the wall next to the door.

Standing on the other side of the door, Drake's heart pounded as he waited for them to be discovered. The only way this was going to work was if they slipped out with anyone noticing. Because he certainly couldn't fight in his present condition. What had happened in Greece had been luck. He'd taken them unaware.

But he did not have the element of surprise right now. Gedeon had read everyone the riot act, and they would take no chances with him. If they saw him out of his cell, he would be loaded up with so much Inceptus that it would probably kill him.

And he couldn't allow that to happen.

He waited, hearing the footsteps approach the door. But then the footsteps continued past, and he let out a breath.

Arturo nudged him and then pointed to the back of the storage room. About eight feet from the ground, just above a wooden shelving unit, was a small window. It wasn't large by any stretch, but it would be big enough to slip through.

Drake nodded, and Arturo scurried over to it. Drake stayed by the door as Arturo climbed. He looked back at Drake once he reached the top, and Drake nodded at him.

Arturo tried the handle of the window. It let out a squeak.

Drake winced, and Arturo went still, but no sound came from down the hall. He waved for Arturo to continue. Moving slowly, Arturo gently opened the window. He locked it open, and Drake waved him out.

Waiting another second by the door for any trace of alarm, Drake dashed across the room and quickly climbed the shelving unit, following Arturo outside.

They were on the side of the building. There was no one nearby, but the woods were a good twenty yards away across open ground.

Drake scurried to the edge of the structure and glanced around the corner.

There was no one in sight. He nodded to Arturo and pointed to the woods. Arturo's eyes widened, but he nodded.

Raising three fingers, Drake counted down to one. The two of them took off for the woods. Drake ran as fast as he could manage, but it still felt incredibly slow, his limbs feeling clumsy and heavy.

He waited for a yell or the sound of a bullet being released from a chamber. He waited for the impact between his shoulder blades, but there was nothing. They slipped into the woods without a single cry of alarm being raised.

Drake bolted forward, keeping pace with Arturo to make sure that he didn't lose the boy. He had no destination in mind. He just knew that right now they simply needed to get one place ... away.

CHAPTER 116

VALLETTA, MALTA

The Hypogeum was quiet. There were objects scattered across an altar across the room. Jake ran over to it and blanched. "There are two cups of blood here."

Jen scanned the space, not responding as she looked for signs of Laney. "Where is she?"

Cleo walked in, limping, her nose in the air. She walked over to some upturned orange cones and yellow tape that lay on the ground. She peered through a hole beyond it and let out a roar.

Jen hurried over, and then Jake appeared with his flashlight, shining it down.

"Jen." His voice was tight as he kept the ray of light on a prone figure on the ground.

Jen leapt into the hole, careful to avoid the stalactites on the ground and dropped down to her knees next to Laney. "Laney. Laney!"

Staring at her best friend's clothes, Jen noted the large cut in her side as she pulled the fabric back and frowned at the healed-over cut underneath.

Blood had pooled underneath her arm. Jen lifted it, frowning again at what looked like another recent injury that was completely healed.

Laney's eyes flickered. "Jen?"

Jen let out a breath. "Hey. You scared me."

Laney tried to sit up, and Jen quickly got behind her, helping push her into a sitting position.

"Jen!" Jake yelled from up above.

"We're good. She's all right, I think. I'll bring her up in a minute."

Jen turned back to Laney. "What happened?"

Laney shook her head. "I fought Gedeon. He beat me. He has the Arma Christi."

Jen frowned, picturing the altar up above. "Are you sure? What happened here?"

Laney stared at the healed wound on her wrist then she looked back at Jen. "I have no idea."

Danny's voice burst across Jen's earpiece. "I do. But you guys are going to need to see it to believe it."

CHAPTER 117

MASSA, ITALY

By the time Arturo and Drake had been full out sprinting for twenty minutes, Drake wondered if he was going to make it. Not because he was worried about someone coming after him.

But because he was pretty sure his heart was going to explode.

His lungs felt like they were on fire. The muscles in his thighs felt like they were being stabbed and pulled with each step. He'd never felt like this before in his life. He really needed to stop making fun of humans when they exercised. This was horrible.

Next to him, Arturo's breaths were also coming out in pants, but the boy didn't stop, nor did he ask to take a break.

Drake kept waiting for the sound of someone following them. But the forest stayed mercifully quiet, which was good because neither he nor Arturo was capable of being silent right now.

The quiet around them, however, did not ease his mind. The people back at his prison could cover the distance they'd managed in thirty minutes in a tenth of that time. They needed to get as far away as possible.

Despite starting to slow, neither of them stopped as they

continued across a creek and then up a small incline. They went down another incline and across a wide-open field.

This was not good. His heart was in his throat as they darted across it. He hated being out in the open like this. The fear of being easily spotted helped the both of them eke out a little more speed.

Drake's fear reduced once they were safely back in the shadows of the forest. But it didn't completely abate. It wouldn't until Drake was back at his full strength and Arturo was somewhere safe.

They continued on without talking, both of them focused on getting away as fast as they could. Next to him, Arturo's face was bright red, his chest heaving at an alarming rate.

Drake knew they needed to take a break or else Arturo would be unable to go any farther. And he was pretty sure he couldn't last much longer at this rate either. Already, dots had begun to appear around the edge of his vision.

Spying a creek up ahead, he angled toward it, and Arturo followed. He stopped at the creek's edge, his hands on his waist as he tried to suck in a full breath. His lungs weren't cooperating, and all he managed were some short shallow ones. "We'll … take a … little break here … for a … moment."

Arturo sank next to the creek, nodding his head. He cupped his hands and brought some water to his lips.

Drake sank down next to him and did the same. After only two mouthfuls, he'd had enough. He placed his hand on Arturo's shoulder. "That's enough. If you take too much, you won't be able to run."

Arturo nodded and then simply fell back onto his butt, laying back on the ground, his knees up, staring at the sky. "Do you think we've escaped them?"

Drake leaned against a downed log and shook his head. "No. But we've got a good head start. We'll walk in the creek for a little bit to hopefully throw them off. Do you recognize this area?"

"No. I don't think I've ever been here before."

Drake knew it had been a long shot, but he'd been hoping that maybe Arturo might recognize something. Maybe they'd only switched houses in the same area. It would give them some idea of where to head. Depending upon where they were, they could spend days going through the woods and never come across a road. They could simply move a little too far in one direction and bypass a road that was just over a hill.

But Drake did not let all of those thoughts and doubts fill his mind. They would get out of this. He would find a way.

Tonight, he'd make sure that they had some high ground that would give them a bird's-eye view of the area surrounding them. He'd be able to see the lights of a city or a road, and from there they would be able to figure out which direction to head.

Feeling better now that he had a plan, he sunk a little lower against the log, closing his eyes. "Five minutes. Five minutes and then we start again."

Arturo didn't answer, and Drake knew that the boy had to be exhausted. Drake himself was a little worried that he might fall asleep.

And he worried what would happen if Mario and the others caught up with them. It would be hours before the drug left his own system. Hopefully by nightfall he'd have at least a little more of his natural strength.

By tomorrow afternoon, he should be fully recovered. If they couldn't find a road, hopefully they could at least stay hidden long enough for Drake's powers to return. If not fully, at least enough of them to give them a fighting chance against their pursuers.

Of course, that wouldn't help Laney.

The thought of her going up against Gedeon chilled him to the bone. Gedeon was ruthless. And while people sometimes described Laney as ruthless, she wasn't, not really. She would do what needed to be done, but she always tried to figure out a way to do it that caused the least damage possible.

THE BELIAL BLOOD

He hoped that when she saw Gedeon, she let go of that impulse. That she simply tried to destroy him.

"Is there any way you could call your brothers and sisters?" Arturo asked, breaking into Gedeon's thoughts.

Drake frowned, cracking open an eyelid. He'd thought the boy had dozed off. "What do you mean?"

Arturo sat up, crossing his legs. "Your brothers and sisters. They're angels, right?"

Drake nodded.

"Do you have a way to contact them? I mean, if you contacted them, would they come and help?"

Arturo had asked the question a lot. He seemed fixated on the idea that someone would rush to their rescue. Drake paused yet again for a moment, considering it. He'd never actually reached out to any of his siblings in all of his time on Earth. He wasn't even sure if there was a way for him to do so.

But even as he thought it, he knew he couldn't do that. The ramifications of it would be too great. "I can't contact them."

"Not even to help us? I mean you're weak, and we don't know where we are. And they've got to be chasing us by now."

"All true. But it doesn't change the fact that I can't contact them. Even if I did, they won't come to our aid. I'm afraid it's up to us."

"You're sure?"

"I'm sure. Now, I think we've rested long enough. We should get moving." Drake stood up, wiping off his pants before extending a hand to Arturo.

Arturo gripped it, and Drake pulled him up. The slightest of tingles ran through him. He released Arturo's hand and scanned the trees. "We need to go. We need to go now."

"In just a moment. There's one more thing I need to do."

Drake whirled back toward Arturo. "No. There's no time. We need to—"

A thick tree branch caught Drake on the side of his face.

Pain exploded across his cheekbone as he crashed to the ground, shaking his head.

In shock, he looked up. Arturo stepped toward him and swung again. This time, the swing took Drake completely off his feet, and the world turned black.

CHAPTER 118

VALLETTA, MALTA

THEY GATHERED UP WHAT WAS LEFT OF THE ARMA CHRISTI FROM the altar before heading to the airport.

Danny had already reported that Gedeon had hightailed it off the island. Danny seemed to know what had happened down in the lowest chamber of the Hypogeum, but he was refusing to say, insisting that they needed to see the video to understand.

But he made one thing clear: Gedeon had left because he was terrified.

And Laney couldn't help but wonder what exactly would terrify someone like Gedeon.

Jen wanted to investigate the Hypogeum further, but Laney had shook her head. If something had terrified Gedeon, they needed to learn what it was before they went looking for it. And besides, most of their people were in need of medical attention. It had been a rough battle, and none of them had come out unscathed.

On the way to the airfield, Cleo lay next to Laney, her paw

bandaged. It looked like she had broken it. Jake had given Cleo a sedative, and Laney absentmindedly stroked her fur. "Nyssa?" she asked Jake.

"In the air. David, Molly, and JW took off with her as soon as they got to the airfield."

Laney nodded. "That's good."

"The UN force is going to cover us while we take off. Nancy's already sent a separate transport for them."

"That's good too. How did they handle it?"

"Surprisingly well. Their training really became evident. They held their own."

"Any casualties?"

"Two of their people are in serious condition, but they'll hopefully make it. Lots of bumps and bruises, more than a few broken bones, but overall, we got lucky."

Yes, we did, Laney thought, wondering what exactly Danny had seen on the recording.

But that would have to wait until they were in the air. Laney wanted to get away from Malta in case Gedeon turned back. After all, they now had the remnants of the Arma Christi. And she had no idea where she was going to hide them, but she needed to get them somewhere safe. She also couldn't help but think about the fact that her blood had been part of the ceremony.

It looked as if Professor Moeshe's research was correct. Lilith's bloodline was the linchpin.

Once they took off, Jen brought over a computer. Henry and Jake joined them as well. Danny hadn't shown the recording to anyone, and the group stayed quiet, waiting.

Laney sat with a blanket around her, sipping some tea as Jen looked at the group of them. "Everybody ready?"

They all nodded back at her, and Jen hit play.

The recording started from when Laney appeared in the Hypogeum door.

THE BELIAL BLOOD

Henry leaned forward. "What is that?"

"It reminded me of when Azazel activated the belial stone. It was a similar chant and seemed to have a similar effect," Laney said, remembering the belial stone levitating in the air above Azazael as a result of the sounds he was emitting.

They watched in silence as Laney shot at Gedeon and then as they saw him cut her arm. Henry grabbed Laney's wrist and looked at the healed cut with a frown.

Laney tugged her arm back. "I don't know," she said, answering the unasked question.

He looked at her with concern, and she shrugged again, meeting his gaze. "Henry, I really don't know how they healed."

"They?" he asked.

She winced, realizing he didn't know about the injury to her ribs.

Focusing back on the screen, she watched Gedeon bolt toward her, and then they were falling. She remembered all of this. She was waiting for the part that she didn't remember.

"My God, Laney," Jake said, his face growing white.

"I was hoping I could buy you guys some time to get inside to stop him."

Jen just reached over and gripped Laney's hand, squeezing it gently. Laney held on to her friend's hand, happy for the warmth.

They listened as Laney spoke about Drake, and Laney's heart tugged again. Drake hadn't been there. They hadn't brought him. She still had no idea where he was. But she knew that they had plans for him.

"This is where Danny said it gets strange," Jen said.

Laney leaned a little more forward, her eyes focused on the screen. This was where she'd passed out.

Gedeon loomed over her. And then his head lifted up, his mouth dropping open. He backed away out of the frame.

Jen increased the volume, and although they couldn't see

Gedeon, they could hear him. "What are you doing here?" he asked, his voice shaking.

A voice, ancient and powerful, spoke. "This is not the way."

"You know nothing. This is my duty," Gedeon said.

A second voice spoke, a slightly higher tone making Laney think it was a woman. But there was something almost otherworldly about both voices. "You have lost your way. And you will harm this woman no further."

Some of Gedeon's attitude returned to his voice. "I'll do what my duty tells me to do."

A thunderclap sounded through the recording, along with a flash of light. The other voice boomed through the space. "You will not harm her."

No response was given by Gedeon, and there was the slightest flicker at the edge of the screen.

"I think that was Gedeon leaving," Jen murmured.

Laney nodded her agreement, her eyes glued to the screen.

There was a sound of shuffling. Two old faces appeared on the screen, one man and one woman, both with long white hair, their faces a pale gray. Laney gasped, and she wasn't the only one. They looked human and yet at the same time, they didn't.

The woman reached down toward Laney. They couldn't see where, but she knew that it was her wounds. A flash of light burst across the screen and then disappeared.

The man looked down at Laney. "It is not your time yet, ring bearer. There is still much for you to do."

Then the two of them disappeared.

The next face on a camera was Jen as she appeared above Laney. Jen reached out and stopped the video. No one spoke for a long moment.

Finally, Henry broke the silence. "Who were they?"

Laney shook her head. "I didn't even see them."

"Neither did we," Jen said. "But whoever they are, they're powerful enough to have scared Gedeon."

"Which means we need to learn who they are. Because they could be a new weapon in this fight."

Laney pulled the blanket tighter around her. "Or a new enemy."

CHAPTER 119

MASSA, ITALY

THE RIGHT-HAND SIDE OF DRAKE'S FACE THROBBED. HIS CHEEKBONE had been shattered. His whole face felt like it was on fire.

But at least my lungs feel better. He would have laughed at his own joke, except his body hurt too much. His thoughts were a mess. He remembered running with Arturo. He remembered his fear for Laney.

"Laney." He pushed himself up. He needed to get to her.

"Laney," a voice mocked.

Drake turned his head slowly, each move sending spikes of pain through him.

Arturo sat on a rock across from him. Mario stood next to him, his arms crossed over his chest. Behind him were two other angels.

Drake got to his knees, looking between them as a wave of dizziness rolled over him. He remembered Arturo swinging the branch at him. "It's okay, Arturo. I know they made you do it."

Arturo laughed. "My God, you really aren't Michael anymore, are you?"

THE BELIAL BLOOD

Drake's eyes narrowed as he looked at the boy who he'd been so worried about these last few days.

Arturo looked back at him with haughty disdain.

Blinking hard, Drake's mind seemed unable to grasp what Arturo meant. He probably had a concussion. Drake had never had one before, but he'd heard that blows to the head could cause such a thing. "What is going on?" he asked.

"Well, we've just been wasting our time waiting for you to wake up," Arturo said. "No one wanted to carry you back."

Drake looked between Arturo and Mario. Why was Mario letting Arturo, a child, do the talking?

"*What* is going on?" Drake asked again.

Arturo hopped off the rock, showing more energy than he had in all the time that Drake had known him. "You really are stupid, aren't you? What happened to the great and powerful Michael? The one who sat at God's hand? The one entrusted with God's most critical missions? The one in charge of the heavenly forces?"

Drake couldn't understand where all this venom from Arturo was coming from. "Why are you so angry at me? I've never hurt you."

Arturo laughed long and loud, but there was nothing humorous in it. "You've never hurt me? All you've *done* is hurt me."

Drake was at a complete loss as to what was going on. Did Arturo lose someone in the battle of Egypt? Was his family hurt by the Fallen somehow and he thought Drake was responsible?

Arturo strode toward Drake. Mario accompanied him, staying at his side. "Perhaps you need a reminder."

Drake frowned, not understanding what he was referring to.

Arturo leaned forward. "Don't you recognize me?"

Drake looked into the young boy's face. But there was nothing young in the expression that stared back at him. In fact, the expression was old, incredibly old, and filled with loathing. More disturbing, there was something in his eyes that was incredibly familiar.

No, it can't be. Even as he thought it, Drake knew it was entirely possible.

Arturo smiled. "The great and powerful Michael fooled by an innocent-looking face."

Drake's mind struggled to come up with any other explanation for what was literally staring him in the face. But there was nothing and there was only one name that went with the face looking back at him. And it wasn't Arturo.

"Samyaza."

FACT OR FICTION

Thanks for reading *The Belial Blood*. I hope you enjoyed it.

The following sections contains some of the facts used to create *The Belial Blood*. They are presented in no particular order. If you're curious about anything that's not covered below, drop me an email at rdbradywriter@gmail.com. And now onto the facts!

Hypogeum.

The Hypogeum is a fascinating historical site. It is in fact older than the Great Pyramid. The only parts of the temple structure that remain are the subterranean levels. It is located on the archipelago of Malta which has dozen of UNESCO sites.

Falling out of use by 2500, it was rediscovered in 1902. Several chambers are still decorated with a black and white checkerboard pattern, red ochre spirals, and honey-combs. It is the only prehistoric paintings found on the island.

As mentioned in *The Belial Blood*, there is an oracle room within the Hypogeum. The oblong chamber has niches carefully carved into the walls to create, amplify, and echo acoustic effects.

R.D. BRADY

The Hypogeum is also situated to align with the winter and spring equinox.

Asmodeus.

Asmodeus is reported to be the top demon whom Solomon used to control the other demons. According to the Haggadic Legend, a Jewish legend related to Passover, Asmodeus regularly visited a well before returning to heaven. Solomon then sent his men to capture Asmodeus at the well. Which of course begs the question of why Solomon called Asmodeus a demon when he regularly returned to heaven.

Vibration of Ancient Structures.

It is true that a number of ancient sites all vibrate at the same frequency: 110 Hz. Interestingly this is in fact the same frequency that when applied to human subjects results in an out of body experience. There are people that argue it is a form of delusion that people experience while others claim an individual actually crosses through to another dimension.

Hampi India.

The Hampi India structure is real, as is the Stage pavilion. British soldiers were completely blown away by the site where each of the pillars sounds like a different musical instrument. They did indeed cut one of the pillars to see how the amazing effect was done. The pillar however looked like regular granite. Years later it was discovered that the pillars were made of a geopolymers, a substance the modern world did not discover until the 1960s. The Hampi India site was constructed back in the 14th century.

. . .

THE BELIAL BLOOD

Mary Magdalene.

Much has been written on the role of Mary Magdalene in the life of Jesus. Some are adamant that she was in fact his wife while others are equally as adamant that Jesus was never married. The historical research seems to fall more firmly on the side of Jesus being married to Mary Magdalene and that the wedding at Canaan was actually Jesus's own wedding.

An interesting argument is put forth that Lazarus was Mary's brother and that he along with Joseph of Arimathea escaped to Egypt after Jesus' death with Mary and the holy Grail, the daughter of Jesus.

Knights Templars in the Holy Land.

The Knights Templars did in fact reside in the Temple Mount during the Crusades when the Christians were in possession of the Holy Land. During that time, the templars engaged in excavations underneath the Mount. Their discoveries were whisked away back to Rome although rumors persist that not everything was returned to the Vatican and that the Templars kept some secrets for themselves.

Obelisk.

The Obelisk has been mentioned before in the belial series. It was originally created in Egypt and brought to Rome by Caligula. He did in fact, install it in his garden before it was eventually moved to its current location in St. Peter's Square. Caligula was quoted as saying "Remember that I have the right to do anything to anybody" and he did. He would torture, rape and generally harm without guilt.

The Pillar Upon Which Jesus was Scourged.

The column of Flagellation had been held at the Church of St. Paxedes in Rome since the early thirteenth century. Currently kept in a glass reliquary, the column had been discovered by St. Helena in the fourth century. It is alleged to be the stone pillar where Jesus was scourged by Pontius Pilate. Scholars, however, doubt that it is the true one.

Thank you again for reading. You can leave a review on *The Belial Blood*'s amazon page. To hear about upcoming publications, be sure to sign up for my email list on my website at rdbradybook s.com.

The next book in the series is *The Belial Angel.*

ABOUT THE AUTHOR

Author, Criminologist, Terrorism Expert, Jeet Kune Do Black Sash, Runner, Dog Lover.

Amazon best-selling author R.D. Brady writes supernatural and science fiction thrillers. Her thrillers include ancient mysteries, unusual facts, non-stop action, and fierce women with heart.

Prior to beginning her writing career, RD Brady was a criminologist who specialized in life-course criminology and international terrorism. She's lectured and written numerous academic articles on the genetic influence on criminal behavior, factors that influence terrorist ideology, and delinquent behavior formation.

After visiting counter-terrorism units in Israel, RD returned home with a sabbatical in front of her and decided to write that book she'd been thinking about. Four years later she left academia with the publication of her first book, *The Belial Stone*, and hasn't looked back.

To learn about her upcoming publications, sign up for her newsletter here or on her website (rdbradybooks.com).

Printed in Great Britain
by Amazon